· —— · ◆◆◆ · —— · ·

PRAISE FOR DONNA GRANT'S
BEST-SELLING ROMANCE NOVELS

· —— · ◆◆◆ · —— · ·

"Grant's ability to quickly convey complicated
backstory makes this jam-packed love story accessible
even to new or periodic readers."
—*Publishers' Weekly*

"Donna Grant has given the paranormal genre
a burst of fresh air…"
—*San Francisco Book Review*

"The premise is dramatic and heartbreaking;
the characters are colorful and engaging;
the romance is spirited and seductive."
—*The Reading Cafe*

"The central romance, fueled by a hostage drama, plays
out in glorious detail against a backdrop of multiple ongoing
issues in the "Dark Kings" books. This seemingly penultimate
installment creates a nice segue to a climactic end."
—*Library Journal*

"…intense romance amid the growing war between
the Dragons and the Dark Fae is scorching hot."
—*Booklist*

SKYE DRUIDS SERIES

Iron Ember ~ Shoulder the Skye ~ Heart of Glass
Endless Skye ~ Still of the Night ~ Blood Skye ~ After Midnight

DARK KINGS SERIES

Dark Heat ~ Darkest Flame ~ Fire Rising
Burning Desire ~ Hot Blooded ~ Night's Blaze
Soul Scorched ~ Dragon King ~ Passion Ignites
Smoldering Hunger ~ Smoke and Fire
Dragon Fever ~ Firestorm ~ Blaze ~ Dragon Burn
Constantine: A History, Parts 1-3 ~ Heat ~ Torched
Dragon Night ~ Dragonfire ~ Dragon Claimed
Ignite ~ Fever ~ Dragon Lost ~ Flame ~ Inferno
A Dragon's Tale (Whisky and Wishes: *A Holiday Novella*,
Heart of Gold: *A Valentine's Novella*, & Of Fire and Flame)
My Fiery Valentine ~ The Dragon King Coloring Book
Dragon King Special Edition Character Coloring Book: Rhi

DARK WARRIORS SERIES

Midnight's Master ~ Midnight's Lover
Midnight's Seduction ~ Midnight's Warrior
Midnight's Kiss ~ Midnight's Captive
Midnight's Temptation ~ Midnight's Promise
Midnight's Surrender ~ A Warrior for Christmas

CHIASSON SERIES

Wild Fever ~ Wild Dream ~ Wild Need
Wild Flame ~ Wild Rapture

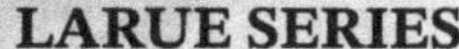

LARUE SERIES

Moon Kissed ~ Moon Thrall

Moon Struck ~ Moon Bound

WICKED TREASURES

Seized by Passion ~ Enticed by Ecstasy

Captured by Desire

Books 1-3: Wicked Treasures Box Set

✦ + ✦ + ✦

✦ HISTORICAL PARANORMAL ✦

THE KINDRED SERIES

Everkin ~ Eversong ~ Everwylde

Everbound ~ Evernight ~ Everspell

KINDRED: THE FATED SERIES

Rage ~ Ruin ~ Reign

DARK SWORD SERIES

Dangerous Highlander ~ Forbidden Highlander

Wicked Highlander ~ Untamed Highlander

Shadow Highlander ~ Darkest Highlander

ROGUES OF SCOTLAND SERIES

The Craving ~ The Hunger

The Tempted ~ The Seduced

Books 1-4: Rogues of Scotland Box Set

THE SHIELDS SERIES

A Dark Guardian ~ A Kind of Magic

A Dark Seduction ~ A Forbidden Temptation

A Warrior's Heart

Mystic Trinity (a series connecting novel)

DRUIDS GLEN SERIES

Highland Mist ~ Highland Nights ~ Highland Dawn

Highland Fires ~ Highland Magic

Mystic Trinity (a series connecting novel)

SISTERS OF MAGIC TRILOGY

Shadow Magic ~ Echoes of Magic ~ Dangerous Magic

Books 1-3: Sisters of Magic Box Set

THE ROYAL CHRONICLES NOVELLA SERIES

Prince of Desire ~ Prince of Seduction

Prince of Love ~ Prince of Passion

Books 1-4: The Royal Chronicles Box Set

Mystic Trinity (a series connecting novel)

DARK BEGINNINGS: A FIRST IN SERIES BOXSET

Chiasson Series, Book 1: Wild Fever

LaRue Series, Book 1: Moon Kissed

The Royal Chronicles Series, Book 1: Prince of Desire

DRAGON FORGED

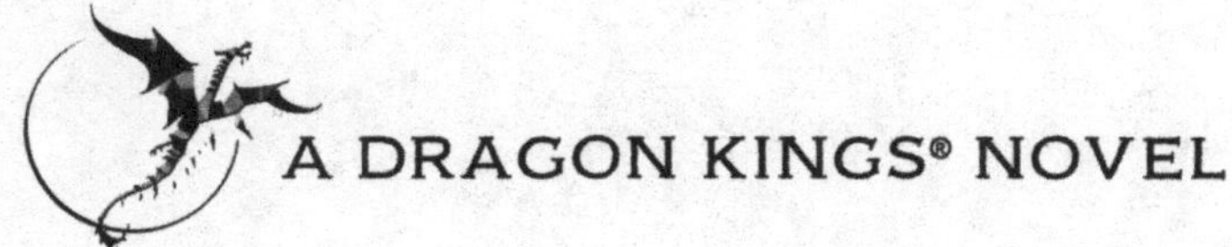

A DRAGON KINGS® NOVEL

NEW YORK TIMES & *USA TODAY* BESTSELLING AUTHOR

DONNA GRANT

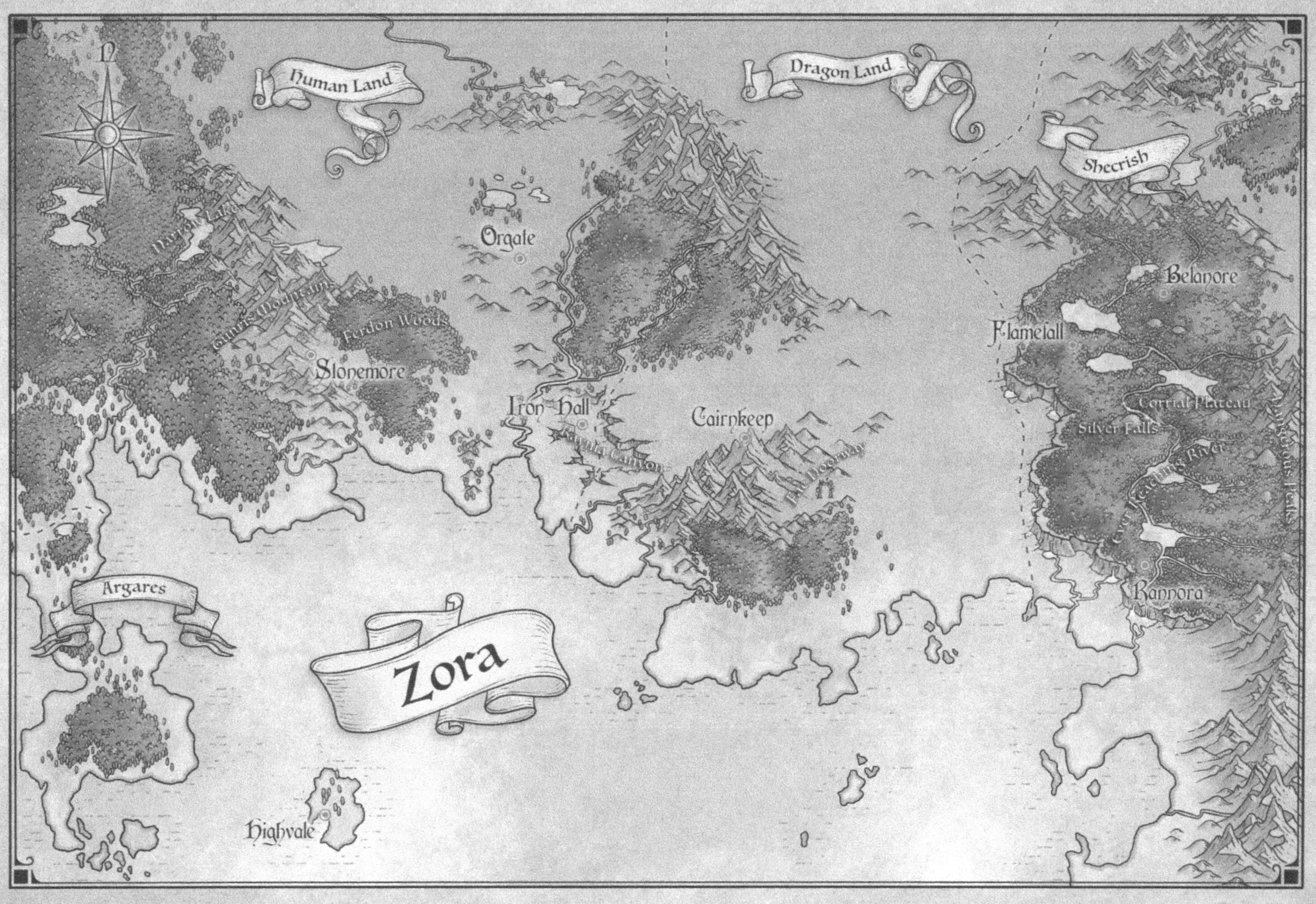

Human Land
Dragon Land
Sheerish
Orgale
Belanore
Flamefall
Fodon Woods
Stonemore
Corral Plateau
Iron Hall
Cairnkeep
Silver Falls
Rannora
Argares
Zora
Highvale

DRAGON KINGS INDEX

Alasdair (AEL-aeS-Deh-R) – King of Amethyst
- Dragon tattoo on his chest
- Power is energy absorption
- Story in DRAGON ARISEN & DRAGON KISS
- Mated to Lotti
  - Youngest Star Person

Anson (AN – sən) – King of Browns
- Ying yang dragon tattoo on back
- Power to take possession of someone's mind for a short period
- Story in BLAZE
- Mated to Devon
  - Gift from Con is a smoky quartz bracelet, both round and princess cut stones

Arian (AR-ee-ən) – King of Turquoises
- Dragon tattoo on his left leg
- Power to control the weather
- Story in DRAGON KING
- Mated to Grace
  - Gift from Con is a rose gold link ankle bracelet with a turquoise heart pendant

Asher (ASH-er) – King of Hunter Greens

- Tattoo on his left arm from wrist to shoulder
- Power to heal burns caused by dragon fire
- Story in DRAGON FEVER
- Mated to Rachel
  - Gift from Con 4-strands of faceted chrome diopside necklace

Banan (BAN-yen) – King of Blues

- Tattoo of two intertwined dragons upon his chest
- Ability to make someone hallucinate
- Story in DAWN'S DESIRE and DARK HEAT
- Mated to Jane
  - Gift from Con is a silver cuff bracelet with a dragon, wings spread, covered in sapphires

Brandr (BRAND-er) – Dragon King

- Son of Con and Rhi
- Gold and beige dragon
- Ability to dispel magic

Cain (KAYN) – King of Navy

- Tattoo on chest
- Ability to use a cone of hot sand
- Story in FLAME
- Mated to Noreen
  - Dark Fae
  - Gift from Con was platinum wire wrapped lapis earrings

Cináed (KIN-ay) – King of Moonstone

· Tattoo on left leg from his knee up to hip

· Power that he can learn and master anything

· Story in DRAGON CLAIMED

· Mated to Gemma

  · Gift from Con silver Celtic cuff bracelet with moonstones at the ends

  · Druid who can sense another Druid's magic

Constantine aka Con (KAHN-stən-teen) – King of Golds, King of Dragon Kings

· Tattoo on his back

· Power to heal anything except death

· Best friends with Ulrik

· One of two Kings who never slept away centuries

· Puts the Dragon Kings and their future above his own happiness

· Story in INFERNO, HEART OF GOLD, OF FIRE AND FLAME, and DRAGON FROST

· Mated to Rhi

  · Gift from the Dragon Kings: a crown with a jewel for every color Dragon King

  · Royal Light Fae

Cullen (KUL-ən) – King of Garnets
- Tattoo on left arm
- Power to breathe fog
- Story in DRAGON UNBOUND
- Mate to Tamlyn
  - Banshee who knows when magical children are about to die

Darius (də-RIE-əs) – King of Dark Purple
- Tattoo on his back looking over his shoulder
- No discernable special ability
- Story in SMOLDERING HUNGER
- Mated to Sophie
  - Doctor
  - Gift from Con are cushion cut dark Siberian amethyst dangle earrings over 5 carets each

Dmitri (DMEE-tree) – King of Whites
- Tattoo draped along the back of his shoulders
- Has the ability to cancel someone's thoughts
- Story in FIRESTORM
- Mated to Faith
  - Archeologist with ties to Skye Druids
  - Gift from Con is a narrow bracelet made of gold interlocked with a single pearl

Dorian (DAWR-ee-ən) – King of Corals

- Tattoo down his left side from his chest to his leg
- Has the ability to turn invisible
- Story in DRAGON NIGHT
- Mated to Alexandra
  - Gift from Con is a large, round sunstone gem set in a narrow rose gold beveled band

Eurwen (AYR-wen) – Dragon Queen

- Daughter of Con and Rhi
- Peach dragon with gold wings
- Tattoo along her spine
- Has the ability to shield herself
- Story in DRAGON MINE
- Mated to Vaughn
  - Gift from Con is a Montana sapphire

Evander (eh-VAN-der) – King of Brass

- Power of crystallokinesis (manipulates minerals and crystals)

Guy (gai) – King of Reds

- Tattoo on back
- Power to erase memories
- Story in NIGHT'S AWAKENING and DARK HEAT
- Mated to Elena
  - Gift from Con is a teardrop ruby nestled in a platinum band

Haldor aka Hal (HAL-door) – King of Greens

- Tattoo on front and wrapping
- Ability to breathe sleeping gas
- Story in DARK CRAVING and DARK HEAT
- Mated to Cassie
  - Gift from Con is a large emerald pendant necklace

Hector (hek-tr) – King of Sea Greens

- Tattoo of a dragon bursting from his chest
- Ability of learning and adapting in any battle
- Story in DRAGON FORGED
- Mated to Emilia
  - Powerful seer
  - Chosen by the magic of Zora to guard Highvale

Kellan (KEHL-ən) – King of Bronzes

- Tattoo on chest and extending to his left arm
- Power to pull wounds into himself
- Story in DARKEST FLAME
- Mated to Denae
  - MI5 agent
  - Gift from Con are smoky quartz earrings

Keltan (KEHL-tən) – King of Citrines

· Tattoo on right ribcage

· Ability to cook anything

· Story in FEVER

· Mated to Bernadette

  · Cryptozoologist

  · Gift from Con is a large oval citrine pendent on a gold
    chain necklace

Kendrick (KEHN-drik) – King of Siennas

· Dragon Tattoo on back

· Power to camouflage

· Story in DRAGON LOVER

· Mated to Esha

  · Sun Elf

  · Asavori Ranger

Kiril (kih-RIHL) – King of Burnt Oranges

· Tattoo on his chest

· Breath of ice

· Best friends with Rhys

· Story in BURNING DESIRE

· Mated to Shara

  · Gift from Con is a Padparadscha (one of the rarest gems in
    the world) emerald bracelet.

  · Dark Fae who turned Light Fae

Laith (LAY-th) – King of Blacks
- Tattoo on his back
- Ability to breathe paralyzing gas
- Runs The Fox and The Hound pub
- Story in HOT BLOODED
- Mated to Iona
  - Ancestor to Warrior, Hayden Campbell (Dark Sword series)
  - Gift from Con is a large black peal and diamond pendant necklace

Marcus (mar-cus) – King of Lavendars
- Power of fraxikinese (manipulate matter)
- Architect who built Dreagan and is rebuilding Iron Hall

Melisse (MEH-LihS) – Queen of Violets
- The very first Dragon King and Dark Fae offspring
- Tattoo winding up her left leg
- Ability to breathe a cone of burning venom
- Was kept prisoner by the Dragon Kings for eons
- Store in DRAGON BORN
- Mated to Henry
  - JusticeBringer with his sister; part of an ancient line of Druid enforcers
  - Brother to Esther (Truthseeker)

Merrill (MEHR-əl) – King of Oranges

· Power of breath a beam of searing light
· Loves to give pep talks
· Best friends with Varek
· Tattoo on back mid-flight
· Story in DRAGON MARKED
· Mated to Katla
  · Gift from Con is a pear shaped Spessartite garnet pendant

Nikolai (nyi-ku-LIE) – King of Ivories

· Tattoo on right arm and right side of his body
· Ability of projected thermography (once he sees something, he can paint or draw it)
· Story in HEAT
· Mated to Esther
  · Gift from Con is mother of pearl earrings
  · Sister to Henry (JusticeBringer)
  · TruthSeeker with her brother; part of an ancient line of Druid enforcers

Ranulf (RAEN-ahlF) – King of Opals

Rhys (REES) – King of Yellows

- Tattoo on his chest and shoulder
- Ability to call the night and shadows
- Best friends with Kiril
- Story in NIGHT'S BLAZE
- Mated to Liliana aka Lily
  - Daughter of nobility
  - Helicopter pilot
  - Gift from Con is a 5-carat cushion cut yellow sapphire ring set in a thin band of platinum

Roman (RO-mən) – King of Pale Blues

- Tattoo on his chest
- Ability to control metals
- Story in DRAGONFIRE
- Mated to Sabina
  - Gypsy
  - Gift from Con are teardrop aquamarine dangle earrings

Royden (ROI-dən) – King of Beiges

- Tattoo on his back
- Power of blinding light
- Story in DRAGON LOST
- Mated to Annita
  - Gift from Con is a raw druzy cluster ring

Ryder (RIE-dər) – King of Grays

· Tattoo wraps his entire torso
· Ability to project weakness into someone
· Has an affinity for jelly donuts
· Designs, creates, and implements all electronics
· Story in SMOKE AND FIRE
· Mated to Kinsey
  · Talented hacker
  · Gift from Con is a gray star sapphire ring, large oval set
    in a thick platinum filigree band

Shaw (SHAW) – King of Sapphires

· Tattoo on right hip, waist, and thigh
· Ability to create illusions
· Story in DRAGON ETERNAL
· Mated to Nia
  · Crafts specialized teas

Sebastian (sə-BAS-chən) – King of Steels

· Tattoo on his right leg winding upward to his abdomen
· Can breathe lightning bolts
· Story in DRAGON BURN
· Mated to Gianna
  · Gift from Con is a large octagonal gunmetal blue stone
    pendant necklace

Thorn (THAWRN) – King of Clarets
- Tattoo on his chest
- Power of sound manipulation
- Story in PASSION IGNITES
- Mated to Lexi
  - Gift from Con are curving French wire 5-caret multifaceted rectangular garnet earrings

Tristan (TRIS-tən) – King of Ambers
- Tattoo on his chest
- Power to get into someone's mind
- Reincarnated Warrior, Duncan Kerr
- First new Dragon King in eons
- Story in FIRE RISING
- Mated to Samantha aka Sammi
  - Half-sister to Jane

Ulrik (OOL-rik) – King of Silvers
- Tattoo on his chest and neck
- Power to bring people back to life
- Best friends with Con
- One of only two Kings who never slept centuries away
- Banished from Dreagan for the war with humans
- Story in TORCHED
- Mated to Eilish
  - Gift from Con are platinum teardrop earrings
  - Powerful Druid
  - Wears silver Celtic finger rings that allows her to teleport

Varek (VAHR-ihk) – King of Lichen

- Tattoo on his left arm
- Power is energy draining shadows
- Best friends with Merrill
- Kidnapped from Earth and brought to Zora
- Story in DRAGON REVEALED
- Mated to Jeyra
  - Warrior
  - Gift from Con are green amethyst stone armbands

Vaughn (VAWN) – King of Teals

- Tattoo on chest
- Ability of dream manipulation
- Attorney for all things Dreagan
- Story in DRAGON MINE
- Mated to Eurwen
  - Gift from Con is a full finger ring with teal stones wound in a delicate, beautiful pattern from the base of her finger to her nail

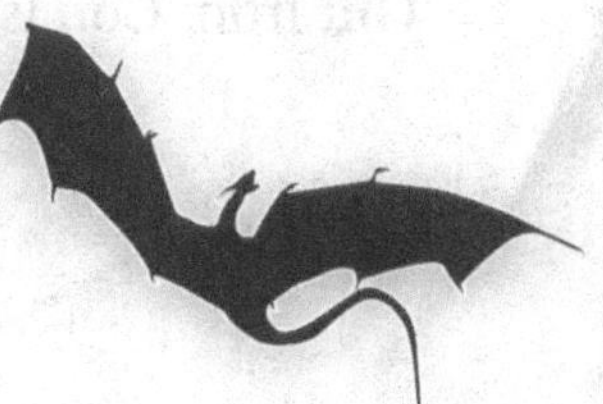

Vlad aka V (vuh-lad) – King of Coppers

- Tattoo on his back with wings on the back of each arm
- Ability to mask himself while in dragon form
- Story in IGNITE
- Mated to Claire
  - Gift from Con is a 5-caret copper zircon set in rose gold
  - First human mate to carry a baby to term

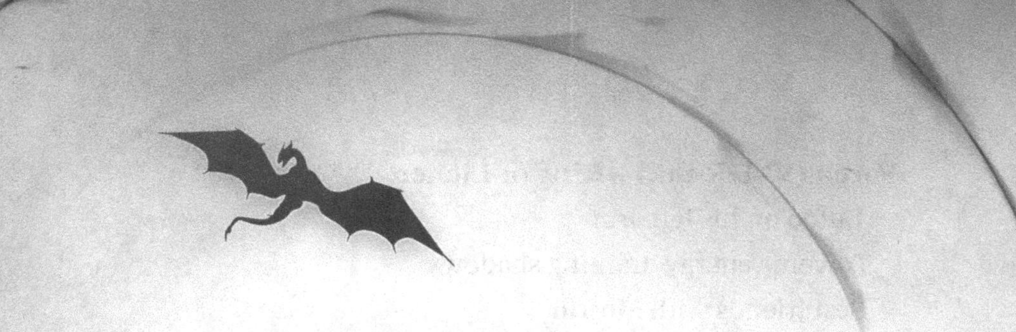

Warrick aka War (WAWR-ik) – King of Jades
- Tattoo on the right side of his body from shoulder to hip
- Power of protection
- Story in SOUL SCORCHED
- Mated to Darcy
  - Was the Druid who unbound Ulrik's magic
  - Gift from Con is a gold bracelet with five jade beads

DRAGON FORGED

A DRAGON KINGS® NOVEL

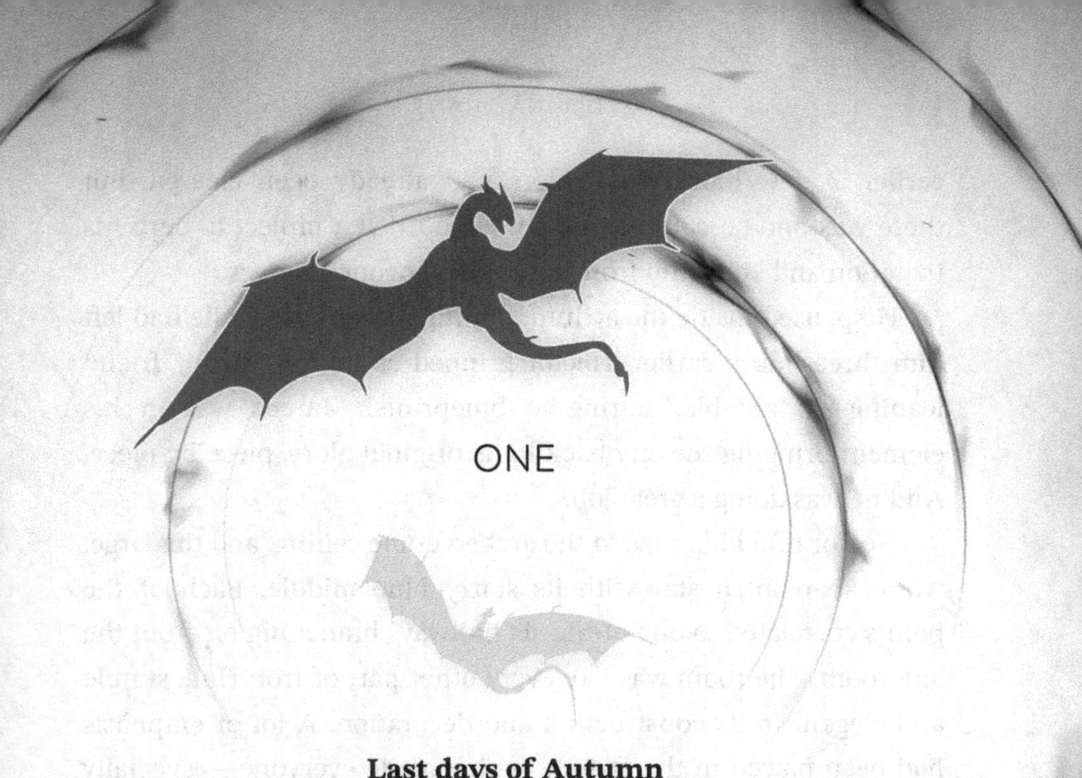

ONE

Last days of Autumn
Iron Hall

Boredom had never been a good companion for Hector. He was a man of action and deed. Not that he didn't enjoy some downtime. After everything he and the other Dragon Kings had endured of late, a little respite was agreeable. But after a week of twiddling his thumbs, he was restless. He needed something to occupy him, and he wasn't due for his patrol rotation along the border for another six days. That was too long to wait.

His boot heels thumped softly on Iron Hall's stone floors. The underground city was enormous, and every time they thought they had explored all there was to see, they discovered more. For the most part, the city had survived relatively well. However, some sections had some damage or had even caved in, making them impassable.

Hector had been exploring an area of devastation found weeks earlier. A few blocked corridors had already been cleared, but there was one he could focus on. He needed a project to curb his irritation and keep him from getting on anyone's nerves.

He paused inside the atrium, finding Marcus where he had left him three hours earlier. Hector grinned as he took in his friend leaning on a table, staring at blueprints. Marcus was in his element bringing the city back to its original glory, piece by piece. And he was doing a great job.

Hector lifted his gaze to the arched dome ceiling, and the large, white six-pointed star with its starry blue middle. Each of the points correlated to one of the six hallways branching off from the anteroom. The room was like every other part of Iron Hall, simple and elegant in its construction and decoration. A lot of emphasis had been placed in the atrium, which made everyone—especially Marcus—believe the entire area was important.

The corridor Hector had just traversed connected a city wing to the antechamber. All four smaller, flanking hallways had suffered damage, but the two closest to the corridor directly across from him had the most. Marcus specialized in architecture—every aspect of it. He had designed and built Dreagan Manor, the distillery, and every other building on their estate in Scotland on Earth. Then, he came to Zora to construct another manor at Cairnkeep, in the heart of dragon land, but his focus had since deviated to Iron Hall. Hector grinned and leaned a shoulder against the wall when he recalled how Marcus's eyes had lit up at the sight of the underground city.

"Tell me again why you doona just use magic to clear this last hall?" Hector asked, looking at the remaining blockage.

Marcus didn't lift his head from the blueprints as he said, "That takes the fun out of it."

This was far from Hector's idea of enjoyable. He was a warrior, a fighter. Give him wide-open skies and an enemy to vanquish over ruins to be put back together any day. He wasn't made to be stuck inside. Yet he never hesitated to lend a hand when needed—or when he had nothing else to occupy him.

He pushed away from the wall and walked across the atrium to the blocked corridor. He only saw rocks and debris, but Marcus viewed things in ways no one else could. It was why building and rebuilding were his fortes. It was also why, if they wanted a spectacular meal, they turned to Keltan, who could make a feast out of nothing. If someone needed healing, Con stepped in. All the Kings had unique skills. Even him. Though he wouldn't call his skill at battle all that special. He picked up battle tactics and fighting styles as easily as breathing. Sometimes, he wished he had something more meaningful or fun.

When the Kings first came to Zora, all that mattered to them was the discovery of their dragons. Enemies had soon emerged, and it seemed they had been fighting one foe after another ever since. It kept them from exploring more of this new world than the bit of land the dragons had claimed. Most of the Kings' time had been spent at Stonemore, a mountainside city near dragon land, where they'd fought multiple battles.

From what the Kings had seen of Zora so far, the realm was stuck in a medievalesque era. Stonemore had many striking buildings, especially the palace at the very top of the mountain. They had glass windows, plumbing, and even heated water. Yet they still used horses and carriages for travel.

Iron Hall was different in more than its architecture. The stones used for the floor glowed from within, but not with magic. Sconces of flames that never went out hung along the walls. The aqueducts would've made the Romans weep with envy. Everything about the city, from the very design to the murals and lighting, made a person forget they were deep beneath the earth. Yet for all Iron Hall's wonders, they had yet to discover the builders, how long they might have lived here, or what had happened to them. He was beginning to wonder if they ever would.

"The debris looks different in here," Hector called out as he walked to the entrance of the blocked corridor. "The floor tiles aren't cracked. They're smashed."

He walked the last few feet into the hall where the rubble began. Squatting, Hector picked up a small piece of broken rock. The edges were burnt as if from a blast of some kind. Or fire. He tossed the rock into the air and caught it. Scanning from one side of the wide passage to the other, he saw deep into the darkness beyond as well as he would have if it were lit. His enhanced dragon senses stretched out, though searching for what, he wasn't sure. *Something* wasn't right.

It occurred to him that Marcus hadn't replied to his previous comment. He looked over his shoulder at his friend, whose dark head was still bent over the designs.

"Did you hear me?" Hector asked.

"What?" Marcus briefly lifted his head and speared him with a perturbed green gaze. "Of course."

Hector grinned. "Did you now? What did I say?"

"Fine. I wasna listening. I have to…"

Hector didn't wait for Marcus to finish, because he wouldn't. Whatever was going on happened inside Marcus's head and never made it past his lips. It was better to leave him to his musings and only interrupt if it was life or death.

Hector faced the debris field once more. The blackened stone bothered him. The few areas that needed work, like shoring up a few cracks, was nothing compared to this section or the two beside it. The hall was situated far from the city's main hub and only connected by the corridors, which explained why the damage was so contained. They hadn't discovered what it had been used for yet. It would likely take the reconstruction of the last hall before they could piece it all together. The other four hallways that branched off the atrium had one or two rooms along the sides, but all had a room at the end. Each was a different size and shape, with nothing inside that might tell them what it was for.

Hector straightened and carefully picked his way around the rubble, moving deeper into the corridor. It led him to more scorch marks on the rocks littering the floor. That confirmed that something—or someone—had blown up this hallway, either by accident or on purpose. It would explain why the others had sustained damage.

It wasn't long before Hector had to duck under the collapsing ceiling. There was no telling how much dirt was above him. With their magic, the Kings could survive a cave-in, but others wouldn't be so lucky. He needed to mention that to Marcus in case he hadn't inspected the areas back here. They needed to set up a barrier, at least to make sure none of the bairns accidentally found their way to this section.

He reached a wall of rock and was about to turn back when he spotted a small opening through a pile of rocks. He did a double take and leaned to the side, trying to get a better look into the gap.

"Fuck," Hector mumbled when he struck his head on a rock.

The indescribable, overpowering need to see inside gripped him. Without a second thought, he dropped to his hands and knees to crawl around and over the large rocks. He cut his palms and arms numerous times on the sharp edges, but his body healed instantly. If it wasn't for Marcus, he would've already reached for his magic to clear his way, but he respected his friend enough not to do that.

It took some time before Hector reached the cavity. His elation was short-lived. When he peered inside, he only found more debris. But even with nothing visible to his dragon vision, he couldn't turn away. The overwhelming need he'd felt earlier intensified, pushing him to investigate further. There was space enough for someone to stand upright, but beyond that was a solid wall of rock.

He continued to scan the space, trying to decipher what had made him want to remain and get inside. The pull was so persuasive that he jerked away from the gap. Hector tried to leave, but found he couldn't. He *had* to know what was inside that room.

Something was in there and luring him. He looked down the hall to the antechamber and briefly thought about calling Marcus. As soon as the thought crossed his mind and passed, he realized he would have to share whatever he found. Hector was at the opening in the next heartbeat. He eyed the width and height, comparing it to his body. It would be tight, especially since he couldn't use magic.

He stuck one arm through the gap, and then squeezed a shoulder and his head inside. When he tried to pull himself the rest of the way through, he got stuck. He had to contort himself to get his other shoulder through. Dirt rained down around him, the ceiling groaning ominously. He flipped onto his back and stared above him, his magic at the ready, just in case.

But it held. When he was sure nothing would fall, he pulled himself through the gap and got to his feet. He had to lean his head to the side so he didn't bonk it. Again. The room was about eight feet square and, remarkably, didn't have as much debris as the rest of the corridor. Hector skimmed the walls and floor, trying to find what had drawn him in. He found himself turning left and walking toward a wall.

He squatted and rolled away a rock the size of a beach ball, finding a slowly blinking turquoise light. The color was vivid, but not bright enough to sear his eyes. He reached for it before he could stop himself. Even as he made contact with the light, he tried to pull back.

One moment, he was in the scorched corridor. The next, he stood in an all-white stone room. A salty breeze caressed his cheek as waves crashed against rocks nearby, and gulls squawked loudly. He turned his head toward the open window and the brilliant sunlight flooding through it. He moved toward it, only to spin around at the sound of an opening door. Hector found himself staring into vibrant blue eyes as bright as a summer sky.

The woman drew up short at the sight of him. He shook himself, unsure if he was dreaming or if the stunning female staring back at him was real. For a moment, she so arrested him that he couldn't move. She had an oval face, a delicate nose, and a mouth that made him think of long nights with their bodies tangled in sheets.

Her airy, white dress was clasped at the shoulders with bands of leather, while a simple leather belt gathered the material against her waist, showing shapely curves before stopping at her ankles to reveal leather sandals. Her blond curls were gathered away from her face and hung past her shoulders, revealing darker strands underneath.

Hector started to reach out to touch her, only to stop himself in time. He couldn't remember the last time someone had mesmerized him so. He had to know her. In every way possible.

"Who are you?" he asked.

As if his words had broken the spell between them, she shut the door behind her and hurried past him. "There isn't time. You must come with me now."

He turned with her. "Just hold on a damn minute. You've no' told me your name. I need to know how I got here. And where is *here*, anyway?"

"I'll show you. Come," she urged as she motioned to another door he hadn't noticed.

He hesitated, then sighed and trailed after her, moving through the doorway. Hector found himself in a narrow hall. "Can you at least tell me your name?"

"All the answers are just ahead."

Why wouldn't she give him her name? It irritated him. He intended to get it from her. He warily followed her, eyeing the doors on either side of him. Everything within him threw up red flags. His lips parted to pose another question, when she halted and spun to face him. She barely spared him a glance, not even meeting his eyes. She hadn't been able to look away when she first saw him. Now, she wouldn't look at him. What was going on?

Hector dipped his chin and caught her gaze. She swung her attention to the opposite side. "Lass? What's going on?"

"I'm sorry," she said.

"Sorry?" he repeated. "For what?"

She walked to the side, and he turned to face her. Her eyes briefly met his. Hector glanced down the hall in both directions. When he looked back at her, he noticed the pulse in her throat was erratic.

"I'm no' hearing any of those answers you promised, lass."

"You will."

Hector planted his feet, refusing to budge. "I think it's time for you to at least tell me your name."

"I'm no one of consequence," she said, at the same time she reached around him and opened the door.

He turned to see what was inside, not realizing he was so close to the threshold. He lost his balance and tumbled through the air. He was about to shift when he landed on the hard ground with a loud grunt. Hector rolled to a stop and gingerly sat up, his legs bent as he shook his head. The room was gone. Now, he was in a field beneath a dazzling sun and big, fluffy clouds.

Hector scrubbed a hand over his jaw. There hadn't been any malice or anger in the woman's words. Nor had she touched him. But there was little doubt she knew exactly what the door was and that it would take him away. The problem was, *why* had she done it? He also had to figure out where he was. He couldn't see the door he had fallen through anywhere. He got to his feet and dusted off his hands. That's when he noticed the man leaning on a shovel, watching him.

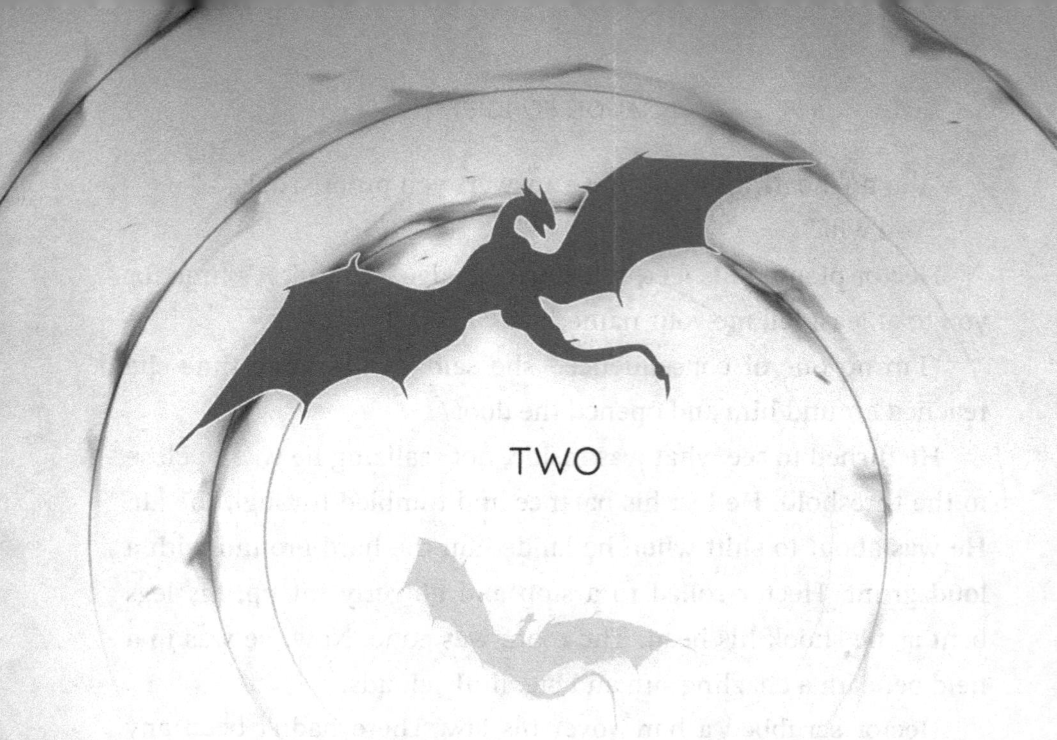

TWO

The minute the Dragon King was gone, Emilia stumbled back a few steps, her knees threatening to give way. She braced her hands on the wall and dragged in huge mouthfuls of air. Her entire body shook from fear.

Sweet silver sands, she couldn't believe she had faced a Dragon King and managed to get him out of Highvale without anyone knowing about his arrival. She stared at the open door, thinking he might reappear at any second, but she knew he wouldn't. He hadn't known where he was, which meant he might not return. Unless he found the beacon again.

Emilia couldn't move for several moments as the sound of her breath filled her ears. Only when her breathing calmed did she lift her head. Her hands, however, still trembled. It was more about lying to the one person she didn't want to. But there was no other way. Her vision had been clear. If the Dragon Kings came to Highvale, a global war would decimate all of Zora.

She swallowed and dropped her hands from the wall as she

quickly closed the door before returning to the inner rooms. Unable to help herself, she glanced over her shoulder to make sure the door remained shut. She saw his face each time she blinked. Rugged. Striking. Handsome. The deep, earthy pools of his soulful eyes had seized her, making it difficult to breathe, much less think. She hadn't expected him to be so exquisite.

He was tall, his power and authority resting around him as easily as the blue tunic he had worn over his impressive torso. Sunlight had lit upon his glossy, shoulder-length, light brown waves. And there had been a myriad of colors in that brief look. She had been so focused on his upper body that she hadn't paid attention to his lower half.

Confusion had lined his brow, as well as a bit of curiosity. But no anger. He hadn't snapped at her or lost his temper. Which was a good thing, considering he was so tall and commanding. Had he wanted, he could've snapped her in two. And yet, he had easily followed her. Which was only because she had rushed him while lying through her teeth. Luck had been on her side, thank the gods. And if the gods really were on her side, they would ensure that no other Kings found their way to the city.

Emilia released a sigh and walked through the room the Dragon King had appeared in. She shivered in remembrance of finding him standing there in his strange clothes. His accent had been different, too. If she hadn't had the recurring vision about the Kings, she would've welcomed him to the island and gotten to know him. But that was never meant to be.

She drew up short for the second time that day when she walked out of the room and found Agathi in the hall. Beautiful, wealthy, and captivating, she was everything Emilia wasn't. She was dressed in a gown of deep teal that showed off her curves.

Dangling gold earrings glinted through her dark tresses. She also had a gold filigree belt at her waist and gold bracelets on each wrist. Agathi was the epitome of wealth and position. Her waist-length brunette hair had been curled and held away from her face with gold clips.

Something about Agathi drew others to her like moths to a flame. The two of them couldn't walk anywhere without someone stopping them to speak to Agathi. It wasn't Agathi's fault. She just had an extraordinary spark that few others possessed.

"Did it work?" Agathi asked hopefully, her deep brown eyes wide with expectation.

It was harder to lie than Emilia had thought. The words lodged in her throat. She couldn't even manage to shake her head. The tolling of the bells gave her a reprieve. "You're being called."

"Frick," Agathi muttered angrily and whirled around to walk away. She halted after a couple of steps and looked back at Emilia. "Come with me."

"You know I can't. I'm not part of the cabinet."

"You are a seer. Besides, it's high time those elitists realized you're being wasted in your current position."

Unlike Agathi, Emilia had never longed to go to one of the restricted meetings, take a seat at the table, or have her opinion counted. She preferred to remain unnoticed. "I'm not interested."

"You could be a great asset."

Agathi had always championed her. Emilia wouldn't have her position in the Oracle guild if it wasn't for her. She owed Agathi for everything she had, but most especially for her friendship. Everyone wanted to be Agathi's friend, and she was friendly with all—to the point where many believed themselves to be her best friend. The truth was, Agathi simply didn't have it in her to correct them. And the only one she confided in was Emilia.

"I'll change your mind someday," Agathi said as she faced her.

Emilia shook her head. "You won't."

"You keep saying that."

"Go. Before they come looking for you."

"Fine." Agathi glanced at the door. "Will you remain to see if one of them comes?"

Emilia's smile was tight. "Of course."

"The summoning will work. You'll see," Agathi said over her shoulder and then hurried away.

Emilia didn't move until she was out of sight. She put her hand on her stomach and bent over, nausea choking her. There was no way she could carry on without telling Agathi the truth—all of it. Including her vision. The weight of knowing what could happen had been a terrible burden. She hadn't, only because the visions urged her to remain silent.

She straightened, walked to a column, and looked through the arch to the turquoise water surrounding the island. The skies were clear, the sea calm. But a storm raged on the horizon. The more magicals that found their way to Highvale, the more the stories spread of the horrendous acts done to their kind. Highvale was divided on whether to remain only a safe place for the persecuted or create an army and wage war. Agathi—and others on the cabinet—believed the Dragon Kings would ensure victory for all magicals.

Emilia's visions, which had been on repeat since she was young, said differently.

She looked down at the streets of Highvale and those going about their days. The only way to find the hidden city was with magic. A few humans had managed to locate the island, but finding it and getting to it were two very different things. Only those with true magic could cross from the mainland. It was a refuge. A haven for anyone tired of hiding their abilities. Everyone could be themselves at Highvale—in whatever way they wanted.

Agathi had been brought to the island as an infant and raised here. Emilia hadn't been that fortunate. Her parents had loved her, and she them. When they realized she had magic, they tried to hide it from others in their settlement. There was no controlling when a vision came, though. Nor could it be hidden.

The hardest thing she had ever done was leave them after she had a vision of their violent deaths at the hands of those in their village. She was only five. She had seen herself at Highvale in the vision and set out to find it. It had taken her months to reach the island, but she had been welcomed as everyone was.

She loved much about the city, but like everything, there were issues. Money, power, and position played into everything. As did politics. The more divided Highvale became about the war, the more the rumbles of unrest could be heard among the citizens. The island was a powder keg waiting to explode, and the Dragon Kings were the match.

Emilia straightened from the column and made her way down the hall. A gentle breeze swirled around her as it moved through the open windows on either side of her. She yearned to go down to the shore for a swim, but that would have to wait until she finished her chores. As part of the guild, she had to earn her keep.

There were only two guild houses now. Oracles and Banshees. There used to be others, but those involved either couldn't or wouldn't meet the directives and duties required. The guilds eventually faded.

Being accepted into the guild could be exhausting. Everyone wanted to be at the top, but not everyone could be. Many didn't like having to climb their way up—or the menial chores that went with it.

But there were also advantages. Emilia didn't have to worry about shelter, food, or clothing, as all were provided. Being in the guild also granted the members a certain level of respect. While Emilia was low in the guild, she ranked much higher among the regular citizens.

With that position and power came political ties. Each guild had its own, as anyone would expect. Because the guilds were so prestigious, each held three seats on the cabinet, and the guild members were elected solely by their houses. It was how Agathi had gotten onto the cabinet.

Besides the six guild members, the entire island voted to elect three representatives who led the cabinet. The candidate with the highest votes out of the three governed the cabinet.

With so many at the table, there were many meetings to debate and vote on any number of things—if they got anything done at all. Agathi often claimed they did nothing but bicker during the two-hour assemblies. Things did get accomplished, but slowly. Or at least that had been the case until recently. Newcomers to the island—or those who had left and returned—brought tales of dragons leaving their lands and battling others. Several had witnessed a dragon shifting into a man or vice versa. It had sent a shockwave of hope throughout Highvale that Emilia had never experienced before.

All the years of having the vision should have prepared her, but she kept hoping it would never come to pass. Yet with the stories, her recurring vision of destruction and devastation, where everything was on fire and dragons roared around her, came more often. It was how she'd known a King would arrive soon.

She went down the stone steps, pausing to look over her shoulder. If one King had found the portal, another might, as well. It hadn't been providence that she'd happened to be there when the Dragon King appeared. The vision had visited her five nights in a row, which had never happened before, so she took it for the warning it was.

Agathi spoke often about the magic the cabinet used in their attempt to summon a dragon. It was the only way Emilia had known where he might appear. That's when Emilia offered to keep an eye on the room. She felt bad for using Agathi, but in the end, what she was doing would save countless lives. If Agathi ever found out, hopefully she would forgive her. Emilia could weather a lot, but she wouldn't survive losing her one and only friend. Because Agathi was more than that. She was also Emilia's family.

The only way to stop another King from being summoned would be to shut off the beacon. Unfortunately, that went beyond her abilities. Only the cabinet could do that, and they wouldn't change their minds anytime soon.

Emilia sighed and faced forward once more. The Dragon King's features flashed behind her eyelids when she blinked. It was a face she wouldn't soon forget.

THREE

Hector looked around as he crossed the field to the man. There wasn't another soul in sight. The land was flat, with only a couple of trees dotting the horizon. The man made no move to meet Hector. He wondered if the stranger had seen how he had come to be there. More worrying was if the man would be threatened about the possible use of magic.

Yet the gentleman smiled as Hector drew closer. If he feared for his life, he likely wouldn't have stuck around. Still, Hector wouldn't take any chances. He'd already been duped once today. It wouldn't happen a second time.

Hector nodded in greeting. "Hello."

"Hello, yourself," the man replied congenially.

By his response, he didn't seem afraid or irritated. That eased some of Hector's worry, but not all. "I doona suppose you could tell me where I am."

"Seems someone such as you should know that."

"Aye, I should." Hector halted about six feet from the man. "Unfortunately, I doona."

The male was short, the top of his head barely reaching Hector's chest. He had white hair sticking out from beneath a wide-brimmed straw hat. Sharp gray eyes scrutinized him. The sleeves of his beige linen shirt were rolled up over his elbows, and faded blue suspenders held up his dark brown trousers. The height and the shovel brought to mind Derek's description of the tomte, a race of individuals inexplicably drawn to crops who were invisible to those without magic.

"I know what you are, Dragon King," the stranger said.

Hector dipped his chin. "And I know what you are, tomte."

Suddenly, his mouth split into a wide grin. "Good. We can get past that. The name's Jushur."

He liked Jushur immediately. "Hector."

"After Ash met Derek, word of the Kings spread rapidly through our kind. I wondered how long it would take one of you to make it down here."

"And where exactly is *down here*?"

Jushur laughed. "You really don't know?"

"I really doona."

That brought on another chuckle. "This is Argares. It's far south from your land."

"How far south?"

"Very far," Jushur replied.

Hector ran a hand over his face. "Did you see how I got here?"

"It was hard to miss. Haven't seen that in…" He thought for a moment, his lips twisting ruefully. "Over a thousand years."

By Hector's recollection, the tomte lived for three thousand years.

"What did you do to irk them so?" Jushur asked.

"Irk who?"

Jushur's shoulders shook as he laughed. "You don't know much, do you, son?"

It had been eons since anyone had called him *son*. The fact that Hector was millions of years older than the tomte didn't seem to matter to Jushur. "It has been a trying day."

"You came through one of the hidden Highvale exit doors. You do know what Highvale is, yes?"

"Now *that* I know." Hector thought back to the blonde and her mesmerizing blue eyes.

Jushur tilted his head to the side and regarded him. "What did you do?"

"Nothing. I got there, then she appeared and led me down a hallway. Next thing I knew, I was here."

"Did she give you a name?"

Hector looked to where he had landed on the ground. "She promised me answers, then promptly tricked me."

"Interesting."

It was maddening. He swung his head to the tomte. "Which way to Highvale?"

"You don't feel it?" Jushur asked with a frown.

Hector rubbed his head as it began to ache. Why couldn't anyone just answer a simple question? He dropped his arm to his side when Jushur's words registered. He closed his eyes, quieted his mind, and reached out with his senses. Magic pulsed all around him like ribbons weaving through the earth and sky. It wasn't as potent as at Dreagan on Earth, but it was strong. He delved through each layer, sensing other tomtes nearby. Beyond that were dozens of others—and it all pointed south. Just like the magic on Earth pointed to Dreagan.

His eyes snapped open as he turned south. The question was: Did he go?

"Seems you have a decision to make," Jushur said. "Care for a nice cup of tea while you mull it over?"

Hector considered Jushur's offer before looking at the tomte. "I doona suppose you have coffee?"

"Never heard of it. What is it?"

"Decadence in a cup."

The tomte scoffed as he wrinkled his nose. "I doubt that. Nothing beats my brew. Have you not had tea?"

"It's prevalent where I'm from. I drink it if I must. But I prefer espresso."

"Too bad you don't have any. I'd like a taste."

Hector grinned and held out his hand, producing an espresso in a cup with a saucer beneath. "Here you go."

"How did you do that?" Jushur asked in a stunned whisper, his eyes locked on the coffee.

"I just can."

Jushur released the shovel. It fell to the ground as he walked closer. "Amazing," he whispered.

Hector had stopped thinking of much as amazing—especially his dragon magic—a long time ago. What would the world look like if he saw it with fresh eyes? He lowered his gaze to the demitasse cup. He had created something out of nothing with just a thought. That was pretty incredible. And he could change shape. Not many magical beings could claim that. Yet, for all the wonders of magic, he also understood why those ignorant might fear such things and the power that came with it.

"Take it," Hector urged when Jushur only continued to stare at the espresso.

The tomte wiped his hands on his pants and carefully took the small cup and saucer. He brought it to his nose and inhaled.

"Careful," Hector told him. "It's verra hot, and the brew is strong."

"I like strong," Jushur said as he tilted the demitasse to his lips.

Hector ducked his head to hide his grin when Jushur pulled a face at the taste of the espresso. "I did warn you it was strong."

"I do believe it could stand by itself," Jushur remarked as he stared at the coffee.

Then, to Hector's surprise, he took another drink. Jushur allowed the third sip to linger in his mouth before swallowing. Hector raised a brow, waiting.

"It grows on you," Jushur admitted.

"That it does."

"I'd love to make you some of my tea."

Hector glanced south. It wasn't as if Highvale was going anywhere. Or the blonde, for that matter.

"Another time, perhaps?" Jushur said.

Hector met the tomte's gray eyes. "I can stay."

"But you don't want to." He grinned. "Go. You need answers. Just promise you'll come back and share some details."

"Consider it done."

Jushur's smile faded. "Highvale might be a place for those like us, but guard yourself, Dragon King. Politics is the trade. It's part of every transaction, deed, and conversation."

"I appreciate the warning."

Jushur tried to return the espresso.

Hector held up a hand. "It's yours."

"Thank you."

Without preamble, Jushur walked back to his shovel. Hector didn't call out a farewell. He had a feeling Jushur didn't like those. Instead, he faced south and started walking. After a few moments, he looked over his shoulder to find the tomte watching him. Hector started to lift his hand but decided against it at the last moment.

He looked at the sky. If he was headed to a city for those with magic, no one would think twice about seeing a dragon. Or would they? The blonde seemed to know who he was. He supposed she could have him mixed up with someone, but... He inwardly shook his head. Nay, she had known. It was how she spoke to him, almost as if she had been expecting him.

The last thing he remembered while at Iron Hall was touching the pulsing light. That must have been what had transported him to Highvale. Something had called to him. It was the only thing that made sense.

The only thing he was certain about was that the blonde didn't want him in the city. Too bad. Because he was headed back. And he intended to find her. She'd promised him answers, and she would give them to him. He lengthened his strides. He was all for a good walk, but he had questions. Many of them.

The afternoon sun beat down warmly. They were on their last weeks of autumn at Iron Hall, and the temperatures were beginning to drop drastically. It had already snowed in the mountains within the dragon land borders. Given the warmth of Argares, they had to be near the equator. Or on the other side of the globe. If that were the case, Jushur wouldn't have said south. He would've indicated that Hector had traveled a much greater distance.

He walked for hours. The flat lands stretched interminably before him. The scent in the air changed. Every so often, he caught a whiff of salt. The fields finally gave way to estuaries. He hiked along the edge of the brackish water, where a multitude of birds scattered at his approach. He didn't stop and marvel at them. His route still stretched before him.

The sunset was a colorful display that held his attention until he crested a small hill and finally glimpsed the water laid out before him like a blanket of cobalt. The grass yielded to lavender sand. Water gently lapped at the shoreline that stretched for miles on either side of him. He didn't see Highvale, but he could feel it. He looked out across the sea as he walked forward.

His feet sank into the thick sand. Hector bent and gathered a handful of the lavender grains in his hands. The color was the exact shade of Erith's eyes. He wondered if the goddess had done it intentionally when she created Zora or if it was just a byproduct of her magic. The next time he saw her, he would have to tell her about this beach. He looked up before turning his head to the side. His fingers loosened as he released the sand and straightened. For now, he had to find Highvale. And the woman.

The ebb and flow of the waves had a relaxing quality as he walked. He studied the constantly changing colors of the sunset before the last rays of light vanished into the horizon. Then he was bathed in the blue light of night and Zora's double moons. The water was black as it rolled onto shore, scattering into foam before the ocean called it home. The sight of a dragon statue rising up at the edge of the sand took him aback. He walked faster to reach it quicker. With so many fearing dragons, it was the last thing he'd expected to see.

His feet slowed to a stop when he finally stood before it. The sculpture was all that stood on the shoreline. A dragon squatting menacingly atop an archway with its wings spread and its mouth partially open on a snarl, teeth bared as if ready to deliver death. Shock went through Hector at the sight of it. He studied the dragon for a long minute as chills raced down his back. He looked behind and around him for others, but no one was there but him and the dragon.

He walked up the stone steps, never taking his eyes off the dragon, then passed through the archway beneath it. When he was on the other side, he turned to look at the statue and found its tail hanging along the outside wall of the stone.

Hector gave the dragon a final look before facing the water. Highvale stood out in the waves somewhere before him. No boats were waiting to take him, and no bridge awaited to carry him over the water. He thought about the sculpture and debated whether to shift and take to the sky. After the woman's reaction to his appearance, however, he would rather approach without being noticed.

He waded into the water until it was chest high, then dove beneath the waves and swam out of the shallows. Once far enough out, he shifted into his true form and headed to the city. Most sea life gave him a wide berth. A school of fish parted at his approach and came back together after he swam past.

The farther he got from shore, the more he felt the magic. He didn't slow until he finally spotted the land rising up from the bottom of the ocean. He circled the island twice, noting the many reefs and caves. There were enemies everywhere, and he wanted to know what was below the water before he went on land. When he was satisfied, Hector returned to his human form and broke the surface, swimming the last three hundred yards to the empty beach.

As soon as he was on land, he called clothes to cover his nakedness. He could follow the sights and sounds into the city, but he wanted to look around first.

FOUR

Highvale was a good-sized island with mountains, coves, and spectacular rock formations along the water's edge and inland. The main city seemed to be situated in the middle of the island and branched out from there. Some areas were uninhabited because of the steep mountainside and the geographical structures.

They did, however, build monuments atop some of the peaks. Hector stared up at one of those now, eyeing the detail that had gone into the dragon standing on all fours, its wings tucked and tail curled at his back legs. Even from the distance, Hector saw the scales and the stinger on the end of the tail. It bore an uncanny resemblance to Con, the leader of the Dragon Kings.

First, the dragon at the shoreline, and now this one. The biggest difference between this realm and Earth was that everyone knew about the dragons. And most feared and hated his kind thanks to Villette, a goddess-like being of the Star People who could travel the universe.

People knew about magic on Zora but shunned those who had it. They were even killed. Most hid their gifts in an effort to stay alive. And just like on Earth, the humans had taken control. Their fear and ignorance of magic and those who wielded it were on full display once more. A war was looming and had been for many generations.

He had hoped those who called the island home would welcome the Dragon Kings, but he hadn't foreseen finding images of dragons among them. Were there others? He intended to find out.

Hector continued his stealthy prowl. It would be nice if he could hide in the shadows like Rhys could or go invisible like Dorian, but he had other talents. While many of the Kings had remained on Dreagan, even after they woke from dragon sleep, he had roamed the Earth far and wide, visiting other lands and discovering new cultures. He immersed himself wherever he went and learned fighting techniques and battle strategies.

Not because he particularly enjoyed the humans. How could he after the war? But he recognized their aptitude at certain things. And while magic was a part of every dragon, he liked to be prepared for anything. Earth's magic had chosen him as King of Sea Greens because he was the strongest and most powerful dragon of his clan. But that didn't mean there wasn't some bigger, badder enemy out there waiting for him.

Dragons were the most powerful species on Earth in terms of both size and magic. He had worried that wouldn't always be the case and had been proven right. Another worry had been whether he could use his magic. Hence his endeavor to train his body and mind in other ways. It had taken a long time—and incredible control—to enter a fight and not immediately reach for his power.

Then, he and several other Kings had come to Zora, and it had been an entirely new world with different players and magic systems. All the knowledge he had acquired and honed was being put to use now.

He walked the water's edge for another fifteen minutes before he spotted the next dragon. This one had been carved into the cliffside and appeared as if the dragon climbed the rocks, his head turned back to look down at the water. Hector walked to the bottom of the mountain and jumped. He secured a hand and foothold about a third of the way up. His next jump landed him next to the dragon's body.

He scanned the dragon's back, taking in the row of tendrils that ran from the base of its skull to the tip of its tail. Hector scaled the rockface alongside the dragon until he was even with its head. There was no doubt now that he saw the tendrils around its mouth and the bony knobs at its nostrils that he was staring at an image of Ulrik.

None of the Kings had been to Highvale. Not even the twins, Brandr and Eurwen, who had lived on Zora their entire lives, had been to the island. The only explanation was that a seer lived on the island. Still, staring at two dragons that looked similar to Kings he knew was unnerving.

Hector finished his climb to the top of the mountain and viewed the island from a higher vantage. Two other dragons were on or atop mountains. The four each faced a direction: north, south, east, and west. He lowered himself to a rock and scanned the city with his enhanced vision. The architecture leaned more toward Greek or Roman with the tall, ornate columns, formalized structures, symmetry, and arches.

Those occupying the isle varied in every possible way. He

spotted the same simple tunics and trousers he had seen at Stonemore. There was even a yellow sleeveless tunic and armband like those worn at Orgate. Then there were those he figured had been raised on Highvale since they all wore some variation of a Greek chiton—like the blonde he'd encountered earlier. The men, however, either kept their legs bare or wore trousers ending at their knees beneath the folds of fabric.

Hector looked down at his clothes. He could keep what he had, which was suitable for walking the streets of other cities like Stonemore. Or he could blend in by sporting the type of dress those who had been there since birth wore. He stayed atop the mountain for hours, watching the movements of the inhabitants at night. The streets finally quieted after midnight as most sought their beds. But not everyone. Two taverns remained open, full of music and boisterous conversation.

When the sky began to lighten with the approaching dawn, he stood and faced the water. He could leave and return to Iron Hall with news of everything he had discovered.

An image of the light within the corridor came to mind. It had beckoned him. Maybe he was *supposed* to be here. Perhaps he wasn't. Not having anything to do had chafed, and he had a few more days before he had to be on patrol. That was plenty of time to find the blonde and get answers before returning home.

He moved to the edge of the cliff and held out his arms. Then, he dove. Wind whistled around him as he linked his hands over his head and plunged into the water. He didn't shift this time. Instead, he swam underwater to the side of the island that faced the mainland. He surfaced from the depths and stilled when the first rays of sun broke the horizon and lit upon Highvale's grand entrance.

Wide steps emerged from the water, leading to enormous pillars on either side. Atop the pillars, two identical dragons sat regally in greeting, their heads turned toward each other. Below each statue stood a marble column with a curved bowl atop it where a fire blazed. Hector stared at the faces, noting their resemblance to Asher, King of Hunter Greens. He didn't think he would ever get used to recognizing the sculptures.

He swam toward the steps. The moment he placed a foot upon the stone, his magic transformed his attire. By the time he emerged from the water, he wore the traditional garb of Highvale. It had been a very long time since he had worn such garments. He adjusted the wide leather belt at his waist and the length of material that fell over the back of his left shoulder. He continued up the steps and past the enormous statues to a stone entrance with four towering columns and a decorative, triangular gable atop it.

A few people milled about, and all of them stared at him. He nodded in greeting and received nods in return. He had just passed beneath the columns when he heard a sharp intake of breath. His head snapped to the right to see a young lad, skinny as a rail with dark curls and blue eyes wide with shock and delight. Hector was about to turn away when the boy's gaze lifted above him, then met Hector's again. He turned to see what the lad was looking at when his gaze landed on a dragon statue hanging from a business sign.

Hector slowly turned to the kid. Somehow, the lad knew what he was. The last thing he wanted was for anyone to out him before he was ready to announce his presence. He put a finger to his lips. The boy nodded in agreement. Hector turned and continued on his walk through the streets. The city had come alive with the dawn. Vendors opened shop doors while citizens carried baskets for shopping. And conversation flowed all around him.

Everyone he saw were humanoids with magic, like the Druids on Earth. If there were other species, as the Kings had long suspected, they would be at Highvale. He expected to see at least some Sea Elves walking around, but so far, nothing. Which surprised him. Hector sensed someone following him and glanced over his shoulder to see the lad before he ducked behind some crates. Hector kept walking. The boy seemed more curious than anything.

The streets were laid out in a grid pattern that made them easy to navigate. Hector heard as many different languages as there were clothing styles. His magic deciphered each, allowing him to grab snippets of conversation as he passed. Despite the varied cultures, there appeared to be a singular language that everyone seemed to know. It was the same as the one from Stonemore.

For the next hour, the lad trailed him, ducking into alleys and behind others in an attempt to stay hidden. He did a pretty decent job of it, too. Hector turned a corner and leaned a shoulder against the side of the building as he waited for the boy. Within moments, the lad rushed around the corner. He drew up short when he spotted Hector. But the kid didn't rush away after being discovered. He stood his ground.

"Do they have school here?" Hector asked.

The lad nodded.

"Should you no' be there?"

The boy shrugged, his lips twisting. "I don't like it."

"That's where you learn things."

"I learn more on the streets," he replied with another shrug of his thin shoulders.

Hector grunted. "It isna the same." He eyed the lad, seeing his dingy clothes and bare feet. "Do you have a family?"

"It's just me," he replied easily.

Too easily. That meant the kid had been on his own for a significant period of time. He wasn't that old, either. "There isna a place for bairns such as you?"

The lad's face scrunched in a frown. "Bairns?"

"Kids," Hector explained.

"There is. I go there sometimes."

That's what Hector was afraid of. "You hungry?"

"I could eat."

By the looks of the lad, he had missed many meals. He motioned to the boy. "Come on."

They fell into step together as Hector looked for a place to eat. He found it on the next street and chose a table outside. The boy seemed hesitant to sit, but he eventually got past it and slid into the wooden chair. Hector said nothing as he waited for someone to come to the table and take their order. A balding, heavyset man wearing a tunic and trousers eventually made his way over, greeting them with a quick smile.

"Get whatever you want," Hector told the lad.

The man looked between them before focusing on the boy. Once the lad had ordered, the attendant swiveled his head to Hector.

"Make it two," he said. Once the waiter was gone, Hector speared the lad with a look. "What's your name?"

"Teo."

"How old are you?"

Teo held his gaze for a long moment. "Eleven."

"Were you raised on the island?"

Teo shook his head.

He didn't readily give an answer, and Hector recognized that the lad didn't want to say more. So, he didn't push. For now.

"What's your name?" Teo asked.

"Hector."

"How old are you?"

Hector smiled at the lad. "Verra old. What do you think I am?"

Teo motioned to a dragon with his head.

"All right," Hector said. "Why do you think that?"

"I can see you. The real you." He shrugged. "And this form."

That was unexpected but interesting. "Are there others like me here?"

He shook his head.

"What can you tell me about Highvale?"

The lad grinned. "Whatever you want to know."

"Tell me everything."

Teo sat up straighter in the chair and leaned forward. "Everyone gets along for the most part. Tensions have been rising, but we realize how important the island is. Which is why things haven't progressed as they might elsewhere."

The fact that those words came from a young boy spoke volumes. Hector rested an arm on the table. "In what regard?"

"What's happening on the outside to those with magic. Surely, you know about that."

"Sadly, I do indeed." Hector drummed his fingers on the table and nodded for Teo to continue.

"If you make it past the first entrance and find your way to the island, you can't be forced to leave."

Hector raised his brows as he thought of his unexpected departure earlier. She hadn't exactly *forced* him to leave. He was the one who had gotten thrown off balance. "Have they wanted someone off the isle?"

"Not that I know of. I know I'm safe here and they can't make me leave. That's all I need to know."

Hector glanced at the table. What had the lad suffered to have such thoughts? And how many others like him, those who didn't know about Highvale, were out there?

"There's a cabinet made up of three members from each of the two guild houses," Teo continued. "Each guild elects members to sit on the cabinet. There are also three others, elected by everyone."

"What guild are you in?"

Their food was brought out and laid on the table. Teo hungrily took a bite and said around a mouthful, "'M not. You have to want to join and pass their tests. Besides, I'm not a Banshee or a seer."

"Those are the only two?" Hector pushed his platter toward the lad after he'd devoured his in just a few bites.

Teo nodded. "They're difficult to get into, and not everyone stays. They're not always treated well."

"Why would anyone want to join to begin with?"

Teo lifted his blue eyes. "Power."

It said a lot about the lad that he could recognize the distinction at such a young age. Hector glanced to the side, his gaze landing on a woman with blond curls. Even with her back to him, he recognized her. He got to his feet and belatedly remembered that he hadn't paid for the food. He crafted a bag of coins with his magic and held it out to Teo. "Eat your fill. I'll be back."

FIVE

The streets were already crowded as Emilia made her way from the guild to the temple. She had overslept because of a fitful night, where sleep had remained out of reach until the early hours. She couldn't stop thinking about the Dragon King. She didn't have the power to keep him from Highvale. No one did.

That was the point. If someone had magic, they were allowed on the island. No matter who they were or what kind of magic they had. The cabinet believed the laws they had in place would prevent anyone from taking over. That declaration always made her roll her eyes. Any being—or group—with enough sway could take control of Highvale, regardless of the cabinet or who had a seat.

It wasn't that she thought the Dragon King would attempt such a thing. That wasn't what she had seen in her visions. But the fact of the matter was that he would return. The question was *when*. He would be furious that she had not only lied to him but also tricked him. How far had she sent him when she helped him out the door? It didn't really matter since he could fly and would likely be back within hours. Would he come alone? Or would he bring others this time?

The more she thought about how she'd handled the situation, the more she knew she had made a mistake. What if her vision of destruction had been caused because *she'd* angered the Dragon King by tricking him and then gently showing him the exit? All those years of wondering when the dragons would show and debating how she would handle things, and *that* is what she had come up with? It had been a catastrophe. How would she ever face anyone if she caused the world to burn?

She glanced at the sky but didn't see any dark spots that might indicate something huge with wings was descending upon them. But they would come. Sooner or later. She had let things be idle for far too long, hoping she was wrong. That others' decisions would change the outcome of her visions. But she knew better. Everything that happened from this day forward was on her.

Her footsteps quickened as she shouldered her way through the crowd. Her heart stopped when she spied someone with shoulder-length, light brown hair. Every muscle tightened as she halted, her heart in her throat. Then the man turned, and she realized it wasn't the Dragon King. Emilia breathed a sigh of relief and resumed walking. She should head straight to Agathi, but she always started the day at the temple. A few moments of prayer wouldn't hurt, surely.

She rushed up the long flight of steps and past the double row of columns into the sacred temple. Alternating statues of dragons and humans rested between the pillars as if the two had lived together at one time. A quick sweep showed that she was alone. In the middle of the space, beneath the open, domed ceiling with sunlight pouring in, stood a morel tree with its pale bark and pink leaves.

Emilia grabbed a couple of incense sticks and took them to the brazier at the edge of the stones around the tree. She lit the incense and stuck it in the sand with dozens of others, then walked to the right and knelt upon a stone, her hands pressed together at her heart with her head bowed. Then she closed her eyes.

I send up my prayers to whichever of the gods are listening. Watch over my parents, should they still be alive. If they have been taken from this realm, then I pray they are happy together somewhere.

Emilia paused and swallowed.

I also ask for strength for what I will face today and in the coming days. Please give me the words to prove the importance of not aligning with the Dragon Kings. And...please keep the Kings far from Highvale so thousands of lives will be saved.

It was a bold, daring ask, but she had to try. She rarely requested anything for herself. It had always felt wrong. But no morning passed when she didn't come to the temple and pray for the parents she had left behind.

She opened her eyes and lowered her arms as she sat back on her haunches to look through the statues and columns to the water. It stretched far into the horizon in every direction. Highvale had meant safety and security for thousands of years. The island had been the only way many magicals had survived. Because despite having abilities, it wasn't always easy to stand against a rioting village.

Emilia had dedicated herself to Highvale the moment she stepped out of the sea and onto the island's stairs. Everything she did was to ensure not only its survival but to make sure it thrived. She had remained in the background, happy to be overlooked and ignored. Today, after she told Agathi the truth, she would likely be forced to step into the spotlight and accept everything that went with that—the scrutiny and the attacks. The suspicion and skepticism.

A sigh fell from her lips as she got to her feet. She turned to leave and jerked to a halt at the sight of the man leaning a shoulder against one of the columns, his bare arms folded across his chest, showing rippling muscles. Deep brown eyes were locked on her. There was no smile on his face, no curiosity in his features this time. The breeze gently moved the ends of his hair.

Her lungs locked as she realized this wasn't a figment of her imagination. She was looking into the face of the Dragon King she had misled just hours before. Ice poured through her veins.

"What? Nothing to say this time?" he quipped. "No lies? No false promises?"

Her mouth went dry as her mind scrambled to find something to say. But nothing she could tell him would appease his anger or absolve her of what she had done. Frick it all. She *was* the reason there was a war. She tried to think of something to pacify him, but fear had silenced her thoughts and frozen her limbs.

He grunted as he straightened and dropped his arms to his sides. She tried to swallow, but her tongue was stuck to the roof of her mouth. It occurred to her then that he hadn't flown to Highvale. If he had, someone would've seen him.

As he made his way to the left of one of the statues, she noticed that he wore an off-white chiton. The garment had been designed to show off a male's physique, and it did a glorious job of revealing his from his muscular shoulders and corded neck to his brawny arms and powerful legs. Even the wide belt accentuated the V from his shoulders to his waist.

His head swung to her, his dark eyes locking on her again. "This is when you should think about speaking."

His accent was so different than anything she had ever heard, but now wasn't the time to ask about that. She had made a decision and acted upon it. It was time everyone knew the truth—including him.

Emilia managed to wet her mouth enough that her tongue was no longer dry. When it came, her voice shook slightly. Then again, she *was* speaking to a Dragon King. "I had no choice."

"There's always a choice, lass. Try again," he urged as he continued to walk around the temple, inspecting the statues.

She followed him with her gaze. "It may sound like an excuse to you, but it's the truth."

He grunted without looking her way. He halted before one of the dragons and looked up at it, his head tilting one way and then the other.

"You never should've been called here," she said.

"But I was."

She briefly cut her eyes to the side. "If I could've stopped that, I would have."

"Why is that?"

Emilia hated that he wouldn't look at her. She eyed his broad back and found her gaze lingering on his trim hips and lower. Furious at herself, she yanked her focus to the back of his head. "Many believe your arrival means an end to the persecution magicals have endured on the mainland."

He continued walking but glanced in her direction. "I take it you doona."

"I do not."

"And what, pray tell, do *you* believe my arrival means?"

She had never said the words aloud. Had never given voice to the fears that had plagued her for so long. Emilia licked her lips and clasped her hands together in a bid to gather whatever strength she could. "Death. Annihilation. Destruction."

He halted and slowly turned to look at her. His dark gaze searched her face for a long moment. "You've seen it."

It wasn't a question. She hadn't considered that he might actually believe her. "I have."

"Is it just my arrival? Or multiple Kings?"

"I-I don't know. My visions never showed me that. I've only seen what will happen if Dragon Kings come to Highvale."

He walked to the back of the temple perched on a cliff and stared out at the water. "You could've told me that."

"I couldn't take the chance you would dismiss my words," she explained. She had to move to the side to see him around the tree.

"I returned. I could well have begun the verra thing you tried to avoid."

She briefly closed her eyes. "I know. No one else knows you're here. We might still have time to stop it."

After a time, he faced her. "Then we must ensure that no one else becomes aware of my presence."

"I agree. It would also help if you left. Immediately." She knew she was pushing things, but she would do anything to keep from seeing the dead scattered about and the world on fire.

He headed toward her, and it was all she could do not to back up a step. Emilia turned with him as he approached. He came to a stop a few feet from her. "I need to know how I was brought here the first time so I can shut off the beacon."

Her legs wobbled when his words penetrated her mind. She wasn't the cause of the world ending. And he was going to help her. Maybe she wouldn't need to tell anyone else about her visions. By convincing him, the Dragon Kings could stop everything before it came to pass. "You'll help me?"

He nodded. "I have questions. If you answer them—properly, this time—I will make sure no Kings ever step foot on the island again."

Emilia hesitated. She should be rejoicing. This had been easier than she anticipated. Too easy, actually.

"You doona seem overjoyed, lass," he pointed out.

"I don't understand why you're so eager to help. You don't know me. You can't even be sure I'm not lying."

He quirked a brow. "You're no' helping your case."

"I expected a fight."

"Is that what happened when you told others?"

She glanced away and bit her lip. "I've never told anyone."

"Now that is alarming. If you saw the end of Zora, you should be shouting it to one and all. Why keep it to yourself?"

If telling him about the doom of the world had been challenging, this was agonizing.

"Come, lass," he bade. "You've gone this far."

She had started this. She might as well spill everything and hope he didn't change his mind. Emilia inhaled deeply and said, "I'm not supposed to. The feeling I get each time I have the vision is that I need to keep it to myself."

"That's curious since it involves so many others."

"I know."

"You've no' told anyone else?"

She shook her head. "No one."

"And you've seen the same vision before?"

"Repeatedly since I arrived on the island."

His lips flattened. "You asked why I would want to help you, a stranger. If you'd lived for as long as I have, you pick up on things. I sense your honesty. About the visions, at least. That kind of fear can no' be faked." He released a long breath. "Enemies trying to kill or enslave us are everywhere we go. We've vanquished so many, but that doesna mean we enjoy battle. All we've faced on Zora is fear and hatred." His head turned to the dragon statue beside him. "Yet, on this island, there are images of us at every turn." Dark eyes slid to her. "You fear me, though. I see it every time I look at you."

"I'm not afraid of you. You are one of us. What you see are remnants of terror from a vision that repeats with the realm soaked in blood and covered in flames."

"Then the quicker I'm gone from the island, the better. Shall we get to the questions? My name is Hector. And you are?"

"Emilia," she replied.

He dipped his head and then asked, "Why all the statues of us?"

"Zora is the dragons' home. This is your world. You've only allowed others to share it with you. We recognize the importance of your kind and the power you wield. Each statue is a reminder that we are connected through magic."

"Who designed them?"

She shrugged. "It was done well before my time."

"How is the island connected to Iron Hall?"

"What's Iron Hall?"

He took a half step closer, his brow furrowing. "You doona know?"

"Our records indicate that a beacon was set up in or around dragon land many generations ago to call one of you."

"Any dragon? Or a King?" he pressed.

She moved a strand of hair that got tangled in her lashes. "A King, I believe."

"How long has it been in place?"

There was an intensity to his words, his face lined with disquiet. "I don't know when it was placed. It could be hundreds, maybe even thousands, of years ago. The cabinet recently turned it on."

"All of that is interesting, considering the majority of the Kings only just arrived."

Before Emilia could answer, someone whistled. She looked toward the entrance to find a young boy before he ducked out of sight.

"We have company," Hector said.

SIX

The conversation was just getting started. Hector wasn't happy about being interrupted. He strode to the steps and peered down to see a middle-aged woman heading up. If he wanted to remain unseen, he needed to disappear quickly. Teo was hidden behind some rocks, waiting for Hector. He'd have to remind the lad to stop following him. Though, if he had been paying attention to his surroundings instead of focusing on Emilia, he'd have heard the approach himself.

Hector looked over his shoulder at Emilia. Apprehension filled her eyes as she watched him. She was as ethereal as a goddess standing among the statues and the pink-leaved tree. With blond curls framing a face of incomprehensible beauty and eyes of cobalt swimming with sun-lit currents, she fascinated him. She had a spine of steel she didn't mind showing him. Emilia was an enigma. How he would love to have the time to solve the mystery surrounding her.

He should leave Highvale. He had some of the answers he

coveted, but he needed more. And, truth be told, he wanted more time with her.

"You said you would leave," Emilia said in a hushed tone as she hurried to him.

He glanced at Teo and jerked his chin down the stairs. The boy nodded and slipped away to await him. Hector turned to Emilia. "We're no' done yet."

"Please," she began.

"I gave you my word, and I'll keep it. I'll stay hidden. But there are things I need to know."

She looked at the stairs, her chest heaving in panic. "Fine. Ask," she urged as she turned to him.

"No' here." He walked to the back edge of the temple and looked over the side. He could easily reach the bottom, but not without being seen.

"Where, then?" she whispered angrily behind him.

He started to answer when the approaching footsteps grew louder. The moment Emilia glanced worriedly at the stairs, he dropped over the side of the temple behind a boulder. He remained there and listened to Emilia leave the temple. Hector leaned around the rock and observed her descent. She didn't look back for him. She kept her head straight and her feet moving quickly.

Every fiber of his being wanted to follow her. And he was about to do that when he saw a woman slip out of an alley and fall into step behind Emilia, who seemed unaware of her follower. He watched the two of them until they moved out of sight.

As long as he didn't shift—and Teo kept quiet—no one would know he was there. Hector picked his way down the hillside and searched for Teo, but the lad was gone. Hector followed Emilia's path and stopped where he'd lost her. That brought him to another set of steps leading to an impressive building. Men and women walked in and out of it, making him believe it wasn't a private residence.

The island wasn't that big. He just needed to bide his time until he and Emilia could finish their conversation. Until then, it was crucial for him to stay hidden in case others like Teo could see who he really was. He scanned the faces of those around him, but few paid him any mind. That didn't mean someone wasn't watching. Someone was always watching from the shadows, whether they were spies or hiding for other reasons.

He stayed relaxed and headed to the beach. There had to be a place where he could be alone until dark, when he would search out Emilia again. He checked behind him often, but no one followed. The sights and sounds of Highvale were no different than any other place he had visited. It looked like a regular city, except for the magic he felt from every direction. All different kinds, too.

His sandals sank into the thick, golden sand. No one was about, but it was an open shoreline with nowhere to hide. Hector turned left and followed the shore, headed toward a cove he had spotted the previous night. He didn't get far before encountering a group of adolescents swimming. They didn't notice as he passed. Their voices and the sound of splashing water soon faded as he put distance between them. Finally, he reached the cove. He had seen it during his initial swim and when he stood on the mountain, but neither time had prepared him for the calm majesty of the sheltered, circular bay.

The water turned from turquoise to cobalt as it deepened, reminding him of Emilia's eyes. The rocky area past the short beach extended into the water. A smile pulled at his lips when he spotted the wide opening of a cave. He removed his sandals and dumped out the sand before tossing them aside and heading to the water. He waded to his calves and stood as the waves gently rolled past him, his conversation with Emilia replaying in his head.

Hector knew firsthand what was happening to those with magic outside of Highvale. It made sense that some would want to help their fellow magic users. Just as there would always be those against any kind of bloodshed. Because no matter what good intentions were set, other players on the board would only deal in violence. They proved that every day by killing.

Even Teo was aware of the tension on the island. How long until things came to a head? Not long, Hector guessed. Perhaps that's why the cabinet had activated the beacon—in hopes the Kings would either have an answer or offer to help. It made sense in every way Hector looked at it.

Until he factored in Emilia's assertion.

Visions rarely laid out a who, what, why, and where scenario. Only the *when* had been left unanswered. The visions gave the seer snippets to decipher. Blood and fire. That wasn't too difficult to interpret. Emilia had stated it was because the Kings came to the island. Had she seen a dragon in her vision? He needed to know how it was all connected. There was no need to return to Iron Hall until he did.

He looked to the side, taking in one of the mountaintop statues. The other Kings would want to see this place. And he wanted them to see it. After all the hate they'd received, it was nice to see people who actually liked them.

The wind carried the sound of someone running toward him. Hector whipped his head around, ready to hide, when he caught sight of Teo. The lad was running full-out, his gaze searching. Hector knew the moment the boy saw him by the quick smile on Teo's face. Much about the lad reminded Hector of his childhood. He, too, had been an orphan. It hadn't been a great upbringing, but things could have been worse.

It taught him to stand on his own early and, at the same time, recognize that friendship could be the difference between life and death—the same traits Teo seemed to be figuring out. Except the lad wasn't doing it in the middle of a clan war, where every day might be his last. Hector didn't want that for Teo or anyone. Emilia's prediction of Zora burning had sent a chill down Hector's spine because it reminded him of how his clan lands had looked once.

"I thought you left," Teo said breathlessly when he finally reached Hector.

"No' yet. There are still a few things I need to sort out."

Teo's brow furrowed as he put his hands on his hips and dragged in mouthfuls of air. "You can't leave. We need you."

"Do you know if there are others like you on the isle?"

"You mean those who can see what you really are?"

Hector nodded.

Teo shrugged. "Not that I know of, but I've not tried to find out."

It was as Hector had expected, but he was still disappointed. "I need to stay hidden until tonight. Just in case."

"It's because of what she told you."

"You heard her, I take it?"

Teo looked toward the water and dropped his arms to his sides. "I did."

"I told you I'd be back. I keep my word. You didna need to

follow me." The lad wouldn't look at him. Hector briefly closed his eyes. "I'm glad you did, though. Now, I doona need to repeat the conversation."

Surprise lit Teo's blue eyes. "You want to discuss it with me?"

"If you're willing."

"Aye," Teo said excitedly.

Hector ran a hand over his jaw. "What do you think about Emilia's vision?"

"That it's real, but that doesn't mean the Kings caused it. It could be the humans."

"How long have you been on the island?"

Teo shrugged and kicked at the sand with his bare feet. "Five years."

"And how much of the outside world did you see?"

"If you're asking if I know the cruelty done to those with magic, I do."

For someone so young to experience such brutality was unimaginable. Yet, it happened every day throughout the universe. You couldn't have the light without the darkness. And there would always be innocents caught in the crosshairs.

"What do you think should happen to those without magic?" Hector asked.

"They should get in kind what they've given to others."

At one time, Hector had thought the very same. Sometimes, he still did. He put a hand on Teo's shoulder and looked into the boy's eyes. "Who will take their lives? Me? You? Trust me, lad, you doona want to be responsible for ending another's life."

"So, they shouldn't be punished?"

"That isna what I'm saying. There will always be violence, and there are times when the only way to stop it is with more savagery.

But that should only be a last resort. Ignorance and fear led those without magic. We need to change their way of thinking. Rationally and calmly."

Teo bit his lip and frowned. "Years of running for our lives without turning our magic on them hasn't changed their thinking. I doubt anything will."

Hector wanted to tell him he was wrong, but he couldn't. The proof was right there. Villette's handiwork at it again. Her hatred for the dragons had invaded Earth and then Zora. When she failed to wipe out the Kings on Earth, she turned her full attention to Zora. All because the Star People had once enslaved the dragons. It had been her brother who created Earth and set the dragons free.

Few knew that, and there was no need to heap additional worries on Teo. He carried too much already.

Hector squeezed his shoulder before dropping his hand. "You're wise for one so young."

"The world has made me that way."

"Highvale keeps all that away."

Teo's lips twisted. "For how long?"

"They'd have to find the isle first. We both know that isna easy." Hector turned and walked toward the cliff.

Teo followed him. After they were seated, the lad asked, "Are there many kids where you live?"

"There are. You're welcome to return with me."

"Really?" he asked eagerly.

"Aye, but you'll be safer here. And just so you know, I'd make you attend school."

Teo chuckled as they shared a look.

Hector turned his gaze back to the water as he thought about Emilia. The longer he remained on Highvale, the greater his chances of being discovered. But he had more questions. The same ones the other Kings would ask. If he didn't have the answers, then someone might return and set everything Emilia was trying to prevent into motion.

"What is it?" Teo asked.

"I need to find Emilia so we can finish our conversation."

"That's easy."

Hector swung his head to the lad. "Why is that?"

"Because I followed her. I know exactly where she is."

Hector threw back his head and laughed, then ruffled the lad's hair.

SEVEN

How was she supposed to concentrate after coming face-to-face with Hector? Again. Emilia had carried the secret of her vision for years, but this new secret added on top was something she feared was written all over her face. She kept expecting people to stop her and demand to know about Hector.

The day dragged sluggishly. She alternated between fear of someone discovering Hector and her involvement in keeping him hidden and having to come clean about her vision. Both were serious offenses, especially to the guild. Something as significant as the end of the world wasn't something a seer kept to themselves. Everyone—not just those in the house or the cabinet—would demand to know why.

She doubted they would accept her explanation as Hector had. They would think it was an excuse or disregard her vision altogether. The guild also wouldn't take kindly to her wish to keep the extent of her abilities hidden. The quiet, modest life she had chosen would be upended. However, she had chosen that herself when she manipulated Hector into leaving Highvale. If he hadn't returned, another King would have come. Hector had found the beacon. How long until another Dragon King did the same?

This was a disaster, no matter how she looked at it.

With her mind otherwise occupied, she didn't pay attention and continually dropped things or ran into others. If only she could stop thinking about Hector. His captivating eyes, his handsome face. His deep, sensual voice with his rolling r's. She tried to imagine what he looked like in his dragon form. Did he resemble one of the numerous statues on the island? What color were his scales? Highvale had been based on tales of dragons. They were worshipped on the island, just as the deities were.

And now, a King walked among them. They should be celebrating. Everyone should know who Hector was. It made her question if she had interpreted the vision wrong. She could argue that if she had only seen it once. But it had occurred multiple times a year for nearly two decades. She hadn't misunderstood what it showed her, even if she wished otherwise.

Why was she responsible for knowing such a violent outcome? Why had the gods bestowed such a vision upon her? It must be a punishment for something she did to anger them. There was no other explanation for her being burdened by a truth no one would believe.

Except Hector.

If only they'd had a few more minutes alone. She might have been able to answer his questions so he could leave and see that no other Kings returned.

Or perhaps it had all been wishful thinking on her part. She was no one. A seer without means, family, or social rank. She was the rarity of the guild. While others exuded confidence and exaggerated their abilities, she downplayed hers.

She picked at her noon meal, her stomach rebelling at the smells. There was no way she could swallow anything right now. And if she did, she feared it would come back up. Emilia scanned the room, looking for Agathi, but she wasn't there. It was time Emilia came clean to her friend—for her own sanity.

Emilia shoved aside her food and went in search of Agathi, but she couldn't find her, no matter where she looked. She was glad for the reprieve. Agathi would be furious and hurt that Emilia hadn't trusted her. She would likely use those exact words. As young children, they had promised never to keep secrets, and Emilia had harbored a huge one from the very beginning.

Throughout the long afternoon, Emilia tried to come up with the right words to explain everything, but nothing sounded good enough. Agathi was her best friend, the sister of her heart. Hopefully, she would find it in her to grant Emilia forgiveness. Because the only way Emilia was getting out of this mess was with Agathi by her side.

Emilia knew she could find her friend at the evening meal. The closer it came to that time, however, the more nervous she became. She looked out one of the arches but didn't see the blue sky or the ocean. She saw Hector's face. No matter how anxious she was about Agathi, Hector and everything his arrival meant wouldn't leave her. Yet, he was part of this debacle—all the dragons were. She couldn't separate them from any of it, which was difficult to accept.

Her vision wasn't just about magicals or non-magicals. It was about humans, dragons, and every other living soul on the realm. It was about life and death for all.

The weight of that nearly buckled her knees. The vision had been about something that would happen in the future. But that future was no longer distant. It was here now. Her stomach turned so violently that she had to cover her mouth with her hand in case she got sick. Someone else should carry the burden of the vision, someone who knew how to handle such an important prediction. Because she didn't.

By the time she made her way to the evening meal, she was so wound up from worry and fear that it was all she could do to remain on her feet. The smell of food hit her as she turned the corner. She had to pause as she gagged. She had never handled anxiety well, which was why she usually steered clear of it.

Emilia pressed her heated forehead against the cool stone, then straightened and continued on shaky legs. She halted atop the steps to the dining room and looked out over the crowd, searching for Agathi's tall form and dark hair. She searched thrice, to no avail.

She gratefully reached her chair and sank into it. The tables were already laden with platters of vegetables, fresh fish, bread, legumes, and cheese. This time, she didn't attempt to fill her plate. She was having a hard enough time with the various smells.

The conversation in the room seemed louder than usual. Maybe it was her imagination, but it almost seemed as if a new thread of excitement ran through the island. Emilia's gaze went to the front table, where the three elected to the cabinet sat. It wasn't just Agathi missing. The other two Oracle guild members hadn't arrived either.

Emilia stayed for as long as she dared before her stomach upset became too much. She rose and left the courtyard, making her way to Agathi's room at the top of the building. Her family's powerful position had granted her a very nice room, but she had gotten a spectacular upgrade upon her election to the cabinet. Agathi's room was easily four times the size of Emilia's, and the view was stunning.

Everyone was at supper, so the corridors were empty. No one saw Emilia race up the stairs to the very top and hurriedly knock on Agathi's door. She waited a few seconds before knocking again. No one answered. Emilia nervously pressed her lips together before pulling out the folded piece of paper she had stuffed alongside her breast earlier. She stared at it for a moment before pushing it under Agathi's door.

Then she retraced her steps to the ground floor and her room. Her original quarters had been in the basement, but her years in the house had given her some seniority. Her room was small but away from the hubbub of the house and situated on the cliffs. Her view wasn't as grand as Agathi's, but she liked it.

She entered her chambers and closed the door behind her, leaning against it for a heartbeat. Then she did something she had never done—she turned the lock. It could be easily overcome with magic, but if someone did come for her, the time it took them to get past the bolt would allow her a moment to compose herself. Though her paranoia was probably her fears being amplified and her imagination running amok.

This was why she had wanted to find Agathi and spill her secret. Secrets. Plural. Holding them was exhausting and terrifying. Emilia longed to be free of them. They were eating her alive. She had backed herself into a corner with no exit. No matter what she decided, her life would be forever altered. Yet she couldn't shake the worry that telling Agathi about Hector might set her vision into motion.

She walked to the bed and sat on the end to look out the window. The mattress suddenly sank beside her, and she turned her head, shocked to find the young boy she had spotted with Hector. Emilia jumped up and glanced at the door.

"You should be more careful," he told her. His blue eyes were clear and bright, his wavy, dark locks mussed by wind. "I watched you come in."

"How did you get in here?" she demanded.

He jerked his chin to the window. "I climbed."

"What are you doing here?"

At this, he smiled. "I've come to take you to Hector."

So, the Dragon King remained on the island. He was resolute in getting the answers he wanted. She hoped he was staying out of sight. "And you are?"

"Teo," he answered with a dip of his chin. "And you're Emilia. We shouldn't waste any more time." He rose and headed to the window.

Emilia frowned as she got to her feet. "I'm not going out that way. I can't climb down the cliff."

"Trust me," Teo said before scrambling over the edge of the window. He held on to the side and smiled, then dropped down.

Emilia rushed over, thinking he had slipped and fallen to his death. Instead, Teo stared up at her from a tiny ledge she hadn't known was there.

"Are you coming?" he asked.

Emilia needed Hector gone, and since he couldn't come to her, she had to go to him. And she had to do it without being seen. That meant scaling a cliff. She watched Teo easily climb down. If the boy could do it, so could she.

She pulled the back of her skirt up between her legs and

tucked the edge into her belt so she could move more easily. Then she sat on the window ledge and swung her legs over, one at a time. Once on her feet, she faced her room as Teo had done and looked down at the ledge. It was right below her. All she had to do was jump down. Seemed simple enough when she eyed it from the safety of her room. Not so much where she stood now.

"Come on," Teo urged. "Just jump. It's only a few feet."

Emilia took a breath and hopped, releasing her hold on the window at the same time. Her feet struck the ledge a second later. Her arms windmilled until she got her balance. When she looked up, she realized it was about two feet from where she had stood. After that, her fear lessened, and she was able to follow Teo down.

The moment she was on solid ground with the waves licking at her feet, Teo was off again. She hurried to catch up as he ran down the short beach. The sun was setting, bathing Highvale in brilliant colors. She rounded the corner of the cove to find Teo sitting on a boulder, looking out at the water.

Emilia scanned the area for Hector. When he didn't rise from behind one of the large rocks, she looked into the cave but only saw darkness. Then she turned to the water. Hector rose from the waves bathed in the golden light of the setting sun. Her breath caught in her throat as she took in his bare chest and corded muscles.

She watched the water dip lower as he walked toward the shore. Just when she thought he might be naked, she spotted the top portion of his chiton hanging around his waist. A thread of disappointment needled her. She ran her gaze back up his incredible body until their eyes met.

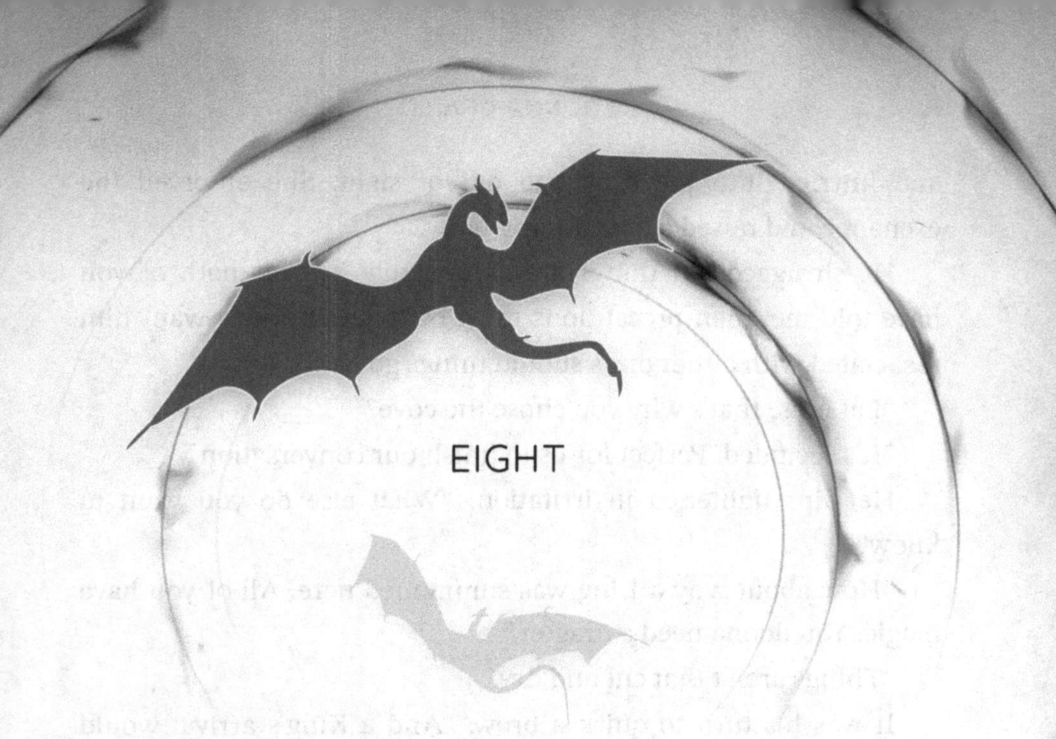

EIGHT

The sight of Emilia standing on the beach, highlighted by the sunset, was an image Hector wouldn't soon forget. Lust raced through him in a primal, wholly carnal response when her eyes lingered on his body. For just a heartbeat, he almost remained nude but clothed himself at the last minute.

He halted in the water with the waves breaking around his ankles. She was breathing fast, her fingers fiddling with the material of her clothes. He tried not to notice the sight of her bared legs or hard nipples, but it was impossible.

"I see Teo found you," he said.

She glanced at the lad. "He did."

"He assured me the climb wasna too dangerous. You were able to descend easily?" he asked and nodded to her skirts that were still tucked between her legs.

She glanced down and hurriedly released them before shaking them out. "Aye, I made it fine."

Hector looked at Teo and nodded. The lad rose from his perch and hurried into the cave and out of sight. She observed the exchange and raised a questioning brow.

He shrugged. "If things are as unstable here as both of you have told me, then precautions must be made. I doona want him associated with either of us should things go badly."

"I assume that's why you chose the cove?"

"It's secluded. Perfect for us to finish our conversation."

Her lips tightened in irritation. "What else do you want to know?"

"How about why a King was summoned here. All of you have magic. You doona need a dragon."

"Things aren't that cut and dry."

It was his turn to quirk a brow. "And a King's arrival would change that?"

"You can't walk this island and not notice the dragons. Your kind is more than legend and lore here. The dragons are the embodiment of supremacy and dominion. It only takes one to call those with abilities together, whether they've been hiding or ignoring their magic. We've endured generations of cruelty, banishment, and murder."

"And chose no' to do anything," he added.

Her eyes narrowed. "A few rose up. A handful fought back. For every death dealt to those without magic, they inflicted it threefold on those with abilities."

"And they ran. I'm no' saying they were wrong in doing so, I'm merely pointing out a fact. A Dragon King wouldna change any of that."

"That's where you're wrong. Things are reaching a breaking point. The cabinet feels the time is right for everyone to band together."

Hector fastened the top portion of his attire over his shoulders once more. He had masked his tattoo the moment he stepped foot on Highvale and would continue doing so. "With a King's help, of course."

"Of course. The current anger, combined with your presence, could grant them the outcome they desire."

"How does your vision fit in with this?"

She wound her arms around herself and shrugged her shoulders. "As I've already explained, I see the fire and blood. I see the dead lying about."

"What dragons do you see?"

"None," she replied after a slight hesitation.

He frowned and walked the rest of the way out of the water. "Then how do you know it involves us?"

"The same way I knew that I had to keep the vision a secret. It was just there."

"And that's where things get dicey. You have this vision of such vivid destruction, but you can no' tell anyone."

Wind lifted the ends of her hair as tension crackled around her. "I thought you believed me."

"I do, but I'm trying to get to the bottom of things."

"You think I'm withholding information."

He twisted his lips. "It has crossed my mind."

"Unbelievable," she murmured as she shook her head and looked away. "I thought you would help."

"I am."

"But you're still here!" she cried, pinning him with a savage look.

Hector stepped closer to her. "My brethren will want answers to these questions, too. If I can supply them, then you'll never see another dragon. If no', we might return."

She rubbed her forehead as if it pained her. "Then ask."

"Are you telling me everything about your vision?"

She dropped her hand to her side and speared him with a look. "I'd gladly show you if I could. Perhaps I'm not conveying the absolute horror of the fields of corpses and body parts. Maybe I need to be more vivid in describing the heat of the flames I feel near me as everything burns. And all around me, I hear dragons."

"You hear them, but you doona see."

"That's right. I've never seen them."

He nodded for her to continue. "What do you hear?"

Her eyes drifted close. "Roars. Some close, others far away. And a rhythmic beating."

"Like wings?"

Her lids snapped open. "Aye. It could be."

"So, you doona know if the dragons are causing the destruction or if they're fighting someone."

"I know that if a King comes to Highvale, my vision will come to pass. You've come. Twice now."

He smoothed back a wayward lock of wet hair that had fallen into his eyes. "No' if no one sees me."

"You make it sound as if that's the catalyst. You may not have to do anything. Maybe setting foot on the island is all that needs to happen."

"And you doona know what sets the vision off. We're both guessing."

She sighed and gave him a little nod. "I suppose you're right."

"Then let me ask you this... Can you say with absolute conviction that dragons will be the downfall of Zora? That we will be the cause of all the death you see?"

Her blue gaze lowered to the ground for a heartbeat. "I cannot. But that doesn't change that your kind is tied to what I've seen."

"Perhaps."

"Have you ever had a vision?"

Hector shook his head. "I doona have that gift, but I know others who do."

"Then you understand that we might not always see things, but we feel them." She flattened a palm on her chest. "We *know* them."

He thought he heard something over the waves and opened his hearing. Multiple people were headed their way, walking fast.

"Did you hear me?" Emilia asked.

Hector walked to her and spun her around, giving her a little push. "Get to the cave and hide. Doona come out. No matter what happens. Do you understand?"

"What's happening?"

"Several others are headed toward us."

Her eyes went wild as she frantically looked at him. "They found you."

"We're about to find out. Now, hide," he ordered brusquely.

She lifted her skirts and ran to the cave. He watched until she was safely inside, then walked knee-deep into the sea. Hector didn't know all the different beings who called Highvale home, so he couldn't guess what type of magic they might have or if they could combine it to harm him. His concern was for Emilia and Teo. As well as preventing anyone else from learning that he was a Dragon King and making the vision come to pass.

Hector watched the sunset for the second night in a row as he waited for the group to reach him. He counted thirteen different footsteps. They didn't try to hide their approach—or if they did, they were terrible at it. He pretended not to notice them as he studied the skyline.

"Hello!" a man called.

Hector sighed and turned to face them. A tall, thin man with a paunch stepped forward and raised his hand. He had short, sandy brown hair graying at the temples and a long, narrow face with wide-set blue eyes. "Hello," he shouted again.

Thirteen stood before him—eight men and five women. Seven were dressed to the nines in Grecian-style clothes that defined their status. The other six wore much more modest attire in a mix of styles, but they all moved and acted like soldiers. No doubt they were there to protect the seven in case Hector got rowdy.

"I'm Loukas," the man said, walking forward another couple of steps. "I am the leader of the cabinet—the governing body here. Behind me is one of my counterparts, Pelagia."

A petite, middle-aged woman stared at him with hazel eyes before she dipped her head. She wore a mint green gown, which brought out her olive complexion. Her dark hair was streaked with gray and pulled away from her face. Several thin gold chains encircled her neck, and long, gold earrings hung from her lobes. There was still a hint of her youthful beauty in the lines of her face.

"Several of the cabinet members and I have come to introduce ourselves," Loukas continued. "Newcomers to our haven usually come straight to the cabinet and proclaim themselves."

Hector grinned, hearing the not-so-subtle rebuke in the cabinet leader's voice. "I was just having a look at this majestic isle. Perhaps you should consider putting someone at the entrance to direct those arriving so no mistakes are made in the future."

Loukas waved away Hector's words with an overbright smile

and drew closer. "It's no worry, my friend. We merely wanted to introduce ourselves. What might your name be?"

He considered lying but decided it didn't matter if they knew his name. "Hector."

"Welcome to Highvale, Hector. What brought you to our island?"

His probing techniques left a lot to be desired. Hector shrugged. "Why do those like us come here?"

"Too true, too true." Loukas folded his hands over his extended stomach. His head tilted to the side. "But what brought *you*?"

The fool wasn't letting it go. Hector had to consider if Loukas knew who he was. He'd been careful when he arrived the second time. No one had seen him in his true form. Though, Teo didn't need to. If there was one, there was likely another. Fuck. Emilia would lose.

"Curiosity," Hector answered. It was time for him to do some probing of his own. He looked past Loukas. "Does everyone get such a welcome?"

Loukas's smile widened as his head leaned to the other side. "Not all, no."

Fucking hell. The bastard knew he was a King. He wasn't done playing the game, though. "I feel special. Why do I get such a display?"

"We've been waiting for you for a long time."

"You must have me mistaken for someone else," Hector began.

Loukas raised his hand to quiet Hector. "There's no need to pretend. We know you're a Dragon King."

Hector walked to stand before Loukas. "Did you ever consider that I might want to keep my identity a secret?"

"The truth hasn't come out. Yet."

The threat in the words was hard to miss. Hector leveled the man with a glare. "What is it you think I've come for?"

"To help us put an end to the humans."

"Humans." Hector clasped his hands behind his back so he didn't wrap them around Loukas's neck. "And what are you?"

Loukas waved away his words as if they didn't matter. "We have magic. They do not."

"How do you know they doona? Some have it and choose to pretend it doesna exist to fit in. You would kill them, too?"

"If that's the side they choose."

Hector had expected such a response, but hearing it still infuriated him. "What about the children? The babes? You want to *put an end* to them, too?"

"They can be raised to believe differently."

"If you doona think innocents will be killed in this war you so desperately want, you're deluded."

Loukas's smile dropped as anger filled his face, ruddying his cheeks. "You're a Dragon King."

"And?"

"We summoned you."

Anger simmered hotly, but Hector wouldn't let it show just yet. "Are you sure about that?"

"Without a doubt. The scrolls are very clear. If we're in need, we must only summon a King to protect us."

"I'd like to see those scrolls."

Loukas sniffed and lifted his chin. "That can be arranged. Now, if you'll come with me."

"I'll remain here."

Loukas's nostrils flared indignantly. "You cannot defy what has been written."

"Who wrote it?"

"Our ancestors."

"About the Dragon Kings? Are you sure?"

Loukas's blue eyes grew hostile as his rage amplified. "The scrolls might be ancient, but we know how to read them."

That was the second time Hector had heard about a link between the island and the Kings. He supposed the scrolls could refer to the twins since they ruled as a Dragon King and Queen, but no one mentioned a Queen. And it had always been King*s*, plural. Then there were the statues, each an image of a dragon Hector knew—himself, included.

"Look around," Loukas said, motioning to the dragon effigies. "You are worshipped here. You will be treated like a god."

"You mean one that does your bidding."

"As it has been ordained," Loukas snapped.

Hector had had enough. He released his fury, letting it fill his words, his person, and the very air around him. "I'm no' some goddamn genie from a lamp. I'm a fucking Dragon King with a mind of my own. I decide who I go to war with! No' you!"

Loukas stumbled back a few steps, fear tightening his face. The rest of his group did the same before clustering tighter together. Hector was glad they were frightened. He wanted them to know what they were toying with—and that he wouldn't stand for it.

"You would forsake your own?" Loukas asked.

"You know nothing about war or the consequences of it. Have those with magic been wronged? Without a doubt. The answer isna violence. Find another way."

"There isn't one," Pelagia said.

"There always is," Hector replied.

Loukas nervously watched him. "Haven't enough of us died?"

"Doona dare ask me such a thing. You know nothing of the Kings or what we've been through," Hector stated loudly enough for everyone to hear.

"You can balk all you want, but you're here. And you aren't going anywhere until we say," Pelagia declared.

Unease slid down Hector's spine. He opened the mental link that connected the dragons. *"Con."* He waited a beat for the King of Kings to reply. Hector tried again. *"Con!"*

Still no answer. Concern filled the faces of the thirteen, but they weren't backing down. They didn't have the metal from Orgate that could render someone's magic null. If they did, the entire island would be affected. He had promised Emilia that no one would know he was here, and he had broken that vow. Now, he had to make sure her vision didn't come to pass. Hector was about to shift and take to the skies when Loukas's voice rang out.

"Bring Emilia and the boy!"

Hector watched two of the six soldiers rush to the cave. He cut his eyes to Loukas to find his thin lips curved in a grin once more.

Emilia stepped out of the cave. "I'm alone."

Hector scanned the beach, looking for Teo. The lad was adept at moving about unseen. He might well have gotten away. The soldiers reached for Emilia, and it unleashed something feral within him. "Doona touch her."

The men paused and looked back at Loukas.

"I said bring her!" Loukas ordered a second time.

The soldiers each grabbed Emilia's arms and roughly hauled her away.

"Find the boy," the older woman barked.

Two more soldiers raced into the cave to search. Hector wasn't sure what they intended to do to Emilia. If he left now and they harmed her in any way, he would never forgive himself.

But if he stayed...

The soldiers came out and shook their heads. Loukas angrily motioned to the two holding Emilia. The soldiers roughly dragged her to Loukas. In the next second, Hector raised a hand and released a volley of magic that landed in the sand in front of the men holding Emilia, halting them.

In the same moment, something rose from the ground and entered his body. It felt like hundreds of tiny cords wrapping around him from his feet upward. He looked down, thinking to see what it was, but there was nothing there. Yet there was no mistaking the feel of them.

"It worked," the older woman murmured.

Hector jerked his gaze to her.

Loukas nodded, a satisfied smile on his face. "You're the island's now. Which means you're ours. You *will* protect us. And, if we deem it necessary, you will go to war for us."

Dread filled Hector. He wanted to deny everything but couldn't. He *was* connected to the isle in a way he hadn't been before. He could feel the rocks, the sand, even the water. It was almost as if he *was* the island.

He looked at Emilia. Her face was creased in regret as she stared at the sand. She couldn't even meet his gaze. Not that he blamed her. She had tried to warn him, but he had demanded answers.

Hector called to his magic. It filled him, surging through his body with might. He then reached down to the island and felt a spark of something familiar. No words passed between them, just feelings. There was time to look into that more later. Someone else needed his attention now.

Hector strode to Loukas. He bit back a laugh when the human shrank away in fear. He got in Loukas's face, forcing him to bend backward. "If you hurt one hair on her head, I'll rip you apart, limb from limb. Do you understand me?"

"Y-you can't hurt anyone on the isle," the leader replied.

"Watch me," Hector vowed. Loukas might be right, but there were always loopholes. Hector would find one if he had to. He turned his head to the group and turned a heated glare of warning on them.

Pelagia's eyes narrowed as she sent him a scathing look. "All of that for one girl? But you'll stand by and do nothing for thousands of us?"

"That *one girl*, as you call her, has done nothing to deserve your treatment. I stand for the innocents."

"That's what we are."

He snorted and returned her contemptuous look. "You're far from that, lady."

"It doesn't matter what you think. You sealed your fate," Pelagia stated.

Hector watched her walk away. They had angered a Dragon King and were about to find out what that meant.

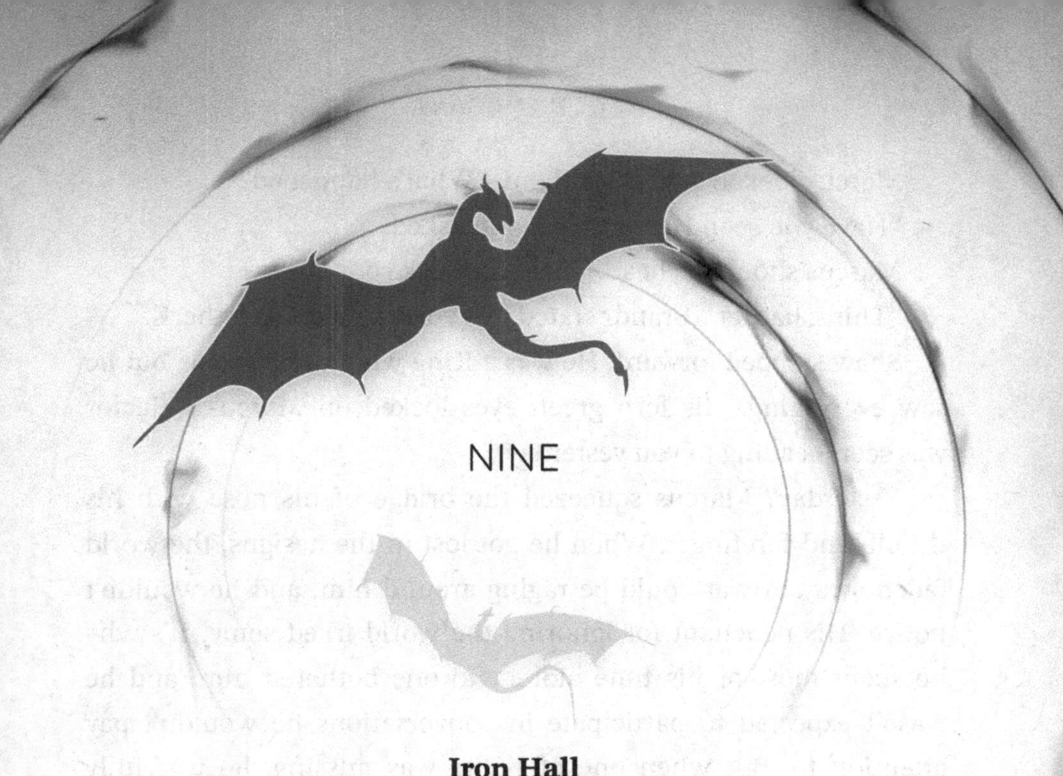

NINE

Iron Hall

The designs from the drawings rose off the page and moved around Marcus as he made corrections with his mind, one layer at a time. Suddenly, the plans fell back onto the paper as someone slammed a hand on the table.

"MARCUS!"

He jerked back and looked to find Con beside him, his black eyes narrowed into slits. "What is it?" Marcus asked worriedly.

"I've been calling your name for some time," Con replied tersely.

It wasn't in Constantine's nature to show emotion. He hid it. Always. The angrier he was, the softer he spoke. But that wasn't the case now. Con was visibly upset, and that sent warning bells through Marcus. He faced Con and saw that they weren't alone. To Con's left was his son, Brandr, who had Con's black eyes and Rhi's black hair. Behind Con were Shaw and Vaughn.

Marcus looked at each of them. "What's happened?"

"Have you seen Hector?" Vaughn asked.

Marcus shook his head. "I doona think so."

"Think harder," Brandr stated, his voice so like his father's.

Shaw stepped forward. He was a King who rarely spoke, but he saw everything. His fern green eyes locked on Marcus. "Hector was seen heading to you yesterday."

Yesterday? Marcus squeezed the bridge of his nose with his thumb and forefinger. When he got lost in the designs, the world faded away. A war could be raging around him, and he wouldn't notice. His penchant for ignoring the world irked some. It's why he spent most of his time alone. No one bothered him, and he wasn't expected to participate in conversations he wouldn't pay attention to. But when one of theirs was missing, he was fully invested.

"He might have been here." Marcus gazed around the room and tried to recall the last time he had seen or spoken to his friend.

He had a vague memory of someone bothering him. He looked at each of the corridor branches, and the stirrings of a conversation began to form in his mind. He couldn't hear the voice or make out the words, but it had happened. The moment Marcus looked at the caved-in hallway, it all came back to him.

"Hector was here. He went in there," Marcus said and nodded toward the last hallway to be cleared.

Without a word, Shaw strode to the opening, Vaughn on his heels. The two picked their way around the debris to move deeper.

"What did he say?" Brandr asked.

Marcus ran a hand down his face. "I doona remember."

"You might want to give those around you more time. Otherwise—"

"Brandr," Con said over him before he could finish.

But Marcus got the point. Brandr and his twin sister, Eurwen, ruled Zora, not Con. Yet, the Dragon Kings answered to Con, not the twins. It was a delicate and complicated situation.

"How long has Hector been missing?" Marcus asked.

Con focused on the ruined hallway where Shaw and Vaughn had disappeared. "We're no' quite sure. We've all tried to reach out to him through our mental link, but he hasna answered."

Because everyone did their own thing at Iron Hall. Some of the Kings weren't even there. They patrolled the dragon land borders while many of the Kings remained on Earth with their mates. Rhi had created a Fae doorway that linked the two worlds, making passage between them easy.

"Did you check Earth?" Marcus asked.

Con crossed his arms over his chest. "Rhi is there now."

They had just gotten Merrill back after Villette captured and held him. Had another of them been taken? Had it happened right here, and Marcus had been too preoccupied to notice?

"Hector wouldna leave Zora without telling someone," Brandr said.

Marcus glanced at the blueprints. He had been overjoyed to find so many areas of the city where he could put his skills to use. It had been a chance to sink into his mind with a project that would last months instead of hours. His brethren had had to come and get him twice to join the battles. He needed to pay more attention to what was happening outside his designs. But more and more, he found he only wanted to be with the drawings.

A large rock fell in the hallway, followed by Vaughn cursing. The entire wing they were in groaned threateningly.

"Get out. Now!" Marcus bellowed and raced to the entrance, studying the new cracks appearing before his eyes.

Brandr didn't spare him a glance. "Their magic can stop whatever happens."

"No' if it's on the other side of the city," Marcus pointed out. He looked from Brandr to Con. "Iron Hall is built through connecting sections. If you look at the damage as a whole, you'll see the domino effect of it moving outward from the spots with the most devastation."

Con glanced at the ceiling. "You've secured and repaired the other corridors in this section."

"And I've been trying to figure out why that one," Marcus said, pointing to the damaged hallway, "has so much destruction. It isna like other sections we've seen. It's almost like it was ravaged on purpose. The passage is built differently than the others, too, which makes me believe it leads to another section."

Brandr's brow furrowed as he shrugged. "What does that have to do with the rest of the city?"

"If I'm wrong, hopefully, nothing. But if I'm correct—and I know I am—the expansion stops its outward trajectory and circles back around and down," Marcus explained.

A muscle in Con's jaw jumped. "Which could impact the rooms on this level."

Marcus nodded. "Precisely. Until I can get in and see how the city was constructed, there's a chance every floor could collapse."

Brandr rushed to the edge of the wrecked corridor. "Vaughn! Shaw! Get back here. Now!"

Within moments, the two Kings strode into the round atrium covered in dust and dirt. They exchanged a look.

"What is it?" Con asked.

Shaw ran a hand through his black hair to shake off the dust. "We saw bootprints that went deeper into the hall."

"No' mine," Marcus said. He pointed to the new cracks. "I'm trying to shore up this side and stop the fissures."

"Hector, then. Could you see where he went? Maybe he found a way through," Brandr said.

Marcus shook his head. "I've already been in there as far as I could go. There isna a way through."

"He's right. There isna," Vaughn agreed. "We saw where Hector crawled. We were headed there when I hit a pile of debris with my shoulder. Next thing we knew, the entire ceiling shook. I thought it was all coming down on us there for a second."

Shaw blew out a breath. "I saw an opening. I might be able to get through, but it would be better if someone smaller could."

"Nay," Marcus, Con, and Brandr said in unison.

Vaughn and Shaw looked at each of them. Vaughn quirked a brow and looked at Marcus, waiting for an explanation. Marcus quickly repeated what he had shared with Con and Brandr.

"Fuck me," Shaw murmured.

Con ogled the corridor. "You're sure Hector wasna in there?"

"Positive," Vaughn replied.

Shaw nodded. "The opening I saw led to a wee room. We might be able to stand up in there, but it was otherwise blocked. We would've seen him."

"Were there bootprints leading back out?" Brandr asked.

Vaughn shook his head. "None but ours."

Marcus strode forward and stood at the entry to the hall. He knew exactly where the wall of rock blocked further progress. If Hector went into the passage and didn't come out, then where had he gone? Marcus took a step, only to hear his name. He paused and turned to look over his shoulder at Con.

"Talk to me," Con urged.

Marcus licked his lips. "I must have missed something. In all my exploration of Iron Hall, I've no' seen a single trap door or hidden passage, but that doesna mean there are no' any. If Hector went in and didna return, there's a reason. And I need to find him."

"No' alone," Brandr said as he started toward him.

Marcus held up his hand. "I'm no' going until I can guarantee the hallway willna cave in. And I'm better on my own."

Everyone looked at Con, awaiting his decision. Finally, he said, "I agree with Brandr. You shouldna be alone. We doona know what's down there or where it might lead. We need to be prepared for whatever it is."

"What about the ceremony?" Vaughn asked.

It took a moment for Marcus to remember that Shaw and Nia had planned their mating ceremony two days hence.

"We put it on hold until we find Hector," Shaw said.

Con blew out a breath. "We'll keep it on the schedule for now and see what happens. We have a few days. The others need to be apprised of the situation."

"I'll see to that," Brandr said.

Con nodded at his son and then turned to Marcus. "Someone will be with you, and there will be at least two others in this room, just in case. What else do you need?"

Marcus marched to the table and flipped through the blueprints. When he didn't find what he was looking for, he glanced at the box beside the table where others were rolled up. He yanked one out and spread it across the table. Con, Shaw, and Vaughn moved up on either side of him to see.

"Here," he said, pointing to a weight-bearing section. "Here. Here. And here." He grabbed another drawing and unrolled it. "Also, here, here, here, here, and here." He pointed out areas of concern on three other blueprints. Then he straightened and blew out a breath. "The bairns need to be moved somewhere safe until I can be sure the city willna crumble."

"Do it," Con stated to Shaw and Vaughn, who hurried out.

Marcus looked at the hallway again. "I should've paid more attention."

"Doona carry that weight," Con said.

Marcus grunted. "No one else can carry it."

"This isna on you, old friend."

"I was so involved in the drawings I didna know he vanished."

Con turned and braced a hip on the table. "You're saving us and this incredible city. I didna realize things were so dangerous, though. You should've told me."

"You've had a lot of other things to deal with." Marcus shrugged. "And I would have, had I run into an issue. No one comes down here unless I request it. I didna think it would be a problem until it was time to move the rubble."

"Put that amazing ability of yours to use. We're all at your disposal. We'll find him," Con vowed as he clamped Marcus on the shoulder.

Marcus turned back to the drawings and braced his hands on the table. Then he took a deep breath and began.

TEN

Emilia felt everyone's eyes on her as she was escorted through the streets. She was numb. How could this have happened? She had been careful, so very careful. No one had known. Not even Agathi. At that moment, she looked up and saw their approach to the Oracle guild house. As if her thoughts had conjured her, Agathi stood on the steps, her face solemn. She briefly met Emilia's gaze before looking behind her. No doubt searching for Hector.

She wouldn't see him now, though. He had remained on the beach, his fury radiating from him like a furnace. No one had dared get near him. The soldiers holding her couldn't get away fast enough, but they hadn't dragged her after his display of magic. Everything she had fought so hard for was over. The vision she had feared would come to pass now. She had known Hector needed to leave.

Maybe she was wrong to blame it on him. She'd have questions if she had been brought somewhere without her consent. She couldn't blame him for that. Whose fault was it then? The cabinet's for summoning him? Hers for not getting him away sooner? The earliest residents, who carved the statues and wrote the scrolls? There was enough blame to go around.

The citizens' cold stares followed Emilia as the soldiers guided her to the lowest part of the guild house, below the basement. She had only been there once. A dare had sent her into the darkness, and it had been a dreadful experience she swore never to repeat. A dare hadn't sent her there this time. Her actions had.

She kept her gaze forward so she didn't have to look other guild members in the eye. The descent went quicker than she wanted, and her heart jumped into her throat as the dank gloom greeted her. She inhaled stale air and choked on it.

The ones holding her jerked her to a halt before another opened a door. She looked inside and took an instinctive step back, but that was as far as she got. Their grips tightened on her arm before they shoved her inside. She stumbled forward to right herself as the wooden door banged shut behind her. Emilia whirled around to stare at it as the reality of her situation sank in.

Each guild had a prison, but they were rarely used. She was the only one locked away, and there was something terrifying about being the only soul within the bleak cells. Would they remember she was here? Maybe they intended to forget her. A slow death by starvation wasn't something she wanted to experience.

Emilia wrapped her arms around herself and took stock of her dismal surroundings. The only light was the flickering torch on the wall outside the door. Its red-orange glow barely penetrated the hand-sized square cut out of the wood and the metal bars across it. As if anyone would be able to fit through that to escape. The room was barely long enough to fit the tattered mat that was her bed and barely wide enough for her to hold out her arms and touch stone on both sides. Water beaded on the walls and dripped from the ceiling.

From the little she could see of the floor, it was filthy. She eyed the dilapidated mat constructed of woven seaweed. She thought about lifting it to shake it out but feared it would fall apart if she did. Then, there was the worry of what might be hiding under it. A shiver of revulsion raced through her.

If she wanted to sit, it would have to be on the ground. There were no chairs. There wasn't anything for her to use as facilities either. The cleanest place in the cell was the door. She made her way to it and leaned back against it as tears threatened. No amount of explaining would get her out of this mess. The fact that they had thrown her in here instead of taking her before the cabinet told her all she needed to know.

She considered the exchange on the beach. Wind had carried the voices, allowing her and Teo to hear what was happening. At first, she'd thought Hector would talk his way out of it, but things had turned suddenly. It was clear that Loukas and the cabinet had come for him. Well, nearly the cabinet. Two members had been conspicuously absent. Specifically, Agathi. Why hadn't she come with the others?

Emilia had known the instant Hector realized the group knew his identity as a Dragon King. The change in his demeanor and tone had been startling and quick. If he had spoken to her that way, she would've been a puddle on the floor, begging him not to hurt her. But not Loukas or Pelagia. Nobody from the group that had come to the beach, actually. They had recoiled in fear but hadn't run. Knowing Hector was so powerful, it didn't make sense that they had provoked him. He could wipe out the entire island with minimum effort. What did they know that she didn't?

Hector's display of magic to stop the soldiers from taking her had startled her but not Loukas or the others. In fact, the more she thought about it, the more she was sure they had antagonized him just to see such a display. The way Hector had stilled, confusion washing over him, had brought her up short. But it was Pelagia's smile that had Emilia's stomach twisting with dread. They knew something she didn't. Something Hector hadn't. Whatever had happened to him was precisely what they wanted. And whatever plans he had to free her stopped right then.

What did they know? What had happened to Hector? More importantly, did this propel them even closer to her vision?

Emilia dropped her chin to her chest. Thankfully, Teo hadn't been caught. She had told him to hide, even though Loukas had seen him. Teo would need to stay out of sight, or he might be thrown in prison, too. Though it wouldn't be with her. There was a general jail for those not part of a guild. She wouldn't even have him for company, such as it was.

She had no idea what time it was. The sun had all but set when they brought her to the prison. She stood until her legs began to ache. Only then did she slide down the door and sit with her legs pulled up to her chest, making sure to have as little contact with the floor as possible. It might be easier to get through the hours if she could sleep, but she wouldn't find any kind of respite with everything running through her head. Her stomach growled, reminding her she hadn't eaten since that morning.

With nothing else to do, Emilia's mind focused on recent events to see how the cabinet knew about Hector. She picked through every word she had exchanged with him. She dissected her day, listing anyone who had been around her and acted differently. She thought about the note she'd left Agathi, but nothing on it said anything about Hector or her vision. No one had seen her climb down the cliff since they were all at supper. The only possibility came that morning when she and Hector had been at the temple, and someone arrived.

Their exchange of words had been soft, though, so it was unlikely the woman had overheard them. She hadn't even seen Hector since he'd left before her arrival. But obviously, someone knew. Emilia went back to when Hector first arrived. No one had been with them. The only person who had asked about him was Agathi, but that wasn't out of the ordinary.

If it hadn't been someone with her, could it have been Teo? She considered how the boy looked up to Hector as if he were some god. And to Teo, he might as well be. Nay, Emilia didn't think the boy would tell anyone about Hector. Which left absolutely no one.

Emilia banged her head against the door and then closed her eyes. The only viable person that kept coming to mind was Agathi. She must have realized that Emilia had lied to her the other morning. But why not just come to her? Why take matters to the cabinet?

"The same reason I didn't go to her," Emilia whispered as she swiped away a tear.

She had betrayed Agathi. It stood to reason Agathi would react in kind. No wonder her friend didn't show any emotion when the soldiers were escorting Emilia. She had thought Agathi was being stoic. Now, she saw things in a different light and realized Agathi had been furious.

Emilia had made so many mistakes she had lost count. Whenever she thought she was doing something right, she only managed to make things worse. Maybe prison was exactly where she should be, so she didn't do any more damage.

Her body stiffened, and her heart rate slowed as her eyes went out of focus. Screams rang in her ears as the vision welled out of the mist and sharpened. She stared at the fires raging around her, the flames licking high as the heat made sweat run down her face. The bodies of the dead were strewn about everywhere as if tossed like dolls. She walked forward, her feet squishing in the wet grass. When she looked down, blood bubbled up between her bare toes. Then the ground shook, and her body vibrated as a dragon roared directly above her.

Emilia sucked in a breath as the vision faded. She tucked her arms between her legs and body as she shivered in both fear and shock. It was the vision. Only there was a slight change this time. She had never walked in the grass before or felt the dragon over her. A shudder ran through her at the memory of the blood-soaked ground.

She had done everything she could to change her vision. She had changed it, all right—she had made it *worse*. No one could feel as low as she did at that moment. Nothing she did would alter the course or make things right as she was being held.

"Psst."

She stilled, unsure if she had heard the soft whisper or if it had been her imagination.

"Pssssssst."

Someone was definitely there. Emilia got to her feet and peered out the square in the door. No one stood in front of it. She put her cheek against the wood and looked as far to the side as she could, then the other.

"Emilia?" someone whispered.

"Who's there?" she asked softly.

Suddenly, small fingers touched the grate. Startled, she jumped back. When she looked out again, she saw familiar, wavy, dark hair. The head tilted back, and she found herself looking into Teo's face.

"You shouldn't be here," she warned as she cast a look toward the outer door.

"I'm not the one locked up." He removed his hand and returned it a heartbeat later, holding a piece of bread. "Figured you might be hungry."

She covered his hand with hers and squeezed. Her eyes burned with fresh tears as she realized what Teo had risked by coming to her. She accepted the bread. "Thank you."

"You need to prepare. They're going to bring you before an assembly in a few hours."

She tore off a piece of bread and slowly chewed. "Where is Hector?"

"You don't need to worry about him. He's not the one in danger."

"Maybe not now. Did you see what happened to him on the beach?"

Teo was silent for a beat. "It was hard to miss. It sure pleased the others."

"I thought the same. Try to get him to leave while he still can."

"That's just it. He can't. Whatever happened bound him to the island, and he's none too pleased about it."

Emilia leaned a shoulder against the door. "They're looking for you, too. You need to stay out of sight."

"I'm good at that. Don't worry. They won't be able to find me. I know to look for spies following me."

Something in his words drew her up short. "Why would you think to look for spies?"

"Because you've had someone following you. It's why I took you out by the cliff. She didn't see us."

"Why would anyone follow me?"

The door shifted, and Teo grunted as if he leaned against it on the other side. "I couldn't say."

"I keep thinking about what happened with Hector. It's like the cabinet planned all of it."

"It sure seemed that way to me. They tried to get him to leave the beach, but he wouldn't go. He's prowling the shores."

Emilia looked out the door again but saw only a portion of Teo's head. "Be careful."

"Hector won't hurt me. He won't hurt you, either."

"You can't know that."

"I do. I knew what he was the moment he entered Highvale. I saw him. The *real* him."

She stopped chewing. "You saw him in his dragon form?"

"Aye. I see both. The real him and the human him."

"Is his dragon large?"

There was a smile in Teo's voice when he said, "Very. I've got to go. Hold your head high when they take you before the others."

Those were wise words coming from a boy. He was gone before Emilia could say goodbye.

ELEVEN

Hector swam hard and fast, his arms slicing through the water like talons through skin. And with every stroke, the invisible bond connecting him to the isle tightened. When he reached the half-mile mark, it was like slamming into a wall. He had tried swimming along the ocean floor but had been halted at the same place. He had even swum the circumference of the island. It didn't matter. There was nowhere for him to break free.

A cage, even without bars, was still a cage. To think he had once lamented the Kings being isolated in their caves for thousands of years. That had been nothing compared to this. He treaded water and looked up at the lightening sky as the sun crested the horizon. The dragon within demanded release, but Hector held back. The sky was his last chance. If he couldn't fly out, it meant he was well and truly bound. He held on to that last thread of hope, even as he knew in his heart that the skies weren't the answer.

Even if he could fly away, he wouldn't. He couldn't leave

Emilia to whatever fate the cabinet had in store for her. Every time he thought about her being hauled away, it infuriated him. The only reason he hadn't gone after her was because he wouldn't have been able to control his rage, and he would've damaged buildings and likely harmed someone on the island. It was better for everyone if he remained alone.

Hector turned and began the swim back to shore. He didn't push himself this time. Instead, he went over everything he'd learned since he arrived on Highvale for the ten thousandth time. He was missing something. He was sure of it. The scrolls might hold the answer. Loukas would attempt to use them in exchange for something, but Hector wouldn't play that game. If the cabinet wouldn't hand over the scrolls, then he would take them by force. At this point, he didn't care what they did to him. They had caged a dragon, which was the ultimate sin in his eyes.

He reached shallow waters and stood, his eyes landing on the statue of Con. Was it the bond to the isle that disrupted the dragons' mental link? Or was it something or someone else? That was another mystery for him to solve. Yet it was probably a good thing he hadn't been able to contact any of the Kings, even to warn them. If he got through to them, they would come. He was already being detained there. He didn't want any of the others ending up in the same predicament. Not to mention, he wasn't sure his brethren wouldn't attack with one of theirs held against his will.

Emilia's vision might not have anything to do with the war against those without magic. It might very well have to do with him being detained.

Hector ran a hand down his face and turned to stare at the horizon. What would this new day bring? His rage burned bright and ran rampant. The last place he should be was anywhere near humans. Unfortunately, he didn't have a choice. He refused to allow the situation to linger for longer than it already had.

"Hector."

The whisper cut through the roar of the waves. He stilled and turned his head slightly as he opened his hearing.

"I knew you'd be able to hear me," Teo said, a smile in his voice.

Hector could tell the lad was behind him at some distance. At least Teo hadn't been caught. Hector would ensure no one laid hands on him.

"I saw Emilia," Teo continued. "They have her locked away in the guild house, but I snuck in."

The pride in the lad's voice made Hector grin.

"They plan to bring her before an assembly today. And...I heard them say you would be there, too."

The hell he would. Hector clenched his hands into fists, his fury threatening to swallow him.

"I think you should go. For Emilia."

Hector closed his eyes. The lad was right. He needed to be there for her. It would also give him an opportunity to be heard. First, he needed to get cozy with the island. He could feel it, but he had been ignoring it. That needed to change. He nodded to let Teo know he would be there.

"I'll be nearby, watching in case you need anything."

The sound of approaching footsteps reached Hector.

"They're coming," Teo said urgently.

Hector didn't turn to greet the group. He also didn't need to tell Teo to hide. The boy was street-smart, and it showed in how he stayed out of their hands. The waves crashed softly onto shore as gulls cried. Pelican-like birds flew in small clusters and dove into the water for food. It was a beautiful scene. Too bad it was marred by politics and duplicity.

The footsteps grew muffled as the group stepped into the sand. An image of Emilia being dragged away, her blue eyes briefly meeting his, flashed in his head. He should've stopped them, but he'd been so shaken by whatever had risen from the ground that he had done nothing. But he had a clearer head now, which meant there would be consequences.

"My lord," a deep voice said from behind him.

Hector turned and faced the ten soldiers who had come for him. He raised a brow and waited.

The leader, a tall, muscular man with sandy blond hair gathered at his neck and brown eyes, took a half step forward. "We're to bring you to the amphitheater."

"No' happening," Hector replied.

The men exchanged confused and worried glances before the leader cleared his throat. "I'm afraid you don't understand."

"It is you who doesna understand. I'm no' going anywhere with you. If you want to attempt to force the issue, you're welcome to try." Hector paused and hardened his gaze. "But it willna end well for any of you."

The men grew restless. A few at the rear even backed up a step or two. The leader, however, didn't budge. And none of them made a move toward Hector. They feared him, and he planned to use that to his advantage.

The leader's lips flattened briefly as he drew in a breath. "The entire city is gathering at the theater. Your presence has been requested."

Hector kept Teo's words in mind when he asked, "Why is such a meeting being called?"

"The Oracle needs to explain herself."

"In other words, it's a trial."

The soldier dipped his chin in confirmation.

"For what?" They couldn't possibly know that she had turned him away the first time. Not unless she'd told them.

The soldier glanced at the sand. "Interfering in a cabinet matter."

"I suppose the cabinet is saying this?"

"You would need to discuss that with the members of the cabinet. I'm merely following orders."

Hector snorted. "Perhaps you should think of interfering."

"My lord?"

"Stop calling me that." Hector really needed to calm his temper.

"As you wish. We can escort you to the amphitheater."

"I doona like to repeat myself."

He thought the leader might argue. Instead, the soldier turned on his heel and led the others away. Hector looked for Teo, but the lad didn't pop up anywhere. Even from his position on the beach, it was clear that residents were headed toward the theater on the northeast side of the island.

Hector turned toward the cove and walked into the water again. He closed his eyes and let himself feel. The moment he opened himself, a tidal wave of magic washed over him with such force that it knocked him to his knees. He didn't retreat or flinch because he recognized the feel of it.

Nothing would ever erase the memory of Earth's magic tapping him to become King. Another memory surfaced of the first time he'd walked Dreagan, where the magic was centered. It had been such a life-altering experience that he had stood in the Dragonwood and let it wash over him, just as he was now.

There was more power on Highvale than anywhere on Zora. It burst from the water, teemed from the rocks, and rained from the sky. And it held him to the island. He was its protector, just as Loukas had claimed. More thoughts came, one after the other, explaining his role.

They disappeared just as quickly as they came. Hector opened his eyes to see the sky above. He realized he was floating and lowered his legs into the water. He contemplated flying to the amphitheater but hesitated. No one had seen him in his true form yet. Other than Teo, anyway. But Hector could use that to his advantage and claim the cabinet was wrong about who he was. Or, at the very least, he could wait and use it as an element of surprise. Either way, it was better if he remained in his human form.

He dove beneath the water and headed toward a rocky section where the amphitheater had been built. Once there, he climbed the steep, wet rocks, waves crashing over him. The theater had been built in a naturally hollow area, which made it a prime location. The chatter of the crowd as they milled about was amplified. He scaled to the top of the stage and situated himself on the tiled roof. The semicircular design had tiers of seats that surrounded the podium. The stage itself wasn't very large, but the columns and ornate architecture above and behind it gave it a dramatic feel.

A murmur went through the crowd as their eyes shifted to the stage. Hector adjusted his position so he could better see what was happening below. Loukas and Pelagia walked onto the stage, followed by seven others.

The crowd quieted when Loukas raised his hand. "Greetings,

my friends. It is rare, indeed, for a congregation to be called, but this was too vital to wait. We have great news that will benefit every magical, whether they live on Highvale or not. Unfortunately, before the joyous reveal, a matter of business must be addressed."

The audience wore confused expressions as they looked at each other, hoping someone might clue them in. Hector observed as the cabinet members around Loukas walked to spaces near the front and sat. Loukas then motioned to someone off to the side. Moments later, Emilia was shoved onto the stage.

His banked rage roared to life at the sight of her dirty gown. It was even wet in places. Still, she held her head high, even as he saw her hands trembling. She attempted to hide them in the folds of her skirt, but he noticed. She was pale, her face tight as her chest rose and fell quickly. His instinct was to jump down and protect her, but he paused. Loukas wanted him here for a reason. Was it so they could show him off to the crowd like some trophy? Or could it be for some other nefarious purpose?

Hector didn't trust him. He didn't trust anyone on the island other than Emilia and Teo. The entire spectacle was nothing but a performance. Hector would bet his entire rare coin collection that elections were coming up soon, and Loukas wanted to retain his position.

"Behold!" Loukas declared as he angrily pointed a finger in Emilia's direction. "One of the Oracle guild's own is being tried on charges of betrayal!"

Emilia didn't cower. She held Loukas's gaze as if daring him. Hector grinned despite himself. She was fearless. What made him nervous was what they planned to do with her. Would they call it treason? It was a possibility that soured his stomach. Discontent moved through the crowd as all eyes turned to Emilia.

"What did she do?" someone shouted.

Loukas smiled as he dropped his arm and faced the audience. Like an actor on stage, he gave himself over to the part of the sovereign of Highvale. He was the type of actor who never *stopped* acting. The world was their stage, and they wanted to remain on it forever. Though the longer Hector watched Loukas, he suspected it wasn't an act. It was Loukas's personality. He adored the attention and power.

"What did she do, indeed?" Loukas stated, slowly looking around the amphitheater. "This city has long been a refuge for those looking to escape the prejudiced views of non-magicals. Some of us were fortunate to arrive here as infants and only know the peace and beauty of the island." He paused for effect, his face losing its smile. "While others have known the hardships of trying to survive on the mainland. Running from mobs intent to kill, lying about who they were, and even hiding so as not to be found. We've waited for generations, hoping the biased view about us would fade, but it has only grown."

Some in the audience nodded. A few even clapped.

Loukas strode to the other side of the stage. "We've heard myriad stories about what's happening out there. So many of our fellow magicals have been slaughtered. Even children are being killed. Something has to be done!"

Half the audience shouted in agreement, while the other half remained silent. Hector watched it all with interest. Teo hadn't been wrong. The city was, most assuredly, divided.

Loukas turned his back to the audience and shot a smug smile toward Emilia before facing the crowd again. This time, he held up both arms, his fingers splayed. The people eventually quieted.

"Thanks to the Oracle guild, the cabinet came up with a plan,"

Loukas said after he lowered his arms. "The kind that can't fail. Something that will ensure no more of our people are ever killed or run off again."

"War isn't the answer!" a woman yelled.

Loukas chuckled, a wry smile upon his lips. "I didn't say we were going to war, my dear. Someone will be doing that for us. It was written in the scrolls by our ancestors. You see, the plan we have is guaranteed."

Hector peeled back his lips in a snarl as he glared at the leader. "Guaranteed, my arse."

"Do you want to know what the plan is?" Loukas asked.

It was so quiet Hector could hear their heartbeats.

"A Dragon King!"

There was a beat of shock before chaos erupted. Some cheered jubilantly while others exchanged apprehensive looks.

It went on for some time before Loukas's booming voice rang out as he looked at Emilia and pointed once more. "Except she attempted to eliminate our best hope."

Hector jerked back in shock. There were a number of words Loukas could've used. He hadn't said murder or kill. That would've been definitive. Nay, he'd chosen *eliminate* to give that impression, knowing Emilia had done no such thing.

"Punish her!" someone shouted.

"Jail her!" said another.

Hector had heard enough. He stood and jumped down, landing behind Loukas. The amphitheater went as silent as death. Loukas whirled around so fast he lost his balance and fell on his arse. Hector strode angrily to him as soldiers rushed out, magic at the ready. He didn't look away from Loukas. It had been eons since

Hector had felt such an urge to dole out a reckoning. It was so great that he was having difficulty reeling in his indignation.

He didn't know how long he remained there with his hands clenched and murder on his mind before he remembered he stood before the entire city. Hector looked at the audience before turning his head to Emilia.

"Does anyone care to know the truth?" Hector returned his attention to the crowd as Loukas scrambled to his feet and off the stage.

"I do!" Teo shouted.

Hector looked to the very back where the lad stood, a grin on his face before he ducked down. "The truth is that things are no' always black and white. They," he said, pointing to Loukas and the other cabinet members, "believe a dragon is the answer—the only answer." He backed up until he stood even with Emilia. "While some have had the same vision since their childhood, showing blood and fire should dragons come to the island."

"Then she should have spoken up," an older woman from the beach stated. "Not taken matters into her own hands."

A man stood. "Emilia is supposed to bring such visions to the guild's leaders so they can be recorded and interpreted."

"Who are you to interpret another's visions?" Hector challenged. "You can't feel them or see what another can. The only one who should be deciphering a vision is the one who had it."

"That is not our way," the man declared.

"For a city so quick to wipe out prejudice and bias, you harbor a lot of it yourselves. Emilia," Hector said as he raised his voice, "was attempting to save lives. All lives. And she did that by telling me about her vision. I was in the process of leaving when we were stopped." He gave Loukas a pointed look. "And tricked. Emilia didn't try to eliminate anyone."

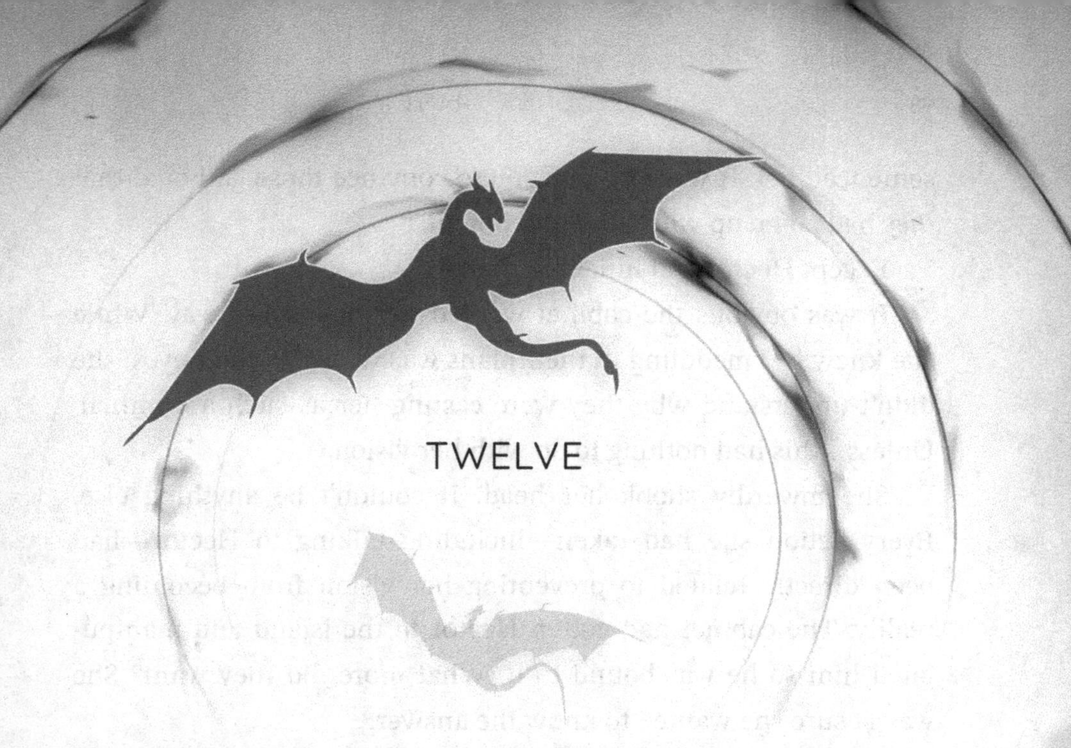

TWELVE

Emilia hadn't been able to take her eyes off Hector since the moment he dropped out of nowhere and onto the stage. His words rang clear and held everyone captive, just as his entrance had. He didn't know her, yet he stood in front of everyone to defend her. Agathi hadn't even done that.

At the thought of her friend, Emilia glanced at her, but Agathi still wouldn't look in her direction. No one had spoken to Emilia since the beach, but thanks to Teo, she'd been prepared for this morning—or as prepared as someone could be. It had still been hard to hear Loukas say such damning words, despite her never liking him. He'd always had a flair for speaking, but his spite was directed at her this time. She had felt the citizens of Highvale turning against her with every word that fell from his lips.

Yet she couldn't fault him. She *had* gone against them. She had conspired behind their backs. Her reasons should matter, but no one wanted to hear them. The cabinet had already judged and sentenced her. It was Loukas's job to convince those gathered that *they* had come up with her punishment.

Except Hector had hindered that.

It was obvious the cabinet wanted her out of the way. While she knew her meddling in their plans was wrong in their eyes, she didn't understand why they were casting her as such a criminal. Unless...this had nothing to do with her vision.

She inwardly shook her head. It couldn't be anything else. Every action she had taken—including talking to Hector—had been directly related to preventing her vision from becoming a reality. The cabinet had gotten Hector to the island and manipulated him so he was bound to it. What more did they want? She wasn't sure she wanted to know the answer.

Hector walked to her. She had to tilt her head back to look into his dark eyes. She saw the anger burning brightly there, but not at her. *For* her.

"Are you all right?" he asked, oblivious to the chaos around them.

The sounds and movements of those in the theater were getting to be too much. She wanted to fade into the background once more and be forgotten.

A frown marred his forehead as he dipped his head to her. "Emilia?"

"I want to leave," she said.

He dipped his chin and put a hand on her lower back to turn her. Several guards moved in front of them, but Hector shouldered through them with a protective arm around her. No one else dared to stop them after that.

"Doona look back," Hector told her.

She put one foot in front of the other. She had no idea where they were going, but it didn't matter as long as it was out of the amphitheater. Blood rushed in her ears, and all she could see was what was right in front of her. Her mind was a whirlwind of outrage, dread, and astonishment. The guild would expel her—if they hadn't already. It didn't matter what Hector had said in her defense. She would be shunned.

"Emilia?"

The sound of her name on his lips pulled her from her thoughts. Hector stood before her once more, his hands lightly holding her shoulders as he looked down at her with concern in his deep brown eyes. She swallowed and looked around to discover they were just inside the cave at the bay. "I'm all right."

"I wouldna blame you if you were no'." He dropped his hands and blew out a breath. "I'm sorry you had to go through that. I should've come for you last night."

"It's fine."

He cut his eyes to her. "It isna. In truth, it's far from fine. It's a bloody disaster." He paused and briefly lowered his gaze to the sand. "Did you know what they planned for me yesterday?"

"I swear I didn't," she vowed, appalled that he even suspected she might.

Teo popped up from behind a boulder. "She didn't."

Hector's shoulders sagged. He lowered himself onto a large rock and rubbed his eyes. "How do you know that?"

Teo looked between her and Hector before moving to a rock to sit. "Before I visited Emilia last night, I hung around the pavilion because I knew the cabinet would gather to talk about what happened. And I was right."

"What did they say?" Hector asked.

Teo licked his lips nervously. "It isn't good."

"Just tell it, lad," Hector urged gently.

"Highvale isn't just a haven for those like us. It's meant for dragons."

Emilia shrugged. "That isn't a secret. There are dragon statues everywhere."

"Not the way you think," Teo replied.

Hector motioned to him. "I think you'd better explain."

"From what Pelagia said, once a dragon uses magic and is connected to the island, he will protect it—and those who call it home—with his life."

Hector grunted. "Like my clan."

"Your what?" Emilia asked, unsure if she'd heard him right.

He shook his head and motioned to Teo. "So, that's what happened yesterday? When I used my magic to stop the soldiers from taking Emilia, I forged this...link?"

"Aye, and they knew you would," Teo said. "That's why they were looking for Emilia and me. They knew one of us would cause you to react."

Emilia waited for Hector to say something, but he just sat there staring into the sand.

Teo shifted anxiously. "The point being, you won't be able to harm anyone here unless they attempt to harm you first."

"Thank you for confirming all of that," Hector replied.

Emilia held up a hand. "Wait. What? You already knew all of that?"

"I...learned no' too long ago."

Teo's brow furrowed. "The cabinet told you?"

"The magic, actually," Hector answered.

Emilia was wholly unprepared to hear those words. She had

never heard or felt magic. She had so many questions, but they would have to wait for another time.

"Everyone has gone out of their way to be pleasant. I doona think anyone will outright try to harm me." Hector scratched the back of his neck, swinging his gaze to Teo. "Did you happen to hear how they knew about me?"

Emilia looked at Teo and waited because she wanted to know the answer. She motioned for him to speak when he hesitated.

"There's...ah...someone who told them. It wasn't me," Teo hastily added.

Hector shot him a smile. "I know, lad. Did you hear who it was?"

"Someone was coming, so I had to leave. That's when I went to see Emilia."

"Thank you for that," she told him.

Hector swung his head to her. "I tried to leave Highvale multiple times, but it's impossible. I should've left when you asked it of me. What about your vision? Do you know how it begins?"

She shook her head as she thought about the new addition to it.

He stared at her for a long moment. "I've set it in motion." He briefly closed his eyes and shook his head. "Fuck."

"Then we stop it," Teo stated.

Hector sat up straighter. "We need to figure out what the cabinet's plans are."

Teo rubbed his palms on his thighs. "I think I might know."

"Go on," Emilia urged.

"A group of five left Highvale last night and headed to the mainland. I heard them say something about knowing where to stir up some trouble," Teo said.

Hector got to his feet and started to pace. "If we're attacked, I'll have no choice but to strike at anyone who comes for us."

"But those without magic can't get to us," Emilia reminded them.

"They can if someone helps them," Hector pointed out as he continued to pace. "Especially if they've been forced."

Emilia shook her head, not wanting to believe it. "The cabinet wouldn't put the city in danger. We're a haven, a sanctuary. The outside world can't reach us here."

"The rules are being changed for those who want to take a stand. They recently heard stories about the Kings and decided to bring one here. They not only succeeded in getting me to the island, but I played right into their hands and bound myself." Hector ran a hand over his jaw. "If things go as I imagine, I'll defend Highvale, but word will spread. More will try to find their way to us in retaliation. That's when the real war will begin. It will spread from here onto the mainland and across the realm."

"The peace of Highvale will be shattered," Teo murmured.

Hector halted and caught Emilia's eye. "Unless we stop it."

"Can you even attempt such a thing being linked to the land?" she asked.

Hector lifted a shoulder and tilted his head. "We're going to find out."

"We're not just going to sit on the sidelines, are we?" Teo asked, his face brightening with hope.

Emilia was about to remind him that he was a child until she remembered how easily he moved about unseen. She looked at Hector and saw he was thinking the same thing.

"We aren't," Teo stated with a bright smile.

She blew out a breath. "I'll do whatever is needed, but I don't think I'll be much help. I'm certain I've lost my standing in the guild."

"You don't need them," Teo said. "Look at me. I'm not in a guild."

Hector ruffled Teo's hair. "I agree with the lad."

Emilia tried to smile through her pain. The guild had been her shelter, Agathi, her family. She had lost both in a single day, and while she had always been alone, she felt it to her core now. It was a cold, lonely feeling that sat like a stone in her stomach. What was she supposed to do now? Where was she to go?

No one would take her in. Loukas had made sure she was a pariah, hated by some and avoided by the rest. She wouldn't be able to get a job, which meant she wouldn't have money to purchase food. Not that it mattered since no one would sell her any. What meager belongings she had were in her room at the guild house.

She didn't know anyone who had been kicked out of the guild. There were ceremonies to get inducted. Was there one to strip her of her association? Or did they just forget her?

The cove started to spin as thoughts swirled maddeningly in her head, each creating a hundred different scenarios where she was treated worse and worse until she ended up wandering the realm aimlessly.

"Hey," Hector said, giving her a gentle shake. "I know what you've lost. And though you may no' believe it, I understand the tangle of emotions beginning to show. But you're no' alone."

"What if all of this is my fault? What if I'm the cause of my vision? Maybe I should've let Agathi find you."

Hector shook his head. "Doona go down that road. It will only lead to madness. You did what you thought you had to do."

"Which may have been the very thing I wasn't supposed to do," she argued.

Hector looked to Teo. "We're no' going to let the vision come to pass, are we?"

Teo shook his head and walked to join them. "We won't let it come to pass."

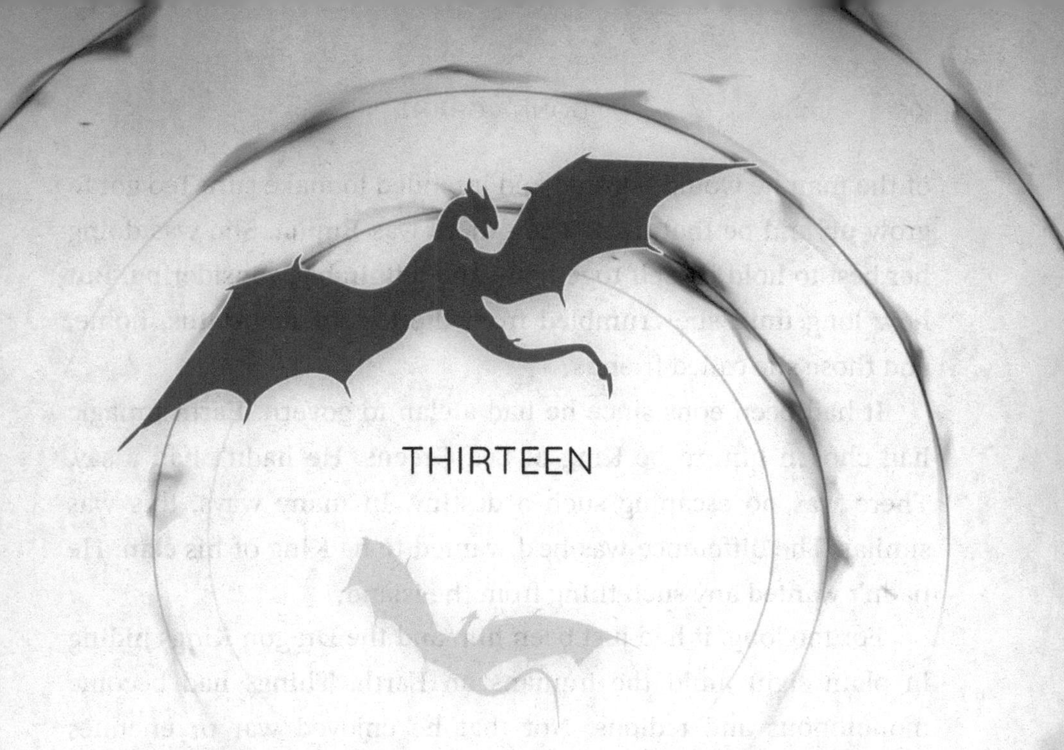

THIRTEEN

Hector didn't make promises he couldn't keep, but even as he said the words aloud, he felt uneasy. There was more at work here than just people and emotions. Like magic, the likes of which he hadn't foreseen or prepared for. He was already ensnared, and that worried him. Though he wasn't panicked. Yet.

"What do we do first?" Teo asked.

Hector looked at the lad. A child in a world that didn't have time for him. A boy trying to be a man when he should have been playing with others his age and getting into trouble while making memories. Instead, Teo had insinuated himself in a dangerous game with deadly stakes. Hector should send him away to ensure his safety, but was anywhere safe? If Hector was now some sort of protector for Highvale, it stood to reason that the best place for Teo was with him. At least until he could get the lad to his brethren.

Emilia and Teo looked to him for guidance. The lad's blue eyes were filled with courage and determination. Hector saw a glimpse of the man he would become and intended to make sure Teo got to grow up and be that man. Then there was Emilia. She was doing her best to hold herself together—and admirably, considering. But how long until she crumbled from the loss of her status, home, and those she called friends?

It had been eons since he had a clan to govern. Earth's magic had chosen him to be King of Sea Greens. He hadn't had a say. There was no escaping such a destiny. In many ways, this was similar. The difference was he'd wanted to be King of his clan. He hadn't wanted any such thing from the island.

For too long, it had just been him and the Dragon Kings hiding in plain sight amid the humans on Earth. Things had become monotonous and tedious. Not that he enjoyed war or enemies coming at those he cared about, but there was a vast difference between his life before the war with the humans and after when the dragons left. The Kings hadn't been able to *be* dragons. Not really. Not as they had been—or they should have been.

That all changed on Zora, where everyone knew about dragons. It was a far cry from Earth, where the humans believed his kind were a myth.

Emilia and Teo waited for him to direct them toward victory. Many of his kin would refuse Teo's help. Maybe he should do the same. But the lad gave them an advantage. Others overlooked and underestimated children. Hector knew better. Besides, Teo had proven how resourceful he could be. Still, there was a limit to what he would ask of the lad.

As for Emilia, Hector wanted to tuck her away somewhere no one could ever hurt her again. She deserved to be cherished and protected. She was strong and had withstood the humiliation at the amphitheater with grace, but that didn't mean she hadn't felt every word and hateful glare.

Hector released a sigh. "We need to get to the mainland. The problem is, I can no' go."

"Then I will," Teo declared.

Emilia shook her head and put a hand on his chest. "Nay. I will."

"It has to be me," Teo said, gently moving Emilia's hand away. "They'll notice if you leave and will likely follow. No one will notice or care about me."

Hector crossed his arms over his chest. "That isna exactly true. The cabinet is looking for you, which means others will be, as well."

"They might be, but they won't catch me," Teo replied with a grin.

Emilia's lips pinched, and her brow furrowed. "I don't like Teo going."

"I have a better chance of getting off the isle."

Hector blew out a breath. "He's right. He does."

Teo squared his narrow shoulders. "When do I leave?"

"As soon as possible."

"You can't be serious," Emilia said, gaping at Hector. "He's a child."

Teo took offense and turned blue eyes filled with indignation on her. "I've done all right on my own. I'm quick and smart. I can do this." He looked at Hector, his gaze beseeching.

But Teo *hadn't* been on his own. Not really. And they all knew it. Still, neither Hector nor Emilia corrected him.

Hector dropped his arms and looked into Teo's eyes. "Listen

closely. I don't want you to do any more than what I'm about to ask. Do you understand?"

"Aye," Teo answered solemnly.

"I mean it," Hector stated, giving the lad a stern stare.

Teo nodded. "I give you my word."

"Be sure, lad. Because your word is all you have. If you go back on it, trust is rarely rebuilt."

"I'll do exactly as you say," Teo replied.

Hector glanced at Emilia to find her face pinched with worry. "When was the last time you went to the mainland?"

"Not since I came here," the boy answered.

"And you know how to get back?"

Teo shrugged. "It should be the same as getting here, right?"

They both looked at Emilia. She threw up her hands and shook her head. "How should I know? I've never left."

"Can people come and go as they please?" Hector asked.

She nodded. "At least, that is what I've been told."

"Can the cabinet or anyone block someone from coming to the isle?"

A flash of apprehension spread over Teo's face that was impossible to miss. The lad had found safety at Highvale. Now, Hector was asking him to leave it.

Emilia swallowed and shook her head. "Not that I'm aware. The city has always been open to all magicals."

Hector faced Teo. "If they try to stop you from returning, I'll get you here myself. You have my word."

All the fear left the boy's face. "All right. What do you want me to do on the mainland?"

"You're going to say a name. You doona have to shout it, but you have to say it with meaning. She'll hear you no matter where you are on the realm, and she'll come. You willna be able to mistake who she is. She has black hair and silver eyes. And she'll be dressed in all black in a manner you've never seen before, wearing boots with verra high heels. Do you have all of that?"

Teo drew in a deep breath and nodded. "Black clothes that look different, black hair, and silver eyes."

"Exactly. She'll be wary of you. Tell her I'm the one who sent you. Tell her she has to come alone and that it's important she no' bring Con or the others. Can you remember that?"

"You sent me. She needs to come alone and not tell...um..."

"Con," Hector offered.

The lad nodded quickly. "And not to tell Con and the others. What do I do after that?"

"You return to Highvale with her and bring her to me."

"Simple enough."

Hector motioned to him. "Tell it to me again."

Once Teo could repeat everything back without stumbling or forgetting, Hector relented.

"What name do I say?" Teo asked.

"Rhi. I've known her for a long time, and I trust her with my life. She's family. Do whatever she says until you get back here," Hector cautioned.

Teo grinned. "Is she a dragon like you?"

"Dragon Queens are rare, but we do have a couple. Rhi, however, is Queen of Dragon Kings."

"Really?" Teo asked, his eyes wide and amazement in his voice.

Hector smiled at the lad's obvious excitement. "Really."

"I'll be back as soon as I can," Teo said, turning to run out of the cave.

Hector grabbed the boy before he could get loose. He gently

turned Teo toward him and bent to look him in the eyes. "Your life is important. Do no' do anything that will put yourself in peril. Even if that means no' reaching the mainland. We'll come up with a new plan. There is always another way. Do you understand?"

Teo glanced at the sand. "I understand."

"Why not just say her name now?" Emilia asked.

Hector looked at her. "I'm no' going to take the chance she'll somehow end up bound here. There are too many unknowns for me to bring her here without her knowing everything that's going on first."

"I'll find her," Teo said.

"Good." Hector released him and straightened. "Good luck and be safe."

Teo smiled and then raced out of the cave.

"Do you think he'll make it?" Emilia asked.

Hector dragged his gaze from the last place he'd seen Teo to look at her. "If he gets to the mainland, Rhi will come. She'll ensure his protection at all costs."

"I'm sorry. I should've asked if you had someone. It never dawned on me that you had a wife."

"I doona. Rhi is a queen, but she's no' mated to me. She's with Constantine, King of Dragon Kings."

Emilia's brows drew together in confusion. "You have a king?"

"Aye, we do. How much do you know about us?"

"Very little. Just that your kind are powerful, and this realm is yours."

He lowered himself onto the sand with his knees up and moved his heels from side to side until he'd dug a little hole. He wrapped his arms around his knees and looked at Emilia. "Do you want to know?"

"I would like that very much," she said as she sank onto a rock.

Now that Hector had offered to share details about the Kings, he didn't know where to start. There was a lot of history, and it could get confusing. Did he tell it as he had lived it? Or did he tell it in the order it'd happened, much of which he and the other Kings hadn't learned until recently? He decided on the former.

"My home is a place called Earth. A planet verra similar to Zora. Dragons ruled all, and for eons we had the entire realm to ourselves. There were dragons of every color and size. Each color stayed together, and a King ruled each clan." He paused, thinking back to that time. The memories were vague, but they were still there. "Life was hard, beautiful, and dangerous. There were days I wasna sure I'd survive."

"But you're royalty," Emilia said.

Hector shook his head. "That isna how that works. The magic of our realm decides who will be the King of their clan. It looks within each dragon to see who is the strongest, bravest, and most noble. Sometimes, Kings are killed in battle. Other times, the magic sees that the dragon they chose to lead has lost what made him a King and chooses another."

"Does the previous King step down?"

"Never."

Her lips parted as she blinked at him. "Then what happens?"

"Battle."

"Doesn't the previous King understand what the magic has done?"

Hector scratched his neck. "Sometimes, a dragon can want to be King so desperately that he believes the magic has chosen him when it hasn't. That's why there is a fight to the death. If the newcomer really is chosen, he'll defeat the current King."

"Did you have to fight?" she asked softly.

"I did. It was long, ugly, and brutal."

She pressed her lips together, her eyes on him. "I'm sorry."

"It is our way."

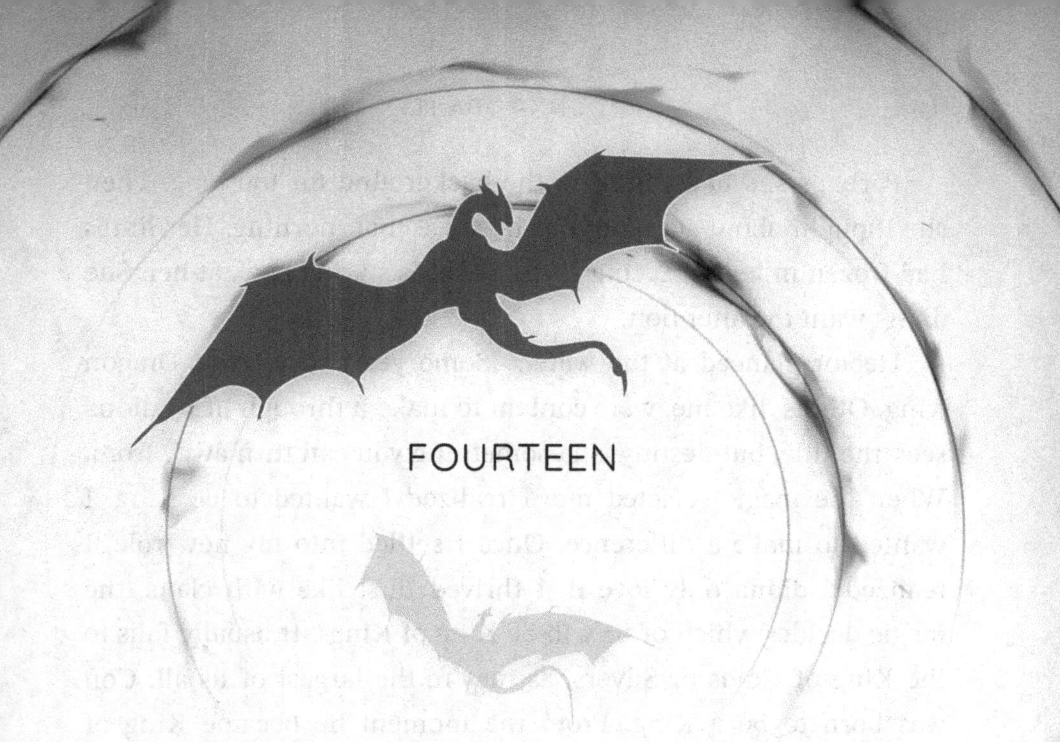

FOURTEEN

It was a violent way, but Emilia was discovering that running to Highvale didn't keep violence away from her. She had been shielded and secluded, but that didn't mean it couldn't touch her life—something she was coming to realize.

She studied Hector's face. His tone was conversational, but she saw him withdraw and sink into his memories a few times. She wondered what he saw there and whether they were good recollections or something he wished to forget.

"You have to understand that your clan looked out for you, and you for them. There was a hierarchy. Everyone knew their place," Hector told her. "It could be a verra political atmosphere for those looking for power, much as it is here. I never liked such things, but there was no getting away from it."

She smiled. "We have that in common."

"It's one thing to want to play at it. It's another to dislike it but be involved. You're involved now. You have to learn to play the game to survive."

Perhaps she had stayed in the background for too long. Then she thought about standing on the stage that morning. Her limbs had frozen in fear at seeing all those faces staring back at her. She didn't want the attention.

Hector glanced at the water. "Some yearned to be a Dragon King. Others, like me, were content to make it through life. I didna seek the title, but destiny isna something you can turn away from. When the magic selected me, I realized I wanted to be King. I wanted to make a difference. Once I settled into my new role, I realized I didna only love it, I thrived. Just like with clans, the magic decides which of us will be King of Kings. It usually falls to the King of Golds or Silvers, as they're the largest of us all. Con was born to be a King. From the moment he became King of Golds, word of him spread throughout the clans. Almost immediately, he became King of Kings, cementing him as one of the greatest of all time."

"You like him."

"He's my brother. Just as every King is. We're a tight-knit family. We've had to be."

Something darkened Hector's face, and she wished she could take back her words.

"One day, out of nowhere, new beings came to Earth. They didna look like us, nor could they communicate with us. Con called the Kings together so we could figure out how to handle things. These beings were terrified of us. I can only imagine what a ferocious sight we were descending from the skies."

She would've liked to see it. She had always been fascinated by the dragon statues and the stories of them.

"Then, we suddenly changed shape. Into this," Hector said, motioning to his human form. "Our magic allowed us to understand their words, and we were then able to converse. They were mortals with no memory of where they had come from or how they had arrived on our realm. We made a vow right then to protect them. We gave them land in which to settle, helped them build homes, and showed them how to hunt and forage. Things were fine for a while, but the one constant in the universe is change."

His voice had shifted subtly as if the very act of saying the words aloud cost him. She should tell him to stop, but her curiosity was too great. Instead, she sat silently and let him continue.

"The humans had considerably shorter life spans, but they bred at a rate we couldna comprehend. Their numbers doubled and then tripled. They kept extending the settlement. Eventually, some asked to move. Nearly all the Kings gave up a small portion of their land for the humans to settle in. Things eased once more. I've always been interested in other cultures and used the opportunity to befriend the mortals on my land. To me, they were part of my clan, though the majority of the clan didna feel the same. Yet they followed my orders.

"I spent time with the mortals when I could, learning more about them and their ways. I wasna the only King to take one as a lover. We discovered soon enough that it was rare for a human to become pregnant by a King, and those who did usually lost the bairns within a few months. The verra few who carried to term had stillborn births."

Emilia was taken aback by his words. "The women on your world can get with child?"

He nodded slowly.

She couldn't fathom such a thing since only animals on Zora

procreated. There were no births from humans. Infants were found, though as far as she was aware, no one knew who brought them or where the babies came from.

"I forgot that isna possible here," Hector said. "Forgive me for being so insensitive."

"For some, that might be difficult to hear, but I've never felt the motherly urge many women do."

Hector released his hands and propped them behind him. "Still, I should be more mindful of such things."

"I take it those women who couldn't carry your children were upset?"

"They were devastated. I made sure the handful of mortal lovers I took to my bed never became pregnant."

Something in the way he said that struck her as strange. "You didn't want children?"

"I was the result of a casual encounter. Dragons mate for life. We seek that bond. It's part of our psyche, our verra essence. Sometimes, those mates are never found, but a dragon will keep looking, always seeking. That was the case with my mum. She was so desperate to have love and a mate that she gave herself to anyone who gave her even a smidgen of attention. The moment she discovered she had conceived, she told the male, and he immediately cut ties with her. She blamed me for it. She couldna bear to even look at me."

Emilia's heart hurt for him. "How was that your fault?"

"It wasna, but that's what she told herself. She had to blame someone, and she wasn't going to blame herself or her lover. She left when I was only a few months old. They found her body weeks later."

"I'm sorry." She didn't know the mother who'd birthed her, but she had loved the woman who raised her dearly.

Hector's lips curved into a gentle smile. "It was long ago. I'm over it."

"I don't think anyone gets past such a thing."

"It taught me a lot. I refused to search for a mate. Figured if it happened, it happened, but I wouldna force it. I also knew I wouldna spread my seed far and wide. If there were to be children, I wanted to be a part of their lives. I wanted them to know they were loved, and I wanted to know their love."

She hadn't ever thought of herself as a mother before, but after hearing Hector's declaration, she began to wonder what it might be like.

"So, nay. To answer your earlier question, none of my lovers ever dealt with a pregnancy. The ones who did had it rough, though. Of course, I felt for the humans, but I didna think too much about it. I assumed—wrongly—that as Kings, we would take a dragon as our mate. That's when Ulrik, the King of Silvers, fell in love with a human. She would've been the first such mate."

"Would've been?" Emilia asked. "I take that to mean it didn't happen?"

"Sadly, nay. Ulrik's uncle was still enraged that he hadn't been chosen as King. Mikkel conspired to ruin Ulrik's life by turning the woman he planned to have as his mate against him. He convinced her to kill Ulrik the night of their ceremony."

Emilia was shocked. "All for a title?"

"To some, it means everything. Mikkel's heart wasna pure, and the magic knew that. It's why it chose Ulrik instead. The thing is, only a Dragon King can kill another King. All the mortal would've done was offend and anger Ulrik. It never came to that. Con and Ulrik were like brothers. Their friendship was something the rest of us were in awe of. Con had long suspected that Mikkel was up to something. He overheard the plan and knew he had to act. He shared what he had discovered with the rest of the Kings."

"He didn't go to Ulrik?"

Hector dug his toes into the sand. "Nay, and I doona blame him. I would've done the same for any of the Kings."

"What happened?"

"We were incensed. To have one of those we had protected and cared for turn on Ulrik, who believed her to be his mate, was abhorrent. Add to that the fact that the humans had been hunting some of the smaller dragons for food, and we'd had enough. We reacted swiftly and brutally. I can no' imagine what a sight we must have been when going after her. She was terrified—as she should've been. We were hurt and outraged on Ulrik's behalf and exacted vengeance for him. At the time, we all believed it was the only way."

Emilia didn't have to ask if they'd killed her. It was there in Hector's words. "And now?"

"Now, we all realize Mikkel manipulated her. He should've been our target. But that's what happens when the clouds of anger blind you." Hector turned his head to look out at the sea. "I knew the moment we cornered her that it was the wrong decision, but there was no going back. Ulrik's face when he learned of her treachery and his uncle's involvement was the worst. It was almost as if I could see his heart being ripped out of his chest. Yet, for all his hurt, he was still furious with us. That we hadna gone to him, that we had made such a decision without him. Something snapped in him that day. The carefree, easy-going person I knew became someone else. He didna take his rage out on us. Instead, he turned it on the humans. He called his clan and decimated the settlement on his land. Then…he went after other mortals."

Emilia didn't speak, didn't move. How could she after hearing such words? She stared at his profile as he grew silent. Took in his strong jawline, corded neck, and the way the wind ruffled the ends of his light brown waves. Hector was glossing over some details, but she couldn't blame him. It was shocking that he'd shared any of this with her. So, she listened and let his story unfold.

He drew in a deep breath and then slowly released it. "We forgot the promise we made the day the humans arrived. We forgot everything but that one of ours—one of the best of us—had been betrayed. The mortals didna stand a chance against us Kings. One by one, Kings called in their armies. The clans bickered among themselves—always had. But for the first time, we were united in the sole purpose of eradicating the humans." Hector paused and looked down at the sand before turning his deep brown eyes to her. "I've seen a world covered in flames and running red with blood. In the quiet of the night, I can still hear the screams of both the humans and the dragons."

She swallowed, her throat tight with emotion as she clutched her hands in her lap.

"Con was the only one who didna join the battle. He proved why he was King of Kings by turning each of us away from the fight until only Ulrik and his Silvers remained. The rest of us took our places against our own. My army fought against the Silvers as we struggled to hold them back. A few Kings sent their dragons to guard the mortals and keep the Silvers away. They were ordered not to harm the humans in any way, so when the mortals attacked, they did nothing."

Emilia turned her head as tears filled her eyes. She dashed them away as soon as they landed on her cheeks.

Hector sat up and dusted off his hand as he sat cross-legged. "Con made all but four of the largest Silvers stand down. Ulrik ignored all of us. He was on a mission, and we had helped him begin it. Con reminded us of our vow to the humans. It didna matter how angry we were, or how much we wanted revenge, we had allowed them to live on Earth, and we didna have the right to take that from them. What we all knew was that the war had been mounting for years. Mikkel had lit the match, but we threw it on the wood by killing the female." He released a long sigh. "It took all of us to contain the Silvers and put them into a dragon sleep. Then, we turned our attention to Ulrik. Once more, we joined together and used our magic to bind Ulrik's. It kept him in human form without allowing him to shift. He couldn't use his magic at all. Then, we banished him."

She winced, but it was easy for her to pass judgment on their actions. She hadn't been there to see or experience it. Besides, it wasn't that far off from what the cabinet planned to do with her. "Did that end the war?"

"For us it did. But the mortals wanted nothing but complete domination. They had no idea we could've wiped them out with a thought. They lived because we allowed it. In the end, it cost us everything. The humans kept attacking. They hunted the Pinks, the smallest of the dragons, to what we believed was extinction and were going after others."

"Yet, you still allowed them to remain."

He shrugged one shoulder. "It's who we were."

"Your promise."

"Aye. Our oath. To annihilate the humans would've made us

unfit to be Kings. The magic would've tapped new dragons to take over. We didna stay our hands because we didna wish to give up our titles. We didna kill because we're no' murderers. But there was no talking to the mortals. They wouldna relent, and we had lost too many already. So, we came to the only conclusion we could."

Emilia raised her brows and waited. When he didn't finish, she asked, "What was that?"

"Removal of the dragons."

FIFTEEN

Saying the words was difficult. Even now, millennia later. Hector was proud of himself for getting it out without his voice breaking.

"Removal? What do you mean?" Emilia asked, her eyes still red from her tears.

The sight of them had been unexpected, but if anyone would feel deeply about dragons, it would be those at Highvale. Her reaction had softened some of the hard edges of his scars. "The only way the humans would stop is if there were no more dragons. There were too many to hide, and the mortals had multiplied at such a rate that they occupied nearly every region."

"So, what did you do?"

"We built a bridge and sent them out into the universe to find a new home with the promise that we would bring them back as soon as we could."

Emilia's blue eyes held his. "You sent your clan away?"

"It was the single hardest thing I've ever done," he admitted. "When the last of the dragons were gone, the Kings gathered at

Dreagan, which was our meeting place. We put up a border so no one could enter, each took a mountain, and slept. Only two didna. Ulrik, because he couldna shift into his true form any longer, and Con. He kept up with the changing times and what the humans were doing. Every ten years, he'd visit and give us the details. We kept waiting to be woken so we could bring back our clans, but I think we all knew it would never happen."

Her face was lined with sorrow.

It became hard to look at her. Hector rose and faced the cave's entrance. "Eventually, dragons became legend. We were forgotten, and the mortals made sure of that. There is no record of us, the war, or how the humans came to Earth. They rewrote their entire history. We walk among them now, pretending to *be* them. We craft an alcoholic drink called whisky, and it's made us a lot of money and allowed us a measure of freedom. But the days of taking to the skies whenever we wanted were gone."

The waves kept rolling in, over and over, just like the years had passed. There was no stopping the tides or time. Hector swallowed and tried not to think about Teo and whether he'd reached the mainland.

"Being a Dragon King without a clan was hard. We had to figure out how to fit into our new lives. But we had each other, which made it bearable. We stumbled many times, but we kept getting back up and moving forward."

"And Ulrik?"

Hector twisted his lips as he faced her. "He suffered his own Hell with his own kind of demons. He was a King, so he didna die. He clawed his way back and built his own empire, all with the objective of destroying the Kings—particularly Con."

"Did he?"

"He came close, but then he found his mate. She didna just help him heal those old wounds. She made him see the world in a new light. His magic was returned, and with it, his ability to shift. He and Con settled their grievances, and Ulrik returned to Dreagan. Which was good because we needed him. We had a powerful enemy we didna know about. Her name is Villette, and she's a Star Person. Do you know her?"

Emilia shook her head and rubbed her arm. "What is a Star Person?"

Hector's thoughts stopped as he took in her dirty dress. He'd been deep in the past while she sat without saying anything about a change of clothes or food. What had he been thinking? That was the problem. He hadn't.

"Are you hungry?" he asked.

She hesitated before nodding. "A little."

Which meant she was probably starving. He inwardly kicked himself for being so thoughtless. "What would you like?"

"Uh..." she hedged. "I'd rather not go to the market. I'm not up to seeing anyone."

"You doona have to go anywhere. Tell me what it is."

She picked at a broken fingernail. "Bread or fruit will be fine."

Emilia jumped at the sudden appearance of a table laden with varieties of food he had seen walking the streets the day before. She stared at it for a long moment before sliding her gaze to him.

"Eat," he urged her.

She looked at the table and then back at him. "You did that?"

"If it isna to your liking, let me know."

"This is more than acceptable," she said and stood.

He watched her make her way to the table and look over the

different offerings before reaching for a piece of fruit. She bit into the deep orange flesh and swallowed. Emilia stuffed the rest of the fruit into her mouth and began sampling from each trencher. Hector looked around the wide cave as she ate.

It was roomy, with the rocky mounds staying toward the sides. The ceiling was low enough that he could touch it without stretching. Alcoves branched off, as well. The tide was in, but the water didn't crest the beach to fill the cave, which made it an ideal location. This would be where they stayed. It was still part of Highvale yet separate. That should make it clear where he stood with the cabinet. Though he wouldn't mind telling them himself.

The first thing he did was walk to the entrance and press his hand against the stone. An invisible shield to keep others out rose. Emilia looked up from eating as he strode to the back of the cave.

"I'm seeing if there's a back entrance," he told her.

It didn't take him long to find that the cave ended, the ceiling sloping down to the sand, ensuring there wasn't another way in. None of the alcoves had back entrances either. He took his time exploring to give Emilia a chance to eat without him hovering. All the while, he was cognizant that Teo hadn't returned. It wouldn't take Rhi long to answer his call. If Teo made it to the mainland.

"Aren't you eating?"

He jerked at the sound of Emilia's voice. Hector found her on the boulder once more. He looked at the table. "That was for you."

"There's no way I can eat all of that."

"Teo will return. He'll be hungry."

She looked out of the cave. "We'll save it for him, then."

"There's only one entrance," he explained as he walked toward her. "There's a barrier over it you willna be able to see. You, Teo, and I, as well as Rhi when she gets here, will be able to enter without problems. Anyone else will be kept out."

"I didn't know such magic was possible. All of this," she said, motioning to the table. "How do you do it?"

He shrugged as his lips twisted. "I doona know. I just can."

"You were telling me about Villette. Will you continue? I very much want to know."

Hector walked to the table, plucked an olive from a dish, and popped it into his mouth. "She is from a race of beings that can travel the universe. Their magic is even greater than mine."

"How did you come to have such an enemy?"

"Because we're dragons."

Emilia's brow puckered in confusion. "I don't understand."

"We recently learned the truth about why she hates us so. You see, a verra, verra long time ago, the Star People enslaved dragons. Her brother sought to free our ancestors. In secret, he created a world—Earth—and then freed the dragons. Earth was kept hidden, but Villette eventually found our realm. The sight of the dragons flourishing infuriated her. She went to another planet, where the entire population was Druids." At the question in Emilia's eyes, he said, "They're humans with magic. They can talk to animals, converse with trees, and even speak to the wind. They're connected to the ecosystem. Some of the Druids there lost their magic. Villette took them and put them on Earth."

Emilia's mouth parted in shock. "The mortals."

"That's right. She knew things would eventually end in war, but it didna turn out as she had hoped. So, she set a new plan in motion that took centuries to unfold. We were nearly defeated, but we triumphed in the end. We still had no idea about Villette's involvement. In truth, we believed our enemies had been vanquished, and we could relax. Then we discovered our dragons had been found. Here, on Zora."

Her lips curved into a smile. "You finally found them."

"One of our friends, Erith, was there when we sent our kin away. She created Zora and brought them here. This realm was supposed to be a new home for the dragons—one without humans."

Emilia's smile faltered. "Then how are we here?"

"Villette. She found Zora and brought more humans."

"She's the one responsible for bringing the babies?"

Hector shook his head. "She swears that isna her. Nay. She brought adults."

"Everything is repeating, isn't it?" Emilia asked somberly.

"In some ways. Dragon territory is off-limits here. That has kept the humans separate, but Villette wasna done meddling. She's the one who created and ruled Stonemore."

Emilia stiffened in surprise. "I've heard of the city."

"She's been trying to kill dragons and create her own. However, we managed to ruin those plans."

"Are you bringing your dragons home?"

Hector tried to smile, but he wasn't sure his lips actually moved. "They could never return to Earth. Their home is here now."

"So, you'll stay. As your clan's King."

"There are no more clans and no need for Kings. The dragons here are ruled by Con and Rhi's twins, Brandr and Eurwen. There really isna a place for the Dragon Kings anymore. The dragons want nothing to do with us. They feel we abandoned them, and they are no' wrong. We've struggled over the millennia without our clans, and now that we found them…" Hector shrugged and swallowed past the lump in his throat.

Emilia got to her feet and took a step toward him. "There is one place that needs you. Highvale."

"I thought you didna want me here."

"Maybe I was wrong."

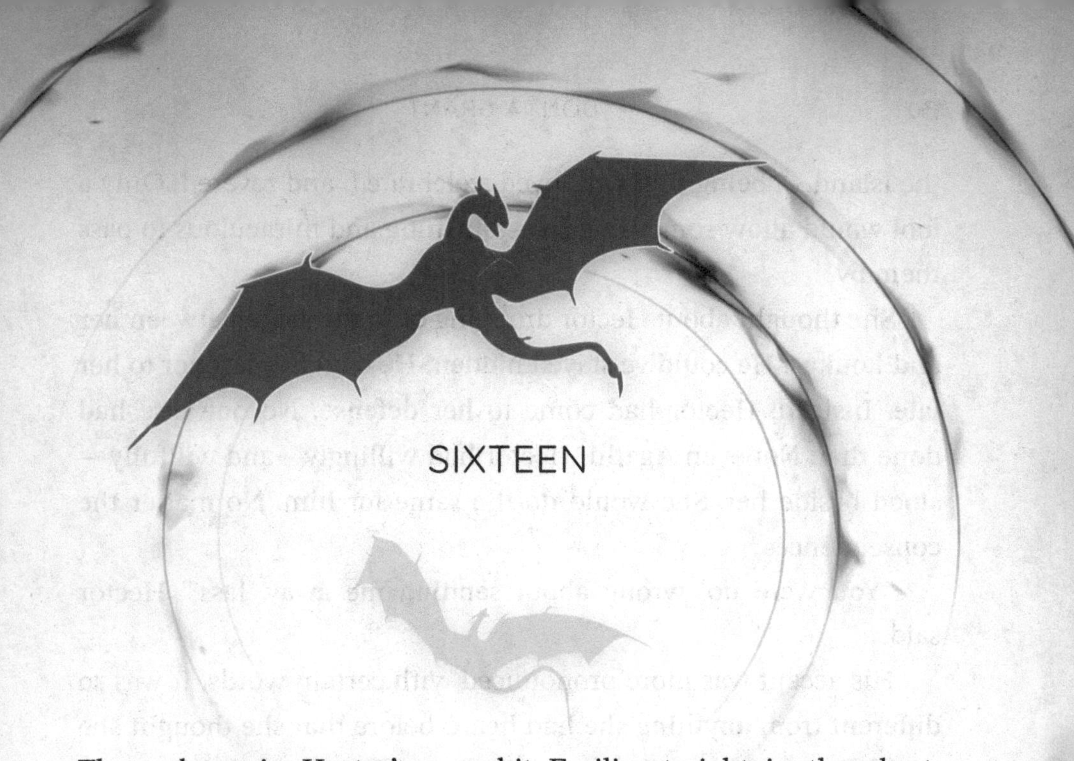

SIXTEEN

The sadness in Hector's eyes hit Emilia straight in the chest, knocking the wind from her. For one as powerful as he to be so despondent seemed unimaginable, yet his hurt was profound.

Her response had been visceral. She hadn't hesitated, hadn't considered her words. She had simply spoken from her heart. Because Highvale needed him. Perhaps not in the way the cabinet believed they did, however. If the dragons didn't want Hector or the other Kings, then the island would welcome them with open arms.

It was the opposite of how she had greeted Hector.

Emilia inwardly flinched at the reminder of how she had received—and promptly dismissed—him. All the lengths she had gone to had backfired to the point that she had lost her home, her friends, and her place in the city. Pain was there, the dull ache of having what mattered most wrenched away. Yet a new opportunity stood before her: a handsome man who could transform into a dragon. A King whose very image was displayed to everyone on the island. A being that was loved, celebrated, and revered. Only a fool would allow something so astonishing and miraculous to pass them by.

She thought about Hector dropping onto the stage between her and Loukas. He could've stayed hidden. He could've left her to her fate. Instead, Hector had come to her defense. No one else had done that. Not even Agathi. Hector had willingly—and willfully—stood beside her. She would do the same for him. No matter the consequences.

"You were no' wrong about sending me away, lass," Hector said.

His accent was more pronounced with certain words. It was so different from anything she had heard before that she thought she could listen to him all day. Particularly when he called her *lass*. She didn't know what the word meant, but she liked it when he said it to her. "I never saw dragons in my vision."

"But you knew we were the cause of it."

"Maybe I was wrong."

He shot her a crooked smile. "I appreciate what you're doing, but you needn't. I've survived without a clan. I'll find a way to continue."

"How long have you lived without your dragons?"

There was a slight hesitation before he said, "I'm no' sure you really want to know the answer to that."

"I do," she insisted.

His lips flattened for a heartbeat. "Millennia."

"A thousand years?" she repeated to make sure she heard him correctly.

"Several millennia."

The words entered her head, but her mind couldn't seem to process them. "Several…?"

His dark eyes watched her closely as he nodded in affirmation.

"How many millennia?"

"Entirely too many," he replied. "I'm old, lass. Verra, verra old."

Yet he didn't look much older than her. How was that possible? Then again, she didn't know of any other being who could change shapes or wield magic as he could.

"And that is why I didna wish to tell you," Hector said.

She quickly shook her head. "I don't care about your age." That wasn't exactly true, but that hadn't been why she had been staring. "You don't look old."

"Dragon Kings heal from any wounds. I suspect that's what keeps us looking youthful."

"All of you?"

He chuckled. "All of us."

"Some carry it better than others," a female said, drawing their attention to the entrance.

The accent was another Emilia had never heard before. Hector's head jerked toward the voice, and a smile split his face. The woman was unbelievably gorgeous, with thick, black hair that fell down her back. Her black clothing was formfitting, her trousers contouring her long legs. The woman's unusual silver eyes briefly met Emilia's before returning to Hector.

He got to his feet to greet her. "You made it."

"You doubted I would?"

Emilia glanced down at her dirty gown and realized how awful she likely looked. She reached up and touched her hair, unable to pull her gaze from the newcomer. This must be Rhi. She was unlike any woman Emilia had ever seen, and not just in the way she dressed. Emilia looked at Rhi's boots and the narrow, tall heel she stood on. Did all the women Hector know dress in such a fashion? How simple everyone at Highvale must appear next to someone so dazzling.

"Where's Teo?" Hector asked as he looked out the cave.

The boy strolled into sight, wearing a bright smile. "I brought her, just like I said I would."

"So, you did," Hector said as he squeezed the boy's shoulder.

Teo stared up at him with a level of adoration Emilia understood and appreciated. Hector hadn't just saved her, he had acknowledged Teo and made him feel important. That went a long way for someone like Teo, and it likely changed his young life.

"We've been worried," Rhi said as she threw her arms around Hector and hugged him.

He returned the embrace, briefly closing his eyes before they released each other.

"Why didn't you contact us?" Rhi asked.

Hector drew in a deep breath and shook his head. "I tried. I suspect something is keeping me from reaching anyone. It's why I sent Teo to the mainland for you." He glanced at Emilia. "Rhi, this is Emilia. Emilia, Rhi."

"Hello," Rhi said with a warm smile.

Emilia was awed by the beautiful stranger. Something about Rhi made Emilia like her instantly. "Hello."

"Rhi," Hector said, getting her attention. "You need to get back to Iron Hall and make sure no one else touches the blinking light in the corridor."

Rhi swung her head to him. "You can tell them yourself."

"Did Teo no' tell you? I can no' leave. I've tried."

Rhi shrugged as if his words meant nothing. "I can build a doorway right here."

"Nay!" Hector shouted, causing everyone to jump.

Rhi's brow furrowed as she searched his face. "Okay," she said, drawing out the word. "Perhaps you need to tell me what's going on yourself."

"This place is like Dreagan. This is where all of Zora's magic springs from. And I'm bound here. It happened when I used magic. I'm..." He shrugged. "The island's protector, for lack of a better word."

Rhi studied his face and gave him a nod. "How long will that last?"

To Emilia's surprise, both looked at her. "I don't have an answer for that. We've never had a dragon here before, much less a King."

Rhi crossed her arms over her chest and released a long sigh. "This isn't good. Con is going to be pissed. He'll come for you."

"You can no' let that happen," Hector replied earnestly. "Return to the others and make sure they doona come. If they do, they might very well become locked here with me."

"The moment I tell Con what's happening, he's going to want to talk to you. And if he can't reach you, he'll come."

Hector ran a hand down his face. "I'm aware. You're the only one he'll listen to, which is why it has to come from you."

Rhi snorted, her face scrunched in denial. "He doesn't listen to me."

"You're his mate. He'll listen to you before anyone else, and you know it."

She dropped her arms to her sides. "What if I think he should come? No dragon should be chained. Ever. No matter how pretty the place might be."

Emilia couldn't argue with Rhi's point, but at the same time, she understood why Hector was so adamant about the others not coming to Highvale. The likelihood that they would become bound just as Hector had was high.

He stalked from the cave into the sunshine. Teo followed, sticking close to his side. Rhi was slower to react, though she did trail after them. Not to be left out, Emilia hurried out, too. She walked to Teo and stood beside him.

"Magic was used to tie you to this isle," Rhi said. "And magic can be used to undo it."

Hector turned to her. "I agree, but I can figure it out. I doona want anyone else caught in the trap. Because that's exactly what it is. A trap."

"And that, right there, will send Con right over the edge," Rhi replied.

Emilia glanced at Teo to find him looking up. She followed his gaze to the sky but saw nothing that would hold his attention—other than the clouds. Yet he was smiling. It was the same adoration he wore when looking at Hector. She leaned close and asked, "What are you looking at?"

"Hector," he whispered.

She was about to point out that Hector stood on the beach and wasn't in the sky when she suddenly stilled. She lifted her gaze once more before shifting her attention to Hector and then Teo. That's when it dawned on her. The only reason for Teo to look up was if Hector had been in his true form.

Teo briefly cut his eyes to her, his smile growing.

"You can see him," Emilia stated. "The *real* him."

Teo nodded. "I can."

She hadn't known such an ability was even possible. "What does he look like?"

"Amazing," Teo whispered in awe.

"Describe him," she urged in a low voice as Hector and Rhi kept talking.

Teo licked his lips. "Huge."

When he didn't elaborate, Emilia rolled her eyes. "Can't you give me more detail?"

"You wouldn't believe me."

"Of course, I would," she insisted.

Teo sighed. "Do you recall the dragon entrance on the mainland?"

"I recall there being a dragon there."

"It's him. That's what Hector looks like."

No matter how she tried, Emilia couldn't remember what that dragon statue looked like. So, she tried another tactic. "What color are his scales?"

"Sea green."

"All right," Rhi said, drawing Emilia's attention. "I'll do what I can, but I can't promise Con won't come. He makes his own decisions. I guess this means you won't be there for the mating ceremony."

Hector's face fell. "It doesna look like it."

Emilia could guess what the ceremony was by the label. One more thing to add to the list of why Hector and his friends would abhor Highvale. And she couldn't blame them. He wasn't staying by choice. He was only protecting the island because he'd been forced to. The moment he could, he'd leave. But that begged the question: When would his obligation be fulfilled?

Would it ever?

Rhi was convinced that Con would come. It could be that Hector being restrained might be what caused the blood and fire in her vision. Yet the Kings couldn't attack Highvale in a bid to free Hector because it would compel him to fight his own. That's what he was desperately trying to make Rhi understand so she could pass it along to the others.

There was no doubt in Emilia's mind that whatever alliance might have been made with the Kings had gone up in smoke the moment Hector was unwittingly bound to the island.

"Teo, you should go with Rhi," Hector said.

The boy shook his head. "You might need me."

"There are other children where I'm going," Rhi told him.

But Teo was unmoved. He shook his head again and lifted his chin defiantly.

Then Hector's gaze turned to her. Emilia straightened, waiting for him to tell her to go. He had enough to deal with without having to worry about her. She wasn't welcome on the island any longer. She was a burden to everyone, something she despised.

"What about you?" Hector asked. "Do you wish to stay after this morning?"

She was taken aback that he'd asked, though she probably shouldn't have been.

"It's your vision," Teo said beside her.

Emilia looked at him. He was right. Her vision had prompted her to keep Hector away. She was tied to all of this whether she wanted to be or not. The weak left when things got difficult, and she wasn't a coward. "I'm staying."

Hector stared at her for a long moment before nodding.

Rhi blew out a breath. "I'll be back soon." Then, she was gone.

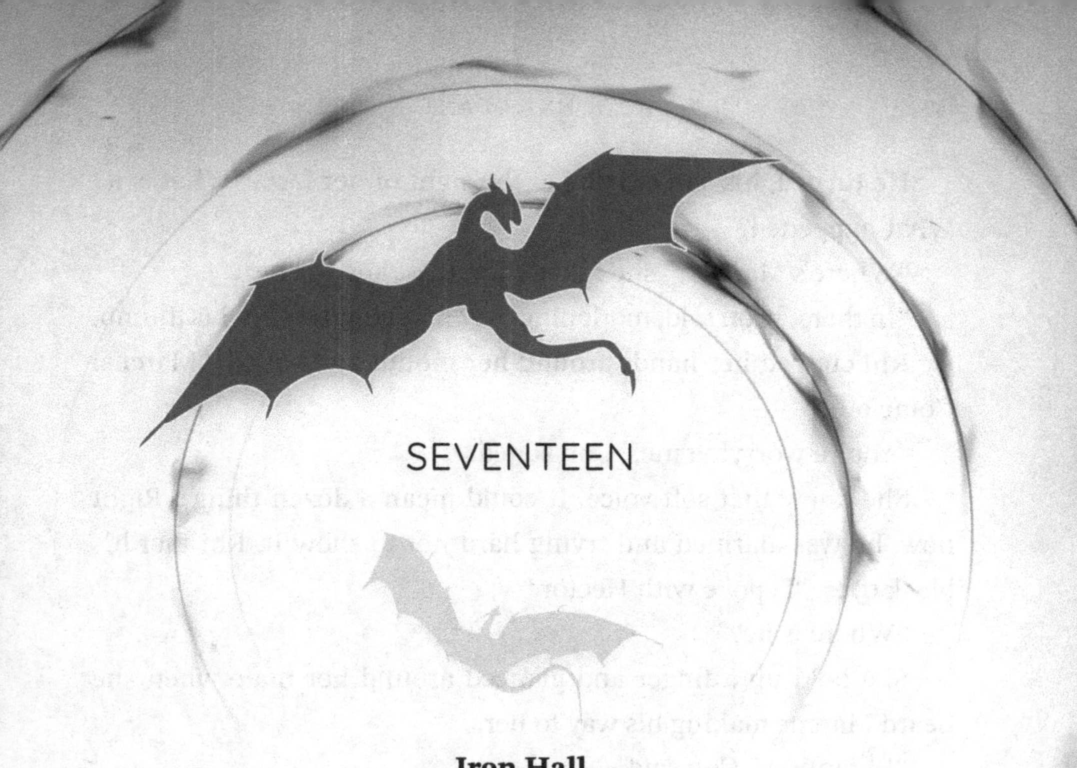

SEVENTEEN

Iron Hall

Rhi teleported to the main area of the underground city. She didn't even glance at the enormous tree overhead, its roots making up a portion of the ceiling as water dripped from them into the large, round pool in the middle. She didn't hear the children laughing from one of the side rooms, nor did she hear Sian moving about in her lab as she did her Alchemist things. Instead, Rhi rushed to Cullen, who stood under one of the weak points Marcus had pointed out.

"Where's Con?" Rhi asked.

Cullen's pale brown eyes swung to her. "He's with Marcus. Wha—?"

She teleported away before he finished. Rhi arrived in the round antechamber to find her mate standing at the entrance to the corridor they had been slowly clearing. "Con."

He turned, his smile dying at the sight of her face. "What is it? What happened?"

"Where's Marcus?" she asked instead of answering.

"In there," Con said, motioning over his shoulder with his thumb.

Rhi cupped her hands around her mouth and yelled, "Marcus! Come out!"

"You're worrying me," Con stated.

She knew that soft voice. It could mean a dozen things. Right now, he was alarmed and trying hard not to show it. Rhi met his black eyes. "I spoke with Hector."

"Where is he?"

She held up a finger and glanced around her mate when she heard Marcus making his way to her.

"Rhiannon," Con said.

"Constantine," she replied. He was fast losing patience, but she understood. "Give me a moment, and all will be clear."

Con grunted but waited, his impatience evident.

Marcus strode out of the corridor and looked from her to Con and back again. "What's so important?"

"I'm waiting to find out myself," Con said as he crossed his arms over his chest.

Rhi had to pick her words carefully. Her mate was the most powerful of all the Dragon Kings, and one of the reasons was because he loved the others as family. His family. He would die for any of them. If any were in trouble, Con moved Heaven and Earth —and sometimes even Hell—for them.

And for her.

She swallowed as she recalled Hector's fear and worry. "Did you find something emitting light in the hallway?"

"Nay," Marcus said with a frown.

Rhi sighed in relief. "If you do, don't touch it. Don't let anyone touch it." Then her gaze slid to Con. "That's what Hector did. It brought him somewhere else."

"Why has he no' returned?" Marcus asked.

Con silently held her gaze, undoubtedly piecing it all together. "Because he can no'."

"Unfortunately, he can't," she admitted.

"And you couldna bring him?" Con asked.

Rhi walked to him and took his hand in one of hers as she loosened his crossed arms. "He was sure he wouldn't be able to leave."

"Then we go get him," Marcus stated.

Con quirked a brow. "My thoughts exactly."

This was the part she hadn't looked forward to. It wasn't that Con didn't think his brethren could handle things themselves—they were Kings, after all. But he never wanted them to think they weren't important enough that he wouldn't drop everything for them.

"Whatever you're no' saying is making things worse," Con told her. "Just say it. Whatever it is."

Rhi rubbed her forehead. "Hector has asked that the Kings stay away. He's right in his fears because the moment he used magic, something bound him to the place. He's tried to leave but is unable. He's also tried to reach out, but nothing gets through."

"Where is he?" Con asked in that soft voice again.

Everyone always believed Con hid his expressions. She had once thought that herself. Now, Rhi understood the subtle shifts in his body language. The way he held his mouth, and even the nuances of his voice, showed her everything he was feeling. Right now, he was anxious and tense.

She squeezed his hand. "He's safe. No one has harmed him, and they won't."

"Where. Is. He?" Con repeated, this time more firmly.

"Highvale."

Ire flashed in Con's eyes. "Tell me the rest."

Rhi laid it all out to both Con and Marcus, explaining what had happened to Hector from the time he pushed the flashing light until Rhi saw him.

"That's why the corridor was destroyed," Marcus said. "I knew from the moment I first looked at it that it wasna a natural cave-in."

Con turned his head to look down the hall. "How much longer until it's cleared?"

"I need another hour."

"Do it," Con ordered as Marcus strode back into the hallway. Then he looked at Rhi. "Can you return to Highvale and look around while veiled?"

She smiled. "Already planned on it."

"Watch yourself."

"Always."

He pulled her into his arms for a kiss. "Doona be gone long."

"I'll be back soon." She started to back up when his arms tightened around her. Rhi quirked a brow.

"Next time, please tell me when you go off like that. What if you'd gotten trapped like Hector?"

"Then you would've come looking for me."

Con ran the backs of his fingers along her cheek. "Always."

He then placed his hand over her stomach. She covered it with one of hers. She was just starting to show, though it was barely noticeable. Rhi was used to only having to worry about herself. It wasn't just her safety she needed to think about now. At least this time, she knew she was carrying a child. She hadn't when she was pregnant with the twins. Her recklessness had nearly gotten all three of them killed. None of them would be on Zora now if it weren't for Erith.

"You're right," she admitted. "I should've told you. I should've thought twice before answering a call."

"You are who you are. It's why I fell in love with you. I just want to be aware of where you're going in case something happens."

She nodded and laid her head on his chest. "From now on, you will."

He rested his chin atop her head as they stood in each other's arms. Rhi could've stayed there all day. It was a miracle she had become pregnant with the twins. It was another miracle that they found themselves parents a second time. With so many of the Kings' human mates unable to bear children, she understood how exceptional the gift was. It was irresponsible to be careless.

Neither she nor Con had gotten to be parents to the twins. They were just now repairing that relationship, and it was delicate business. She didn't want to lose this new life growing inside her or be estranged from another offspring.

It seemed Con was thinking the same thing because he said, "Maybe you shouldna go. Lotti can go in your stead."

While Lotti wasn't Fae, she was a Star Person and could make herself invisible, much like Rhi did by veiling herself.

"Just in case," Con added.

Rhi pulled back to look at him. "There will come a time when I step back from such things, but now isn't it. I will ask Lotti to accompany me, however. With two of us, we can cover more ground. And if something goes wrong, there's someone else there to help."

"I doona like the idea of something going wrong," he mumbled.

Some might find his overprotective nature controlling or smothering, but she knew it resulted from an abundance of love. Besides, he never attempted to control her. He wouldn't be able to, no matter how hard he tried. And they both knew that.

"Am I not your mate?" she asked.

Desire flared in his dark eyes. "You are."

"Am I not your queen?"

His voice dropped low as he brought her body flush to his. "Aye."

"Then, as your queen, it's my duty to help Hector since you cannot. Trust me."

"I have from the moment I first saw you."

By the stars, this man always knew what to say to make her heart skip a beat. How was it possible to love someone as much as she loved him?

"Go," he murmured huskily and set her away from him. "Go, so you can return to me."

"Always," she said with a wink before teleporting out to find Lotti.

It didn't take Rhi long to find her and explain the situation. Within minutes, they traveled to Highvale. Except Rhi didn't go directly to the island as she should have. Instead, she found herself on the beach, staring up at the dragon statue doorway where she had been when Teo summoned her. She looked around, but Lotti wasn't with her. Perhaps she had gotten to the city without effort because she was a Star Person.

Rhi had to know where she was going before she could teleport somewhere. Unless someone called for her. But she had been to the island, so she should've been able to head straight for Highvale. It was infuriating.

She veiled herself and walked up the steps and beneath the arched doorway. A statue of Hector loomed over her. She hadn't gotten a good look at the other statues on the island the first time, but she planned to this time. Did all of them look like Hector? Or were they different dragons? Once she stepped beneath the arch, she could teleport to Highvale. As before, she found herself on some steps leading from the sea to the city.

Rhi walked up the stairs. This time, she paid more attention to the dragons at the entrance and smiled when she noticed they looked like Asher. No one could see her, but someone could still bump into her, which meant she had to be careful where she walked. She couldn't talk either since others would be able to hear her. It came in handy if she wanted to scare someone, and she had used that trick on Halloween with humans numerous times.

But she wasn't walking the streets of Dublin now. She was in an enchanted city situated on an island only those with magic could get to. And one of her Dragon Kings was tied to it somehow. She still stood by her earlier comment. Magic had been used to lock Hector here, and it could be used to release him.

She had been too intent on getting to Hector the first time to notice the city much, but now she lingered in the streets, listening to conversations and watching the citizens. There was a good mix of those who sought Highvale as a sanctuary and those who had lived there all their lives. Oddly, the newcomers weren't singled out or treated differently. At first blush, it looked to be a welcoming, inclusive place.

However, Hector had been tricked. No matter how nice and attractive the surface looked, it was what was underneath that mattered. Teo had given Rhi a quick rundown of the guilds and the cabinet. She could go to the Oracle guild and see what she could uncover about Emilia and the cabinet's part in summoning Hector. Hector was convinced Emilia wasn't involved, and while Rhi was inclined to believe him, she wouldn't be doing her due diligence if she didn't check Emilia's story.

Rhi scanned the structures until she found the pavilion where the cabinet met. Those who ran a city had the most secrets. That's where she would begin.

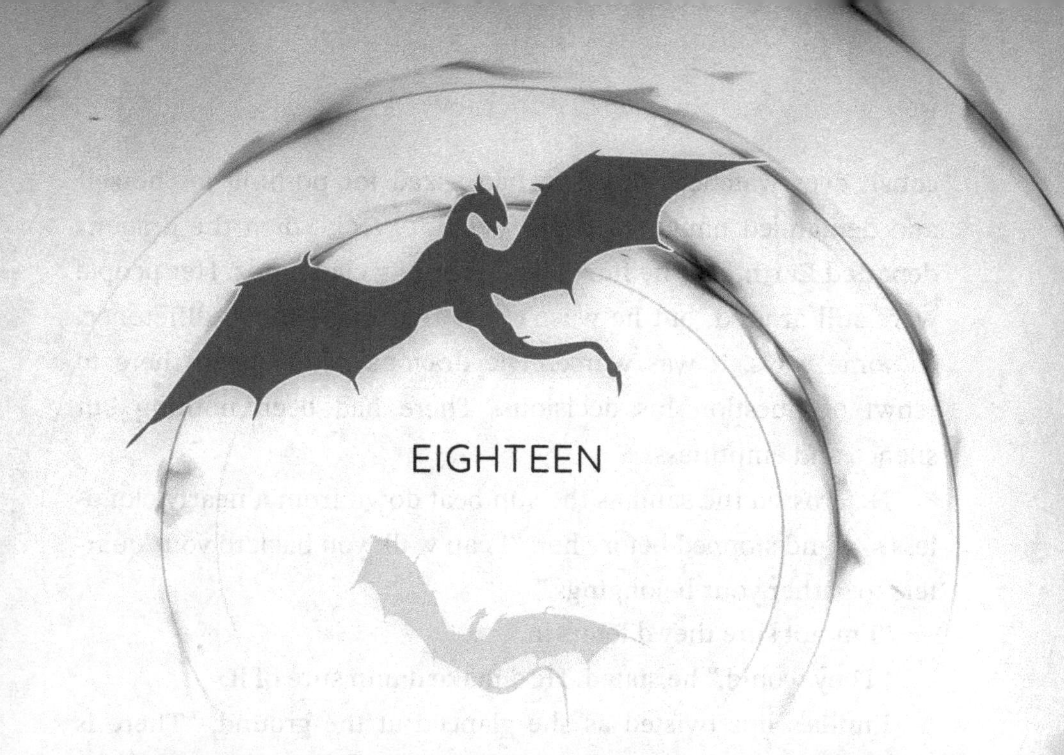

EIGHTEEN

What a fucking mess. No matter how Hector looked at his present situation, there was no way it ended well. The thing was, if he had been asked to help, he probably would have. Any of the Kings would've stepped up. But to be tricked and bound to the island was unforgivable, no matter how anyone looked at it.

Rhi would ensure that none of the Kings ventured to Highvale, but Hector knew she would return. And likely with reinforcements. He could only hope that nothing befell the mates on the island. Otherwise, the residents would get their war—just not how they wanted it.

He could continue staring out at the vast ocean, grumbling like a peevish child, or he could focus on finding a way to regain his freedom. He wasn't the sort to complain, and he'd done enough of it. Hector blew out a breath and turned around. That's when his gaze landed on Emilia.

His life wasn't the only one affected. Hers had been irrevocably altered, too. Strands of blond curls lifted in the sea breeze as her cobalt eyes watched him. She had asked for nothing for herself and demanded naught. He had been a wreck when the dragons departed Earth, and he flew over his empty clan lands. Her people were still around, but he wasn't sure that made much difference. In some ways, it was worse. The dragons hadn't been there to scowl or question his decisions. There had been nothing but silence and emptiness.

He crossed the sand as the sun beat down from a nearly cloudless sky and stopped before her. "I can walk you back to your quarters to gather your belongings."

"I'm not sure they'd let us in."

"They would," he stated. He'd make damn sure of it.

Emilia's lips twisted as she glanced at the ground. "There is nothing to retrieve."

"I find that hard to believe. That was your home. Surely, you have mementos or clothes."

"A shell I found on the beach, and the comb Agathi gave me."

His gut twisted. That was all she had? He had seen some of the residents dripping in gold and pearls.

"I've always lived simply," she said.

There was living simply, and there was being deprived. He wasn't sure which column she fell in. "You never dreamed of more?"

"Who doesn't?" she asked with a laugh. "It was hard not to when my closest friend came from the most powerful family on the island."

"And who is this?"

"Agathi. We met at the guild house. She sits on the cabinet."

And did nothing to help Emilia. But there was no need to point that out. Emilia had been there and witnessed it herself.

Most likely, that blow hurt worse than being removed from the guild.

Emilia's smile wobbled. "I used to try on her clothes when we were younger. She attempted to get me to wear some of her jewelry once, but it didn't feel right."

"Tell me about the guilds," he urged, wanting to take her mind off Agathi. "I gather there is a hierarchy."

The sadness that had crept into her voice vanished at the change in topic. "Oh, aye. Everyone comes in at the lowest level and works their way up."

"How, exactly?"

"Depends on the guild. For us, it was announcing a vision and seeing if it came to pass."

Hector grunted. "What if the vision had nothing to do with anyone at Highvale?"

"Then you didn't move up."

"That's a convenient way of keeping others from getting ahead."

Emilia tucked her hair behind her ears. "I never wanted the power. Advancement gives someone more authority, and the thought of making decisions for an entire city every day made me sick to my stomach."

Hector raised his brows. "Is that no' what you did by convincing me to leave?"

"I never thought of it that way, but you're right. I did decide for everyone."

"And you didna hesitate to keep others safe. I think you could've handled that kind of responsibility with ease."

She shifted her feet in the sand, then took a step back to stay in the shadow of the cave entrance. "The truth is, I never liked the attention. Agathi craved it. She came alive with it while I worried about saying or doing the wrong thing with so many watching."

"I'm guessing those advancing through the guild gained other things like possessions and responsibilities."

"They did."

Just as he'd suspected. "And those who didn't rise?"

"Still had a place in the guild. Many things have to be done to keep it running."

Doing the menial chores the others refused to do, most likely. "Have you kept all of your visions to yourself?"

"I've only ever had three—well, four now. The third over and over again since I was five."

He wanted to ask what the others were, but he focused on the repeated one for the moment. "From the seers I know, recurring visions mean it's important. I can no' believe you didna share that burden with anyone, especially at such a young age."

"As I said, something urged me to remain silent. So, I did."

"The vision hasna changed at all?"

Her mouth tightened slightly as her brow furrowed. "That's why I said I'd only had a handful of visions my entire life. Maybe I shouldn't have called it another one. It was almost the same."

"Almost? What was different?" he pressed.

"I was walking. I'd only witnessed the vision before. This time, I stood in the grass. When I stepped, blood bubbled up from the ground."

For such an event to occur, there would've had to be a lot of blood. She had said the realm was covered in it, but he hadn't thought she meant it literally.

"And there was a dragon behind me. Its roar made my entire body vibrate and the ground shake beneath my feet."

"The dragon would've been verra close. You still didna see any?"

She shook her head.

Had his arrival brought about the altered vision? Or was there another reason? Hector needed time to think, and she needed to rest. "Come," he urged and motioned to the cave. "A soak in some hot water will make you feel better."

Her brow puckered, but she turned and entered. He heard her quick intake of breath when she saw the tub. Maybe he shouldn't have exhibited such magic in front of her, but he wanted to pamper her since it seemed no one else ever had. Beside the copper tub was a stool with a basket atop it laden with various soaps and other things. She ran her fingers along the edge of the tub as ribbons of steam rose from the water. She peered into the basket without touching anything.

"It's all for you. Rhi and the other mates like the bath salts. You put them in the water, and they fizz. The bars are to wash your body, and the bottles are for your hair," he explained.

Bright blue eyes filled with shock lifted to him.

He walked to the basket and lifted an item. "This is shampoo. Use it first, followed by the conditioner," he said, showing her the second bottle. "Take your time. No one will disturb you."

Hector turned on his heel and walked out of the cave. He hadn't taken two steps before Teo popped up from behind a boulder. If he hadn't been whining about things, he might have noticed the boy's absence. He had made it clear to the cabinet that Teo and Emilia were under his protection, but that didn't mean nobody would try to harm them.

Teo ran over to him, his smile bright. Hector faced him and dropped to one knee to look him in the eye. "You've chosen your side, lad, and I applaud you for it. However, I can no' guarantee that someone willna come after you."

"Let them try," Teo declared.

Hector put his hand on the boy's shoulder. "You're brave, but you also need to be smart. I can no' stand the idea of something happening to you."

"No one sees me."

"Yet. They will if you doona change things up."

Teo kicked the sand as he hung his head. "I'm trying to help."

"You are. I just want everyone safe. Let Emilia or I know if you're going off."

"I wanted to see if I could hear anything on the streets."

Hector dropped his hand and rose, guiding Teo toward the water's edge. "Did you?"

"You're all anyone can talk about," the lad said excitedly.

"I bet."

"Some don't think you're really a dragon."

Hector couldn't care less about the doubters. The ones who believed were the ones who ensured he was chained to the island. "Is anyone talking about Emilia?"

"Aye."

The lad spoke so low Hector barely heard him. "What are they saying?"

"Different things," he mumbled.

Teo had been happy to share gossip about Hector, but he didn't seem so eager to impart what he had learned about Emilia. Hector wasn't the only one who wanted to shield her.

He lowered his voice to make sure it didn't carry back to Emilia in the cave. "Tell me, but doona say anything to her about it."

"I don't even want to tell you."

He met the lad's blue eyes. "That bad, huh?"

"People are cruel."

"Unfortunately, you'll find that everywhere in the universe. It isna just on Highvale or Zora."

Teo grunted, a sound so like him Hector had to hide his grin.

He dropped to his haunches and hung his fingers in the waves rolling over his bare feet. "Tell me so you doona have to carry it anymore."

"I heard someone call for her banishment. Some groups are really angry at her for attempting to keep you from the city."

"Never mind that I came to her defense," Hector muttered.

Teo pulled a face. "I think everyone has already forgotten that."

"Is there more?"

"She has been banned from the guild. The cabinet is asking businesses to swear not to serve her. If they do, and someone turns them in, they will be fined."

Hector shook his head at the audacity.

"That decree has also been demanded of families," Teo added. "She isn't safe. The moment she shows her face in the city, everyone will turn her away. She won't be able to buy food or other necessities."

"Good thing she willna need to. Neither do you," Hector said and met Teo's eyes. "The cave is big enough for all of us. I put up a shield that prevents anyone but the three of us from getting in or out."

"What about Rhi?"

Hector straightened. "I feel for anyone on this island who tries to harm her. She can handle herself. But more than that, she's my queen. I will defend her."

"But…can you? I thought you were bound to protect those on Highvale."

"I was obliged to my brethren long before this island." He really hoped he wouldn't have to put it to the test.

Teo nodded, looking older than his eleven years. "Where is Emilia?"

"Taking a bath. She was exhausted."

"You should've seen where they put her. It was filthy."

Hector popped his knuckles. "She'll never suffer anything like that again as long as I'm around."

"Then I hope you stay."

He looked down at the boy, wondering what he had endured in his young life.

Teo's expression was troubled when he turned his face up to Hector. "I know you don't want to be here, and I don't blame you, but you're needed. And I don't mean for a war, either. I mean for the others who can't take care of themselves."

Like Teo. Hector found it telling that the lad didn't include himself in that. He touched the side of Teo's face and smiled at him. "Fate brought me here. Though I doona know what's in store for us. There's likely to be danger."

"I don't care."

But he did. Hector lightly patted the lad's face. "It's going to be an adventure."

Teo smiled in response. The protectiveness Hector felt for Emilia now enveloped Teo. He might not be able to get off Highvale, but if things got bad, he'd make sure the two of them did.

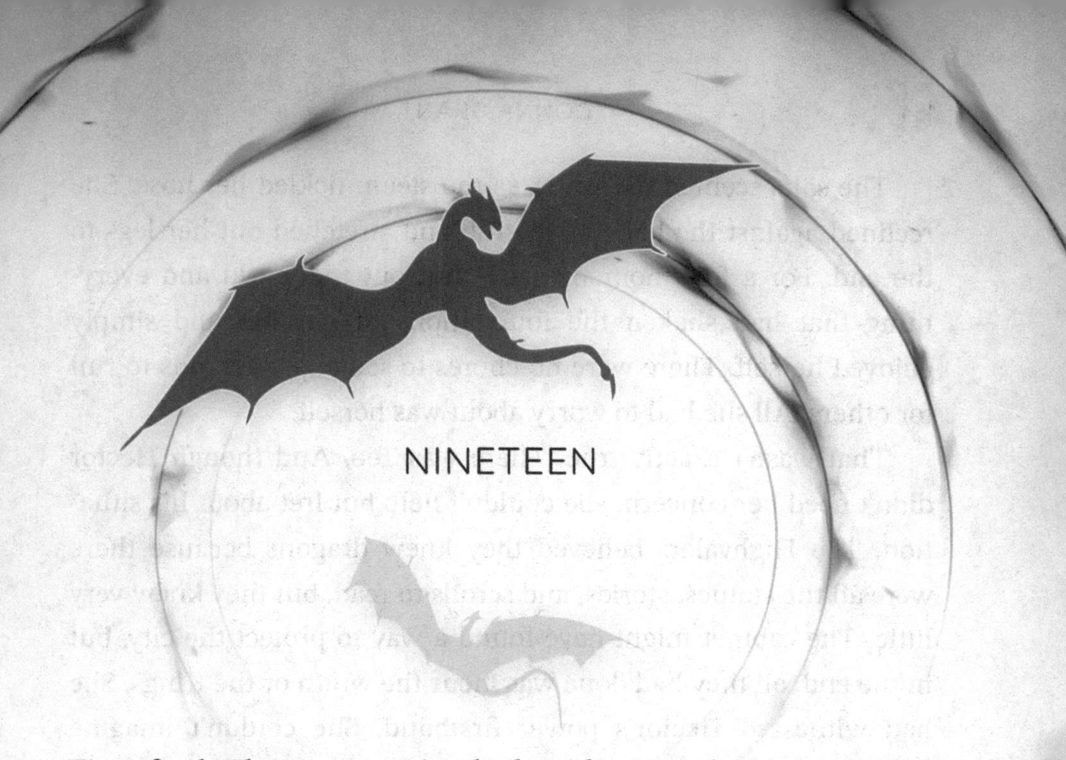

NINETEEN

First, food. Then an amazing bath with water that never cooled and melted all her stress away. Hector continued to surprise Emilia with his thoughtfulness. Not since her parents had anyone looked out for her in such a way. She'd had to learn to take care of herself at a very young age, and that hadn't changed when she made it to Highvale.

Emilia couldn't remember the last time she had undressed so quickly. She didn't want to think about putting her dirty gown back on after the bath, but that was a problem for later. Now, she was going to enjoy the water. Normally, she bathed in the communal tubs at the guild house. Having a tub all to herself was a luxury she had never imagined she would get to experience.

She had smelled the different-scented soap and their corresponding bath salts before deciding on a rich, sweet, and sensual scent. She couldn't read the words on the bottle, but it didn't matter. It smelled divine. She had never used salts before, so she had to guess how much to add.

The salts scented the water as the steam tickled her nose. She reclined against the back of the tub and stretched out her legs to the end. For a few moments, she shut out the world and everything that had shaken the foundations of her life and simply enjoyed herself. There were no chores to see to, no errands to run for others. All she had to worry about was herself.

That wasn't exactly true. There was Teo. And though Hector didn't need her concern, she couldn't help but fret about his situation. The Highvalers believed they knew dragons because there were all the statues, stories, and scrolls to read, but they knew very little. The cabinet might have found a way to protect the city, but in the end, all they had done was incur the wrath of the Kings. She had witnessed Hector's power firsthand. She couldn't imagine what more Kings could do. Not to mention Rhi.

Emilia sighed. So much for her peace. She couldn't relax as she wished with everything going on—and the part she played in it. She reached for the soap and lathered it in her hands before scrubbing her body. The moment the water got cloudy as she rinsed, it cleared. It came as such a shock that she washed herself two more times just to see it happen again.

"More dragon magic," she mused.

She wet her hair in the now-clean water and sought out the bottle Hector had said was used to wash her hair. She stared at the label, trying to discern any of the letters, but it remained garbled. Once she unscrewed the top, she brought it to her nose and smelled it. The scent was soft but refreshing. She poured a small amount into her cupped palm to get a better look.

When she rubbed it between her hands it lathered. She poured more into her hand and massaged it onto her scalp and down the strands. Once again, when she rinsed, the water cleared. She sat up and smoothed the water from her face over her hair. Then she turned to the second bottle. She tried it out like the first, but the consistency was different. Since she wasn't sure how to use it, she decided not to try.

Emilia stood and reached for a cloth next to the basket to dry off. Her gaze darted to the entrance, but there was no sign of Hector or Teo. She stepped out of the tub—not onto sand but a mat constructed of thin wooden strips set slightly atop it. It allowed her to dry off completely without getting sand stuck to her. She didn't remember it being there when she'd gotten into the water, but she could have missed it in her excitement.

She bent to retrieve her soiled gown, only to find it missing. Emilia straightened and searched the area. That's when she saw the daybed off to the side. Lying upon it were four gowns. One was yellow with a floral pattern along the edges, and another was red with a geometric-patterned edge. The third was pale green with dark green ivy edging, and the fourth was white with gold stripes along the border.

Unable to help herself, she walked over and touched each of the gowns. She saw different belts and clasps for the fabric at her shoulders. This couldn't all be for her. Could it? She looked out the entrance, hoping to see Hector. Emilia bit her lip and glanced to where her dirty clothes had lain, then back at the daybed she was positive hadn't been there before she got into the tub.

She drew in an unsteady breath. The gifts—if that's what they were—made her uncomfortable because she had never received one before. Emilia picked up the pale green chiton and let the soft rectangle of material slide over her body. She marveled at the shoulder clasps that looked like ivy leaves before fastening them. The belt was braided, deep green leather.

Just as she turned, she spotted a chair and a small table set in the back alcove. The table held a comb and a mirror, and new sandals sat at the base of the chair. She made her way into the alcove and spotted a bed, as well. Emilia sank into the chair to begin working the tangles out of her hair. When she finished, she put on the sandals and stood.

By the time she walked out of the cave, she felt like a new person. She shaded her eyes from the sun and found Hector and Teo knee-deep in the water, fishing. She just watched them for several moments. Hector's deep laugh floated over the water to her. What kind of man—dragon—was forcibly bound to a place and still able to find a smile and show kindness to an orphaned boy and a shunned woman?

The breeze moved strands of Hector's hair as the sun brought out the many shades she'd noticed the first time she saw him. Her gaze lowered so she could observe the play of muscles across his shoulders and down his back. The waves rolled into him, soaking the ends of his thigh-length chiton. She recalled when he had risen from the sea, his chest bare as water coursed down his rippling muscles. She had thought—*hoped*—he had been naked. Getting the tantalizing views of him only made her wish to see more.

Hector held up the spear, drawing her gaze to his arm. She peered closer to make sure her eyes weren't deceiving her. There was something dark along his outer left arm. Nay, *both* arms. She looked closer at his neck and thought she saw something there, as well, though it could be hair. It was difficult to see. The dark marks hadn't been there before. Did it have something to do with his imprisonment?

Suddenly, Hector turned and looked over his shoulder. Their

eyes met, and the corners of his mouth lifted in a smile. She found her lips softening in return. He bent and said something to Teo, who nodded. Then, Hector made his way out of the sea to her. As he neared, she saw more of the marks on his arms.

"The green suits you," he said, stopping in front of her.

She looked down at the chiton and smoothed her hand over the fabric. "It's beautiful, thank you. But one would've been plenty."

"Why? You should have choices."

Her heart skipped a beat at his crooked smile.

"And you're verra welcome. Anything else you want or need, just tell me."

"I don't think I can."

He chuckled softly. "Then we must change that."

"Are you always so giving to those who have wronged you?"

"You didna harm me. You attempted to stop something awful from happening. It's others who have wronged both of us."

She glanced toward Teo to find him intent on catching a fish. "What do we do now?"

"Nothing for the time being."

She was so surprised by his words that she jerked her gaze to him. "Is that wise?"

"What can I do? If I demand answers, the cabinet will withhold information from me. For now, we relax and enjoy the day. Do whatever you want to do."

"You've accepted things, then?"

He grunted and checked on Teo. "Far from it. Rhi's right. Magic was used, and it can be undone. I'm considering my next move. I doona do things rashly. Few good things happen when you do. It willna be long before the cabinet wishes to talk with me. I'll find out more then. When I do, I'd like you to come with me."

"That's the last place I should be. They detest me."

"I willna push you to accompany me, but I think you should reconsider. The cabinet has dictated things in the city for too long. Your guild ruled your life. You're strong enough to make your own decisions, and you got me out of the city within moments, remember?" he added with a grin.

Emilia wrinkled her nose. "You won't let me live that down, will you?"

"Absolutely no'. You had the courage to stand against a Dragon King to save the realm. *You* should never forget it."

"And if I was wrong? What if you really are supposed to save us?"

He grew serious as he held her gaze. "Never doubt your intuition. That and your visions led you from the time you were a wee girl. You trusted them then. Do so now."

Perhaps he was right. Emilia drew in a breath and looked at the undulating water.

"Are your parents here? I can bring you to them—or them to you, if you'd prefer."

"They're somewhere on the mainland."

"Somewhere?"

She turned her gaze to him. "They knew of my visions and tried to keep it from others in the village, but rumors were spreading. I was a child, and didn't realize that my warning a woman of her impending death and how to avoid it was wrong. All I knew was that I was saving a life. And, as you know, people fear what they don't understand. My parents got wind of the villager's anger and intended to stand between me and the mob coming for me."

"You left."

Emilia shrugged a shoulder. "I had a vision of my parents being brutally killed to stop the mob from getting to me. My parents were good, kind, loving people. They didn't deserve such a death. They loved and protected me. It was my turn to shield them. The vision showed me Highvale, and I knew I had to get there. I left in the early morning and set out for the island. It took months for me to get here."

"How old were you?"

"Five."

His eyes widened. "Bloody hell. It's a wonder you survived. You've been on your own ever since?"

"I had Agathi. She was the sister I always wanted." His lips parted to respond, but Emilia didn't want to talk about her friend or the past. She locked her gaze on his arms. "Those weren't there before. Do they hurt? Is it because of the binding?"

Hector glanced at his arms. "They've always been there. I just hid them."

"What are they?"

"Tattoos."

She wished she could see his chest because the marks disappeared beneath his tunic. Before she could ask, Hector's head whipped to the side, and his body tensed. Teo came running out of the water. Emilia looked at what had drawn Hector's attention: Agathi coming down the beach. Tears stung her eyes. She'd known her friend wouldn't abandon her.

"Stay here," Hector murmured as Teo came to stand beside her.

Emilia was about to argue when Teo took her hand. She looked down at him as his blue eyes lifted to hers. His apprehension kept her rooted to the spot. "I've known Agathi for most of my life. She's a good person."

"She didn't stand with you."

"It would've harmed her position."

Teo shook his head. "They might have killed you, and she wouldn't have done anything."

"She wouldn't have allowed that to happen." At least, Emilia hoped that was the case.

She swung her head back to watch as Hector met Agathi at the shore. She couldn't hear what they were saying, but a deep, aching dread began in the pit of her stomach.

TWENTY

Even though Hector knew someone would come for him, he was still irritated by the woman's arrival. More so because the cabinet had sent a single woman instead of soldiers. As if that would somehow placate him. It once more proved they had no clue about who he was or what he was capable of—regardless of him being bound to the island.

He didn't want the newcomer anywhere near Emilia or Teo. Hector chose to walk to her to keep her away. However, her smile at his approach told him she believed he was eager to speak to her. She would realize her mistake soon enough.

"Hello," the tall brunette said as he approached.

She was lovely. The kind of beauty that turned heads and made simple men do idiotic things. Her hair was curled, placed artfully around her face, and held with a gold headband. Her eyes, nearly as dark as her hair, were large and held a welcoming warmth. Her teal gown complemented her olive complexion while also highlighting her full breasts and small waist. She was a woman used to being looked at and knew how to dress and move to elicit responses. Some men might fall for it, but he had been around for long enough to have seen it all.

Hector dipped his chin, waiting.

Her smile faltered as she bent her arms at her waist and clasped her hands. Sunlight glinted off gold rings, one on each hand, and the thick, gold cuff on her right wrist. "My name is Agathi, and I sit on the cabinet."

So, this was Emilia's friend. He instantly relaxed, thinking she had come to see Emilia. Then it dawned on him that she hadn't said that. Instead, she had said she was on the cabinet. There was only one reason she wouldn't announce that she was Emilia's friend. He tensed again, his anger slowly churning.

"I've come to collect you. The cabinet wishes a meeting," Agathi said.

"Do they?"

She inclined her head regally. "I ensured them there was no need for soldiers."

"You think any of you can make me do something I doona want to do?"

"I think you'll do whatever you wish. You want to know the cabinet's plans. I'm here to bring you to the meeting so you can learn them."

His deceptively even tone had fooled her into believing she had him wrapped around her finger. "Your plans do indeed concern me. We'll go."

"Good. We shall walk together."

"I wasna speaking of you when I said *we*."

There was a subtle tightening of her lips. She never looked behind him. "They aren't part of the cabinet. They aren't allowed in."

"I'm no' on the cabinet either."

"You're different."

The more Agathi spoke, the more her opinion was clear. "Policy should apply to everyone."

"You aren't everyone, though, are you? You're a Dragon King. The invitation is only for you."

He wanted to decline. It was on the tip of his tongue to tell Agathi to fuck off. But he knew the kind of individuals those on the cabinet were. They would keep requesting a meeting, or worse, come to him. He wanted Emilia with him as he walked through the city to prove to everyone that she wasn't the villain in all of this, but he also couldn't force her. She had hesitated when he brought it up, which told him she wasn't ready.

Hector looked over his shoulder to find her standing at the cave entrance. She watched them, her brow slightly furrowed. The green gown looked exquisite on her. Her hair was down, and no jewels covered her, but she was more striking in her simplicity than Agathi in all the gold of Zora.

Emilia gave him a nod. The wind might have allowed her to catch some of the conversation. He hoped she hadn't heard it all. She had been hurt enough that day. He returned the nod and faced Agathi.

"Perfect," she stated with a bright smile.

The brunette turned and retraced her steps to the city. Hector stayed a step behind her as she pointed out locations around them. He waited for her to ask about Emilia or do something that would make him believe she was a decent person. Unfortunately, Agathi never did.

Everyone noticed the moment he and Agathi left the beach and walked up the steps into the city. People halted mid-conversation and gawked as they walked past. She was all smiles and slowed to walk even with him. She took him along many streets like he was a prize to be shown off. Hector had concealed his tattoos before he spoke to Agathi, and he was glad he had. She talked nonstop, either to him or whoever she passed, calling people by name. She was wasting her time if she thought that made a difference to him.

Finally, they made their way up to the pavilion. The large rectangular building had thin, fluted columns with elaborate capitals decorated with leaves and scrolls. Vegetal elements were incorporated all around the building. Two guards who stood outside opened double wooden doors. Hector looked at both of them, locking their faces into memory as he followed Agathi inside.

They entered a foyer with towering ceilings, only to pass through another guarded doorway. The ancient Greeks had open assemblies that anyone could attend. It seemed those on Highvale preferred to keep their meetings private. Nothing good ever came from that.

Hector soon found himself in a huge room with a magnificent mosaic floor. Along the walls were dragon statues as tall as the columns between them. Seeing so many sculptures of his brethren after being hidden and hated for so long was unnerving. But his attention didn't stay there. It turned to the cabinet that sat behind a semicircular table. In the middle of the crescent were three chairs larger than the others, and seated upon them were Loukas, Pelagia, and a woman with white hair and age upon her face.

"Well done, Agathi," Loukas praised.

Hector watched Agathi preen at the compliment as she made her way to the only open seat.

Loukas cleared his throat and turned his blue eyes to Hector. "Now that you're here, we need to go over a few things."

Everything about the building and those within it made his hackles rise. Hector wanted to lash out and show his supremacy. Yet, he remained calm. For now, at least. It was better to know every aspect of his opponent before he showed his hand. And, without a doubt, the cabinet and all those responsible for binding him to Highvale were his adversaries.

"We have a home readied for you," Pelagia said. "Move in as soon as possible."

"The beach suits me fine," he declared.

Loukas snorted. "Be that as it may, we cannot have you living at the shore."

"And why is that?" Hector pressed.

Loukas looked at Pelagia for help in answering. She shrugged in response. Loukas sighed loudly. "We can provide for you."

"I doona need you to provide anything."

Agathi's voice rang out. "I will make sure he gets there."

Hector swung his head to her. "You think you have that kind of sway?" He enjoyed the way her smile slipped. His gaze slid back to Loukas. "As I've stated, I'll remain at the beach."

Nervous looks were exchanged around the semicircle. He had set them on edge. Good. Because he had been there since the moment he arrived on the island.

"Then we will discuss the plans for war," Loukas announced.

Hector chuckled.

Pelagia's hazel eyes narrowed, making the wrinkles around them more pronounced. "You find that humorous?"

"I find your audacity shameful," he replied.

"Ours?" the older woman gasped in outrage.

He swept his gaze around the room, looking at each member. "Aye. *Yours.* You've never seen war. You've no idea what it's like to be covered in blood or have the stench of rotting flesh fill the air. You doona know what it means to send others out to take someone's life—or have theirs ended. You sit here in a protected place and make decisions that affect the rest of the realm as if you have that kind of power. You're no' gods. You doona have the right."

"Then why were instructions left for us to bring a Dragon King here?" Agathi demanded.

Hector walked to her side of the table. "Has there ever been a King at Highvale before?"

"Nay," she answered after a pause.

"Has there ever been a dragon here?"

Agathi swallowed as her face pinched. Slowly, she shook her head.

It was just as he feared. "You found instructions about something you knew nothing about and then decided to act on them because you believed yourself merited."

"Those with magic are dying!" Pelagia shouted.

Hector pinned her with a look as he stalked to her. "So are others, including dragons!" He drew in a breath and fought for calm once more. "You are messing with things you doona understand."

"Neither do you," Loukas retorted. He was breathing heavily, his face blotchy with anger. "You *will* defend this island. You have no choice."

Hector laid his hands on the table that separated him and Loukas. "That's right. Even if that threat comes from within."

"Y-you can't," Loukas said as shock drained the color from his face.

"The magic that bound me doesna care who causes the threat. All it wants is for me to end it. You desire a war because you imagine I'm the means to win it. I know people like you," Hector said as he straightened and looked around the room. "You believe your position grants you power and protection. You all think you have the right to make life-altering decisions for others, but you doona. Doona dare summon me again. I'm no' yours to command."

Hector turned and strode out of the building with long, purposeful strides. He ignored the people on the street and didn't slow down until he reached the beach. He came to the cave entrance, only to halt when he saw Emilia standing at the shoreline, her arms wrapped around herself. His hearing picked up a sound. When he turned his head, he watched Teo pop up from the rocks.

"She's been like that since you left," he said as he approached Hector. "She told me she was fine, but I saw the sadness in her. Agathi didn't even look at her."

Hector put his hand on Teo's shoulder. "I know."

"I don't like Agathi."

Hector felt that way about the entire cabinet. "Be mindful of what you say around Emilia. She still considers Agathi her friend."

"Then Emilia needs to know the truth."

He looked down at the lad. "How much of our conversation did you hear?"

"Most of it."

"The day has delivered several blows to Emilia. Let's no' let another land today."

Teo nodded as he looked toward her. "Agathi wants you."

"She's a woman used to getting whatever she wants."

"Maybe, but I know that look. She won't give up easily."

Hector grunted and found himself watching Emilia. "Doona worry. Agathi isna my type."

TWENTY-ONE

Iron Hall

The city was intact. At least for now. Marcus walked through the once derelict corridor where Hector had vanished. This hallway was by far the longest of those in this wing. The only things left to dispose of were small pieces of rubble. He could see all the way to the back now. The torches lit by magic that lined every wall were still out, but his dragon eyes had no problem seeing. There was more of the city on the other side of the hall, and he wanted to explore it, but not until he knew for sure how Hector had been taken.

Marcus halted beside a small pile of stones. He dropped to his haunches and eyed the faux rock with its button. It didn't appear to match anything in the corridor, the others surrounding it, or anywhere else in Iron Hall he had walked through. So, where had it come from?

He heard a long, low whistle behind him and turned to see

Ryder's short blond hair. Marcus straightened and smiled in greeting. He had requested Ryder's opinion because of the electronic nature of what he had discovered. Ryder could figure out anything technical and mechanical. He had created and built the security and monitoring systems for the Dreagan estate and the distillery, which added another layer to their magical border. He had also designed their computer system.

"Bloody hell," Ryder murmured, his hazel eyes finding Marcus. "This place is incredible. No wonder you were so anxious to come."

Marcus grinned as he nodded. "It is impressive."

"To say the least. But you didna ask me here to give me a tour. What do you have?"

Marcus pointed to the rocks in question. "That. Hector said it emitted a slow, pulsing blue light. He had an overwhelming urge to touch it, and when he did, it transported him to an island."

"Highvale," Ryder said with a nod. "Con filled me in. No' exactly the atmosphere anyone wants with a mating ceremony about to take place."

"It has us all troubled."

"Have you touched it?"

Marcus shook his head. "Hector told us no' to, but it isna blinking now."

"I'm glad you didna take the chance." Ryder dropped to his haunches and then tipped forward onto a knee to look closer. After a long inspection, he lifted the device in question. "It isna activated at the moment."

Marcus watched Ryder turn the mechanism over in his hand, looking at it in different ways. He frowned when Ryder tried to press the button a few times. Then Ryder opened the object.

"Fuck me," Ryder murmured in shock.

Marcus looked inside, trying to see what had caught Ryder's attention. "What is it?"

"Nothing like I've seen before. This is amazing."

Marcus had an idea why others got frustrated with Ryder. "Do we need to worry about anyone else being drawn to it?"

Ryder pulled a wire free. "No' now." He climbed to his feet, his excitement palpable. "This is an incredible find. Have you run across any other tech?"

"That isna something I look for. I only know it's out of place in the city, at least in the sections I've investigated. It doesna match anywhere. However, there is much more of the city to find and explore."

"If you doona think it belongs here, then how did it get here? And why is it here?"

"From what Rhi said, Hector thinks it's somehow connected to Highvale. Apparently, they love us."

Ryder's blond brows snapped together. "Us? As in...dragons?"

"Aye. And Kings. Rhi said there are statues of dragons everywhere on the island."

"That's different. I'd say let's pay them a visit, except they've bound Hector."

Marcus blew out a breath. "Yep. The thing is, I've no' seen any mention of Highvale in the city, and Hector said they didna know where the device was, only that it was near the dragons."

"Which means they didna place it here."

"Then there's the fact that this corridor was intentionally destroyed. I've no' come across anything but that," he said, nodding to the device, "needing to be hidden."

Ryder looked past him down the darkened hallway. "What about down there?"

"I've no' looked yet. I wanted to know about the mechanism first."

"This tech is verra advanced, and I do mean *verra*. Nothing on Earth even comes close. If there's more here, I want to find it."

Marcus scratched his cheek and glanced down into the dark hallway. "You think there's more of those?"

"Someone brought it, and if you're correct, someone tried to bury it. Would you put all your trust into one device? I certainly wouldna."

"Shite. Just when we thought this place was a safe haven."

Ryder grunted as they started walking. "I'm beginning to think nothing on Zora is safe."

"I wish we knew who built the city and where they went. There hasna been a single clue."

"You need an archaeologist."

Marcus met his gaze and grinned. "Good thing we have one of those."

"Faith will find something—if it's here to be found."

"I'll alert Con." Marcus opened his mental link. *"Con."*

"Did you find something?" Con asked.

"Ryder said it's tech he's never seen. We're going deeper into the hallway, but we could really use Faith."

"Keep me posted. I'll get her here as soon as I can."

He severed the link. Marcus watched his bootprints leave a trail on the dusty floor.

"How long do you think the city has been unoccupied?" Ryder asked softly.

Marcus shrugged, his steps slowing. "Difficult to say. The main chamber with the tree that everyone calls the great hall allows air and rain, but the deeper you go, the less the environment plays a part. Then you have this corridor that was blocked off from everything."

"Do you feel that?" Ryder whispered.

"Aye."

The air was stale and still. Marcus glanced at Ryder to see that he had also slowed. Ryder scanned the darkness ahead while Marcus alternated from looking down the hall to studying the walls. There was a distinct unnerving feeling he couldn't shake. Everything inside him said to turn around and leave. It was so overwhelming that he halted in his tracks. Ryder had stopped a step behind him. They exchanged a look.

"Something doesna want us down here," Marcus said, keeping his voice low.

Ryder moved up so they stood shoulder to shoulder. "I doona run from things, but it's getting harder to stay in here."

"It's the same for me, but we have to keep going. If something is down there, we need to take care of it before it gets out and harms the bairns."

Marcus forced himself to take another step. His heart pounded, and his blood turned to ice, the hairs all over his body standing on end. His muscles locked in an attempt to keep him from moving forward until his steps were nothing but shuffles. Ryder's breathing was uneven and rapid, telling Marcus he felt the same all-encompassing fear.

His mind raced with possibilities for what might await them, from a horde of invisible entities to monsters and ghosts. He clenched his hands into fists, determined to keep going. Marcus looked over his shoulder to see how far he had gone, only to see they had only walked about twenty feet from where the device had been.

"Fuck," Ryder murmured as he put a hand on the wall and bent forward.

Marcus looked toward the dark end of the corridor, which appeared to stretch infinitely before them. "Something isna right."

"Obviously," Ryder bit out before he spat onto the ground.

Marcus realized then how sick Ryder was. He looped Ryder's arm around his shoulders and turned them. "We're getting out of here."

Marcus expected Ryder to feel better once they passed where the tech had been, but it was the opposite. He got worse. Marcus was the only thing keeping Ryder upright. That's when he saw that Ryder still had the device in his hands. Marcus knocked it out of his grip.

"*CON!*" Marcus bellowed through the mental link as he raced to get out of the hallway.

The floor vibrated with approaching footfalls, and Marcus heard the sound of feet hitting the stones. Derek was the first to burst into the atrium and rush to Marcus. Con was next, followed by Cullen and Alasdair.

Con and Derek took Ryder as Alasdair and Cullen helped Marcus to the table. Marcus watched as Derek and Con laid Ryder on the floor. His eyes were closed, and his breathing was labored. When had he passed out? Marcus shook his head, trying to sort through his jumbled thoughts. Con placed his hand on Ryder, and they waited. Con could heal anything but death.

Ryder drew in a deep breath and opened his eyes. He looked from Con to Derek and back to Con. "What happened?"

"That's what I'd like to know," Con said. He swung his blond head to Marcus.

Marcus looked down the corridor. He parted his lips to describe it all, but his thoughts vanished. "I...can no' remember."

Ryder sat up, and everyone looked into the hallway.

"Maybe we should've left it blocked," Cullen stated.

Derek got to his feet and went to the corridor in question.

"Doona!" Marcus yelled and reached out to stop him.

Derek looked back at him but didn't go any farther.

Alasdair studied Marcus's face before he said, "Something happened down there."

"Aye. There was fear in your voice when you called for me," Con said.

Cullen grunted. "Ryder was unconscious, and Marcus was on his way to that."

Had he been? Marcus would remember if he had been. Right?

"You recall nothing?" Derek asked.

Marcus leaned back on the table. "I knew I had to get out of there."

"Ryder?" Con pressed.

Ryder shook his head as he got to his feet. "I remember coming in here and finding Marcus in the hall."

"What about finding the tech?" Con asked.

That got Marcus's attention. "What tech?"

"You asked me to bring Faith and said Ryder had found some tech," Con explained.

Marcus looked at Ryder, who shrugged. "I have no memory of that."

Cullen walked to the entrance of the hall, and Marcus once more had the urge to call him back. He bit his tongue to keep silent, but the compulsion didn't relent until Cullen halted beside Derek. Marcus released a relieved breath and found Con and Alasdair regarding him peculiarly.

"I think I see what Ryder found," Cullen said.

He took a step into the hallway.

"Nay!" Marcus and Ryder yelled at the same time.

Cullen halted and turned to them. Marcus looked at his outstretched hand and slid his eyes to Ryder to find him in the same position. Marcus slowly lowered his arm and swallowed heavily. His heart thumped wildly in his chest. The room was silent as the four stared at him and Ryder.

Con came to stand in front of him, blocking Marcus's view of the corridor. "You've been in that hall multiple times without any issue. So have I. What changed?"

"I doona know," Marcus answered.

"You said you were investigating down there. Did you reach the end?"

Marcus had no memory of such a thing. "I doona know."

"What if I retrace your steps?"

Marcus jumped up. "You can no'."

"Why is that?" Con pushed.

"I doona have an answer except the obligation to keep everyone out."

Con nodded and stepped back. "All right. Cullen, put up a shield to keep everyone out. I think it's time to call it a day. We have a mating ceremony to prepare for."

Marcus eagerly left the area. He didn't even grab his blueprints on the way out. The feeling of dread that had nestled in his stomach didn't relent until he was in his room. He showered, changed, and ate, then played with the kids and went out on patrol.

But he couldn't stop thinking about the corridor.

TWENTY-TWO

The sight of Agathi walking along the beach had sent joy coursing through Emilia, erasing so much of the pain from earlier. And then it had crumbled to dust when her friend hadn't even looked in her direction. It showed Emilia just how deeply she had wounded Agathi by keeping her vision a secret. It didn't matter why Emilia had done it. It was enough that she had.

That had been the only thing she'd kept from Agathi all these years. Then Hector arrived, and Emilia added that on top of it. She couldn't imagine how cross Agathi was with her. They had bickered over the years, but she never once worried that Agathi might cut her out of her life. Until today.

The longer Agathi had stood with Hector without acknowledging Emilia, the more the blade had sunk deeper into her heart. Emilia had wanted to save the realm, but she had never considered what she might lose in exchange. She had left her parents and their loving family behind so they wouldn't be killed and found a new family with Agathi. Emilia couldn't lose a second one. The pain would be too much to bear.

If only she'd had a little more time. She could've told Agathi about the visions and Hector. Except she'd had years with her seer secret and never shared it. Not even when Agathi had excitedly told her the cabinet planned to call a Dragon King. Emilia could say she had been frozen with shock, but that excuse only lasted so long. It had been weeks since the cabinet enacted the summoning. Weeks where Emilia had remained silent.

Nothing Emilia could say would make up for what she had done. But she'd like the chance to try. Unfortunately, she wasn't sure Agathi would listen, which made everything harder.

Emilia squeezed her eyes shut when her mind pulled up the image of Agathi smiling at Hector. She knew that flirty smile because she had seen Agathi use it often. Now, it was directed at Hector. No man could resist Agathi's smile. Not even a dragon. It had made Emilia's stomach twist uncomfortably with envy.

She had experienced jealousy before, but it had always passed quickly. Not so this time. It stayed and made itself comfortable. Seeing Agathi with Hector reminded Emilia of everything she didn't have—and never would. The few things that mattered to her more than objects had been taken away, which meant she had even less now than the day before.

Her vision and fear for her parents had sent her to the city. However, she hadn't been able to stop Hector's arrival. Which meant she no longer needed to remain on the island. She didn't want to leave Highvale, but she couldn't stay either.

Movement caught her attention, and she turned her head to find Hector and Teo walking toward her. She shouldn't be relieved that

Agathi wasn't with them, but she was. Teo and Hector were talking, but the wind snatched away the words before she could hear them, much as it had when Agathi was on the beach. Teo grinned as he commented. Hector threw back his head and laughed.

It was impossible not to notice a man like him. She would've been enthralled by him even if she hadn't known he was a Dragon King. Hector was larger than life. His charisma pulled everyone into his orbit—including her. She liked being there, and she especially enjoyed his attention. She certainly couldn't fault Agathi for wanting some of it.

Emilia faced Hector and Teo as they approached. A shiver of awareness ran down her spine when Hector's dark gaze locked on her. Without looking away from her, he said something to Teo that had the boy running toward the cave.

"Hi," Hector said as he stopped before her.

Sweet silver sands, he was gorgeous. "Hi."

"How are you?"

Troubled. Anxious. Worried. Afraid. Lonely. "I'm fine. And you?"

"Better now." He sighed and briefly lowered his gaze to the sand. "The cabinet wanted to see me."

"I assumed as much. How did it go?" She wanted every detail. Really, she wanted to know if they had spoken about her. It was selfish and silly to be so focused on herself when larger issues were at hand, but she couldn't help it.

"About as well as you can imagine."

Emilia couldn't hold in her smile. "That good, huh?"

"Let's just say I ruffled some feathers." His lips split into a wide grin. "I wish you could've seen Loukas's expression when I told him that guarding the island didna stop me from attacking someone who caused it harm—even if the threat came from within."

Her eyes widened in shock. "You didn't."

"Oh, I certainly did." His smile widened as if he were reliving the incident in his head.

Emilia covered her mouth and started laughing, trying to envision Loukas's face. The merriment released some of her tension, easing the tightness in her chest. She lowered her arm. "I needed that. Thank you."

"I can laugh now, but I wasna at the time."

"Nobody refuses the cabinet."

He snorted and faced the water, crossing his arms. "I did today."

"Can I ask what they wanted?"

"You can ask me anything. Always. Never hold back," he said as he looked at her. He sighed then. "They want me to move into a house. I refused."

Emilia frowned as she glanced toward the cave. "Why would you turn down such an offer?"

"I doona want anything from them."

"If this is about me, I ca—"

He dropped his arms and faced her. "It is about you. It's also about Teo. And me. It's about all of this. They might have found a way to bring me here and even bind me, but I doona answer to them. And I never will."

"I'm considering leaving."

There was a long stretch of silence. "Have you decided anything?"

"Not really. I..." She blew out a breath and shook her head. "This is my home."

"Then you should stay."

She wrinkled her nose. "It isn't that easy."

"Nothing worth having ever is. You fought for more than Highvale all these years. Doona stop now."

She drew in a long breath and slowly released it. "It's hard to stay somewhere no one wants you. There's a whole world out there."

"A dangerous one."

"I appreciate everything you've done for me." She looked down at her gown. "The clothes, the food. All of it. But I can't spend my life hiding. Not even on the island I love."

Hector ran a hand down his face. "I've done too much hiding myself. You're right. You shouldna hide. I can have Rhi take you if you really wish to leave. She'll bring you anywhere you want to go. Or...she can take you to Iron Hall."

Was it her imagination, or did it sound like Hector hoped she picked the latter option? Most likely, it was just her desire to hear that in his voice. Because he made her feel special, and she didn't want that to end. The only people who had ever wanted her were her parents, but her very existence had endangered them. Emilia had always been different. She never really fit in. It didn't matter how nice or welcoming she was. It was like others knew she didn't belong, so they never included her. Agathi's friendship had made things tolerable, but Emilia had lost that now.

"You shouldn't want to help me," she told Hector. "Not after how I first treated you."

"How did you do that? What was that door I went through?"

She shrugged and moved some hair caught in the wind from her face. "It's a doorway I'm not supposed to know about.

Sometimes, when I open it, it's nothing but a storeroom. Other times, it shows different places."

He grunted and nodded. "How did you know it wouldna be a storeroom when you opened it for me?"

"I didn't. I hoped it wasn't."

"So, you didna know where I would end up?"

She inwardly winced as she thought about how she reacted without thinking of the consequences. "I didn't."

"But you had to know I'd return."

"I did, but I hoped you wouldn't. I also thought I might have more time."

He quirked a brow. "For?"

"To tell Agathi everything so she could help me come up with a plan."

"You didna tell her, though."

Emilia shook her head in disgust. "I left her a note to find me, but things...happened before I got the chance. I should've told her years ago."

"You kept it to yourself for a reason. Doona second-guess your decision now."

"I've hurt Agathi."

Hector turned away, but not before she saw him frown.

"What?" Emilia pressed. "She's angry with me, isn't she? She has every right to be."

"Nay, she doesna." He gave a quick, irate shake of his head. "I doona know if she's mad. She never said."

Never said. Did that mean Agathi hadn't asked about her *at all*?

Hector faced her, his voice softer as he asked, "At any time, did you do anything out of malice?"

"Never."

"Did you intend for me or anyone else on the island to come to harm?"

Emilia was taken aback by his question. "Not once. My goal was to stop people from dying."

"I believe you. I want you to remember what you just told me in the coming days."

"Why?" she asked hesitantly, not liking how her thoughts had turned.

Weary lines settled across his face. "Because life is unfair."

This was about Agathi. It had to be. She must have said something that Hector didn't want Emilia to know. Now that she'd come to that conclusion, she had to know. Otherwise, trying to figure out what it was would drive her mad. "What did Agathi say?"

"Emilia," he began.

"Please. I have to know."

He held her gaze for a long, silent moment, then released a sigh. "She didna speak of you."

And there it was. Five words that sliced through her and shattered the last vestiges of her comfort. The only thing that had kept her going was Agathi. She wouldn't get to apologize or explain, which meant the only person who mattered to her had shut the door on their friendship.

"If she would but hear me out," Emilia began.

"Sometimes, we think we know people when we really doona."

"She's all I have."

Hector studied her face before nodding. "Then I'm sure you'll have the opportunity to speak with her and get it sorted."

It was a lie. He didn't believe it, but he had said the words out of kindness to her. What did he know that she didn't? She could ask, but she was afraid of the answer now. Maybe that's why she had never told Agathi about her vision. Fear. Of Agathi's response. Of being laughed at.

Of being dismissed.

"We have a few hours before the sun sets. What would you like to do?" Hector asked.

Water hit her feet as the high tide started to come in. "You're asking me?"

"Why no'?"

"I...don't know."

Hector grinned. "I bet Teo will have some ideas."

He let out a whistle. A few seconds later, Teo walked out of the cave. He jogged to them when Hector waved him over.

"What would you like to do for the next couple of hours?" Hector asked. "Anything you want."

Teo's eyes lit up. "Anything?"

"Indeed," Hector replied, smiling.

"I want to learn to swim."

Hector frowned. "You didna swim to the island?"

"We have to use magic," Teo replied as if he had already said it a million times.

Emilia shrugged when Hector glanced at her.

"Swimming it is," Hector said. His dark eyes remained on her. "Want to join us?"

"I think I'll watch."

Her mood had taken a nosedive, and she didn't want to bring Teo down. She knew Hector was trying to take her mind off things, and it showed the depth of his compassion. She watched the two of them head into the water as Hector talked. Emilia made her way to the rocks near shore and settled herself upon them. She hadn't been there long when Rhi suddenly appeared beside her. Emilia jumped, startled.

"This is nice," Rhi said as she stared at Hector and Teo.

"It is."

Rhi lifted her face to the sun and closed her eyes. "I had a special place on an island once. It's where I went to get away."

"You don't go anymore?"

"It grew too exhausting to continue to shut myself off from others. I went after what I wanted instead."

Emilia found her gaze moving to Hector. "I assume you got it, then?"

"I did. Though not without some pain. It was worth it in the end."

When Emilia looked at Rhi, the Fae's strange silver eyes were on her.

"I overheard a bit of your conversation with Hector, and I apologize for that. I wouldn't normally say anything, but I feel obliged to give you some unsolicited advice. It took a remarkable young girl to be aware of the danger to herself and her parents and set out for what I imagine was a very long and scary trip to Highvale."

Emilia dropped her gaze to the rock where her feet rested. "It was terrifying. Looking back, I wonder how I survived."

"But you made it. Not only that, you built a life here."

"That's now gone."

Rhi sighed loudly. "That's only the case if you allow it to be."

Emilia slid her gaze to Rhi. "You weren't here. You didn't see or hear what happened."

"You're right. I didn't. But that doesn't change facts. This is your life. You're the lead in your own story. You left your family and found a new one. But guess what? You can find another. The point is, you get to choose. Not some absurd cabinet, your friends, or even me or Hector. *You* have that power. Use it."

Could she? Did she dare? "You make it sound easy."

"It won't be. But it's better than letting others decide what you can and can't do. If you want to remain on the island, then do it. No one can force you to leave."

"Perhaps not, but they can make it so I want to go."

Rhi grinned. "Only if you let them. Don't give others your power. Find the strength that brought you here and hold on to it."

Emilia had never thought of it that way. She had been too consumed by the fact that everyone had turned on her instead. But Rhi reminded her that she had a say in her life. And she would take the chance.

"There you go," Rhi said, her smile widening. "That look right there is what you need. No one will dare stand between you and what you want when they see that."

TWENTY-THREE

Night had long since fallen over the island, and stars winked from above as Zora's two moons lit up the sky. The only way Hector could get Teo to sleep was to pretend to do the same. The lad was passed out in a hammock in the middle alcove. Hector could hear his deep breaths and occasional light snores. Teo had expended a lot of energy learning to swim and had fallen asleep the moment he climbed into the hammock.

The swimming lessons had gone well. Teo was keen to learn and picked it up quickly. It had been an enjoyable few hours for both of them. It was the first time Hector had ever taught someone to swim, and it was impossible not to wonder what it might have been like if he'd found a mate and had children before the war with the humans.

He'd never allowed himself to contemplate such a thing before. Not since the dragons were sent away. Yet it was all that rolled through his mind as he lay on his bed listening to the rhythmic crash of the waves.

As a precaution, his nook was closest to the entrance of the cave. He heard Emilia's bed creak but ignored it until her feet crunched on the sand as she walked toward him. Hector remained where he was but turned his head to see her pass. Wind cut through the entrance, molding the simple, unbelted white chiton to the front of her body. His gaze lingered on her beaded nipples and the outline of her sensual curves.

Need burned through his veins as blood rushed to his cock. Her image would be burned into his mind for all eternity. Then she was out of sight. He swung his legs over the side of the bed and rose. When he peered out of his alcove, she had already exited the cave.

He found himself slowly following her. He couldn't tear his gaze from her as she leisurely walked to the water. When she reached the shoreline, she paused and lifted her face to the sky. The scene was one of beauty and tranquility. She was bathed in moonbeams, her blond curls dancing in the gentle breeze. Dark waves rolled against the shore, crashing onto the sand that shimmered in the moonlight, before reaching out to her as if beckoning her.

His breath caught when she slipped her arms out of the gown and let it pool at her feet. He ran his gaze down her back to the swell of her tight arse and then her shapely legs. His balls tightened as another wave of desire took him. She stood in the balmy night air for another heartbeat before walking into the bay. Then she dove. A few seconds later, she surfaced and swam with long, slow strokes.

The night offered cover the day couldn't. She had remained on shore earlier while he and Teo played in the bay. He figured her thoughts had been too heavy, and he had only made them worse.

Her body curved as she dove once more. She breached the surface and began swimming again.

It was as if she were dancing in the water. Watching her was relaxing, even though he knew he should give her the space she likely needed. But he couldn't leave. He sat against the rocks with his knees bent and heels propped in the sand, his arms wound around his legs as he let himself see the beauty of what surrounded him. He set aside his irritation and anger at the people who called it home and considered the island.

He couldn't see the magic, but he felt it all around him. He laid his hands upon the sand and closed his eyes. Magic pulsed like a heartbeat. He thought about Dreagan and grew homesick for Scotland. Soon, the wild, craggy mountains of Dreagan were replaced by Emilia.

His eyes opened, and he searched for her. He found her in the middle of the bay, treading water as she looked at the moons. Every second he sat there, he fought the urge to join her. But he wouldn't be able to keep his hands off her if he did. It was hard enough as it was, but if he added in the water and her nude body... his hunger to know her, *claim* her, would be too powerful to resist.

Besides, he was spying on her. Hector was horrified that he had stooped so low. He pushed to his feet when he heard someone approaching. It was after midnight. He'd spotted some residents atop the cliffs, wanting a glimpse of him, but no one aside from the cabinet and soldiers had ventured into the cove. He was immediately on guard. It didn't take long for the figure to come into view. The woman wore a cloak with the hood pulled up to cover her face. She went straight for the shore.

"Emilia," the woman called.

Emilia's head whipped around at the sound of her name. She

swam closer, but she didn't leave the water. Neither had seen him yet. That gave him a chance to walk up behind the new arrival. After what he had witnessed from the cabinet and some of the residents, Hector wasn't taking any chances. Especially not with those he had under his protection.

"What are you doing here, Maro?" Emilia asked.

"I've been waiting to talk to you. Alone."

Hector clenched his jaw. If Maro wished to speak to Emilia, all she had to do was come down to the beach and do it. The fact that she had waited to come at night meant she didn't want anyone seeing her talking to Emilia. He hung back a little in case Maro turned out to be a friend, but he was still close enough to step in should the need arise.

Emilia rocked softly with the rolling waves. "We're alone. What is it?"

"Why didn't you come to us with your vision?" Maro demanded, her voice tinged with confusion and a hint of distress. "That's what you're supposed to do."

"Something told me to keep it to myself."

"And look where that landed you." The bewilderment was gone, replaced with indignance.

Hector opened his mouth to reply, but Emilia beat him to it. "I did what I thought I had to do."

"And we will do what *we* have to do," Maro replied with a lift of her chin.

Emilia's lips twisted. "You never believed I belonged in the guild anyway. We both know you're pleased I'm gone. So, why are you really here?"

"To tell you to do the right thing and leave Highvale."

Fury engulfed Hector.

"You've said what you needed, now leave," Emilia told her. "Before you do, let me make something clear. I will leave when—and if—I wish. Not because someone told me to or because I was treated badly. Highvale is open to all magical beings, whether you like them or not."

Maro turned and angrily strode away. Hector watched her until she was out of the cove, then looked at Emilia. He was glad she had found her strength once more. And she had done it in a crushing, classy way. He had desired her before, but he craved her on an entirely new level now.

Emilia's gaze met his. "I couldn't sleep."

"It's a beautiful night."

The waves pushed her closer to shore. "The water's nice. Want to join me?"

He wanted it more than anything. The temptation to walk into the water was so great he found himself leaning forward, even as he knew he shouldn't.

"It's just a swim," she said.

He shook his head. "We both know that isna true."

She swirled her hands atop the water and watched him.

Despite knowing it was wrong and would complicate things, Hector walked to the edge of the water. A wave rolled in and over his feet as he sank into the soft sand. The water barely concealed Emilia's breasts. He could see the swells each time a wave rolled past. She had an allure he couldn't resist. The combination of her beauty, determination, and inner strength was potent and difficult to resist. It was something he rarely found in a woman, and when he did, it always brought him to his knees. Her courage matched a King's, which was heady indeed.

Things were too messy on the island, though. If he gave in to his needs, they would only get messier. He always did the right thing. Just once, he wanted to do what felt good. And getting into the water with her would feel amazing.

She never looked away, never begged. She simply waited for him to make up his mind. This opportunity on this exquisite night wouldn't come again. And he would regret it for the rest of his long life if he let it pass him by.

Hector strode into the water and didn't stop until he stood before her. With her hair slicked back and the water droplets on her cheeks highlighted by moonbeams, he was lost. Utterly and completely enraptured.

A strong wave rolled through and pushed her against his chest. Hector caught her by the shoulders and held her steady as she stared up at him with those cobalt eyes. Her hands flattened on his chest, branding him through the material of his chiton. Fire licked his veins, scorching him. A hunger like no other coursed through him.

The pulse at her throat beat wildly. He gently wiped a drop of water from her cheek before his eyes lowered to her mouth. Her lips were full and, oh, so kissable. He yearned to taste her, to sweep his tongue into her mouth.

Suddenly, she stepped out of his arms and flashed a quick smile before turning and diving beneath the next wave. He immediately followed. The chase had begun, and he would be victorious.

He observed her naked, supple body moving skillfully through the water. Hector shed his clothes and propelled himself to her side to swim alongside her. Underwater canyons thousands of meters deep lay beneath them while marine life swam around them. He had witnessed it all when he first investigated Highvale, but it was different seeing it with Emilia. She swam straight into a school of fish and then paused to watch them scatter before merging around her in synchronization.

When the fish moved away, she shot straight to the surface for air. He followed more slowly. He crested the surface and shook his head to get the hair from his eyes. They treaded water, staring at each other. They had swum out of the cove into choppier waters.

"How far out can you go?" she asked.

He shrugged. "A bit more. How far do you want to go?"

"Sometimes, I just want to keep going."

"Do you swim often?"

She lifted her chin as a big wave lifted her. "Not as often as I'd like."

"Now you can swim anytime you want."

"I can, can't I?"

He moved closer. "You can do anything you wish, lass."

"Anything?"

"Anything."

She moved close enough for him to touch. It was an invitation. One he wouldn't ignore. He put an arm around her and pulled her against him. The moment their flesh touched, a current passed between them. Her eyes briefly widened, telling him that she'd felt it, too. She put her hands on his shoulders and smoothed them up his neck and around into his hair.

He lowered his head, and her eyes closed a heartbeat before his lips touched hers. He kissed her a second time, then a third, lingering longer each time. When her lips parted, he slipped his tongue inside her mouth to slide against hers. She moaned and tightened her arms around him.

Hector stopped treading water and let them both slip beneath the waves. The gurgling water, teaming with marine life, was a seductive, arousing backdrop. He didn't keep them underwater for long before they breached the surface. She ended the kiss and opened her eyes to look at him. The desire sparking there made his heart skip a beat. Then her lips were on his again.

The brush of her turgid nipples against his chest was a temptation all its own. He skimmed his palms down her spine to the indent of her lower back and then over the swells of her arse he had stared at earlier. He cupped her ass and ground his arousal against her. She moaned in response, which only made him ache for her more.

She explored his upper back and arms, and left a trail of heat everywhere she touched. She rocked against him sensuously, and he groaned before submerging them again. Her long locks of blond hair floated around them as she wound her legs around his waist. He kicked softly, propelling them to shore.

TWENTY-FOUR

She burned. She ached. She hungered. All for Hector. He kissed like he'd crafted the act himself. Desires ran hotter, hunger stronger, with every caress of his hand, every tangle of their tongues. She shivered in need each time she felt his thick arousal against her. The water stimulated her as it ran sensuously along her body. She clung to him as tightly as he held her, each holding on as if they were all that kept the other together.

He brought them to the surface so she could fill her lungs with air. All the while, they were slowly spinning in the sea. She heard nothing, saw nothing, *felt* nothing but Hector. He was the beginning, the middle, and the end, all rolled into one gloriously magnificent being.

The groan that rumbled through his chest when she wrapped her legs around him caused her stomach to quiver in anticipation. Desire unfurled in a long, slow pulse that made her clench her legs. She could hardly believe a Dragon King wanted her. But she wasn't going to question it. Even if it was only for tonight, she would take everything she could.

He adjusted his grip on her arse, putting his fingers very near her center. Her sex throbbed eagerly in response. She ground against him, seeking release. His mouth broke away from hers. She opened her eyes to look at him and found his dark eyes watching her. Both of them were breathing heavily.

He slowly moved his hand until the pads of his fingers brushed against her sensitive flesh. She sucked in a breath as waves of heat rolled through her body. Her sex clenched greedily. Desire flared in his eyes as he caressed a finger along her labia, each pass getting closer and closer to her center until he seized her mouth at the same instant he pushed the finger inside her and slipped them underwater. The combination was intense and potent.

Being underwater and kissing was both stimulating and arousing. His finger thrusting inside her only doubled the sensations. He moved against her breasts, his chest hair scraping her nipples, making them harden even more. Then he found her clit. He slowly moved his thumb back and forth over the swollen nub as his finger continued to stroke her.

They broke the surface again, but she barely noticed. Desire tightened low in her belly, pushing her closer and closer to her climax. He bent her back over his arm and fastened his lips around her nipple, giving it a pull.

She gasped as desire rippled through her. She was so close to peaking. It was within reach. All she needed was a little push. She groaned as he added a second finger. Her breath caught, hoping she could tip over the edge, but the orgasm remained elusive. He moved to her other breast and suckled that nipple deep into his mouth. At the same time, he increased the tempo of his thumb and fingers. She cried out, her body quivering with ecstasy.

When the climax struck, it crashed down on her relentlessly. Pleasure flooded her, every pulse sending her higher and higher. She rode each glorious wave, and when she finally regained awareness, her body still shuddered with the remnants of the orgasm. She opened her eyes and saw the stars blanketed above, then lifted her head to see Hector's smile.

"That was something to witness," he murmured.

For the first time in a long while, she didn't have a care in the world. But reality intruded as she became cognizant of Hector sitting in shallow water with her in his lap. "It was something to feel, too."

"I bet."

"Someone could've seen us."

He shrugged indifferently. "Let them."

"And if it was Teo?"

"He'd get a lesson a wee bit early," Hector replied with a wicked grin.

She laughed. "Very early."

He smoothed a strand of wet hair away that had clung to her cheek. "You have my protection. I offer it freely."

She was immediately offended until she considered why he had made the statement. A lot had occurred in the hours since she met him. She had gone from self-assured to afraid to an emotional mess to finding her confidence once more. It was no wonder he wanted to be certain she wasn't trading sex.

"Do you believe I'm not thinking clearly?" she asked.

"I trust you know what you want, but I wanted to be clear that I've given you my protection and ask for nothing in return."

She nodded and stroked a finger across the side of his face. "Now that you know I'm not trading sex for anything, there is the matter of your pleasure."

He was leaning toward her when his head suddenly snapped to the side. He looked up, and Emilia followed his gaze, finding a figure standing at the edge of the cliff. The person immediately backed away out of sight.

"I doona like being spied on," he stated, gently setting her aside and getting to his feet.

She jumped up and caught his hand before he could walk away. "It won't do any good to go after them."

He looked back at her before he faced her and took her other hand in his. "They can spy on me all they want. I'm concerned about you and Teo."

"They'll never find Teo," she joked. When Hector's lips barely curved into a smile, she glanced at the water and released a breath. "Everyone wants a look at you. Then there are those who are curious about me. And we can't forget the cabinet and what they want. My point is, I can take it. I might get upset for a moment, and I may even cry if my feelings get hurt, but I'll get over it."

"You shouldna have to, lass."

Emilia shrugged and smiled. "Maybe not, but that won't change what's happening."

"I can change it."

"It's nice that you think so, but I don't believe even you can."

His eyes narrowed slightly as he teasingly asked, "Is that a challenge?"

"Not at all," she said with a bark of laughter. "You've only been here a short time. You've not yet grasped the authority the cabinet has."

"You also have power, and I'm no' talking about magic."

She shivered in the night breeze. "I'm remembering that."

"Oh?" he asked as he walked her out of the water to where she'd left her chiton.

Emilia slipped the gown over her head. "I forgot that after I arrived on the island. I was so happy to be here that all I wanted was to fit in. I lost sight of the girl I'd been to become what everyone else was or what they wanted me to be. The only thing I couldn't forget was the vision."

She stopped talking as she realized Hector was still nude, and she was able to see the entirety of his tattoo for the first time. She stared at the dragon, speechless. It covered him from the outside of one arm, across the width of his chest, to the outside of his other arm. It was like looking at a dragon coming straight at her as it burst from Hector. The head sat in the middle of his chest, its mouth open, showing rows of terrifying teeth. A small section of the dragon's neck and chest were visible, and then the wings stretched out to Hector's shoulders and curved around the outside of his arms.

"That is incredible," she murmured.

She placed her hand on the dragon's head, and Hector covered it with his. Her eyes lifted to meet his. Then he cupped her face and gave her a long, languid kiss. He pulled away, and when she looked down again, he was clothed, the material covering his magnificent body and the tattoo. More dragon magic. She was beginning to wonder if there was anything he couldn't do. Emilia tried to hide her yawn, but he saw it.

"Come. You need to rest." He wrapped an arm around her and guided her toward the cave.

She didn't object. She *was* tired. After the previous night with little sleep, the horrible start to the day, and the night swim, all capped off by an intense orgasm, she was exhausted. They were quiet as they entered the cave. Hector put her bed, and she scooted over to make room for him. Instead of getting in, he kissed her forehead.

"I'll be right back," he whispered.

She tried to tell him he didn't have to sleep with her, but her lids had already fallen shut.

Agathi hurried back to the pavilion where Loukas and Pelagia waited. She threw open the doors and stalked into the room as the pair turned to her.

"Did you talk to him?" Pelagia asked.

Agathi shook her head. She was so upset she couldn't find words.

"He refused to see you?" Loukas asked in disbelief.

Agathi yanked off her cloak and tossed it across the table. "I didn't go down."

"Why not?" Loukas demanded. "You got him here earlier. He might put up a fight, but he'll fall for you. Everyone does."

Agathi's stomach twisted at the new betrayal she hadn't seen coming. "We don't have time to wait for that."

"Why? What's happened?" Pelagia asked sharply.

Agathi could barely get the words out. Even thinking them made her want to scream in denial, but Loukas and Pelagia wouldn't stop hounding her until she told them. She breathed deeply and said, "He and Emilia were together."

Pelagia tsked. "So what? He's protecting her. No one can resist you."

"They were *together*," Agathi repeated, her fury rising.

Loukas's brow furrowed deeply. "Are you telling us they were having sex?"

"That's exactly what I'm telling you," Agathi replied.

Pelagia put a hand to her forehead and leaned back against a table. Loukas kept blinking, his confusion turning to annoyance. Both were silent for a long moment. Finally, Pelagia spoke.

"He's a man with needs," she said with a shrug. "So what? They've had a sexual encounter. It doesn't mean he won't come around."

Loukas turned and braced his hands on the table. "What if it does? What if Agathi's right, and he chooses Emilia? It will ruin everything."

"I never said he'd choose Emilia," Agathi snarled.

"Then we take her away," Pelagia said.

Loukas jerked his head to her. "We can't send anyone away. You know the island rules."

"I didn't say send her away. I said *take her away*. Meaning, from him," she said as if speaking to a child. "If we reinstate her in the guild, with a higher rank that keeps her busy, she won't have time for him."

"That could work," Loukas replied.

Agathi was aghast. "After what Emilia did, you want to *reward* her? You can't be serious."

"Do you want to be a Dragon Queen or not?" Pelagia shouted angrily.

Loukas shrugged. "It would appease Hector."

Agathi sniffed and glared at the older woman. They had always disagreed on things. They were only working together now to secure a direct line to the dragons for eternity. Though, Pelagia didn't know the full extent of Agathi's plans.

"Pelagia's right," Loukas said as he straightened and turned to face them. "Agathi, you need to make amends with Emilia. It's the only way this will work."

"The sooner, the better," Pelagia added.

Agathi shook her head. "Emilia won't believe it. Not after what I've done."

"Of course, she will. You're her only friend, remember? She'll ask for your forgiveness, and you'll give it," Pelagia said.

Loukas grunted as he drummed his fingers on the table. "I think we should reinstate her and give her the promotion first."

"You're forgetting you don't have that authority," Agathi told them. "It has to come from those of the guild sitting on the cabinet. Even then, guild members have to agree."

Pelagia twisted her lips. "Looks like you have a lot of work to do."

TWENTY-FIVE

Hector pulled the blanket up to cover Emilia. He wanted to climb into bed with her and spend hours learning her body and bringing her pleasure again and again. There was a deep ache inside him, a need he had just discovered, to watch her flush with ecstasy. But that wouldn't be tonight.

Finding Agathi watching them had left him cold, dousing his desire as he sensed a threat rising. Something about her felt off, though he couldn't put his finger on what it was. Thankfully, Emilia hadn't been able to see it was Agathi, but Hector had, despite the cloak and hood. There was more going on than what he had uncovered. He could feel it in his bones. The problem was discovering what it was—and who was involved.

He listened to Emilia's deep, even breathing before he stood. With one last longing look at the bed and her warm body, he quietly walked to check on Teo. The lad was still in the same position, deep in his dreams. Hector made his way out of the cave and turned and looked up at the top of the cliff where Agathi had stood. He could jump easily, but he needed to work off some anger and energy.

The climb up the rocky cliff was over far too quickly. Hector pulled himself up to the ledge and straightened. His gaze dropped to the shore, where he and Emilia had been a short time earlier. How long had Agathi watched them? It was impossible to tell since there were no tracks on the rocks. What he was sure of was that she had seen him and Emilia being intimate. He remembered Agathi's flirting earlier. Hopefully, he had made it clear that he wasn't interested, but sometimes women like her didn't take the hint. It all depended on what her goal was.

"I thought you'd be up here."

He glanced to the side when he heard Rhi's voice, but she wasn't there. "Still veiled?"

"I thought it prudent. A lot is going on at Highvale."

"You left earlier before we could talk."

A rock tumbled off the side of the cliff. "I didn't want to interrupt you. Besides, you and Teo were having fun. And I needed to do some more investigating."

"Did you see Agathi here?"

Rhi released a breath. "I did."

"How long was she watching?"

"Long enough."

He ran a hand down his face. "I have a bad feeling about her appearance."

"Me, too."

He fought not to look at Rhi since she wasn't visible. Instead, he focused on the horizon. "What did you find?"

"It's more where I wasn't able to go. I followed her back to the pavilion. By the way, good job of keeping your cool with them. I wouldn't have been able to."

"It would've been nice to know you were there."

She chuckled. "You didn't honestly think I was going to leave you on this island alone, did you?"

"Does that mean you convinced Con no' to come or send anyone else?"

"It does."

Hector blew out a relieved breath. "I knew you could do it."

"He's not happy, and neither am I. It's why I brought backup."

"Lotti?" he guessed.

Another small stone fell over the cliff. "I always said you were a smart one."

Hector snorted a laugh. "Tell me you've found something."

"You could say that. I followed you into the pavilion without an issue earlier. When I attempted to follow Agathi, something blocked me. Completely. I couldn't get through even the first door. I don't know who she was meeting or what was said, and that concerns me greatly."

It worried him, too. "What could keep a Fae out?"

"If we were on Earth, I'd say wards or dragon magic. Since no one on Zora knows about the Fae, I don't think that's it. Up until now, I only believed Star magic had the ability. Lotti is having a look around the pavilion right now."

"So, there's someone powerful here."

Rhi grunted. "That's my guess. We'll see how Lotti gets on."

"Do you think it's Villette?"

"Hard to say. She's been unpredictable of late, so it could be her. She does want a war."

Hector scratched his shoulder. "No' one with humans and magicals. She wants it between humans and dragons."

"There is that. Then I remembered that she helped us free Merrill from the entity."

"Agathi wasna up here to take in the view. She was observing us."

A third rock rolled away before Rhi said, "I think she was here for *you*, big guy."

"I shut that down earlier."

"You ignored her efforts, and then you embarrassed her. Not the same thing, sadly."

Fuck. Rhi was right. "Then I'll make it crystal clear."

"I'm not sure that will help. She was furious when she left after seeing you and Emilia. That could be directed at both of you. You, because Agathi has her sights set on you. And Emilia because her friend encroached."

"I'm never getting off this bloody island, am I?"

Rhi made an indistinct sound. "We'll find a way."

"I should've kept my hands off Emilia. What if I've made things worse?"

"Like I said, we'll find a way."

Hector ran his hands down his face, inwardly kicking himself for giving in to his desires. "This can no' turn into a war. No other dragons can come because I know in my heart they'll be bound just as I am. That willna do anyone any good. We must do everything possible to ensure Emilia's vision doesna come to pass."

"For what it's worth, you seemed happy today while teaching Teo to swim."

He paused, thinking about the sun, the waves, and the laughter. "I was."

Rhi sighed loudly. "If anyone can get out of this situation, it's you. I'm going back to see if Lotti got into the pavilion. I'll check in soon."

Hector remained for another few minutes, mulling over options in his head. He was grateful for Rhi's and Lotti's help, but this was his mess, and he needed to find a way to sort it. He had hoped by refusing the cabinet and remaining on the beach they would get the point, but deep down he had known they wouldn't.

It was his fault for believing a group of magicals trying to protect their home wouldn't retaliate. He had studied humans and their reactions for long enough to anticipate their next moves. The snag he'd run into was that this wasn't a city or country fighting another. This was a group of individuals who wanted revenge for abuse and murder. The basis was the same, but the subtle nuances made all the difference.

They hadn't lured a Dragon King to their island just to fight and win battles. They had another plan. And he'd been too angry at being tricked, and then too outraged about Emilia, to see it. But he did now. Clearly.

Hector turned on his heel and walked through the city streets. He didn't stop until he came to the Oracle guild house. Emilia had told him that those with the highest rank had rooms at the top. He could walk through the door but didn't want to deal with someone telling him he couldn't enter. Nor did he want anyone seeing—or knowing—that he wanted to speak to Agathi. They would take it out of context. Nay. The meeting must be done in private. There would be another—more public—one later, but what he had to say couldn't wait.

There were plenty of spots around the building that covered him from view as he began his climb. It took nothing for him to reach the top floor. He got to the first balcony and silently walked to the open doorway. A glance into the room showed the older gentleman he'd seen at the cabinet table.

Hector jumped from that balcony to the next. The bed in this room was empty, and none of the decorations made him think of Agathi. He checked two more chambers before dropping onto the last balcony. It had an incredible view of the city and the water. He looked through a window to find candles lit and Agathi sitting on the bench at the end of her bed. Her hair was down, the brunette locks falling to her waist as she slowly ran a comb through the length.

He walked through the open balcony doors and stood just on the inside so no one could see him. Then, he waited for her to notice him. It didn't take her long to look up and jerk in surprise.

"No' fun being spied on, is it?"

"What are you talking about?" she asked innocently.

He jerked his chin to the cloak she had discarded on a chair. "I saw you. Neither the distance nor the hood, hid your face from me."

"All right," she admitted and set the comb beside her. "I was there. Is this where you ask me why?"

"Oh, I can guess why."

She let out a short laugh. "I seriously doubt that."

"Then tell me why you were spying."

"I was concerned about Emilia."

Hector swallowed his bark of laughter. "You were no' so worried earlier when you came to the beach."

"I have to be careful about who is listening. And watching. Why do you think I went at night?"

"Nice try. You didna ask after her when we were alone. No one would've known."

She swallowed and sighed in irritation. "It doesn't matter what I say. You won't believe me."

"Your actions speak louder than any words."

"Am I to believe that you came in here to lecture me?"

He shook his head and straightened from the wall. "I've no' figured out what's going on or your involvement, but I will."

"We've been clear about our intentions."

"You throw around *we* a lot, but I bet few outside the cabinet know what's happening."

She rose to her feet in a fluid motion and held her elbows bent at her sides, her hands clasped. "We're ensuring the continued safety of Highvale and all magicals on the realm."

"The island has never been in jeopardy, and the cabinet knows it."

She didn't reply.

"One more thing, let's keep this little visit between us," he added.

Agathi dipped her head in agreement. Hector slipped out and made his way back to the cave. He checked on Teo again and then stood beside Emilia's bed. She was on her side, one hand curled by her cheek, the other resting atop the bed. He could climb in beside her. He could wake her and spend from now until dawn wringing cries of pleasure from her. But he couldn't. Not yet. Maybe he would get the opportunity soon.

He drew in a long breath and slowly released it as he squatted beside the bed. He had to test a new theory, but he didn't like it. He wished there was another way, *any* way that wasn't sharing what he was about to reveal.

"Emilia," he said and touched her shoulder.

She drew in a breath, her eyelashes batting open. The moment she focused on his face, she smiled and lifted the covers, welcoming him into her bed.

His gut clenched. He debated bringing her out to the beach to talk. He could even slide in next to her, but that seemed too intimate. Besides, he needed to see her face to gauge her reactions.

A frown marred her features as she lowered her hand and rose on an elbow. "What is it?"

"Do you know who was watching us tonight?"

"I don't. Do you?"

He nodded. "It was Agathi."

Emilia's frown deepened. She sat up and crossed her legs as she faced him. "Are you sure?"

"I saw her face beneath the cloak."

"I see," she murmured and dropped her gaze.

Hector took a fortifying breath before saying, "I went to visit her tonight to discover what she wanted."

Emilia's blue eyes snapped back to his. "You went to see her?"

Her hurt was evident, and it made what he was about to do even harder. "It was a verra quick visit."

"Did she tell you why she came?"

"She said it was to check on you because she was concerned."

Emilia paused and leaned her head to the side, her hair falling over one shoulder. "But you don't believe that."

He smoothed a hand over his mouth and jaw. "Nay, I doona. When she came this afternoon to take me to the cabinet, she had many opportunities to ask about you. She didna. She claimed she came tonight so no one would see her."

The more he spoke, the more he felt Emilia pulling away. He

didn't blame her. It was simply a consequence of someone shielding themselves from more emotional harm. He'd been there himself on several occasions. He just hated that it was happening. But it had to be done. He still hoped his suspicions about Agathi were wrong, but he knew they weren't. Emilia wouldn't believe him about Agathi. She would have to learn it for herself.

"Agathi is my only friend," Emilia stated. "Being on the cabinet was her dream, and she has to be mindful of what she says and does because she doesn't want repercussions for her family or the guild. I can see her sneaking out at night to talk to me. She's done it before."

Hector had expected just such a reaction. "I asked her to keep our conversation private, but I wanted you to know why I went and what was said so you didna think anything was done behind your back. Because nothing was. I doona want anything to do with Agathi. If it were up to me, we'd still be in the water."

TWENTY-SIX

With her mind spinning, Emilia watched Hector rise and walk away. She wished they were still in the water, too, but they weren't. He had ended that. He had declined her offer to pleasure him.

He'd also urged her to sleep so he could go to Agathi.

Her beautiful, kind friend who everyone loved. Was it any surprise Hector wanted to be with her? But this time, Emilia really wanted someone and believed he felt the same way. Maybe she had seen more in his kindness than was there.

She pressed her hand to her chest as pain filled her. Emilia hadn't even had time to digest what had happened between them in the cove. She'd gone to bed with her body content and her heart happy. Only to learn this new information.

Jealousy stabbed her, its blade sharp and aim true, as she realized Hector had tucked her into bed without hesitation and gone to Agathi. Emilia usually deflected the envy, but she couldn't now. It ran too deep and hurt too much. Agathi had everything. Why did she have to take the one person Emilia had taken an interest in?

She stared at the spot where Hector had been. His words filled her mind again. Confusion blossomed through her hurt and resentment. Why would he tell Agathi to keep their meeting private and then come and tell her? She searched for reasoning but wasn't in a reasonable or rational mood.

Emilia sat in the comfortable bed Hector had provided, surrounded by pillows and a soft blanket. She wore the clothes he had endowed, ate the food he offered, and had bathed in luxury because he had given it to her. And he had asked for nothing in return. He had come to her defense and kept her and Teo safe. What did he have to gain by putting a wedge between her and Agathi?

Absolutely nothing.

She glanced up and saw Teo peeking around the corner. She waved him over and patted the bed. "Did we wake you?"

"It's fine. I, uh, overheard," he said hesitantly.

She ran her fingers through his wavy strands. "I see."

"Are you upset with Hector?"

Emilia was angry at everyone but Teo at the moment. "I'm troubled about all of it."

Teo picked at the frayed hem of his tunic. "He gave me new clothes and sandals."

"Do you not like them?" she asked, noticing that he still wore the same attire.

"I think they're very nice, but I don't want to get them dirty."

She grinned and moved her still-damp hair behind her ears. "Wear the clothes. They can be washed."

"She flirted with him."

Emilia stiffened, the quick change in subject startling her. Though she didn't have to ask who Teo was referring to.

He looked down as if making eye contact with Emilia was too hard. "I saw her."

"Agathi is the most beautiful woman on the island. Everyone wants to be with her," she replied defensively. She might be angry at her friend, but she didn't like anyone talking negatively about her.

Teo sighed as he slowly stood. "I didn't mean to upset you, but I think you should be careful around her."

He was gone before Emilia could reply. First Hector, and now Teo. Neither had said anything derogatory about Agathi exactly. But it was implied. The fact that both were tiptoeing around what they obviously wanted to say spoke to how they were taking her feelings into account. That was more than others did.

She swung her legs over the bed and placed her feet on the woven rug but didn't rise. Her alcove was the largest in the cave system and bigger than the room she'd had at the guild. The arched ceiling was low, giving the area a snug feeling. Her eyes landed on the chair to the right, where she had carefully placed her other gowns. There was a small dressing table to the left, where the mirror and comb sat, along with some bottles of oil, a large bowl, and a pitcher of water.

Hector hadn't given her the basics. Everything here was something she would expect to find in Agathi's chambers. Hector was a prisoner, but that hadn't stopped him from showering her and Teo with gifts. No matter how hard she tried to think of why he would want to come between her and Agathi, she couldn't come up with anything.

If Hector and Teo weren't the problem, and she was watching it all play out, she had no choice but to consider others. And with Agathi's name continually coming up, perhaps it was time to take a hard look at their friendship.

Emilia didn't know how long she sat there, lost in thought, before Teo returned. He placed a plate of food beside her before hurrying off again. She sighed and pushed to her feet. The fabric rubbed against her breasts, causing her nipples to harden. Her thoughts immediately went to her swim with Hector. How would it have ended if Agathi hadn't been there? Would Hector have been in her bed that morning? Would she have woken in his arms?

She tugged off the chiton and made her way to the table, pouring water into the bowl. After she'd washed her face and sponged off her body, she turned to the gowns. Emilia went back and forth between the red and the yellow before grabbing the floral one and pulling it over her head. The material was incredibly soft and lay sensuously against her body. She used a purple cord that brought out the color of the flowers to wrap around her waist several times before tying it. She attached purple clips to her shoulders and then put on the new sandals. Only after she was dressed did she return to the table to look at her hair. Her curls were wild, so she pinned them away from her face.

Emilia grabbed the platter of food and walked out to look for Hector and Teo. She would have to face them sooner or later. It was better if she didn't stew in her thoughts any longer. Yet when she exited the cave, there was no sign of Hector. She studied the waves, hoping he would rise from them. Eventually, she spotted Teo sitting on a boulder.

"May I join you?" she asked.

He shrugged without looking at her. "I guess."

She settled in beside him. "Thank you for bringing me the food."

"Hector wanted to be sure you ate."

"Where is he?" she asked nonchalantly.

Teo pointed to the water. "He said he'd be back soon."

Emilia couldn't look at the bay without thinking of the incredible orgasm or the way his hard, powerful body felt against hers. She brought a piece of fruit to her mouth and chewed automatically, then dragged her gaze from the water and focused on Teo. "It's never easy to be honest with someone. I should've thanked you earlier instead of getting upset."

"I shouldn't have said anything."

"I'm glad you did. Friends should always be truthful."

Teo's dark head turned to her, and hope spread over his face. "Are we friends?"

"How could we not be?" she replied with a smile.

His dour mood evaporated quickly. If only her gloomy emotions could so easily be turned around.

"Um...Emilia?" Teo whispered.

She looked at him and found his gaze directed down the beach. She followed his line of sight and spotted Agathi in her favorite creamy white chiton cinched with a wide, gold belt. Her neck was bare of necklaces, but she wore multiple gold bracelets on each arm, and long, golden earrings dangled from her ears. Agathi's brunette locks had been curled and were held with a golden headband that sparkled in the morning sun.

Emilia set aside her food and got to her feet. "Get to the cave."

"I should be with you," Teo argued.

"I'll handle this. Go to the cave and stay there, no matter what happens."

"I don't like the sound of this," he muttered, climbing down with his platter and heading into the cave.

Emilia's first concern was Teo's safety. She didn't relax until he was safely behind Hector's shield. She could also go there, but it was past time she spoke with her old friend. Emilia needed some answers, and she knew there was a good chance she wouldn't like what she heard. She took a deep breath and let Agathi come to her. It was a petty move she wouldn't have done before, but it was also smart in case she needed to run for the cave.

It stunned Emilia that she wasn't sure if Agathi was a friend or a foe. How had they gotten to this point? Could it all hinge on the fact that she had kept the vision to herself? It boggled her mind that it could be that. She knew Agathi better than anyone. She knew Agathi's kindness and giving nature. She didn't hold grudges. She would be angry, but they would find their way to forgiveness. They always did.

Emilia watched as her beautiful friend stopped before her. They were both guarded and tense. Emilia had so many questions, but she refused to speak first. After all, she was the one being judged and condemned.

Agathi's shoulders lifted as she drew in a breath. "I was hoping I'd get to talk to you."

"You had a chance yesterday," Emilia retorted. It came out frostier than she had planned, alerting her that she was far angrier than she had first thought.

Agathi's lips twisted. "I didn't, actually. The cabinet sent me to bring Hector, and I had to get him there quickly."

"You didn't ask him about me."

"I did, actually."

Emilia frowned. Agathi had never lied to her before. At least not that she knew of. She didn't know Hector as well, but Emilia kept coming back to...why would he lie? Unless it was to get back at everyone for him ending up bound. She decided to let that go for the moment and instead said, "Nor did you look at me after I was detained and put in jail."

Agathi briefly pressed her lips together. "We promised never to keep secrets. You kept a big one."

"You're a seer. You should understand that sometimes we know things about our visions that direct us a certain way and urge us to say certain things. And, sometimes, tell us not to say anything at all."

"From the moment I confided in you about the cabinet summoning a King—which I wasn't supposed to do, by the way—you knew you would betray me," Agathi stated, fury tightening her face.

"I'm trying to save everyone!"

Agathi's hands were clenched, her knuckles white. She breathed heavily as she glared at Emilia. "Do you have any idea the kind of difficult position you've put me in? So many believe I helped you. I've spent hours defending myself."

"Difficult?" Emilia choked out. Just because she had anticipated Agathi's ire didn't mean she would sit and take it. "You didn't spend hours alone in a dark prison without food, water, or even a clean place to sit. You weren't forced onto that stage alone with everyone staring at you. You know how I hate attention like that."

"We were supposed to be friends."

"We are."

Agathi raised her brows. "Really? Then why didn't you tell me about the vision?"

"I wanted to. You have no idea how many times I almost did. But every time, I got that same feeling that I needed to keep it to myself. Still, I planned to tell you that night. But I was taken into custody. I left you a note."

"I found it."

Emilia's stomach clenched. She'd found it but hadn't bothered to do anything about it? It was another blow. How many more could she withstand. "If you had come to see me, I would've told you everything."

"But not the guild?"

Emilia shook her head.

"Why?" Agathi demanded.

"Because I hoped that once I explained it to you, you would help me."

Agathi jerked back as if slapped. "Why would I do that?"

"Because the world is going to end with Hector's arrival."

"It looks fine to me."

Emilia parted her lips to speak, but Agathi's hand sliced through the air.

"You hurt me," Agathi stated as she stepped forward, tears glittering in her eyes. "I've done everything for you, and this is how you treat a friend? Others told me not to get close to you, but I always defended you. *Always*. And this is how you repay me?"

"I've lost everything."

"You made the decisions that put you here."

Emilia couldn't decide if she wanted to scream or cry. Her emotions were jumbled, wound into a ball that sat in her chest and squeezed painfully, preventing her from giving in to either reaction. In that instant, she shifted tactics. "Why were you watching us last night?"

"I was here to check on you. I got embarrassed at being seen and ran off."

Emilia had believed Hector when he told her it was Agathi, but something about hearing her friend admit it felt like a punch to the gut. Agathi's explanation sounded plausible. Maybe she had been too quick to believe Hector and Teo. Especially with all the years of friendship she and Agathi had shared.

"Is he demanding sex in exchange for his protection?"

Emilia was so shocked by the question that her mind went blank for a moment. "That isn't his way."

"You claim to know him, yet he has only been here a few days."

"I know him better than you do." It was a low blow, one Emilia regretted the moment the words were out of her mouth.

Agathi smiled coldly. "You can see how it looks. It isn't as if you have anywhere to go after being kicked out of the guild."

"What I do with my body is no one's business."

"There is one more thing you should know," Agathi stated. "Hector isn't loyal to you. He came to me last night."

Blood rushed in Emilia's ears as a howl of refusal rang through her mind. There it was. What Teo and Hector had hinted at. Agathi hadn't lied. Hector *had* gone to her, but Agathi made it seem like he wanted more than a discussion. The fact that she left it hanging allowed Emilia to imagine all sorts of things. And she would have if she didn't know the truth. Because Hector had shared it with her. Almost as if he had known Agathi would find a reason to tell Emilia.

With that realization, she looked at Agathi's visit in a whole new light—and didn't like what she saw.

"Did he?" Emilia finally got out. She decided to play along because she didn't have the energy to do anything else right now.

"I refused, of course. I don't share, as you know."

Emilia's anger took control of her chaotic emotions. "And you decided to tell me this because…?"

Agathi's smile didn't reach her eyes. She turned without answering and walked away. Emilia watched her and struggled to understand how her life had been upended so quickly. Someone took her hand and squeezed. Emilia looked down to find Teo beside her.

TWENTY-SEVEN

"I'd feel better if you told me what you planned," Rhi whispered.

Heads turned as Hector walked through the streets, but no one saw Rhi since she was veiled. He'd had a bad feeling since he'd learned that neither Lotti nor Rhi could get into the pavilion. What was the cabinet doing, and why did it need to be kept secret? Their decisions affected the entire city, and it was time the citizens were privy to what was going on.

Hector stopped next to a small group of people and said, "Gather everyone in the amphitheater." He looked around at the others watching him. "Spread the word that another assembly is being called at the amphitheater now."

There was a beat of silence, and then everyone moved at once.

"Hector," Rhi whispered from behind him. "Are you sure you know what you're doing?"

"I'm making it up as I go."

"I was afraid you were going to say that," she muttered dryly.

He'd been on edge since he discovered Agathi watching Emilia and him at the cove. It had only gotten worse after he'd talked to Agathi. And his conversation with Emilia had gone as badly as he knew it would. He had to set his feelings about her aside for the moment, even if he didn't want to. Instinct warned him that something nefarious was going on, and he had to get to the bottom of it before something else ensnared him.

Rhi muttered something and grabbed his arm, instantly veiling him. Before he could ask what was wrong, she turned his face, directing his gaze down the street. That's when he spotted Agathi coming up the steps from the beach. She could've walked from anywhere on the island, but he had a sinking feeling she had gone to the cove.

Both he and Rhi remained silent as they moved out of the street so no one could bump into them. They watched Agathi walked toward them with a bewildered look at those rushing around.

Agathi grabbed the first person she could. "What's happening?"

"The Dragon King has told us to go to the amphitheater," the middle-aged female replied.

Agathi's gaze jerked in the direction of the theater before she grabbed her skirts and started running down the street.

"I think I'd better follow her," Rhi whispered.

Hector nodded. Rhi released him and hurried after Agathi. His feet ate up the distance until he reached the cove. He entered the cave just as Emilia was walking out. They both drew up short. He searched her face, looking for something, anything that would tell him Agathi had upset her, but Emilia appeared remarkably calm. She was likely still upset with him. It wasn't as if she had been thrilled when they last spoke.

"Hi," he said.

She glanced at the ground. "Morning."

"Are you...?" He stopped and tried again. "Is everything all right?"

"As far as I know."

He glanced over her shoulder, his gaze sweeping the cave for Teo. Then he returned his attention to Emilia. "I've called a meeting."

"For?"

"The island."

Her throat bobbed as she swallowed. "Does the cabinet know?"

"They will soon enough."

"You need to be careful."

Hector twisted his lips. "There is a time and a place for everything. I doona like the things I've witnessed—or that I'm learning. I may be bound to the island, but the cabinet is wrong if they think they can control me."

"You don't understand the power they have."

"And they doona understand mine," he said more forcefully than intended. He looked to the side and sighed before returning his gaze to her. "Do you know who or what would keep Rhi or Lotti out of the pavilion?"

Emilia's brow furrowed, then she shook her head. "Nothing that I'm aware of."

"I might understand Rhi no' gaining entrance, but no' Lotti."

"Because she's a Star Person?" Emilia asked uncertainly.

He nodded. "Nothing should stop Lotti or any Star Person. If the cabinet has something—or someone—with such power, I want to know." It could be useful in any future battles with Villette because they hadn't seen the last of her. "I doona know how things will go at this assembly. One way or another, the truth will come out."

"And you believe you should be the one to force it?"

"If no' me, then who?"

She lifted her shoulders. "I don't know."

"You are a Highvaler. You should come. No one will harm you."

"I'll think about it."

Something had changed between them, and Hector didn't like it. Emilia was reserved and withdrawn, as if a wall had come down between them. He'd sensed it last night, but in the light of day, he had hoped that things might go back to how they had been.

Hector shot her a fleeting smile. She didn't return it as she turned on her heel and walked to her alcove. He fought not to go after her and claim her lips for another searing kiss. He wanted to hold her against him. But he did neither.

Each time he thought about the way her body had moved against his in the water, his balls tightened with need. He'd told himself not to go into the sea with her. He'd known it was a bad idea from the beginning but hadn't been able to resist her. The longer he was on the island, the more he realized she was what drew him back, not the need to discover how he had gotten here.

It was useless to contemplate a decision already made when there was no changing it. Emilia might regret what had transpired between them, but he didn't. And he never would. He'd do it all over again if given the chance. Just to be with her.

He turned and walked to the shore. Teo was nowhere to be found. He'd wanted to speak to the lad, but by the sound coming from the amphitheater, just about everyone had gathered. It was time for his showdown. It was easy to forget that the dragons weren't the biggest, baddest beings here as they were on Earth. Maybe he'd be defeated today. Maybe it'd be tomorrow. But he wouldn't sit around and wait for it.

Hector waded into the water. When the waves reached his waist, he dove beneath the surface and swam out of the cove. Then he shifted and burst from the water into the sky with one beat of his wings. Droplets cascaded from him as he soared toward the clouds. He saw the island to his left. A shout from the amphitheater told him he had been spotted. They wanted a dragon, so he would give them one.

Once he was inside the cloud, he twisted his body and tucked his wings against him as he dove straight for the theater. He locked his gaze on the citizens. Their shock had turned to glee at the sight of him, but that quickly changed to fear when they realized he was headed straight for them. He wanted to scare them a little. They needed to know what he was capable of. The island might worship dragons, but the Highvalers knew nothing about them, and it showed.

Hector spread his wings and soared low over the theater and then the city. He circled around and made a few passes as he waited for the cabinet members to show themselves. The moment he saw Loukas, Pelagia, and Agathi, he released a thunderous roar. Then he dipped a wing and swung around. He angled his body downward as he flew toward the stage. When he drew close, he shifted back to his human form and tucked and rolled to drop to one knee, his hands on the ground.

He had called clothes to him the moment he shifted, but this time, he wore jeans and a black tee to remind them he wasn't from Highvale. Hector lifted his head and looked at the crowd before straightening. Every eye was on him. The only sound was the wind passing through the columns. Some stared at him in disbelief, a few in reverence, but most in astonishment.

Loukas was the first to shake himself from his stupor. He marched forward. Hector raised his hand and sent out a blast of magic that struck near Loukas's feet, keeping him off the stage.

"What is the meaning of this?" Loukas demanded.

Hector pointed to the seats. "Sit, and you shall find out."

"I lead any meetings," Loukas argued.

"No' this time."

Hector looked at Pelagia next. Her face was pinched as if she were trying to decide if she should say something. She wisely thought better of it and also took a seat with a rigid back and contempt burning in her eyes. Agathi and the rest of the cabinet sat before he had a chance to look their way. Good. Maybe they might get somewhere.

He scanned the faces for Emilia and Teo but saw neither. That upset him far more than he liked. He comforted himself with the knowledge that Teo was most likely hiding somewhere, watching everything.

"We're waiting." Loukas's voice rang out through the quiet theater.

Hector walked from one side of the stage to the other, taking the measure of those there. "How many of you have sat in on a meeting of the cabinet?"

People looked at each other in bewilderment. Several moments of confusion passed before someone said, "Not me."

"Or me," another shouted.

Soon, everyone was agreeing.

It was just as Hector had figured. "How many would like to know what the cabinet is discussing and deciding?"

This time, the reaction was instant as some raised their hands while others spoke out.

Anger reddened Loukas's face as he crossed his arms. Pelagia's scorn increased as she glowered at him. The other cabinet members, including Agathi, were looking more and more nervous by the moment.

The crowd waited to hear what he would say next. Hector drew in a breath and released it before he spoke. "Where I come from, such meetings are open to the citizens. It allows transparency between those who hold positions of power, and those they're serving."

The clapping started slowly, but it built to a crescendo.

"I think all of you have a right to know what's happening. How many knew I had been brought here without my consent?" he asked.

The theater went silent.

"That's what your cabinet did to me. Then, I was tricked into binding myself to the island, unable to leave." Hector locked his gaze on Loukas. "A prisoner."

Pelagia got to her feet. "You make it sound as if it's all our fault. Emilia showed you the door the moment you got here, and *you* returned. All on your own."

"Of course I did," Hector admitted. "I wanted to know what had brought me here to begin with. Yet you didna allow me to leave again, did you? You put me in a position where I would use my magic, thereby confining me."

Loukas jerked to his feet, his hands fisted at his sides. "We needed you! We've told you the plight of those with magic on the mainland."

"And I told *you* I had seen it with my own eyes!" Hector

bellowed in return. "We've been fighting against it ourselves! It was never you against the others alone. But you didna give me the courtesy of asking for my help. You simply made the decision about my future."

Pelagia lifted a brow. "Would you have helped us?"

"We'll never know," Hector stated.

He heard Rhi whisper his name behind him at the same time he felt the air stir. Hector swung his head to the side, his eyes locking with gray ones. Shock slid through him. "Eurielle?"

"You know her?" Loukas asked.

There was a note of delight in his voice that set Hector's teeth on edge. He ignored Loukas and focused on Eurielle. She was both Lotti and Villette's sister and had sided with the Kings against Villette. They had been looking for her since she went missing during their big battle at Stonemore.

Hector walked to her, but he became disquieted when there was no greeting. "Eurielle? How long have you been here?"

She studied his face. "A while."

He inwardly winced. At least now he knew how the cabinet had known he was a Dragon King, and who was blocking Lotti and Rhi from the pavilion.

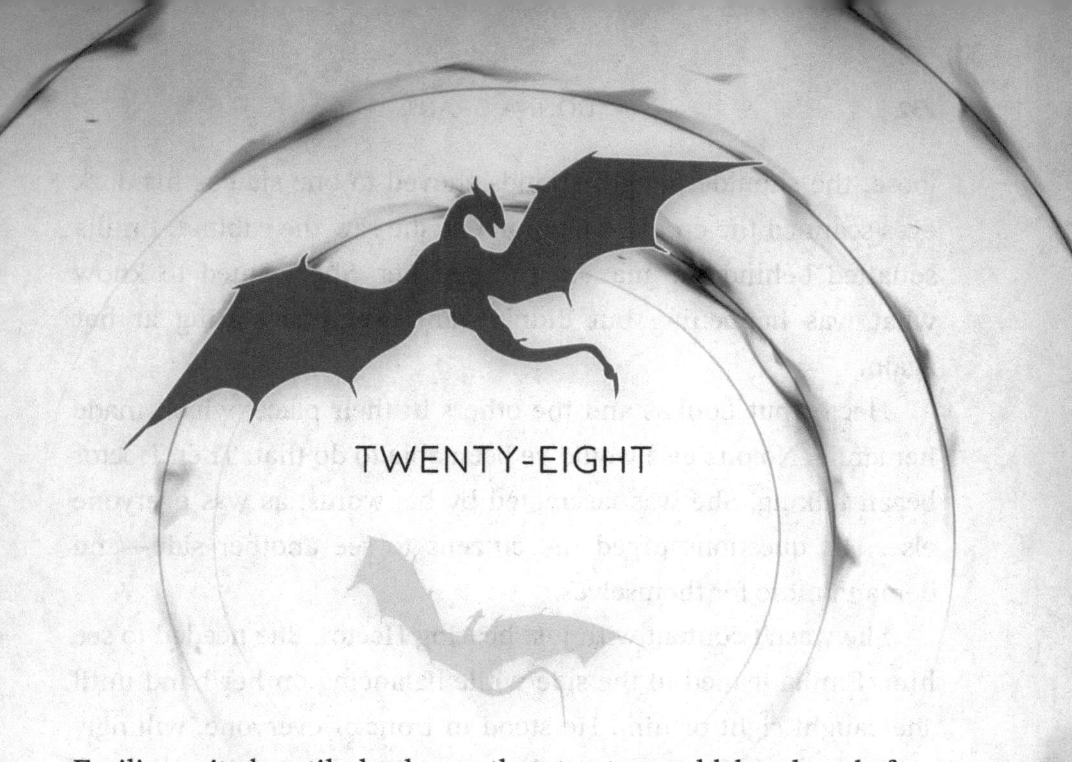

TWENTY-EIGHT

Emilia waited until she knew the streets would be clear before going down to the beach and up the stairs. She was mulling over Agathi's visit when Hector returned to the cave. She should've told him what had transpired between her and Agathi, and she would. She just needed to figure out a few things first. That was why she said she wasn't sure if she would go to the meeting. His disappointed look, however, had changed her mind.

The city was eerie when deserted, but she quite enjoyed not being stared at. A massive shadow passed over her. Emilia immediately looked up but saw nothing but clouds. She hurried through the streets to the amphitheater as she heard gasps from the crowd. She arrived in time to see Hector rise from a kneeling position. All anyone had to do was look at him to see his dominion, his utter supremacy.

Hector's chiton was gone. In its place was a top that molded to his hard sinew, defining his shoulders, chest, and arms. He wore dark trousers and thick-soled boots. His light brown hair was loose, the shoulder-length strands shoved to one side as his dark eyes scanned the crowd. The moment she saw the cabinet, Emilia squatted behind the man in front of her. She wanted to know what was happening but didn't want everyone staring at her again.

Hector put Loukas and the others in their place, which made her smile. No one else would've been able to do that. Then Hector began talking. She was fascinated by his words, as was everyone else. His questions urged the citizens to see another side—and demand more for themselves.

She wasn't content with just hearing Hector. She needed to see him. Emilia leaned to the side while balancing on her hand until she caught sight of him. He stood in front of everyone, willingly and courageously, uncaring who he might anger or the repercussions. Then again, unlike everyone else, he had nothing to lose. He could stand defiantly against the cabinet and preach change. Maybe the city would even get it. *Maybe.*

Emilia saw Hector look to the side. The surprise on his face caused her to lean even farther out to see who he was looking at. That's when she saw the woman dressed in deep orange, her long, straight brunette hair hanging to her waist. Her gown was expensive, though she wore no jewelry, not even earrings. Yet she stood regally as if directing everything and everyone.

And Hector knew her. Was this Lotti? Both he and Rhi had said the name several times, but Emilia hadn't met her yet. Emilia glanced around for Rhi, but she didn't see the Fae. She swung her gaze back to the woman dressed in the finery of Highvale. Hector's surprise bothered her.

If the woman was Lotti, it could be that he was shocked she had shown herself. Or the woman could be someone else. Emilia had never seen her before, but she didn't know everyone on the island.

Someone touched Emilia's other side. She jerked around and saw Teo. His eyes were round with either fear or panic. Or both. "Where have you been?" she whispered.

He swallowed heavily, his chest rising and falling quickly. Teo leaned close and softly asked, "Where's Rhi?"

"I don't know," she said with a shrug. "Why?"

"We should get to the cave."

The panic in his voice made her blood run cold. She glanced around, but no one seemed to be paying any attention to them. "Why?"

Teo's small fingers wrapped around her wrist to tug her arm. "Please."

His plea won her over. Emilia let him lead her away. They kept low, hoping no one would spot them. She tried to look at Hector but couldn't see the stage through the mass of people. He was no longer talking, and she suspected it was because of the woman.

Teo had been so adamant about going to the cave that she was surprised when he reached the steps leading to the stage and started down them. Emilia yanked her arm out of his hold and quickly backed up.

"Hector!" Teo shouted without stopping.

Hector's head swung around. His dark eyes looked at Teo before lifting to her. Without a word, Hector spun and took two running steps before jumping into the air and transforming. The man was gone, and in his place was a gigantic dragon. Emilia stood rooted to the spot. She couldn't look away. This wasn't a statue. It was a real, breathing dragon. She had known what Hector was, but knowing it and seeing it were two different things.

Her eyes swept over the wide, sea green scales that turned much darker underneath. He had several small central horns atop his head, and rows of crystals along his jaw. He had a broad neck and a colossal body before tapering to a long tail that ended with a sword-like edge. His enormous wings had armor-like scales growing on top of the wing's primary bones. She followed Hector as he flew higher. He looked back, his huge, pearly eyes meeting hers before she lost him in the clouds.

Teo grabbed her arm and yanked as he ran past. She stumbled after him as she pulled her eyes from the sky. She glanced over her shoulder to see those nearest her turn their attention to her. She grabbed her skirts to keep pace alongside Teo.

There was no time to ask why they needed to get to safety. She trusted Teo. Maybe she shouldn't. Perhaps she couldn't trust anyone. Everything she had thought she believed had been turned upside down. All she knew was that something had spooked Teo enough to show himself at the theater to warn Hector. Hector certainly hadn't waited around for an explanation. Which was why she wasn't either. There would be time for explanations later.

The soles of their sandals slapped at the stone streets as they wound their way to the nearest stairs to the beach. Sometimes, she pulled Teo, Other times, he pulled her. But they never let go of each other.

Emilia glanced at the sky, hoping to see Hector again. The brief look caused her to trip. She felt herself lurching forward, but Teo steadied her. They shared a look before they picked up their pace. She was usually careful going down the stairs because they were covered in sand, which caused her to slip, but she didn't care this time. She and Teo practically flew down the steps, her feet barely touching them until they landed in the thick sand. For a heartbeat, she got stuck before she could move again.

An ache started in her side, and every breath she took was like a blade slicing down her throat. The sand made it hard to move, and that meant exerting more energy—which was quickly depleting. The cove was nowhere in sight either.

"Don't stop," Teo said, pulling her along.

She dug deep and found the strength to continue, albeit at a slower pace. No sounds were coming from behind them or in front of them. No one shouted from the cliffs above or rose from the water. But something had terrified Teo, and that meant it also scared her.

"We're not going to make it," she heard Teo mumble.

Emilia adjusted her grip on him, hiked her skirts higher, and forged ahead as fast as she could pump her legs. One of her sandals came off, but she didn't stop to grab it. All she could hear over her thudding heart was her harsh breathing.

Then, finally, they rounded the corner and saw the cove, its calm waters waiting. She scanned the area but still didn't see any threats. No one could get into the cave. It was their haven. All they had to do was get to it, and they would be protected. Her feet moved faster as a new burst of energy surged within her, knowing their sanctuary was so near.

Teo moved ahead slightly and led her through the boulders. The entrance to the cave was just ahead. A thunderous roar sounded over them, causing Emilia to duck even as she looked up for a glimpse of Hector. The roar ran long and loud, following them into the cave and bouncing off its walls before finally dissipating.

She and Teo stood in the center of the space, breathing hard as they stared at the entrance, waiting for Hector. Minutes ticked by with no sign of anyone or another roar from Hector. Emilia released her skirts and wiped the sweat from her brow with the back of her hand.

"He should be here," Teo said into the silence.

Emilia's legs shook from their run. She looked down at him. "What happened? Why did you warn Hector and bring us here?"

"Why isn't he here?" Teo said instead of answering her.

Her knees gave out, and she sank onto the sand. Then she tugged his arm to get his attention. Finally, his blue eyes met hers. "Tell me," she urged.

"You shouldn't have been at the amphitheater after what happened."

"Teo, please. Just tell me."

He turned his head away, his gaze once more on the entrance. "Where did Hector go?"

Emilia realized she wouldn't get an answer from him. While that didn't sit well with her, she couldn't make him tell her. And even if she did, he'd probably lie. His worry about Hector made her concern grow.

She rose and got some water. After she'd drunk her fill, she brought it to Teo. He tried to wave her off, but she was persistent. Eventually, he drank. Yet there was still no sign of Hector. No one at Highvale would harm him. So why had he flown away? She looked at Teo and contemplated asking him again, but she knew by the way he stared at the entrance that he wouldn't tell her anything until Hector arrived.

The shadows of the boulders changed on the sand as the sun moved steadily across the sky. Teo hadn't moved from his spot, nor would he eat. Emilia could no longer sit still. Since she didn't know what was going on, her mind ran rampant with all kinds of thoughts, each darker than the last.

She paced, tidied up their alcoves, and thought about Agathi's visit. She paced again. She glared outside at the waves, seeing her and Hector from the night before. She paced some more.

Then she sat in front of Teo and refused to let him look away. "Tell me. Now."

His face fell. "I was hiding at the pavilion."

"You got inside?" she asked in astonishment.

"I was outside, hoping to hear something. They burst out when they heard Hector had called a meeting. That's when I heard them say the vote had gone through to reinstate you into the guild."

Surely, that couldn't be what all this was about. She should be happy about being able to return to the guild, but she wasn't. "What else?"

"A family has been found to take me in."

"And that isn't good news? Why?"

He looked at the sand, his fingers playing in the grains. "I don't need one."

"Everyone needs a family."

"I have you and Hector."

She took his hands in hers. Just as she was about to comfort him, she remembered how he had shouted Hector's name. Whatever the reason, it had caused Hector to fly away instead of heading toward them.

"What aren't you telling me?"

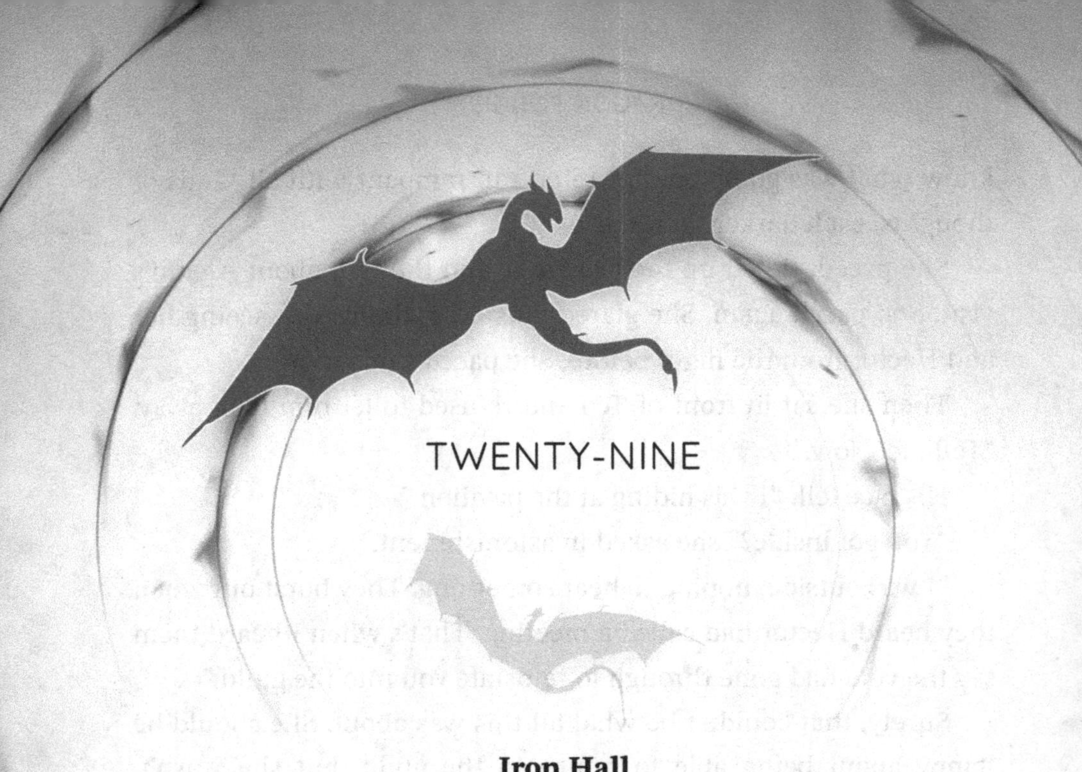

TWENTY-NINE

Iron Hall

Marcus didn't want to be in the atrium, yet he hadn't been able to stay away. It didn't matter how long he stared down the corridor, he couldn't remember anything past Ryder's arrival. And that was very alarming. It had to be something powerful to have him *and* Ryder missing time. He didn't even want to think about what might have happened had he not alerted Con to their findings—a discovery he had no memory of reporting.

"I thought I might find you here," Evander said as he walked up.

Marcus glanced over his shoulder at the King of Brass, noting his kilt worn for mating ceremonies. He met Evander's gray eyes. "You mean Con sent you."

"Actually, it was Eurwen." Evander stopped beside him. "You know we'll get this figured out. We always do."

"That's easy for you to say. There was no' any fuckery happening with *your* mind."

"True, but that doesna mean we're no' all extremely disturbed by it."

Marcus blew out a breath. "First, Hector goes down the tunnel, pushes a button, and vanishes. Then I go down, and nothing happens. Ryder joins me, and we walk farther, only to come back and forget. Something must have happened. Something we can no' remember. Or maybe something we were no' supposed to have seen."

He shivered as if someone ran a cold finger down his spine.

"Standing here willna fix that," Evander said. "The ceremony starts soon, and you're no' dressed."

His missing memories were important, but so was the joining of a King to his mate. "Aye. Of course."

Marcus turned and headed for his chambers on the other side of the city. He'd return once the ceremony was concluded. Maybe some time away from the area would help him sort through the jumble in his mind.

"How far did you get?"

Evander's voice halted his steps. Marcus looked over his shoulder to see his friend staring down the corridor. "A wee bit shy of halfway. Why?" When Evander didn't answer him, Marcus returned to him and gazed down the hall. "What do you see?"

"It's no' what I see. It's what I feel," Evander replied, his voice nothing but a whisper.

"Is something calling you down there?"

Evander shrugged and shook his head. "I sense...trepidation. It's overwhelming. How have you no' felt it?"

"I might have. That could be what caused the missing time."

"You doona remember seeing anything?"

Marcus's stomach tightened with foreboding once more. "Nothing."

"What about the tech Ryder found? Did it contain a crystal?"

"No' that I recall. You think there are crystals?"

Evander ran a hand through his short, dark hair. "They've been known to absorb emotions. That could be what I'm experiencing, but I willna know unless I see for myself."

"I doona expect that to happen anytime soon."

"Something occurred in there," Evander said, pointing down the corridor. "Something traumatic."

Marcus had thought the same thing. "I want down there as much as you do, even as something inside me tells me to never go down it again. I didna have that feeling before, which tells me something within caused it."

"And took Hector."

"It might be the same, or it could be something completely different. We willna know until we investigate."

Evander studied the corridor for another long minute. "After the ceremony."

"Aye," Marcus agreed.

They walked away together, each glancing behind them at different times. They continued in silence until Marcus branched off to head to his chamber to change. He put on the dress shirt and kilt before tugging on the long socks and some shoes. Next, he shrugged into a jacket and inspected himself in the mirror. He was at the door, his hand on the knob when he heard someone whisper, "*Help*."

Marcus whirled around at the voice, his eyes slowly searching his room for who had spoken, but no one was there. No one he could see, at least. There was no doubt he had heard a voice. It had sounded close, too.

"Who's in here?" he called.

When there wasn't a reply, he closed his eyes and expanded his hearing. Minutes passed, nothing but the regular sounds of the city greeting him.

"Help..."

The whisper came a second time, just as clear, but more was spoken after that he couldn't make out.

"Where are you?" Marcus asked. "Tell me where you are so I can help."

There was no reply, nor another whisper. Was he losing his mind? Had something within the corridor affected his cognitive function?

Marcus was rattled as he left his chamber. He made his way to the center of Iron Hall, where the others had already gathered, but he couldn't shake the anxiousness that roiled in the pit of his stomach. That's why it took him a moment to recognize the unease in the great hall.

"What is it?" he asked Kendrick.

"Rhi and Lotti have no' returned, and Rhi didna come when Con called for her."

Because of the mating ceremony, the Kings from Earth had journeyed through the Fae doorway to bear witness. While they could exit through the doors of the city into Raynia Canyon and cross over the border onto dragon land, they didn't wish to draw attention to themselves. No one outside their group knew about the city, and they wanted it kept that way. Usually, Rhi and the other two Fae mates, Shara and Noreen—along with Lotti—teleported everyone to Cairnkeep, where the twins lived and ruled.

It was always difficult because the dragons didn't want to see the Kings, even though they tolerated them. The dragons didn't accept humans—mates or not. That's why they were jumped in instead of having the Kings fly everyone there.

Shara and Noreen were taking groups to the capital. Ulrik had the silver cuff he'd gotten from a Fae that allowed him to teleport, so he also helped out. His mate, Eilish, used her silver finger rings that granted her the same ability. Between the four of them, their massive group got to Cairnkeep relatively fast.

Marcus looked past the cliff to the mountains beyond and the dragons that dotted the sky. They gave the capital a wide berth during the ceremonies because of the humans. The twins must have alerted them about it, giving them time to retreat. He could watch them all day. It didn't matter what color or size they were. They were dragons, and he missed them dearly.

He returned his attention to those around him when Shaw walked to the front with Con, who would officiate the ceremony. Marcus smiled at Shaw, who stood beaming as he waited for his mate. A few moments later, Nia walked down the row, wearing a sapphire blue gown that matched Shaw's scales. Her brunette waves were gathered at the back of her head, with a few tendrils hanging around her face.

Most everyone watched her, but Marcus always watched the King. Shaw was the quiet one among them. It wasn't that he didn't like to talk. More that he chose what he said and to whom. There could be no doubt about the love Shaw and Nia shared. It was written all over his face as Nia reached him.

Con smiled out over the group. "I'm excited that another Dragon King has found his mate. Shaw went into the heart of evil and walked away with Nia by his side. They faced—and tackled—deception at every turn but came out stronger together. Shaw, you've long been our brother, and today, we gain another sister."

Marcus joined in the clapping. He had always been a sucker for mating ceremonies—celebrating love and the joining of two people who had found their way to each other despite all the odds and worlds between them.

"Now, without further ado," Con said, his voice booming over them. "Shaw, do you bind yourself to Nia? Do you vow to love her, cherish her, and protect her above all others?"

Shaw's smile got even bigger as he nodded. "Unequivocally."

"Nia," Con asked, "do you bind yourself to Shaw, King of Sapphires? Do you promise to love him, cherish him, and protect him above all others?"

Nia was nodding before Con had finished. "Aye."

The moment the word left her lips, she hissed and looked down at her upper left arm and the dragon eye tattoo that appeared.

Con looked over the crowd with a smile slightly dimmed by Rhi's absence. "The proof of your vows and your love. Everyone who sees this will know that Nia has been marked as Shaw's mate for eternity!"

Marcus chuckled as Shaw tugged Nia to him and kissed her as he turned and dipped her. Everyone cheered for the couple. Marcus whistled and clapped, but his gaze slid back to the dragons. When he returned his gaze to the couple, Shaw and Nia were making their way down the aisle together, arm-in-arm. The celebration would continue back at Iron Hall.

Traditionally, the ceremonies took place at Dreagan, but when Eurwen and Vaughn mated, she wanted it at Cairnkeep since it was her home. Ever since, those who found love on Zora had their ceremonies there.

Marcus lingered as others gathered to return to the underground city. They wanted to continue the festivities, but he planned to sneak off as soon as he could and return to the corridor. So, he let the others go ahead of him.

"I take it you're going back?" Evander asked as he came up alongside him.

Marcus nodded. "I am. You joining me?"

"Yep."

"Count me in," Ryder said as he walked up.

Marcus saw Ryder's mate, Kinsey, watching him as she stood with some of the other mates. "Are you sure that's wise?"

"I'm no' leaving Zora until I know what happened to me," Ryder vowed.

Evander grunted. "I doona blame you. Have you told Kinsey?"

"She's no' pleased, but she understands. Why do you want to go? Curiosity?" Ryder asked.

Evander's brow furrowed. "I felt something I can no' explain."

"Interesting. I'll spend some time with Kinsey and then join you two," Ryder told them.

Marcus thought about telling them what he had heard but decided to keep that to himself for the time being. He nodded as Ryder walked over to join Kinsey, and their group returned to Iron Hall. He wanted to get back to the corridor as badly as he wanted to stay away from it. It was a unique event that he'd never experienced before, and one he'd be happy to never repeat.

He debated flying back to Iron Hall, but the whisper bothered him. He had to know if it had come from someone or if he was going insane. Marcus and Evander were part of the last group to leave Cairnkeep. He looked toward the dragons before Ulrik touched his silver cuff and teleported them back to the city.

It was easy for Marcus to slip away from the revelry since no one paid any attention to him. He didn't even bother returning to his room to change. Instead, he chose to use magic to switch his clothes. Expending magic in such a manner was something they didn't do on Earth. It was a way to ensure they didn't forget that mortals were around and thus get discovered. That directive had changed on Zora, and all of them were taking advantage of it.

The closer Marcus got to the atrium, the harder it was to keep going. He forced himself to cover the last bit of distance until he stood in the antechamber. He couldn't look down the hallway. His gaze landed on the bare table, and the blueprints rolled up next to it. He grabbed a drawing and unrolled it. He had to know if he still had the same abilities.

As usual, he could decipher all the intricacies of the plans and different options for building. Marcus braced his hand on the table and dropped his chin to his chest in relief. He looked up when he heard footsteps approaching. It wasn't long before Evander appeared.

"Figured you'd beat me here," Evander said with a crooked smile.

Marcus was rolling up the blueprint when Evander hushed him. Marcus stilled, waiting to see what was going on.

"Did you hear that?" Evander mouthed.

Marcus's heart thudded. Had he heard it, too? "Hear what?" he whispered.

Evander was silent for a moment before he shook his head. "I thought I heard one of the bairns coming, but I was wrong."

THIRTY

Nothing felt right. Hector had known calling the assembly might backfire, but he never could've guessed that a Star Person would show up. And of all of them...Eurielle? But it wasn't the Eurielle he remembered. She was different.

He soared amid the clouds, weaving among them. The Eurielle he had just spoken to didn't appear at all friendly toward him, which didn't compute because he hadn't done anything to her. Then Teo had shouted his name. The fear in the lad's voice and the terror on his face had taken Hector aback.

"Danger," Teo had whispered.

He'd known Hector would be able to hear him clearly. Then Hector saw Emilia. He hadn't hesitated to shift and keep everyone's attention on him. Only a few saw Teo and Emilia running away. When it appeared that some might try to follow them, Hector dove low over the audience. The force of the gusts his wings created knocked a few people back, but he didn't care. Not if it allowed Emilia and the lad to get away.

It wasn't difficult to keep everyone at the amphitheater until he saw Emilia and Teo get to the cave. He looked for the danger Teo had warned him of, but Hector didn't see anything. Which meant it was another kind of threat. He turned his gaze to the cabinet then. Like the others in the audience, they didn't know if his flying was a show to entertain or one done to cause fear. The only one seemingly unmoved by it all was Eurielle.

The cabinet was certain he couldn't harm any of them. He wasn't convinced that was true, but he also wasn't willing to test the theory—or his bond with the island. At least, not yet.

Hector grew tired of hiding in the clouds. Besides, he needed to talk to Teo and get some details. He tucked his wings and dove, plummeting toward the sea. He breached the waves and sank deep into the depths before returning to his human form. Rather than swim to the cove, he headed to the nearest shore. It was always better to get a view of things before walking into a potential situation, and everything right now was a potential situation. Emilia and Teo had made it to the cave, he knew that much, but that didn't mean all was well. He intended to be prepared.

Once he reached shallow water, Hector stood and noticed the people on the cliffs above, scanning the water for him. Someone spotted him before he could react. There was no way he could remain unseen unless he stayed in the cave, and he had spent too many centuries sleeping in his mountain to do that again.

The only thing for him to do was ignore the gawkers. It wasn't as easy as it sounded, especially when he'd hidden his true identity for most of his life. He should feel free now that it was out in the open, but in some ways, it felt more restrictive. It was wrong to complain about one thing only to get the other and then complain about that.

Hector was so caught up in that loop that he didn't realize he was naked until he was on shore. He called his jeans and shirt to him. He'd worn a chiton to blend in, but there was no need for that now. There wasn't an option for him to blend in no matter what he wore. Though the chiton was cooler, so he'd probably change later. For now, he wanted to remind the citizens of Highvale how different he was.

He hadn't taken two steps before someone touched his arm. The next thing he knew, he was in an empty room with a decent-sized window on two walls, putting them in a corner of some building. He called to his magic and widened his stance.

"Easy," Rhi said, lowering her veil. "It's just me."

Hector relaxed. "Where are we?"

"A room Lotti found. We need to talk."

"About Eurielle, I'm guessing."

Rhi's lips flattened into a thin line. "Yes and no. Something's going on here."

"I'm aware."

"No, I don't think you are," she said with a firm shake of her black-haired head. "It's something that not even Lotti can sort out."

That made him pause. "Eurielle isn't the same person we knew. I thought it was an act at first, but I don't think it is."

"I don't either. I got close when she showed up, so I heard your conversation."

Hector crossed his arms over his chest. "Where was Lotti?"

"Nearby, but she didn't want to get too close in case Eurielle reacted to her presence."

"Eurielle is how the cabinet knew I was a King."

Rhi grimaced and nodded. "I believe so. Lotti wants to talk to her. Honestly, I'm not sure that will make a difference. Sometimes, I think the island is a paradise. Then it's like I get a glimpse behind the curtain and nothing is as it seems."

"I've felt like that for a while now."

"We need to get it sorted in case it involves you."

He grunted. "I think it involves me. Do you know why Teo would call out to me like that?"

"No clue."

Hector shoved his hair out of his face. "He whispered the word *danger*."

"Ah.. That explains why you left so quickly. I saw him and Emilia dashing away and thought that might be the reason. I stayed near them just in case."

"Thank you."

She wrinkled her nose. "I might have let an opportunity to follow the cabinet pass in doing so."

"Maybe Lotti discovered something." The slight tightening in Rhi's face gave him pause. "What is it?"

"It could be nothing."

"*What* could be nothing?"

She glanced out the window and sighed. "I haven't been in contact with Lotti since Eurielle appeared."

Hector tried not to think too much about that. It could be anything. Lotti was invisible to everyone, including Rhi.

"And then there's Con," Rhi said. "He's been calling for me."

"Then you should go before he comes looking."

She threw up her arms in frustration. "I can't leave you."

"Lotti is here."

"You don't know that."

He quirked a brow. "And you doona know she isna. I'll be fine.

You need to check in with Con. He's likely going mad that you've no' answered him."

"I'm sure it was about Shaw and Nia's ceremony."

Fucking hell. The mating ceremony. He had completely forgotten about it. Hector had never missed one, and he didn't like that he wouldn't be there for Shaw's and Nia's. All because a handful of people had decided they needed a Dragon King. His banked fury ignited in a scorching wildfire. The sudden and overwhelming need to retaliate consumed him.

"Hector?"

It took him several deep breaths to calm and be coherent enough to look at Rhi. When he did, she physically flinched.

"None of this is your fault," she said.

He knew exactly whose fault it was, and he knew how he wanted to fix it. But he couldn't. He wanted to hurt them, inflict pain. He needed to hear them scream and beg for mercy.

Hector stumbled back into a wall and clutched his head. Where had that thought come from? The last time such notions had entered his head was during the war with the humans. He had come so close to losing who he was then. To have such feelings again, whether warranted or not, was terrifying.

Worse, the longing to do harm had yet to dissipate. It lingered, swirling through him like a viper, leaving behind poison in its wake.

"Hector."

He threw off Rhi's hands when she touched him and spun around to keep his back to her. He flattened his palms on the wall and pressed his forehead against the stone as if he could will the thoughts out of his head. But they were there, a part of him now like bone and sinew.

"Hector!"

Rhi's voice sounded as if it came from miles away. He was no longer in the room with her. It didn't even feel as if he was still on the island. A presence was there, slithering around him, silent and dark as the ether. It wound around him slowly, gently. Gradually, his fear subsided. He recognized the presence. He couldn't see its face, couldn't hear a voice, but he knew it somehow. It didn't want to hurt him. Even as that assurance went through his mind, he remained tense. It wasn't supposed to be there. Or maybe *he* wasn't supposed to be with it. It was wrong. All of it.

"NAY!" he bellowed and threw out his arms.

He heard a startled yelp behind him. Hector's eyes cleared, and then he was back with Rhi. He turned around to see her rising from the floor across the room. Hector rushed to her and helped her to her feet. "What happened?"

"You."

"Me?" he asked in confusion.

She nodded and dusted herself off. "You threw me off. What just happened?"

"I doona know." A new kind of horror unfurled within him. "I wasna here."

"You never left."

He shook his head. "Someone was with me. I felt them. I recognized them, but I doona know who it was. They tried to calm me, but I knew it was wrong. I threw them off. Or who I *thought* was them."

"You didn't hurt me, so don't worry about that. I'm more concerned about what just happened. Has it ever occurred before?"

"No' the presence. But the fury? Aye."

Her silver eyes grew troubled. "What do you mean?"

"I wanted to hurt someone. Nay," he replied with a shake of his head, "that isna true. No' someone, the cabinet. I wanted to hear them scream."

Her face grew ashen. "Like—"

"The war," he finished.

Rhi swallowed hard. "That's worrying."

"Aye. And it was uncontrollable."

"It's time for Con."

Hector sliced a hand between them. "Doona dare! Keep everyone away."

"I don't know how much longer I can do that."

"If others come, they'll be bound with me. I'm sure of it. If I'm feeling this way, what would happen if other Kings came and felt the same rage."

Rhi leaned back against the wall. "Shite. It'd be a blood bath."

"Exactly. I'll figure out a way. And if I can no', then I'll have Lotti put me down."

"Put you...?" Rhi's shocked voice trailed off. Her face then tightened with outrage. "You aren't a damn dog."

He ran a hand through his hair. "The fate of Zora is at stake. The lives of thousands are worth more than mine."

"Con wouldn't agree, and I certainly don't."

"Aye, you do. And it's how you should feel," he said softly. Hector forced his lips to curve into a semblance of a smile. "You need to get to Con before he and Alasdair bring the other Kings down on the island, looking for their mates."

She drew in a shaky breath. "I'll be back. I promise."

"I know. First, though, can you take me to the cave? I doona trust myself to walk among the humans."

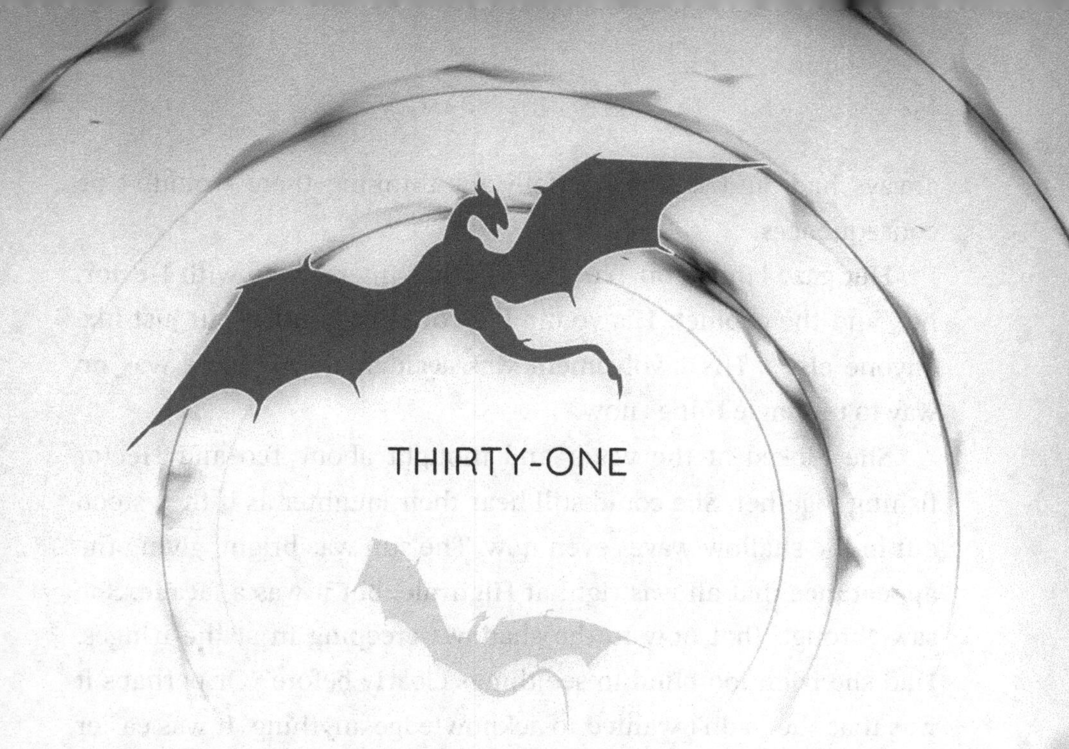

THIRTY-ONE

There was no food or water. Emilia and Teo had become dependent on Hector, and it never occurred to her that he might not be there to supply them with the necessities. It hadn't taken her long to get used to magic that could produce whatever he wanted whenever he wished it. But he wasn't there now, and neither she nor Teo had eaten anything since that morning. She heard the boy's stomach growling already.

Soon, she would have to venture from the cave. She couldn't wait for Hector's return forever. Teo wasn't being completely honest with her, but she couldn't get any more out of him. Nothing had felt right since the day Hector showed up. The world she had known and loved was spinning at a rate she couldn't keep up with —and she didn't want to try. She wanted off the island and away from the tragedy she saw unfolding yet was unable to prevent.

But she was part of the performance now. No longer a spectator, her decisions and actions affected everyone. Perhaps they always had, and it was her folly for thinking there wouldn't be consequences.

Her gaze landed on Teo. Even he was intertwined with Hector, her, and the cabinet. His young life could be snuffed out just like anyone else's. His involvement was accidental, but there was no way to untangle things now.

She looked at the water and thought about Teo and Hector fishing together. She could still hear their laughter as if they stood out in the shallow waves even now. The sun was bright, giving the appearance that all was right at Highvale, but it was a façade. She saw through that now to the shadows creeping in at the fringes. Had she been too blind to see things clearly before? Or perhaps it was that she hadn't wanted to acknowledge anything. It was easier to pretend that nothing was wrong than to accept reality and have to do something about it.

She might perceive the darkness closing in, but how did she fight it? *Could* she fight it? She was a seer. She couldn't conjure beds, food, or clothes like Hector. How was she supposed to stand against whatever the shadows were? They might eat her alive. *Might*? She snorted. They would. It would. Whatever *it* was.

It wasn't that she couldn't or wouldn't stand up for herself or others, it was that she didn't know how. Not when the other option was Hector. She imagined he could simply look at someone and eviscerate them. Or devour them in flames. All she could do was glare and tell them what she wanted to do to them.

Emilia had never felt so powerless or helpless. It wasn't a good feeling. In fact, she loathed it. She could grab something to protect herself and learn to wield it, but that meant nothing when the weapon of choice was magic. Her visions wouldn't shield her from an attack, nor would they wipe out her enemies. All they could do was potentially warn her of something. *If* she interpreted them correctly.

"Hector!"

She whirled around at Teo's shout and watched the lad launch himself across the cave at Hector, who caught him easily. The sight of him enfolding Teo against his chest brought a lump to her throat. Hector lifted his head, his dark eyes meeting hers. She detested the awkwardness between them. She had caused it, and it felt like a great chasm separating them now, impossible to cross.

"Are the both of you all right?" Hector asked.

Before she could answer, Teo pulled out of his embrace and said, "I didn't think you were coming back."

"I'll always come back for you." Hector's gaze returned to her. "For both of you. For as long as you want me to."

Those words seemed to take a huge weight off Teo. His smile was still dim, but at least it had returned. "We'll always want you to return. Won't we, Emilia?"

Both looked at her. She nodded because she *did* always want Hector to return.

Some of the tension eased from Hector. He lowered his gaze to Teo and asked, "Now that that's settled, want to tell me why you said there was danger?"

Teo glanced in her direction. "I was hiding outside the pavilion when the cabinet rushed outside. I overheard them."

He didn't say more, and Hector looked at her.

Emilia took pity on Teo. "Apparently, I'm being reinstated in the guild."

Hector's face showed nothing as he nodded at Teo. "Is there more?"

"Maybe," Teo said, looking at the sand and digging the toe of his shoe into it.

Emilia once more found Hector looking at her to explain. "They found a family for him."

"Ah," Hector said. "I see."

Teo lifted his head, his face creased with concern. "You think I overreacted, don't you?"

"I didna say that, lad. Just because they found you a family doesna mean you have to go. You get to choose."

"They won't let me."

Hector shrugged. "I'll make sure they know it's your choice."

"What about Emilia? Isn't it suspicious that they want her back?"

Warmth spread through her at Teo's concern.

"It sure is," Hector murmured as he looked her way.

Teo's stomach growled loudly.

"Bloody hell," Hector murmured. He held out his hand and produced two plates of food. He handed one to Teo. "Here you go."

Teo grabbed the plate with a muffled thanks before he sank down where he stood and shoveled the food into his mouth as fast as he could.

Hector approached her with the other plate. He handed her the food and said, "I should no' have stayed gone so long."

She accepted it and grabbed an olive to pop into her mouth. "I thought it better if we remained inside."

"That was a wise move."

"What's going on?"

Hector took her arm and brought her to the table and chairs. His voice was low when he spoke. "I can no' say for certain. Is he telling me everything?"

"He told you what he told me." Emilia glanced at Teo to see him focused on the food. How many meals had he missed in his short life? "I think there's more," she mouthed.

Hector nodded. "Me, too."

They fell into silence, and she took the opportunity to eat more of the bread, olives, and meat. She shot a secret look at Hector and noticed the concern that colored his face as he watched Teo.

"What about you?" she asked.

Hector turned his head to her and raised a brow in question.

"Are you all right?"

He released a long sigh. "I doona know."

Suddenly, he jumped up, went to the cave entrance, and peered outside. Then he turned to look at her. She shrugged and shook her head in confusion.

"It's Agathi," he whispered.

Teo grumbled angrily.

"Emilia?" Agathi called.

Hector motioned Teo to him as they walked to her alcove at the back of the cave to give her some privacy.

After their last conversation, Emilia was surprised Agathi had returned. What was left to say between them? Unless she had come to notify Emilia about the guild.

"Emilia? Are you there?"

She walked to the cave entrance, but she stayed on the inside. "I'm here."

There was a beat of silence before Agathi asked, "Can you come outside?"

"I don't think so."

"Then, may I come in?"

It was Emilia's turn to pause. "I'm afraid not."

"I need to speak with you."

Her friend's voice was different than earlier. The anger that had tinged her words was gone, putting Emilia on edge. "You can come to the entrance. It's just the two of us."

Agathi appeared as she made her way closer. She glanced past Emilia before meeting her gaze. "I suppose you saw Hector in his true form today."

"I did," she replied.

Agathi fidgeted, something she never did. "I'm supposed to tell you that you've been reinstated in the guild."

"Supposed to?"

"That's right. They've also promoted you."

Now, *that* was a surprise. First, she was kicked out, then reinstated, and then reinstated with a promotion. Something was definitely going on. She had to admit that Teo was right to panic. Emilia decided not to reply. Agathi had something to get off her chest, and Emilia would let her do it.

Agathi took a step forward, only to immediately be pushed back. She glanced up at the top of the entrance as if she expected to see something there. Her gaze dropped to Emilia. "Is he keeping you prisoner?"

"I can come and go at will. The barrier is to keep others out."

"Others?" Agathi repeated hesitantly. "You mean me."

Emilia dipped her chin. This Agathi was like the friend she knew, and it *almost* made Emilia think she could trust her.

Agathi grimaced. "I deserve that." She looked around nervously and shuffled as close as she dared. With her voice barely a whisper, she said, "I'm sorry. About all of it. I was ordered to act angry with you. I was told to ignore you. You know the power Loukas and Pelagia have. I know how much the guild means to you, but don't come back. It's all a ploy. Loukas and Pelagia have been setting up secret meetings not even the cabinet knows about. I don't trust them, and I've been playing a part, trying to uncover what's going on. What I know is that you're in danger. Please believe me, Emilia. You're the sister I never had. You know me better than anyone. Please. Trust me now. Don't take this offer, and don't let Teo go to the family."

Emilia was so taken aback by it all that she wasn't sure how to respond. "They can't send me or Teo away. No one can be removed from Highvale. Loukas and Pelagia can't hurt us. So, what's the danger?"

"They can hurt you in other ways. Trust me. I've seen it."

"You mean they can imprison us."

Agathi's eyes darted to the side. "That's part of it. You're free right now. Stay here, and you'll remain that way. The cabinet won't dare to go against Hector. But if you return to the guild, I'm not sure what will happen to you."

Emilia wanted to believe her. The woman standing before her was the Agathi she had grown up and got into mischief with. The Agathi who had shared dreams and plans for the future with her. The Agathi who had always taken up for her. Who had been her friend when no one else would.

"You know me," Agathi insisted. "The *real* me. Not the one I show others. Certainly not the one I've shown you the past few days. I had to play that game for both our sakes. I'm trying to save you."

Even a day before, Emilia wouldn't have hesitated to trust her, but a lot had changed in that time. Maybe too much.

"The cabinet expects me to return with an answer," Agathi said. "What should I tell them?"

Emilia felt decades older than the woman she had been before Hector. It was as if she had lived a dozen lifetimes in the days he'd been on the island. The naïve, trusting girl was gone. She saw layers of deception and truth in everything around her. And it was up to her to uncover each of them. She could no longer follow her heart and believe in those she had always put her faith in.

"I'll think about it," she answered.

THIRTY-TWO

Hector didn't have to strain to hear Emilia's conversation. He sat on the chair in her alcove and waited for her and Agathi to finish while Teo sat at the opening, desperate to catch a word or two.

"Can you hear them?" he whispered.

Hector nodded.

Teo tried to get a glimpse of Emilia before he jumped up and walked to Hector. "What are they saying?"

"It's a private conversation."

"But you can hear them."

Hector bit back a grin. "No' on purpose."

"But you aren't trying *not* to hear them."

The lad had a point. Hector leaned forward and rested his forearms on his thighs. "She's no' in danger."

"Of course, Emilia's in danger. The other one is here."

"I know you doona like Agathi," Hector began.

Teo clenched his jaw and whirled around. "No one listens to me."

Hector was up and in front of the boy before he could take another step. "I am. And I have been, but I can no' do anything about something if you doona tell me."

The anger went out of Teo in the next breath. Wariness crept into his expression.

Hector sighed, both in frustration and exasperation. "Lad, I know you've had a rough life. People have let you down, and you've struggled. I'm sorry you've had to go through that. I meant it when I said I would be here for you for as long as you want."

"I know," Teo mumbled.

"Sometimes, the most difficult thing about finding a clan is realizing that being a part of something means no' just receiving trust but giving it, as well."

Teo's lip trembled slightly. "Don't make me say it. Please."

The *please* was the gut punch. Hector hadn't wanted to believe the cabinet would use Teo, but the truth was laid bare with those six words. He put his hand on Teo's shoulder and gave him a comforting squeeze. "You doona have to say anything you doona wish to, lad. Ever. No' with me."

Hector dropped his arm and returned to his chair, but it wasn't to listen to Emilia's conversation. It was to consider how and when the cabinet had gotten to Teo. Their desperation to get to him and Emilia at first—as well as Teo's trepidation of them—suggested it was a recent occurrence. How recent was what Hector needed to uncover by any means other than grilling Teo.

"I can get you off Highvale immediately," Hector said.

The lad slowly lifted his head to look at him.

"The offer I made when we first met still stands. It will always stand."

Teo's narrow throat bobbed as he swallowed.

"Give it some thought," Hector urged him.

Emilia appeared at the alcove entrance. "Give what some thought?"

Hector got to his feet. "Leaving the island with Rhi."

She looked from him to Teo, studying the boy for a moment. "Things here are getting volatile. We value your help, but Hector and I would feel better if you were safe."

"Nowhere's safe," Teo said.

Her brow puckered at his words, but she didn't push him for an explanation. She looked at Hector. "Until a few moments ago, I didn't realize that I had lived a sheltered life. I thought I struggled. And I suppose I did."

"What happened?" He hadn't been paying attention to the latter part of her conversation.

"How do you know when someone is telling the truth?"

He lifted one shoulder in a shrug. "Depends on the person."

"Agathi visited me this morning."

Hector briefly looked at the lad to find him watching Emilia intently.

She walked to the bed and sat on the end, folding her hands in her lap. "It was an odd conversation." She frowned as she gave a small shake of her head. "Agathi was angrier than I've ever seen her. It wasn't our first fight, but it was by far the worst. She couldn't see where I was coming from. She wouldn't even try. A lot of heated words were exchanged before I asked why she had spied on us. She claimed she had come to see me, but she quickly let me know you had paid her a visit, though she suggested it was something more illicit."

Hector seethed with ire. He had known Agathi would go to Emilia at the first opportunity.

"She claims she refused you, but if you went to her again, she wouldn't."

Hector fought to keep his voice neutral when he said, "Nothing happened. I stayed at the balcony doors while she sat on the bed. There was nothing for her to refuse as I made no advances."

"I believe you. I was so hurt by our entire exchange that it made me reevaluate the years I've known her. Every conversation, every confidence shared, every hope revealed. I thought about the first time we met and how we always ended up together despite everyone wanting to be her friend. Why would she choose me? The loner, the misfit. The oddity."

"You're not odd," Teo said as he sat beside her.

Emilia smiled and took one of his hands into her. "Thank you, but I am. I've never quite fit in, no matter what I've done. I think it just happens sometimes."

"It's no' you," Hector said. "It's that you've no' found your clan. They'll be the ones who love you and want to be with you *because* of all the ways you're different."

Her gaze lowered to a spot in front of her. "I'd like to hope that's possible. With everything that happened at the theater, I had put aside thinking about Agathi until she showed up again. She came to tell me I was reinstated with a promotion."

That was suspect, but Hector didn't need to tell Emilia that. He could see she had come to the same conclusion.

"If that bombshell wasn't enough, Agathi then told me that her ignoring me and the anger earlier was all a show the cabinet demanded of her. She said both Teo and I are in danger." Emilia's blue eyes swung to him. "She told us to stay with you. That if I go to the guild, and Teo goes to the family, we'll be harmed."

Hector sank onto the chair. "If she was acting before, it was a good performance. One she didna break both times she and I were alone."

"The things she's said and done behind my back and to my face the last few days, war with the person I've known for years. I can't reconcile the two."

"Then doona. Take each separately."

She puffed out her cheeks and sighed. "How do I do that?"

"What does Agathi have to gain from you being exiled from the guild?"

Teo made a sound in the back of his throat. "That's easy. No competition."

"Competition?" Emilia asked with a choked laugh. "Are you serious? She'll be running the guild one day. She's far ahead of me in every aspect: wealth, position, and beauty."

"The last is debatable," Teo said.

Hector nodded. "It's a landslide in Emilia's direction, if you ask me."

A slight stain of color tinged Emilia's cheeks at their praise. Her lips softened into a smile.

"So, what does Agathi gain if you're in the guild?" Hector asked.

Teo rolled his eyes. "Again, an easy one. She'd have access to you," he said, nodding toward Hector. "If we're out of the way, you'd no longer be protecting us, which means you'd have more time for her."

The words hung in the room. Emilia's pallor turned ashen.

"Then why would she urge me not to go to the guild? Why tell me to remain?"

"To make it seem as if she has your best interests at heart," Hector replied.

"This makes my head hurt," Teo said, rubbing his temple.

Emilia nodded as they shared a look. "Agreed."

Hector parted his lips to talk when Emilia's body went rigid, and her gaze turned distant.

"She won't let go," Teo said hysterically while attempting to yank his hand from hers.

Hector rushed to them and gently rested his hand atop theirs as he caught Teo's gaze. "Easy, lad. She's no' trying to hurt you. Look at her."

When Teo did, Hector also turned to Emilia. Her pupils and irises were white, ringed in black. He had only seen someone have a vision once before, and while it had looked different, there were enough similarities for him to know what was happening.

"She's having a vision," Teo said.

"Aye. Let's just sit with her and wait for it to finish."

Teo never took his eyes off her face. "Does it hurt her?"

"Does it hurt you when you use your magic?" Hector asked.

He shook his head. "Nay."

"Then I doona believe it causes her any harm either."

Teo's face contorted with pain. "She's squeezing hard."

"It'll be over soon." At least Hector hoped it would. He had no idea how long visions lasted, much less how long Emilia's did.

"It hurts," Teo cried.

Hector could see how hard Emilia was gripping him. He tried to loosen her fingers, but she only clutched him tighter.

Teo violently tried to yank his hand away.

Hector gripped him by the shoulders to get his attention. "Easy, lad. She's no' squeezing on purpose. She needs you. Otherwise, she would've let go."

"I can't feel my fingers."

The tears in Teo's eyes propelled Hector to try again to free his hand. Emilia clenched him so tightly he feared breaking her fingers in his effort to free the lad. He got a finger between Teo's hand and Emilia's when she sucked in a deep breath, and her eyes returned to their normal cobalt color. He looked into her face as she blinked and focused on him.

There was a split second where she came back to herself before she recalled the vision. She tried to hide the fear and distress, but he saw it. He tenderly smoothed a strand of hair from her face just so he could touch her. Her blue eyes were bright as she held his gaze. Her hands cupped his face before she leaned toward him. Their lips met in a soft kiss, but her taste was all he had been thinking about since their night in the cove. He flattened his hand on her back as he brought their bodies closer and deepened the kiss.

Somewhere in his lust-filled brain, Hector remembered they weren't alone. He regrettably ended the kiss and lifted his head. Emilia was slower to open her eyes. Desire flashed in her blue depths, and her lips were swollen from the kiss. If they were alone...

But they weren't. And even if they were, he still wouldn't. Emilia had been put in the middle of a struggle, and it wasn't right that she was being used. Same with Teo. There were too many obstacles for them to be together as he longed for them to be. Worse, those obstacles might always be there.

Hector looked to the side where Teo was sitting, watching them. Emilia turned her head to the boy and grinned.

"You didn't have to stop," the lad said. "It was better than watching you have the vision. At least I knew you were okay."

Emilia's smile died at the mention of the vision. Hector's heart clutched as her gaze slid back to him, and a slight frown furrowed her brow. She smoothed a hand down his face. Her eyes grew troubled, and she didn't try to hide it this time.

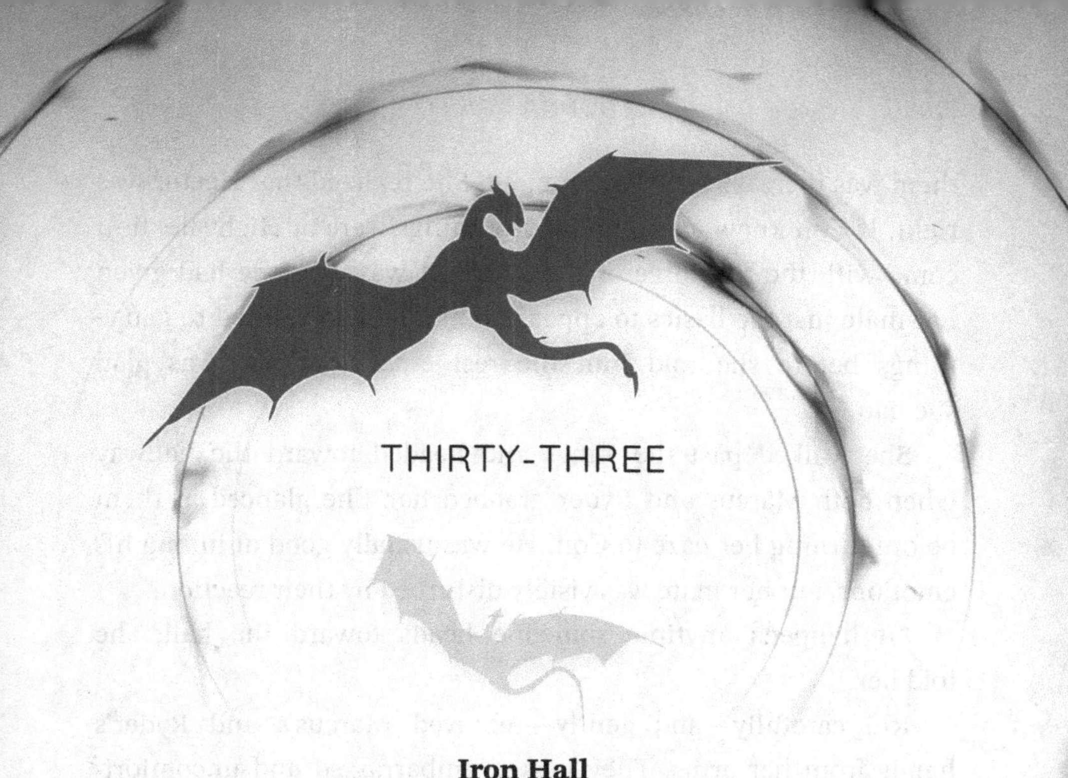

THIRTY-THREE

Iron Hall

Rhi looked from Con to Marcus to Ryder and then Evander before her gaze returned to her mate. Con held her tightly for long minutes before she gave him an update on Hector. Then he had taken her to the atrium and told her everything.

"Is it connected to Hector?" Con asked.

She shrugged and shook her head. "Your guess is as good as mine."

"What about the tech I supposedly found? Have you seen anything like that at Highvale?" Ryder asked.

"I've not been looking for anything electronic." She'd been too busy rushing around, trying to sort through the tangled political schemes.

Evander had yet to pull his gaze from the corridor. Marcus kept turning away, but he made himself look back. Ryder wouldn't peer down the hall at all. Con's worry for the three of them was increasing by the moment. She realized that Hector was right. If Con knew exactly how dire things were at Highvale, he'd come with the full force of the Kings. It was why she had given her mate just the basics to appease him. She had wanted to gauge things before she told him the rest, and now, she was glad she had.

She walked past the Kings and headed toward the hallway when both Marcus and Ryder grabbed her. She glanced at them before turning her gaze to Con. He was usually good at hiding his emotions, but her mate was visibly disturbed by their reaction.

"It happens anytime someone heads toward the hall," he told her.

Rhi carefully—and gently—removed Marcus's and Ryder's hands from her arms. They looked embarrassed and uncomfortable with the entire episode. She observed them as she took another step. Both noticeably held themselves back from reaching for her a second time. She got to the opening and looked down the hall. She could barely make out the end of the corridor, or at least what she believed was the end.

"I can teleport there," she said.

"Nay!" Marcus, Ryder, and Evander yelled in unison.

She turned to the side at their shouts, wearing a frown of her own now. It wasn't like any King to act in such a way. Which meant there was, indeed, something happening in the corridor.

"Evander hasna been inside," Con said.

The King in question scratched his forehead. "I doona know why I said that. I just feel that no one should go down there."

"I do, too," Marcus said.

Ryder nodded. "Me, as well."

Rhi looked at Con. "What about you?"

"I doona feel anything other than concern about what's affecting the others," he replied.

She swung back to the hall. The barrier he'd put up should have stopped anything from getting through, but it obviously hadn't if Evander still felt something. Would it affect the other Kings? The humans in the city? What about the kids?

Rhi thought about Hector. She'd promised to get back to him immediately, but how could she leave Iron Hall with this going on? Yet how could she not return to him when he was now bound to the island? And how long until she had to come clean to Con about everything? She didn't like keeping secrets from her mate. That had nearly destroyed them before, but she also knew him well enough to know what his response would be—and it was everything Hector feared. For the time being, it was better if he didn't know everything.

She could get down to the end of the corridor. By jumping there, she would skip walking down the hall as Marcus and Ryder had. Maybe they had tripped something when they traversed it. First, the hallway had taken Hector, and now, it had shaken three others. Maybe they weren't supposed to find what was at the end. Everything was keeping them out, and that might be to protect them.

Rhi turned to face Con. As she did, her eyes passed over Marcus. He wore a pained expression, his head turned slightly as if he were listening. Her gaze jerked back to him to confirm what she had seen. She then looked at Ryder to see his reaction, but he had backed away from the hall. However, Evander was staring intently down it, his head also cocked as if he heard something.

"What do you hear?" she asked Marcus.

He straightened at being caught. "You."

"You heard something coming from the corridor," Con said.

Marcus shook his head.

Rhi exchanged a look with Con before she homed in on Evander. "What about you? What do you hear?"

"Every once in a while, I think I catch something, but it turns out to be nothing," Evander answered casually.

Con sighed loudly. "I think it's better if everyone stays out of this area for the time being."

Ryder couldn't get out fast enough. Marcus was right behind him, but Evander was slower to leave. Rhi took Con's hand and dragged him after the other Kings. The longer she stayed there, the more uneasy she got. She couldn't shake the feeling that someone was watching her.

Con waited until they were walking alone before he asked, "When are you going to tell me the rest?"

"Later." She didn't even pretend not to know what he was talking about.

"Is Hector in trouble?"

"If he was, I'd tell you."

Con halted and turned to face her. "No' if you believed it would make things worse."

"Sometimes, I really hate that you know me so well," she said with a smile as she rose on tiptoe and wound her arms around his neck.

He didn't return her grin.

She sighed and dropped her arms to her sides. "I've already communicated Hector's wishes for no other Kings to go to the island. You also know I agree with him. That hasn't changed."

"Tell me everything."

Rhi shoved her fingers into her hair and tilted her head back. "I've seen firsthand what is happening at Highvale."

"And that's killing me. I expect to get all the details from you. No' have you pick and choose what to tell me in hopes of keeping me in the dark," Con snapped.

"Ugh," she muttered. She looked at him and dropped her arms. "That's not what I'm doing."

He raised a brow and looked at her.

"Fine. It's what I'm doing, but I have a bloody good reason."

"I know. It's why I've been patient, but I can tell something has happened."

Rhi rolled her eyes, but it was only a halfhearted attempt. "I really need to work on that."

"I'd rather you didna."

"Right. We're a team." She walked to him and wound her arms around his middle, then rested her cheek on his chest. His arms came around her to hold her firmly. "Everything I'm doing comes from a place of love, and you have a lot going on here."

"I willna bother explaining in great detail my fear when you didna answer my call."

She squeezed him tighter. "I heard it in your voice. I would've come if I'd been able."

"As for what's happening here, we're dealing with it. It isna as big of a threat as what's going on with Hector."

"You have to promise you won't go after him."

Con leaned her back so he could look into her eyes. "I can no'—and willna—make that promise. You've disclosed the dangers and what might happen if any other Kings visit. Give me some credit that I'll remember that."

"I give you all the credit, honey, but I also know you would destroy worlds for your family."

"You're damn right I would," he stated softly.

It was one of the many reasons she had fallen for him. Rhi took a deep breath and then told him everything, not leaving out a single detail. By the time she finished, Con was so still he almost appeared dead. Outwardly, he projected a serene exterior, but inside, he was raging. This was the side of her mate everyone should fear. It meant that he was calculating all the ways to get to one of his Kings and crush anyone who stood in his way.

"Are you sure it was Eurielle?" he asked.

Rhi leaned against the opposite wall of the corridor, one foot propped against it. "Positive."

"And you've no' seen Lotti since?"

"Nope."

Con cut his eyes down the hall. "Alasdair will want to know about his mate."

"Lotti probably went to speak to Eurielle. She was the one who told Lotti about them being sisters, after all."

"You can no' be sure they're together."

Rhi dropped her foot to the ground. "It's why I need to return."

"Things are going from bad to worse on that island."

"The very—and I do mean *very*—last thing we need is for all the Kings to be bound there with Hector."

Con stalked two steps to stand in front of her. "Take me to Hector. Veiled," he added when she tried to speak. "No one will see us. No one will know we're there."

"Eurielle will. She's how they knew about Hector in the first place. He didn't arrive as a dragon. Look, handsome, I know you're a doer. You run headlong"—his face darkened—"okay, I exaggerated. You're a planner."

"And I always win," he added.

She gave him a flat look. "Stop interrupting me. Aye, you win, but we've had enough encounters on Zora to know that things here aren't like they are on Earth. We've been triumphant, but barely. Something about Highvale is different from other places. I don't trust it. Let me and Lotti do what we can for Hector. If we're not successful, you'll be the first person I come get."

"I doona have to tell you to be careful, do I?"

Rhi tossed her hair over her shoulder. "Need I remind you that I was in the Queen's Guard and fought alongside the Kings in the Fae Wars?"

"Of course, no'."

"Do I need to remind you of *this*?" she asked and yanked up her shirt sleeve to show off her dragon eye tattoo.

Con roughly dragged her against him and claimed her mouth, kissing her until she was breathless. Then, he lifted his head. He said nothing as he placed his hand over her stomach.

"I haven't forgotten, my love," she said.

"Just make sure you return to me."

She brought his head down and gave him a lingering kiss. "Always."

"Then go to Hector."

His arms fell away. She suddenly had the strongest urge to remain with him. It was never good when any of the Kings were separated. Rhi blew him a kiss and teleported out before she changed her mind. She didn't go to the cave. Instead, she went looking for Eurielle. If she could find her, she'd likely find Lotti.

THIRTY-FOUR

Every time Emilia thought that things couldn't get worse, they did. She had never gotten angry at being a seer. The years of the vision on repeat, while alarming, had allowed her to become acclimated to what she saw. It wasn't until after Hector's arrival that it had altered. Then came the most recent one.

Normally, she was alone when a vision struck, so it was a jolt when she came to and found him there. The way he had looked at her brought her back to their moonlight swim and the riot of desire that had taken her. A longing, a craving that only grew the longer she was with him. Emilia couldn't think beyond needing his touch. Then his lips were on hers, and she had been floating on a cloud of unquenchable hunger until he ended the kiss.

That's when she remembered Teo beside her. One sentence from him, and the vision barreled into her like a tidal wave. There was no way to shove it aside again, no way to forget what she had seen.

"The same vision as before?" Hector asked gently.

She wanted to ask how they had known she was having one, but she couldn't think beyond the horror of what she'd seen. For the first time in her life, she didn't want to see the future. She wanted nothing to do with knowing what would happen—and who would get hurt. The emotional trauma was too great for her to keep hidden. Nothing she tried could bury it, and she wasn't even sure she should.

"Nay," Emilia answered.

Comprehension dawned across Hector's face as his gaze sharpened. "Teo, can you give us a moment?"

Teo was slow to get up, but eventually he walked out of the alcove. Hector sank onto his haunches and waited. He wouldn't press her. If she refused to tell him, she knew he would accept it. She wasn't sure she could do the same if their positions were reversed. In fact, she knew she wouldn't. She would hound him, begging and pleading, until he relented.

Seeing the destruction of Zora had been agonizing, but she hadn't seen faces. There wasn't anyone alive, and she never saw the dragons. It had been terrifying to relive that over and over. It paled in comparison to the knowledge she held now. She wanted to give it away, remove it from her mind, and forget it ever existed, but the gods had shown her. It was now up to her to ensure she changed the course of the future before it was too late.

"You need to leave Highvale. Immediately," she stated.

Dark eyes watched her carefully. "I've tried, lass. I can no', remember?"

"You can if you've been released, and I know how to release you."

Hector didn't jump up with excitement. Only simple acceptance. Was that the wisdom of living such a long life? How childish and tedious humanity must look to the Kings.

"The vision?" he asked.

She nodded once and rose to her feet. "We shouldn't tarry. The sooner, the better."

His hand snaked out and grabbed her wrist as she tried to walk past him. She turned as he stood. "There's something you are no' telling me."

There was a lot she hadn't said—and wouldn't. She owed him that. Everyone on the island owed him. Her heart caught as she leaned into him, craving one last moment in his embrace. He wrapped his arms around her, and she squeezed her eyes closed. She would miss his strong arms and hard body, his smile and his warm laugh. She would miss so very much.

One of his hands held her head, pressing it against his chest. She wanted to stay there forever. Hector was the first person to truly see her, and it had changed everything. The past few days had been utter turmoil, with hurt doled out by the bucketfuls. But it had also revealed deceptions and half-truths from every direction. A vision had urged her from her parents for their safety, while another vision was granting her the freedom for yet another path. It was the right thing to do, the only thing to do, and still it was impossible.

"You deserve freedom. We need to see to it," she said around the lump in her throat.

His hands cupped her face and tilted it so she could look at him. "Come with me. Let me take you away from here."

"I want nothing more." She felt tears sting her eyes when his mouth curved into a smile. It died a quick death when she added, "But I can't."

"There has to be another way."

She couldn't think when he was touching her. She swallowed, pulled out of his arms, and headed out of the cave. "There isn't. We must hurry."

Teo heard them and came rushing out of his alcove. "Where are we going?"

"You must stay," Emilia said.

He gaped at her before running to catch up. "I can help."

"We'll be back, lad," Hector promised.

She wanted to reassure Teo, but there wasn't time. There wasn't even time for goodbyes. Emilia grabbed her skirts and ran the rest of the way to the shore and into the water. Hector was right beside her.

"What are you doing?" Hector asked.

She dove into the water without answering. Emilia swam to the seabed as fast as she could and followed it as she scanned for the cave entrance. She had wasted time, possibly too much time. Her lungs burned for air, but if she surfaced, the window for Hector's freedom would close.

Hector swam up beside her. He held up his arms and shrugged, asking her what they were looking for. There was no way she could explain now. Emilia kept swimming, fighting against the currents and the demands of her lungs. All the while, she felt the sands of time rapidly running out. Her eyes became unfocused and her brain sluggish. The next thing she knew, she was at the surface.

"Fucking breathe!" Hector shouted.

She sucked in air to her starved lungs and then gulped in more.

"What were you doing?" he demanded. "Trying to kill yourself?"

"Take me back down. I have to find the cave."

His dark eyes flashed with anger. "Tell me where it is, and I'll search for it."

"It has to be me. That's what I saw in my vision."

"I willna sacrifice your life for mine."

She struggled against him as he began swimming to shore. "Are you listening to me?"

"I've heard every word, lass."

"I seriously doubt that." She gave him a hard shove to break free.

Hector released her as they treaded water, facing each other. "You almost died down there. Do you understand that?"

"I'll take a bigger breath."

"If you're determined to go down, then there's som—"

She frowned as he gave a slight shake of his head.

"There's something I can gi—"

"Hector?" she asked frantically. *Nay. Nay, please.*

Panic flashed over his face. "Emi—"

Then, he was gone. Vanished before her eyes. She turned in a circle, searching for him. She even dove under to see if he was there. Emilia surfaced as dread soured her stomach. "Hector!"

She knew he wouldn't answer, even as she shouted for him over and over. He was gone. She was too late. Tears ran down her face as she swam the last bit to shore. When she finally reached shallow water, her skirts tangled around her legs, tripping her. Teo rushed out and helped her to her feet.

"Where is he? Where's Hector?" Teo demanded, fear making his voice crack.

She dropped onto her hands and knees, curled her fingers into the wet sand, and hung her head. "He's gone."

"Then get him back. Get him back, Emilia! We have to get him back!" Teo shouted hysterically.

She rose and wrapped her arms around him. He buried his face against her neck and sobbed as her own tears coursed down her cheeks.

"What happened?"

Emilia startled at the sound of the new voice. Her head jerked to the left, where her gaze landed on a woman with wavy, shoulder-length blond hair and turquoise eyes that refused to let Emilia look away. The woman wore a cream undershirt beneath a leather corset with black trousers tucked into knee-high boots.

Emilia set Teo to the side and got to her feet. "Who are you?"

"My name is Lotti. What happened to Hector? He was there, and then he wasn't."

Lotti. This was the woman Rhi and Hector kept speaking of. She wiped the hair from her face with the back of her hand so she didn't get sand in her eyes. "I don't know."

"What did you do to him?"

"I was trying to free him," Emilia answered defensively.

Lines of worry creased Lotti's face. "You have no idea where he went?"

Emilia shook her head. "He's never disappeared like that. Rhi has, but not him."

"Shite." Lotti looked one way and then the other down the beach. "This isn't good. Rhi," she called out.

A heartbeat later, the Fae appeared. Her silver eyes moved from Lotti to Emilia and Teo. Then, she scanned for Hector. "Where is he?"

"Gone," Teo said with a sniff.

Rhi directed all her attention to Emilia. "Tell me what happened."

"I had a vision that showed me how to free Hector. I was trying to do it, but I think we ran out of time," Emilia explained.

Lotti crossed her arms over her chest. "They were out in the water. He brought her up to the surface. Then he vanished."

"You need to tell us about the vision, Seer," Rhi stated.

Lotti put up a hand before Emilia answered. "Not here. Too many eyes."

The four of them headed into the cave. Emilia was worried that Lotti wouldn't be able to enter, but she passed the barrier without incident. Emilia then watched her touch the rocks as a ripple ran across the entrance.

"That should make things a little difficult," Lotti murmured.

Rhi looked to Emilia. "We're waiting."

Emilia wiped her hands on her wet gown. "I've only had a few visions in my life. The first got the attention of my village and made them fear me. The second urged me to flee my parents before they were killed and find Highvale. The third one reoccurred several times a year and showed the world on fire and bathed in blood."

Lotti nodded in understanding. "It's the reason you wanted Hector away."

"Exactly," Emilia agreed. "The day he returned, I had a vision. It was the same, though slightly different."

Rhi stood tensely. "And no sign of dragons in any of them?"

"I heard them, but I never saw any. Hector asked the same thing." Emilia shivered against the cool wind coming through the entrance. "Just recently, I had another one. But it was different in all ways."

Lotti asked, "How so?"

"It showed me two paths. One with what would happen if Hector wasn't freed."

"And that was?" Rhi asked.

It nearly killed Emilia to see it. How would she put it into words? She stared into Rhi's eyes and knew that as nice as the Fae was, she would fillet Emilia alive to get the information she needed about Hector. "We all thought the bond between Hector and the island was permanent, but it wasn't. It had a time limit."

"Time limit for what?" Lotti urged.

Emilia's throat tightened. "He could be freed unless he took a mate of the island."

"Dragons mate for life," Rhi said. "They can't force him."

Emilia wrapped her arms around her center to hold back the screams that threatened to break free. "They will. And they are."

"Which means Highvale will forever have a dragon guarding it," Lotti replied.

Rhi snorted. "And his mate. Both of them would essentially be immortal."

"To rule Highvale for eternity," Emilia said with a nod. "Exactly."

Lotti blew out an angry breath. "They're taking away everything that made Hector, Hector."

"And the second part of the vision?" Rhi asked.

Emilia's throat tightened, but she forced the words out. "If I had gotten to the cave, I could've severed the temporary bond. That would've allowed him freedom."

"And gotten him away from this bloody place," Rhi muttered.

Lotti tucked her hair behind one ear. "Do you know who took him?"

"The same one who will be his mate. Agathi." Emilia couldn't believe her friend could be so diabolical. She hadn't known Agathi at all. Their years of friendship had been nothing but a sham. Everything had been a lie to deceive and manipulate. And Emilia hadn't realized any of it until it was too late.

Rhi swung her head to Lotti. "I fucking knew it."

"It's my fault," Teo said as he sat in the chair, hanging his head.

Emilia gaped at him. "This isn't your fault at all."

"It is," he insisted as he looked up, his blue eyes meeting their gazes. "A couple of guards found me hiding at the building. They took me to Agathi, who threatened to hurt you unless I made sure Hector thought you and I were in trouble. They wanted to see how far he would go for us."

"You mean she wanted to see if he had fallen for Emilia," Rhi bit out furiously.

Lotti walked to Teo and squatted before him. "You were forced to do something against your will. You aren't to blame for any of this."

"I could've told Emilia or Hector." Teo shrugged. "Hector figured it out. Well, not all of it, but he knew I had been forced to do something. I thought he'd be angry, but he wasn't."

Rhi's lips twisted. "Because he, like us, knows you were used."

"We need to move fast," Lotti said as she straightened.

Rhi rubbed her hands together. "Do we go in together or separately?"

"It's too late," Emilia said.

Rhi's silver eyes locked on her. "It's only too late when you give up."

"I'm not giving up," Teo said as he jumped to his feet.

Hector wouldn't give up on her, so she wouldn't give up on him. "Neither am I."

"Good, because we could use your help," Lotti said.

Rhi looked over at Emilia. "First, you need to change for battle."

"Do I get a sword?" Teo asked.

Lotti whispered something to him as Rhi guided Emilia to her chamber.

"I'm not a fighter," Emilia said.

Rhi walked to the chair where the remaining two gowns lay. She lifted one, then the other, considering both. "You're not fighting with a sword or even magic." She turned and held out her pick to Emilia. "Today, you're fighting with your heart."

# THIRTY-FIVE

He wasn't supposed to be here. That thought kept running through Hector's mind as he looked around the room. His gaze skimmed over the naked bodies sensuously wound together that covered every wall. The turquoise mosaic floor depicted the ocean, and the ceiling was painted to resemble the sky, complete with clouds, birds, and the sun.

There was an oversized daybed against one wall, a sofa against another, and a long bench against a third. There was only one door and no windows. He had no memory of getting to the room. One moment, he had been in the cove with Emilia, and then...here.

The hairs on the back of his neck rose as the sensation of being watched prickled his skin. Hector turned and spotted Eurielle standing against a wall dressed in pale aqua. Her dark hair was gathered behind her head while the ends fell over one shoulder.

"Did you bring me here?" he asked.

Eurielle tilted her head slightly but didn't answer.

Hector had known something was wrong with her when he saw her at the amphitheater. "Eurielle, tell me what's going on."

"It will all be explained soon," she answered.

"You're allied with the Dragon Kings. What are you doing here?"

She sighed as if listening to him was aggravating.

"We've been looking for you," he tried.

She rolled her gray eyes. "So you keep telling me."

"You fell over the side of the mountain at Stonemore. You remember that, right?"

"Vividly," she replied.

What was he missing? Why was she so angry? "Miena was defeated."

"I know."

"You know?" he repeated. "Why did you disappear on us?"

Her gray eyes slid to him. "Disappear on you?"

This conversation was going nowhere. He had no idea why she had suddenly gone from an ally to a foe, and he had other things to worry about. "Why am I here?"

She issued a slight shrug of one shoulder. "It's time."

"Time for what?"

"Time for you to take your mate."

Emilia's face flashed in his mind. He stumbled back a step as the truth slammed into him. He had found his mate and hadn't even realized it. Or maybe he had. He'd been drawn to Emilia from the start. He made excuses to be near her, but his heart had known. His head was just slower to catch up.

The door opened behind him. He turned and saw Agathi sauntering inside with a pleased smile, her cold, brown eyes assessing.

She walked to him, not stopping until she was close enough to touch. He moved back, but she stepped with him.

Finally, he grabbed her by the shoulders and held her away from him. "What are you doing?"

Her dark eyes searched his face for a long moment. She leaned to the side and asked Eurielle, "Why isn't it working yet?"

"Give it time," Eurielle replied.

Unease wound tightly in his chest, crushing his lungs. He immediately called to his magic and put up a shield around him. It would keep just about anything out. Anything except a Star Person. Eurielle was working with Agathi, but he couldn't figure out why or what she could gain from it.

"One of you care to tell me what the fuck is going on?" Hector demanded as he shifted to the side and looked between them.

Agathi grinned haughtily. "I'm ensuring the survival of all magicals."

"How do you intend to do that?" Hector asked.

"With you, of course."

Alarms began going off in his head. He was certain she couldn't do anything to him, but he knew Eurielle could. "I'm no' going to help you do anything."

Agathi smiled and moved her hand to him. He leaned out of the way, and a snarl contorted her face. "That's the last time you do that to me."

Hector had had enough. He headed to the door and grabbed the handle, but his fingers wouldn't work to open it. He tried again, and once more, his hand wouldn't obey. Undeterred, he pushed magic into his palm to tear it off its hinges. Yet that didn't free him either. He looked over his shoulder to find both women watching him.

If he couldn't get out the usual way, he would get out another. He called to the dragon within, but just like with the door, he couldn't shift. Hector knew Eurielle was preventing him from leaving the room.

When he ended up bound to Highvale, he'd believed that, ultimately, he could make his own decisions and do whatever he wanted—other than leave. It was his folly for not digging deeper into the island's legends. He might have found a way out if he had spent more time learning why the cabinet believed a Dragon King was the answer to their prayers. But Agathi had directed his attention to keeping Emilia and Teo safe, which prevented him from seeing what was really happening.

Hector had one chance left to get help. He'd have to be quick, though. "Rhi!" he bellowed.

Eurielle's expression didn't change. Agathi, on the other hand, rolled her eyes. "Why can't you accept that you're mine?"

"I have never, and *will* never, be yours," he told her.

She laughed. "I always get what I want, and I want you."

"I think others should've told you *nay* more. You doona seem to understand what that word means."

"I know exactly what it means. I just choose not to accept it."

He was waiting for Rhi to show up. Maybe she already had and realized she needed to bring Lotti. At least, that's what he was counting on. If Rhi couldn't get in the room, then she would know Eurielle was with him, and she and Lotti would figure something out. They just needed time. So, he kept Agathi talking. "Why me?"

"Emilia isn't the only seer to have visions. I was ten the first time I saw you." Agathi walked along the wall, trailing her fingers across the naked bodies. "Do you not see our faces here?"

Hector looked closer. His stomach turned in dismay as he

recognized himself in various positions having sex with Agathi. A cold sweat covered him. He couldn't use his magic, nor could he shift. He was powerless, and it was fucking terrifying.

"I was shown my future with you. Us, together. Righting all the wrongs and recreating Zora. I've been waiting for this day my entire life," Agathi continued. She paused beside one of the images of them kissing. "You were meant to be mine. Fate has decreed it."

"You're no' my mate," Hector stated.

Agathi traced the naked body that was supposed to be him. "I was supposed to be your first contact. If I had been, you wouldn't be confused. You arrived an hour early."

"It wouldna have mattered if you were the first person I met. You're no' my mate. You may worship dragons and have stories, but you doona know anything about us."

She lowered her arm from the painting and faced him. "Everyone had a part to play. After I informed my parents of the vision, they did everything I told them to do to ensure all of it came to pass, just as I had seen it. It wasn't hard to work my way through the guild's ranks to the cabinet. Loukas and Pelagia were too easy to mold, and the old fool with them is nothing. To this day, Loukas and Pelagia believe that bringing you to the island was their idea. That's how good I am."

"I wouldna brag about manipulating people."

She ran her eyes over his chest. "Aye, everyone had a part. Even poor little Emilia."

Her name was like a punch through his chest. Icy fingers of warning wrapped around his heart and squeezed. Hector had never liked or trusted Agathi. Now, he loathed her on a level he hadn't thought possible. Merely being in the same room with her was revolting. But he needed to give Rhi more time.

"How did Emilia play a part?" he asked.

Agathi chuckled. "You remember her now, but soon, she'll be gone from your thoughts."

Not if he had anything to say about it. He was a Dragon King and wouldn't go down without a fight. He reined in his ire and crossed his arms over his chest. His battles usually involved armies. He hadn't prepared to battle a single person. But a good warrior always knew when to pivot. So, that's what he would do. In the meantime, Agathi liked to talk. All he had to do was give her a little time.

Just as he suspected, Agathi continued. "Emilia was also in my visions. She is a vital part of everything, just not how she thought she was. You have no idea how easy it was to separate her from everyone. She believed everything I told her." Agathi chuckled. "She had no idea I was telling everyone how much she disliked them. It was entirely too easy to become her only friend."

"Except she kept her vision from you," Hector said.

Agathi's lips pinched. "She nearly upset my perfectly planned future. If Eurielle hadn't shown up, Emilia very well might have."

Hector was beginning to worry that Rhi and Lotti couldn't get to him. Which meant he had to get himself out of this mess and face a Star Person. It wouldn't be easy, but he had to try. Giving in wasn't an option. He tried to hold on to Emilia's and Teo's faces as he searched his memories for ways to battle against Eurielle. All the training he'd received over the countless centuries must have *something* he could use.

"Do yourself a favor and give in to me," Agathi told him. "We are meant to be mated. Together, we will decimate those without magic and restore order."

"In case you didna hear it the first time, you're no' my mate," Hector repeated.

"Of course, I am. I've seen us together."

Magic rushed through his body, moving thick and fast. He fisted his hands against the hatred that welled up for her. "A dragon mates for life."

"I know. It's in the scrolls."

"Is it also in the scrolls that once a dragon finds his mate, if he isna with her, he will die?"

Agathi gave him a flat look. "You're confused. Shortly, you'll realize I'm your mate."

"I've already found my mate."

"Eurielle," Agathi called worriedly.

It was Hector's turn to grin. He asked Agathi, "Are you worried?"

"Eurielle!"

"You've known all along," he said as he stalked to her. "You've known it was Em—"

"It's done," Eurielle said, cutting him off.

THIRTY-SIX

"I don't think I can do this," Emilia said as she walked up the steps from the beach.

Veiled beside her, Rhi said, "You're not alone. I'm right here with you."

Emilia knew the moment someone noticed her. Whispers spread along the street ahead of her as more and more people turned to look her way. Lotti and Rhi hadn't let her see herself after she got ready, but now she wished she had pushed for a mirror.

Rhi had chosen the white gown with the gold stripes along the edge. She had two thin gold bracelets on her left wrist and five on her right. Her fingers were bare of adornments, but Lotti had fastened a thick necklace around her neck. Gold bands were fastened at her shoulders, and she even had a bracelet around her right ankle. The final piece was a gold dragon armband that wound up her left arm.

Rhi and Lotti had then taken charge of her hair. She had sat as they gathered and pinned strands in place. The weight of the gold headband surprised Emilia. She almost asked to remove it, but the delight on their faces when they stepped back to look at her had changed her mind. Even Teo's eyes had widened with amazement.

"I do believe you're battle-ready," Rhi said.

Lotti smiled as she looked Emilia over. "Now I know why Hector chose that color for her."

"I never knew he had such great taste," Rhi said.

Their lighthearted banter soon passed as Emilia got to her feet. "Are you both sure about this?"

"Positive," Rhi stated.

Lotti's turquoise gaze slid to Rhi. They shared a look before Lotti grabbed Emilia's hand and said, "Good luck." She then walked to Teo. "You know what to do?"

"I do. I'll be there no matter what," the boy answered.

Then Lotti was gone.

Now, Emilia was headed deeper into the city with Rhi.

"All you have to do is get to him," Rhi whispered.

That might be easier said than done, and they both knew it. They were counting on her to know where Agathi might take Hector. Emilia second-guessed herself when it came to her so-called friend. She hadn't known Agathi as she thought she had, which made trying to guess where they were even harder.

It was unnerving to have everyone staring at her. Emilia had always faded into the background, happy for Agathi to take center stage and even happier to know they were friends. The more time she had to sit with what she had learned, the more she wondered if anything between them had been real.

With so many eyes on her, Emilia was conscious of every step she took. She kept her focus on the street because it was easier. But perhaps it was time for her to do the opposite of what she normally would. She took a fortifying breath and glanced up. Her gaze met that of an older man. He didn't gawk at her in scorn. Instead, she saw surprise.

She chanced another look on the opposite side of the street. This time, it was a young girl with wonder spread across her face. Emilia began looking into other faces and meeting gazes. Everyone was curious, and a few seemed dubious, but most looked on in approval.

She had been comfortable with her old life and position. Yet there was so much more out there that she had never even dared to consider. Not because she didn't believe she was worthy, but because she hadn't dreamed big enough. She knew exactly where she belonged now, and she would get there. She had seen it. Even if her vision hadn't shown her this part, with Rhi, Teo, and Lotti's help, she would fulfill her vision.

Emilia acknowledged some of those lining the streets. Her heart thudded against her ribs, and her palms sweated. Every step brought her closer to facing the person she had loved like a sister. She concentrated on Agathi while searching her memories for a clue to where she might be on the island. There weren't many places to hide. She had to consider Agathi's family home since Agathi spent so much time there. Emilia had only been there a handful of times. She had never felt welcome there. Now, she knew why. The property had plenty of rooms, most of which she had never seen, but the location didn't feel right.

The secluded rooms of the temples were another consideration. She knew Agathi's favorite, but that didn't seem like the place she would bring Hector either. It needed to be somewhere large. A place where Agathi had complete control. Somewhere no one would dare question her.

Emilia spotted the pavilion ahead of her. As a cabinet member, Agathi would have access that others wouldn't. Emilia had never been within the building's walls and could only guess at its size and what Agathi might have available to her. Yet she kept walking.

She passed several structures Agathi likely had access to, but there wasn't time to search them all. All she could do was trust her intuition, which took her to the guild house. Emilia halted before the steps, her gut clenching. This had been her home. The place she had been accepted. Within these walls, she had laughed and cried, learned and taught. She had dedicated her life to the guild and all its members. She looked up at the door, then higher to the top floor where Agathi's room was.

"Are you sure?" Rhi whispered.

Emilia twisted her lips. "I am."

"I took a look around inside. I can get us in if they won't open the door," Rhi said in a low voice.

The door would likely be barred against her. The street remained lined with curious citizens, all of them watching her. This wasn't about her, though. It was about Hector and the continuation of Highvale. Her vision hadn't just shown her the two options as she had told the others. She had seen its destruction, as well. It's why she had tried to release Hector while she could. If she had only been a few minutes quicker or swum faster, she might have done it.

She looked at those on the street. None of them had any inkling of what was going on. She could urge them to leave, but they wouldn't. Just as she wouldn't in their shoes. Her gaze returned to the door. She lifted her skirts and proceeded up the steps. Rhi didn't make a sound behind her, but Emilia knew she was there. Knowing she wasn't alone had helped her get this far. Hopefully, it would help her do what she had to do in the end.

Her legs were shaky, and her stomach felt tied in knots. She thought she might vomit by the time she reached the door. She didn't have time to raise her hand and knock before it opened, and she looked into Maro's aging face.

"Emilia," she asked worriedly and looked past her. "What's going on?"

"I need to come inside."

Maro swallowed, her eyes locking with Emilia's. "I've been ordered to lock you below if you showed your face."

"I suppose Agathi telling me I had been reinstated with a higher position was a lie, then?"

Her brow furrowed deeply. "I'm afraid so."

"Be that as it may, I must come inside."

"Just leave. I don't want to put you in prison, but with all these witnesses, I won't have a choice."

She shrugged. "Do whatever you must, but I will enter."

"Why?"

"I'm trying to save Hector, the island, and everyone on it."

Maro fretfully looked at the crowd. She dipped her head and lowered her voice. "How?"

"Let me in, and I'll tell you."

Emilia waited for another few seconds before the older woman finally opened the door and stepped aside. Emilia crossed a threshold she had entered and exited thousands of times before. She halted just inside the door and waited for Maro to lock it behind them.

"I've been shown two visions," she told the other woman. "One where Agathi gains control of Hector and dooms everyone without magic, and another where he's freed," Emilia said.

Maro rocked back on her heels. "How does either of those affect us?"

"If Agathi is successful, do you honestly believe the other Dragon Kings will sit back and let her control one of theirs? They will stop her. The only reason they've not come yet is because Hector urged them to stay away. Without him reassuring them he's all right, they'll be here in a heartbeat. And what do you think they'll do to Agathi and anyone who was complicit in what she's done?"

Maro nodded slightly. "But if he's freed, we're fine?"

Emilia smiled. She didn't want to lie.

"How do I know you aren't lying?" Maro asked. "You never told us about your other visions."

"I've seen the deaths in my visions. I saw the world running with blood and blackened by fire. I did everything I could to keep the dragons away to ensure that didn't happen."

Maro's thin lips twisted as she shrugged an aging shoulder. "You still should've told us. It could have been recorded and saved you a lot of trouble."

"All it would've done was put the spotlight on the dragons, exactly where I didn't want it. If I had seen them coming, everyone would've said they could find a way to change the outcome of my vision. Don't try to tell me differently. I've seen it too many times."

"We've been successful in changing things before."

"But not always." Beside her, Rhi made a sound that sounded suspiciously like a growl. "We could debate this for eternity. I had my reasons for not sharing the information. Are you going to help me, or are you locking me away?"

Before Maro could answer, she grunted and crumpled to the ground.

Rhi dropped her veil, a look of frustration on her face. "We don't have time for her to decide. Where to?"

"Down," Emilia said hurriedly. "Agathi has access to every level of this building."

Rhi motioned for her to go. "I'm following you."

Emilia walked around Maro and headed toward the back and the hidden staircase. Everyone who lived at the guild house knew about it, but only certain members were permitted to use it. She ignored all that when she opened the door and headed down the stairs. Her knees threatened to buckle with each step, but somehow, she kept going.

No, not somehow. She kept going because of Hector. Because he deserved better. Because she would right the wrong done to him and so many others.

Because she loved him.

She descended the final step and stood at a junction. There was a short hallway on either side with doors. Agathi and Hector could be in either one. She faced the right and headed down the passageway.

"I'll be veiled behind you," Rhi whispered.

Emilia barely heard her over the blood rushing in her ears. It felt like her heart might burst from her chest at any moment. She alternated between needing to vomit and wanting to scream. The suspense, anxiety, and fear were just too much.

She reached for the door latch and saw her hand trembling. Emilia squared her shoulders and thought about the little girl who had set out from her village to travel hundreds of miles over three months to reach Highvale. That child had been strong. She could face anything—even her best-friend-turned-enemy.

Emilia opened the door before she changed her mind and saw Hector kneeling before Agathi, staring up at her with a look of utter devotion. Emilia then noticed the painted walls and what—as well as *who*—they depicted.

"You're too late," Agathi stated gleefully. "He's mine. He was always meant to be mine."

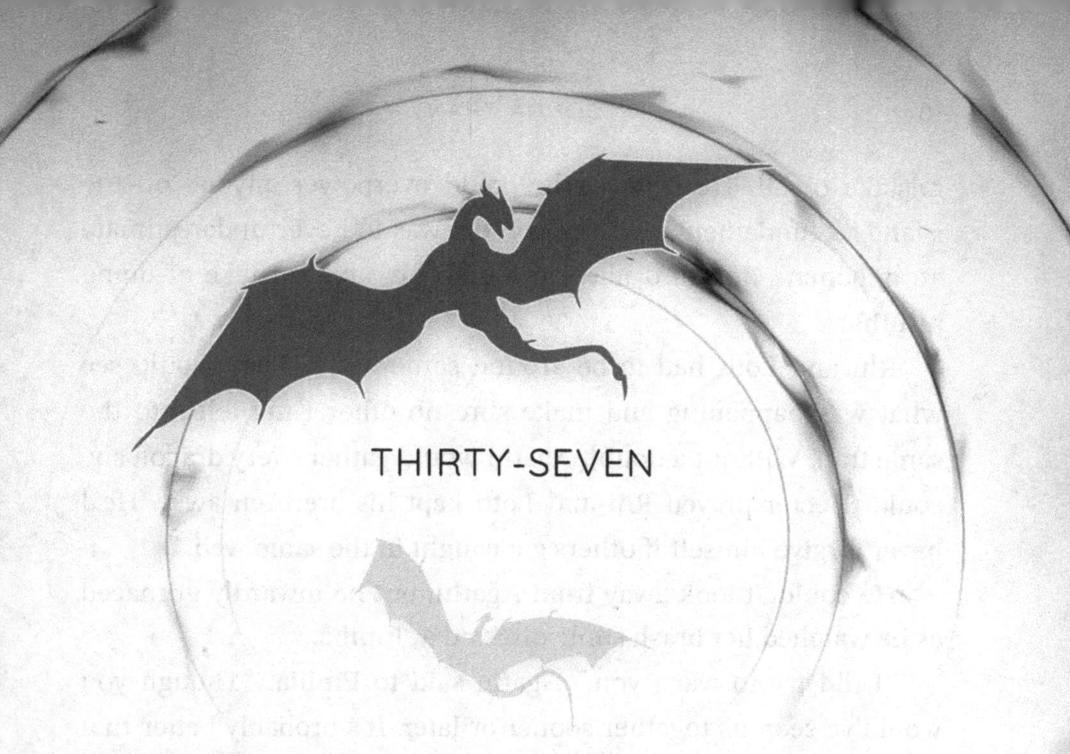

THIRTY-SEVEN

Hector seethed. He raged as he fought to regain control of his body. No matter how hard he struggled to turn his head or even move his eyes to Emilia, he remained riveted on Agathi. He tried to jerk away and get to his feet. He attempted to tell Agathi exactly what he thought of her. But he couldn't. She had dominion over every part of him except his mind.

It was the cruelest form of torture because he knew exactly what was going on. He would've wanted no part in her plan if he had power over his body. Even when he was a youngling without a family, he had never felt so helpless. Or panicked.

Nor so utterly enraged.

When he got free—because he *would* find a way—he was going to level all his immense rage on Agathi and anyone who had aided her in her delusional, absurd bid for power.

Hector had let his guard down on Highvale. He'd seen all the dragon sculptures and believed no one would do him any actual harm because they revered him. And he'd made the greatest mistake of all: He believed he could overpower anyone on the island. A fundamental rule of combat was to never underestimate an opponent, and he'd made the unforgiveable mistake of doing just that.

Rhi and Lotti had to be around somewhere. They would see what was happening and make sure no other King fell into the same trap. Without a doubt, Agathi would gather every dragon she could. Hector prayed Rhi and Lotti kept his brethren away. He'd never forgive himself if others got caught in the same web.

He couldn't look away from Agathi, but he inwardly grimaced as he watched her brash smile directed at Emilia.

"I did try to warn you," Agathi said to Emilia. "Though you would've seen us together sooner or later. It's probably better that it's in private, so you don't have to worry about people seeing you cry."

"I'm not weeping," Emilia replied.

Hector wished he could smile at her declaration. Instead, he cheered in his head.

"I have to admit," Emilia continued, "you had me fooled."

Agathi preened. "Don't take it personally. I dupe everyone."

"Decades of friendship. Shared secrets, hopes, and dreams slipped away like sand in the wind. How does it feel to have nothing real?"

"Real?" Agathi asked with a bark of laughter. "I have real." She held out her hand toward Hector. "I have a Dragon King."

Emilia drew in a long breath and released it. "Do you? Would he kneel before you if you didn't have Eurielle forcing him?"

Out of the corner of his eye, he saw Eurielle yawn as if the entire performance bored her. No one could force a Star Person to do their bidding, which meant she was getting something out of this. Hector couldn't figure out what Agathi had told Eurielle that would make her agree to help the seer. Eurielle could have anything, go anywhere. Her power was greater than all the dragons combined.

"Careful," Agathi warned. "You don't want me as an enemy."

Emilia chuckled softly as she stepped farther into the room, moving out of Hector's peripheral vision. "Isn't that what we've always been?"

"Hmm. You might have some claws, after all."

"Your mistake was thinking my easy-going nature meant I would roll over."

The tension in the room was palpable. Hector wanted to warn Emilia about Eurielle. So far, the Star Person had remained quiet, but there was no guarantee she wouldn't intervene. Emilia was treading on dangerous ground—and doing it alone. He demanded that his muscles and tendons answer him as he strained to get to his feet. He had to move between Emilia and Eurielle before it was too late.

Sweat broke out on his forehead as he fought against the magical hold. He felt Eurielle's eyes on him. If he couldn't stand in front of Emilia, he'd draw Eurielle's attention any way he could.

"You've never fought for anything in your life. How many times were you passed over for advancement in the guild?" Agathi asked, smiling arrogantly.

Emilia's light footsteps moved farther behind him. He didn't understand what she was doing until he heard a second set of light footfalls. *Rhi*, he mused.

"Did it ever occur to you that I didn't want to advance?" Emilia asked.

Agathi made a sound in the back of her throat. "Why would you want to be stuck doing the jobs no one else wanted?"

"You see the world as something to conquer. I see it as something to be a part of and enjoy."

"You don't think I'm going to enjoy being at the top?" Agathi rolled her eyes. "People like you make it easy for those like me."

Emilia said, "You mean those who deceive and betray?"

"I know what I want, and I get it by any means necessary. If you can't understand that, then you're one of those I step on to get to the top," Agathi replied.

Hector felt someone near him. When he listened closely, he could hear footsteps. *"Nay, Rhi!"* he bellowed in his head. *"Stay back! Doona let them know you're here. I willna be able to stop myself if Agathi orders me to hurt you."*

Rhi wouldn't die. She was mated to Con, which meant she would survive. But the child she carried might not. Con never should've allowed her to come. Hector never should've had Teo call for her in the first place. Nothing was going as it should, and he was squarely in the middle of everything, unable to even curl his hand into a fist unless Agathi gave him permission.

A bead of sweat rolled down his forehead and into his eye, causing it to sting. He blinked away the irritation as Eurielle's attention tightened on him. He kneeled between her and Rhi on his right and left, and Agathi and Emilia in front and behind him. He was a fucking Dragon King, yet as helpless as a newborn kitten. The contradiction left him reeling—and more than a little rattled.

"What does the cabinet have to say about you taking control of the island?" Emilia asked.

Agathi's smile was slow and menacing. "You'd have to ask them."

An odd sensation began in his stomach and grew. Flashes of the outside of the pavilion filled his head.

There was a long stretch of silence, and Hector imagined Emilia staring at Agathi. Finally, Emilia said, "Who did you convince to kill them? Because you wouldn't be happy with them stepping aside. You want complete and utter domination."

Now Hector saw flashes from within the pavilion.

"You do know me," Agathi replied with a smug grin.

"Oh, I know you better than you know yourself. You wanted Hector to carry out the deed, but he can't."

Agathi snorted. "You sound very sure of yourself."

"I am. First and foremost, he is bound to protect Highvale and the residents from *all* threats. That includes you. I know you well enough to know you contemplated testing the theory that Eurielle's hold was stronger than his bond with the island, but in the end, you went another route."

Murdeeeeeeeeer, the island said.

Hector knew for certain multiple people had been slain. That feeling in his stomach continued to swell.

Agathi crossed her arms over her chest and narrowed her eyes. "Interesting theory. And who would I have sought to commit such a heinous act?"

"The only one who wants power as much as you. Loukas."

Rhi remained beside Hector as he watched Agathi's face. He saw the tightening of her lips at the mention of Loukas. A second later, her mouth curved into a smile, her dark eyes lowering to him.

"I didn't tell Loukas to harm anyone," Agathi stated. "But the cabinet has been slain."

The deed had been done. That feeling in his stomach consumed him. A powerful rush of outrage surged through his veins. Hector rose to his feet. Agathi no longer controlled him. The island took precedence, and it demanded the murderer be found.

Hector rushed through the door, up the steps, and out of the building. A large crowd of people stood outside and gasped at the sight of him. He leapt into the air and shifted, taking flight as he scanned the island for any sign of Loukas. On his second flyover, he spotted the head of the cabinet standing among the gathering.

He couldn't land atop a building because he might crush it. Instead, Hector returned to his human form, called clothing, and dropped to land on the street behind the crowd. Everyone spun to look at him. As he strode toward them, they parted to let him pass. Loukas made a desperate attempt to flee, but Hector grabbed him by the back of his clothes and threw him to the ground. He stood over the human and saw the blood spatter.

Loukas put his hands up to shield his face as he trembled in fear. "What did I do?"

"Why is there blood on your hands and clothes?"

The cabinet leader paused and flipped his hands over. Tears rolled from his eyes when he spotted the blood. His chest heaved, and he lifted fear-filled eyes to Hector. "I-I-I don't know."

Hector hadn't seen the dead, but the truth was burned into his mind as if he had been there. He heard the screams and knew some of the members had tried to make a run for it, only to find the doors locked. Their bodies lay scattered throughout the meeting room.

"I don't know how this blood got here," Loukas whispered. "You have to believe me."

Hector grabbed him by the front of his chiton and pulled him to his feet. Then he dragged Loukas after him as everyone headed toward the pavilion. The guards there didn't even try to stop him. Hector kicked open the door and stalked to the meeting room. Before they even reached it, he smelled the blood before he saw it seeping from beneath the door. Loukas said nothing until Hector swung the door open to show him the bodies within.

"Nay. I-I...I couldn't have done this," Loukas murmured, tears rolling down his face. He couldn't look at the figures.

The mob behind them strained for a look at the carnage. Their shock quickly turned to outrage. Loukas, who had once stood proudly and arrogantly in front of all, now saw his life crumbling around him. He covered his face with his hands and sobbed pitifully.

Someone grabbed for Loukas. Hector swung his gaze to the individual and stared until the man released Loukas. No one else dared to touch him as Hector walked his prisoner out of the building. Loukas didn't ask for mercy, nor did he ask what would happen to him. It probably hadn't hit him yet that his life was over. The island demanded peace and safety, and Loukas had broken that.

Hector took him to the beach. Once there, he shifted. Loukas looked up at him tearfully before Hector wrapped a large hand around him and flew out over the ocean. There, he released Loukas to the waves. Hector stared north across the vast sea, where the rest of his brethren were. He had missed Shaw and Nia's ceremony and feared he would miss a lot more.

"Return to me."

He heard Agathi's voice on the wind, and his body obeyed without hesitation now that he had completed the island's task. As he flew back, Hector's gaze met Emilia's before they slid to the right, where Agathi stood next to her.

THIRTY-EIGHT

Come to meeeeeeee…

The voice from her earlier vision in the cave repeated the same call in her head. She had tried to get there to free Hector but failed. However, if the island called to her, then she still had a chance.

She looked away before Loukas's body hit the water. The drop was from so high that it wouldn't have mattered how he tried to enter the ocean, it would've killed him instantly. She hadn't liked him, but she had never wished for his death.

"What did you do, Agathi?" Emilia asked.

Agathi's look of mock horror turned her stomach. "I don't have any idea what you're talking about. As you can see, Highvale has its protector. Hector will stop anyone who threatens the island. Including you."

She had been expecting the threat. Yet her ex-friend's words still cut deep. Emilia faced her, seeing Agathi for who she really was. "I've done nothing, and you know it."

"That isn't for me to decide." Agathi looked toward Hector.

Emilia followed her gaze and watched the sun reflecting off his sea green scales. He was magnificent, his raw power startling and breathtaking to watch. She had stared at the statues for years, wondering what a dragon might look like in real life. None of her fantasies had come close to his impressive grandeur.

"Return to me," Agathi stated.

Emilia briefly closed her eyes, her heart clenching. The sight of Hector returning to Agathi was tough to behold. Emilia had failed him. It was up to her to make things right. One way or another.

"You dressed to impress him, didn't you?"

It took a moment for Agathi's words to penetrate Emilia's haze of sorrow and regret. She remained silent. It was her way of getting back at Agathi since the woman hated being ignored or snubbed.

"No amount of finery would make you hold his attention," Agathi asserted. "He's mine."

"*He* isn't an object to be owned," Emilia replied before she could stop herself.

Agathi grinned, her gaze raking over Emilia in disgust. Hector dropped beside Agathi. He rose from his crouch as clothes covered his glorious body and tattoo. Emilia fought not to reach out to him. She looked behind Agathi to where Eurielle stood, watching everything. Emilia had no idea where Rhi was anymore, and she had given her and Lotti plenty of time for the next part of the plan.

Emilia felt the same pull toward the sea she had after her vision earlier. She needed to get to the beach, but Agathi would prevent it if she tried to leave. Her ex-friend had everything planned out, and Emilia wagered that her death was part of that plan.

Agathi winked at her before facing those gathering in front of the guild again. "My fellow citizens. I'm heartbroken to announce that one of the elected members of the cabinet, Loukas, has slain the others."

"Conveniently, you weren't there!"

Emilia tensed at the sound of Teo's voice.

Agathi kept her composure, but her gaze searched the crowd for him. "It's true. I was here, at the guild, running late to the meeting Loukas called. Fate's hand intervened and kept me out of harm's way."

"We need another election," someone said.

Agathi took a step forward. "Another election will take place as soon as it can be set up. In the meantime, I want everyone to know that as the sole remaining cabinet member, I will do all I can to keep the city running smoothly." She motioned to Hector. "With the Dragon King by my side. You saw the island's swift response to murder. We've suffered a huge blow this day, but we will come through it."

"Liar!"

Teo again, his voice louder this time. Emilia clenched her hands and turned to the crowd. She searched the faces for the boy. He was moving around, making it difficult for anyone to locate him, but it wouldn't be long before someone turned him in.

The awkward silence that followed Teo's declaration agitated Agathi. Emilia took advantage of that. "I think you should withdraw from the cabinet and let a new one be elected from the guilds and citizens."

Hatred shot from Agathi's eyes as she glared at Emilia. "This doesn't concern you."

"She's a citizen, which means it concerns her and the rest of us. That's the law," a woman in the middle of the crowd said.

Emilia could feel Agathi's rage growing. She stood her ground against her and pushed even more. She had to get the seer to react. "And as a citizen, I move to exclude Agathi from being considered by the Oracle guild for any elected seat of the people."

"Stop while you still can," Agathi murmured under her breath.

"What are you going to do? Convince someone to kill me?" Emilia asked loudly enough for others to hear.

Agathi moved to stand closer to Hector. "Detain her."

"For what?" someone shouted.

When Hector locked eyes with her, Emilia started to move back. Somehow, she remained in place. He stalked across the short distance separating them and wrapped his hands around her wrist in a tight grip.

"Don't let her speak again," Agathi told him.

Murmurs of surprise and dismay spread through the crowd. Emilia had known it wouldn't take much to force Agathi to show everyone who she really was. Hector's other hand lifted and clamped over her mouth. She looked into his eyes, but the man she had come to know was no longer there.

She leaned into his hand. It might very well be the last time they were this close. It pained her to see him ensnared in Agathi's plan. She regretted that she had been deceived by someone she'd considered a sister. Of all those she thought might hurt her, Emilia had never thought it would be Agathi. But what was done was done.

Emilia leaned back a hair and whispered to Hector, "I will make this right."

Fight, damn you! Take back control!

Hector screamed at himself as he continued to strain against Eurielle's hold. He hadn't yet figured out why she had handed control to Agathi. Nothing about the pair made sense. And without the ability to speak to Eurielle, he might never know.

At least he was next to Emilia again. He could once more look into her eyes. He had silently begged her to stop antagonizing Agathi, even though he understood exactly what Emilia was doing. It would only make things worse for her later, though. He felt her lips move against his palm and heard her words over the roar of the crowd around them.

"I will make this right."

If only he could let her know that he was still here. Rhi hadn't made contact, and he didn't begrudge her that. She didn't know that he was aware of what was happening. Everyone saw the robot he was and assumed he was completely under Agathi's control.

At least he knew the island trumped her. It did little in the way of helping him get free, but it was something.

"I'm sorry I wasn't quick enough this morning to sever the link," Emilia whispered.

Agathi was speaking to the crowd, but he drowned out her voice to focus on Emilia. He tried to shake his head. He even got it to move slightly.

"I should've been honest with you from the beginning," she continued. "I should've told you why you couldn't stay the moment you appeared."

He wanted his lips on her mouth, so the feel of her warm breath against his palm was agony. He craved her, and only her.

But he'd been too blind to see it. She was his mate, and to be without her meant death for him. However, that was preferable to being under Agathi's control.

You moved your head. It was only a fraction of an inch, but you did it. Do it again!

He was drowning in the memory of Emilia's blue eyes as he recalled their moonlit swim. He could still taste her kisses, could still feel her body clenching around his fingers as she peaked.

Fingers grabbed his chin and jerked his head to the side. He suddenly found himself looking into Agathi's face.

"Did you hear me? I said kill Emilia. She's a threat to the citizens," Agathi demanded.

The crowd had been worked up and shouted among themselves. He should've been paying attention to her and what she said, but if it was a choice between Agathi or his mate, he would choose Emilia every time.

"You doona get to decide who dies," he replied.

Agathi's dark eyes flared before they narrowed. "You can't defy me."

"I am bound to the island. I protect it and the citizens from danger."

"She is a danger to our safety," Agathi argued.

"She's no'."

Fury contorted Agathi's face. "She will be. You'll see."

His stomach curdled with fear. He knew Agathi had something to do with the cabinet murders, but she hadn't actually killed them. Loukas had done the deed, which is why he had been punished. So far, all Agathi had done was talk. But therein lay the rub. She had somehow convinced Loukas. Had she manipulated

Eurielle, too? She would attempt to do the same to Emilia if given the chance. He had no choice but to take her life.

It would end his right then. A dragon couldn't kill his mate. But if Emilia was a threat to the island and it demanded retribution, he wouldn't have a choice. It wouldn't matter what Agathi said.

He let out a bellow in his head when Emilia pressed a kiss to his palm. Agathi had set the perfect trap, and he had walked right into it. He had to find a way out of the tangled web while ensuring Emilia's survival. Because she was as caught as he was now.

The mob grew louder as they fought among themselves. How long until one of them hurt someone? How long until they came after Agathi?

"Bring her," Agathi demanded. Even she knew that things were quickly getting out of control.

Hector hoped Teo was somewhere away from the crowd. It didn't surprise him that the boy was helping Emilia. He was a good lad. Hector wished Teo was at Iron Hall and away from all this nonsense. Agathi spun and strode into the building. He followed, his hand still wrapped around Emilia's wrist.

"Take her to the prison below and return to me," Agathi told him as she and Eurielle walked the other way.

The deeper he got as he descended below the main building, the more repulsed Hector became. Emilia didn't attempt to talk him out of it or beg to be released. She didn't struggle to get out of his grip. She merely walked beside him as if they were out for a casual stroll. And that slayed him as nothing else could.

Teo had told him how bad the prison was, but it was even worse than the lad had described. Hector told his feet to stop walking. He visualized his body halting, but it still didn't obey him. He came to the first cell of the prison and put Emilia inside. His fingers loosened instantly, and he shut the door, locking her within.

He looked at her through the square hole in the door. She turned to face him, her lips softening into a quick smile.

"You aren't alone," Emilia said.

His gaze lingered as he took a step back and turned to leave.

THIRTY-NINE

Rhi followed Hector up the stairs, her mind racing to find a way to bring Con to the island. Then she looked at Hector and knew that no other dragons could ever get close. Not as long as Eurielle was here. That left her, Lotti, Emilia, and Teo to sort things out.

The worst battle Rhi thought she would ever be in was when she took down her mother. In that battle, the Light and Dark Fae banded together with the Dragon Kings to defeat Usaeil in a bloody, exhausting, and epic victory. But the lines of division had been clear. Things were not so well-defined on Highvale.

Rhi hated anything political. It was one of the main reasons she had refused to become Queen of the Light, even though she was a royal. In her years in the Queen's Guard, before she discovered that Usaeil was her mother, she had navigated politics daily. And hated every moment of it.

Being queen alongside Con was different. There wasn't the same duplicity and deception that could be found in both the Light and Dark courts. So, finding herself once more embroiled in a political web sickened her. But she couldn't—and wouldn't—leave Hector.

Once she followed Hector to see what Agathi's and Eurielle's next moves would be, Rhi would return and release Emilia. She had hoped Hector seeing Emilia would free him, but Rhi had miscalculated. Eurielle's hold was too strong, and he and Emilia hadn't yet realized they were mates. It was easy for her and Lotti to see, but there had been too much outside interference for Hector to recognize what stood right before him.

Rhi started getting nervous when Lotti still hadn't returned. While a powerful Fae, she was no match for Eurielle. Agathi, on the other hand...that was another story.

It had been traumatic the first time Emilia was thrown into prison. Not so much during her second stint. Once Hector was out of sight, she closed her eyes and let the memory of her earlier vision replay.

Come to me...

"I am," she whispered to the island.

She knew where to go now. If only she had known sooner. If she had, none of this would be happening. Her stomach twisted painfully when she thought about Hector's vacant eyes. He hadn't recognized her. That hurt more than Agathi's duplicity. She had bared her soul to him and told him things she had never dared to admit to another. It had been easy to talk to Hector.

One of her biggest regrets was her reaction when he told her about visiting Agathi. Years of being around her ex-friend's beauty and witnessing everyone falling at her feet had resurged a long-buried insecurity, which Emilia had taken out on Hector. And Agathi had used it against her. Hector was the one who had seen Agathi's intentions and alerted her.

Come to me...

The voice penetrated her thoughts, instantly shifting them to the sea. It wasn't a memory of her vision. It was as if someone was in her head.

Hurry.

"Emilia!"

Her eyes snapped open to find Teo standing before her.

He released a relieved sigh, his shoulders dropping as he took a step back. "I didn't think you'd wake."

"I wasn't sleeping." She looked beyond him to the open door. "I knew you would find me."

Teo's brow was creased, his blue eyes filled with worry. "I don't know where Hector is."

"I'm not going to Hector."

"What? Why? You're not giving up, are you?"

She put a hand on his shoulder and shook her head. "Never. I'm going to free him from the island."

His eyes went wild as he held out his arms at the door to block her. "You've already tried that, and it nearly killed you. I saw Hector drag you to the surface."

"I know where to go this time."

"But...I'm not a good enough swimmer to go with you."

She gently touched his smooth cheek. "Hector needs you more than I do right now. I'll be fine. I promise."

It killed her to lie to him, but convincing him would take longer than she had. She had tarried too long as it was.

"Don't treat me like a child," he stated, lifting his chin defiantly.

Emilia sighed and dropped her hand. "I do it out of love."

"I can take it. Just tell me."

It broke her heart to hear his voice wobble. He was too young to experience the things he had, but life had a way of molding individuals in ways they couldn't understand. "I'm the only one who can break his bond with the island."

"Should you, though?"

"What do you mean?"

Teo dropped his arms to his sides. "Hector protecting the island is the only thing keeping Agathi in check. If that is gone, then Agathi can make him do anything."

"Not if she doesn't know the connection has been severed."

"She may not, but he will."

Teo had a valid point, but she knew what her vision had shown her. She had believed it was meant to happen before, but she had been wrong. That was why the island hadn't allowed her to get to where she needed to go. Timing was everything.

"Do you trust me?" she asked.

He nodded his head of dark curls. "You know I do."

"Then trust that I know what I'm doing."

His face fell. "Where do you need to go? I can get you there."

"I can get there on my own. Stay out of sight. I don't want Agathi to find you." She pressed a kiss to his cheek. "Be safe."

"This feels like a farewell."

She gave him a quick smile. "Ready?"

He turned, and together they walked out of the cell. They moved silently up the stairs to the building's main floor. Teo paused at the top and spun around, his arms wrapping around her waist. She embraced him and kissed the top of his head.

"Good luck," he whispered as he released her.

She looked into his eyes. "You, too."

Emilia watched him hurry down the hall and disappear around the corner. She squared her shoulders and strode from the stairwell to her chambers without encountering anyone. Once the door was shut, she walked to the window and climbed out. Except this time, she didn't climb down the rocks to the beach, she jumped into the water.

FORTY

"Calm everyone. They're getting out of hand," Agathi told Eurielle as Hector walked into the room.

He looked at the Star Person, but if he hoped to see Eurielle's anger, he was disappointed. She sat with her arms resting along the arms of the chair. Agathi had yet to notice him as she was still watching the mob through the window.

Agathi spun around to glare irritably at Eurielle. "Did you not hear me?"

"I heard you," Eurielle replied calmly.

"Then do something."

"Why?"

Agathi gaped at her, eyes wide. "Why?" she sputtered angrily. "Can't you hear them? I need them calm."

"Then perhaps you should've thought about your words before they left your mouth."

If he had been able, Hector would've laughed.

As if she knew his thoughts, Agathi's dark eyes slid to him for a heartbeat before she refocused on Eurielle. "They have to be calm."

"You keep saying that as if it matters to me."

"It should, since it's part of me taking over Highvale."

Eurielle arched a dark brow. "Then I suggest you do something."

"I can't. They won't listen to me," Agathi bit out.

Her frustration showed in her rapid breathing and the flare of her nostrils. Hector was clapping inside his head.

Eurielle sighed. "I fail to see how this is my problem."

"You know why," Agathi said through clenched teeth.

"I know your plan, and I agreed to my part in it," Eurielle said as she waved a hand toward Hector. "That is where my involvement ends."

Agathi fisted her hands and released a shriek of exasperation. "Then we need to amend our agreement."

"I think not. I've yet to get my portion of the deal."

And there it was. The reason Eurielle had helped Agathi. Hector waited with bated breath, hoping to get specifics. What could Agathi possibly have that Eurielle wanted or needed? She had Star magic. She could get anything.

His gaze locked on Agathi. He had never asked if her magic extended beyond being a seer. Loukas had been sure he hadn't killed the other cabinet members. He believed it so strongly that it had shown in his eyes. Yet the proof was on him. The only way he could have unknowingly committed such a crime was through some type of manipulation, be it with magic or words. If Agathi had that kind of influence, then she could convince anyone to do anything. Even a Star Person with god-like supremacy.

Which meant that Agathi's reach could extend to every single person on the island if given the chance.

Why, then, hadn't she turned it on him? It couldn't be that she needed him bound to Highvale because that connection eclipsed Eurielle's. The simplest—and most logical—answer was that her kind of manipulation didn't work on dragons. It was why she worked so hard to get a King to the island and then made sure he was bound to keep him there. Thereby giving her time to sort out the rest.

There was at least one other Agathi couldn't manipulate—Emilia. Otherwise, no one would've stood between him and Agathi.

Hector had to break Eurielle's hold. If he couldn't speak and convince her to release him, then he needed to find another way. Trying to force his limbs to obey wasn't working, either. He had to disrupt Eurielle's magic somehow. Her presence was like a phantom in his mind, there but out of reach.

He fixated on that existence, hoping he might be able to push it out if he could lock on it. Each time he got close, it skittered away like a cockroach—and the angrier he became. The emotion focused him, making him more resolute to tackle the presence. He shut out Agathi and Eurielle and put all his attention on confronting the unwelcome resident. It might all be for naught, but he was a warrior by nature. He would continue to fight until his last breath left his body.

The more he chased, the more elusive the presence became.

Until it suddenly stopped running.

One moment, Hector was in a room with Eurielle and Agathi. The next, he was in a black room facing...himself.

Something was wrong with Hector. His eyes were open, but they were blank. Rhi tried not to panic but was quickly plummeting into that deadly abyss. Con would never forgive her if Hector died. None of the Kings would.

Where was Lotti?

Rhi could no longer wait. She had to do something. And quickly.

She put her hands over her stomach and prayed the child growing within her survived. Just as she was about to drop her veil and show herself, Lotti and Villette appeared inside the room. Rhi's knees went weak with relief.

Agathi looked at them like a monarch would a peasant who had just sprayed them with mud. "Get out."

Neither Lotti nor Villette paid her any heed. Their attention was on Eurielle. Rhi couldn't look away, even as she edged away from Hector and toward Agathi.

"Hello, sister," Villette said to Eurielle.

Agathi's face drained of color. She took a step back. Apparently, she wasn't as idiotic as Rhi had first thought.

Lotti moved toward Eurielle. "It's time to go."

There was a heartbeat of stillness as Eurielle looked between the two of them. She raised her hands, but Lotti and Villette were prepared and grabbed her, vanishing in the next instant.

FORTY-ONE

The sea felt different around Emilia. It was more than the motion of the waves that lifted and dropped her or the push and pull of the current. There was a power there she hadn't noticed before. She hadn't jumped out far enough from the rocks, yet the waves didn't slam her into them. Instead, she swam away easily.

When she was far enough out, she turned and looked back at the cliff and her bedroom. She listened for a roar or the flap of Hector's wings, but the only sounds were the birds and her ragged breaths. She swallowed the regret of not being able to say goodbye to Hector. There were so many wasted opportunities between them. Still, she wouldn't trade her time with him for anything. As messy and dangerous as it had been, she had found passion and…love.

She could say it now. She could let the wind carry her words into the sky and beyond. They might even reach Hector one day. Because he *would* survive and rejoin the other Kings. She turned her gaze to one of the dragon statues at the four corners of the island. She had been granted the privilege of not only seeing a real dragon but also knowing him. She knew what it was to be held and kissed by him.

Pleasured by him.

Emilia removed her sandals and let them fall into the depths. With one last look at the sky, she drew in a deep breath and dove. A crackling sound filled her ears as she headed straight down. Pressure built slowly, and she had to pinch her nose to equalize the pressure in her ears.

She kicked hard, her mind drifting to the past few days. Hector wasn't the only one who had changed her life. Teo had made her remember what it was like to have a family. The laughter, the learning. The love.

Then there was Rhi. Without the Fae, she might never have remembered the fortitude that had put her on a journey to Highvale. Emilia had buried that little girl to become like everyone else on the island. In doing so, she had forgotten and ignored her true self. She had desperately wanted to fit in, so she'd hidden everything that made her different.

Now, Emilia embraced all the things that made her distinctive, everything that set her apart from those on the island and everywhere else. She was never meant to be like others. No one was. She didn't know why she even wanted to be or when it had begun. It had taken her a long time to realize the mistake, but in the end, she had.

Her arms propelled her through the water as she swam deeper. The current helped her glide effortlessly to the seabed.

Hurry.

She kicked faster to heed the island's summons.

Teo didn't know where to go now. He roughly wiped away a tear that'd landed on his cheek as he walked out of Emilia's room. He had followed her, hoping she wouldn't jump. But she had. He hoped when she looked back that she would change her mind and climb out of the water. Instead, she had dove beneath the surface and hadn't come up for air.

He could no longer help her, but there was still Hector. Teo turned on his heel and made his way through the building. No one paid him any mind. They were too riled up by the deaths of the cabinet members and Agathi's words. The entire island was incensed, tensions running high. Someone needed to take control, or the words being thrown around would turn into fists. And it wouldn't be long after before someone lost their life.

He kicked into a run when he heard Agathi's bellow of rage from somewhere deep in the building.

Hector circled himself. Each time he got into a fighting stance, ready to attack, his doppelgänger did the same. Eurielle didn't just have control of his body, she had access to every memory. Which meant she could retrieve his centuries of training. What little advantage he had was wiped away in an instant. That didn't make him withdraw, however. It only spurred him on.

"What are you waiting for?" he asked his lookalike.

The clone smiled before launching itself at Hector. He braced for the hit. The doppelgänger landed a vicious punch to his gut, and all the air left Hector's lungs. He had no time to even gasp as he ducked a spinning kick. He straightened, grasped his lookalike by the arms, and rammed a knee into its back.

Neither used magic. This was about pain and domination.

The clone swung his arm. Hector raised his hand, grabbing the back of its elbow and kicking the back of its leg. The doppelgänger dropped to one knee and rolled forward, taking Hector with him.

They grappled in a tangle of limbs, each trying to get the advantage while simultaneously anticipating each other's moves.

Rhi took immense pleasure in Agathi's distress when she screamed as Eurielle vanished with Lotti and Villette. Rhi dropped her veil and leaned against the wall, waiting for the human to notice her. The moment Agathi did, her eyes widened, and panic infused her features.

"Who are you?" Agathi demanded.

Rhi contemptuously raked her gaze over the mortal. "Your worst nightmare."

"You don't want to hurt me," Agathi said serenely.

Rhi chuckled and pushed from the wall. "Oh, believe me, I want to do a lot more than hurt you."

Terror tightened Agathi's face. "You don't want to hurt me."

"You can say it a million times, and in a million different ways, but it won't change what I intend to do to you," Rhi stated.

Agathi took a frantic step back as her chest heaved. "Hector!"

Rhi raised her brows as she looked at Hector, who still hadn't moved. Then she advanced on Agathi. "You aren't nearly as smart as you think you are. How many times do you have to be told that he won't hurt someone for you?"

"But you want to do me harm."

"That's right," Rhi said with an icy smile as she continued to advance. "I do. But I never said I was doing it on the island."

Agathi's face went white as she blindly reached her hands out for something to grab, only to come up against a wall. "W-what?"

"You've made so many mistakes, but your biggest was wanting to control a King. We could've been your allies, but you only saw power."

"Y-you're a dragon?"

Rhi twisted her lips and pulled a face. "Oy. Did I forget to introduce myself?" she asked in a mockingly sweet tone. "I'm Rhi, a Light Fae. And...oh, yeah, I'm also queen of the dragons." She put her hands on the wall on either side of Agathi. "And you fekked with my family. For that, you'll pay."

Agathi fainted before Rhi could touch her. Teo burst into the room, panting as his gaze moved from Agathi to her. They both turned to Hector at the same time.

"He hasn't moved," Teo said breathlessly.

Rhi bent and used her magic to bind Agathi's hands and feet. Then she turned to Hector. "He looks different."

"What do we do?"

The chaos of the crowd outside was rising to unmanageable levels. Rhi went to the window and peered out. "We need to leave. Stay with Agathi while I get Emilia."

"I already released her."

Rhi's heart skipped a beat. Not because of Teo's words, but because she noticed his red-rimmed eyes and puffy face for the first time. "Where is she?"

His eyes filled with tears as he choked out, "Gone."

"Gone where?" she asked gently.

Teo sniffed and dashed a hand across his face to swipe at a tear. "In the sea."

Rhi squatted in front of Teo and took his hands in hers as she looked up at him. "Tell me everything."

It spilled from the boy in one long, run-on sentence with barely time for a breath. Ice coursed through her veins before he even finished. Hector had barely gotten Emilia to the surface earlier. Even if she found what she searched for in one breath, she wouldn't make it back up.

Rhi looked at Hector. She couldn't leave him. Her gaze slid to Agathi. Nor could she leave her. But Rhi also couldn't leave Emilia out there alone. There was only one option.

She straightened and grasped Agathi's feet to drag her closer to Hector. "Come," she bade Teo when he didn't move right away.

The boy immediately rushed to her side.

"Grab Hector's hand," she instructed. "And don't let go."

The moment Teo had Hector, Rhi touched him and teleported them to the cave.

Of all the people Lotti thought she would reach out to for help, Villette wasn't on the list. She was never even *considered* for the list. Yet Villette was the only one who could help in this convoluted conspiracy. It had taken Lotti far too long to find Villette, and even longer to convince her to help. Villette might be there now, but Lotti expected her to leave at any second.

Or switch sides.

If Alasdair were there, he would question her decision to bring in their mortal enemy. Villette had attempted to kill her several times. But nemesis or not, Lotti needed Villette.

"This is insane," Villette whispered beside her.

They stood on some sand dunes across from Eurielle. An unforgiving sun beat relentlessly on them as wind lifted grains, only to hurl them like tiny bullets into their exposed skin. Lotti wouldn't have chosen the desert as a battlefield and wasn't sure which of the other two had. But they were here now. Besides, it was deserted, which meant they didn't have to worry about bystanders getting hurt. Because when Star People fought, it was violent and ruthless.

Lotti took a step to the side, and sand swallowed her foot. This battle wouldn't be hand-to-hand. It rarely was when their kind battled. Power was their forte, and it was used freely and often. Lotti didn't have much experience in either battle or going up against her own kind, but the few skirmishes she had lived through had been intense and brutal. She was coming to learn that was just the way of the Star People.

"We didn't have another choice," Lotti answered.

Villette shook her head of long, blond hair, a portion of which hid the burns on the right side of her face. "I'm talking about Eurielle. Something isn't right with her."

"I told you that." It was all Lotti could do not to roll her eyes.

Villette raised her voice and called out to their sister. "This isn't you, Eurielle."

"How would you know?" Eurielle spat.

Villette's fingers curled into her hand. "I know you're a good fighter, but you've never sought battle. You always preferred to find another way."

"Seems things have changed," Eurielle replied.

Lotti decided to change the subject. "Why help Agathi against Hector? He's our friend."

"Friend?" Eurielle barked a laugh. "Is this when you play the sister card?"

Villette's eyes narrowed briefly. "We are sisters."

"Not the kind I want," Eurielle declared.

Lotti blinked against the blinding sun. "Any suggestions?" she asked Villette.

"There is one thi—"

Her words were cut off as a blast of magic struck Villette, knocking her backward. Lotti raised her hands and blocked a barrage from Eurielle, the force of which caused her to dig in her feet. The sand slid beneath her, pushing her backward.

Then Villette was beside her. She struck back at Eurielle behind Lotti's shield, landing a few good hits.

"She's strong," Villette said through clenched teeth.

"She's not holding back," Lotti said as she fought to stay on her feet. "We can't stay like this."

"On three, we split."

Lotti nodded.

"One. Two. Three," Villette called.

Lotti dropped her shield and dove to the side. She rolled and came up on one knee as she lobbed magic at Eurielle at the same time Villette did. Eurielle blocked Villette's, but Lotti's struck her shoulder, spinning her around.

She and Villette closed in on Eurielle as they continued to issue strike after strike. Eurielle didn't relent. She kept firing her own shots. Villette kept Eurielle's attention, which allowed Lotti to tackle her to the ground.

"What are you doing?" she demanded of Eurielle. "We're not your enemy."

One moment, Lotti had Eurielle. The next, she was flying through the air and landing on the slope of the dune, rolling the rest of the way to the bottom. Lotti blinked the sand from her eyes and got to her feet. She looked up to find Villette and Eurielle locked in combat. There was a lot of history between them.

Lotti called to her powers and levitated to the top of the dune, landing behind Eurielle. She fired a shot at the spot behind Eurielle's knee that dropped her. Eurielle vanished right before Villette's next volley struck. Lotti and Villette looked at each other before scanning the desert for their sister.

But Eurielle was gone.

Hector was as riddled with wounds as his double. And none of their injuries were healing. This wasn't the real world, though. This was in his mind, which meant magic didn't heal him. Hector was exhausted and weary, but his doppelgänger looked ready to go another ten rounds despite his wounds.

"You can no' win," his lookalike said. "Give up. You know you want to."

"You know nothing about me," Hector stated.

His clone chuckled as they circled each other again. "You know that isna true."

Hector attacked. He aimed high, but went low at the last moment, sweeping his double's legs out from under him. The other landed on his hands and then jumped to his feet. He tried to elbow Hector again. It was a glancing blow, but closer than Hector liked.

He landed a jab in his doppelgänger's side. The double came around with a wicked punch to Hector's jaw. He heard a crack as pain exploded in the side of his face. Almost immediately, the clone landed a hook to the other side. Hector felt himself falling backward. He fell hard but rolled to the side before the lookalike stomped on his face.

Emilia tried not to think about how her lungs burned as she reached the seabed. She had come this far. She couldn't stop now.

Closer. Nearly there.

She wasn't sure when she knew that the voice was the island. It was odd to acknowledge a piece of land's sentience, but who was she to question it? The island needed her. Hector needed her.

The reef was filled with brightly colored fish and other aquatic animals. She propelled herself along, moving toward something she couldn't define or explain. But it was there, waiting. She released a little more air from her lungs to ease the tension. Within seconds, the pain returned as her body told her she had to breathe. Emilia pushed past the anguish and scanned the reef for the cave entrance. There were many openings, but none were the cave she sought.

Another current came from behind her and boosted her forward several feet. She did a double take as she found herself outside the cavern she had been looking for.

Come.

Emilia hung in the water for a moment before swimming into the mouth of the cave.

Hector got to his feet and rammed a shoulder into his double, lifting him slightly before slamming him to the ground. They fell together. Hector slipped out of his grip before his twin could lock his ankles around his neck. A foot caught Hector in the back of the leg, dropping him to a knee.

The doppelgänger jumped up and aimed a fist at Hector's broken jaw. Hector rolled out of the way and to his feet. Then, they were trading punches. Face. Body. Then face again. More body shots. Each hit harder than the last.

Hector grabbed his double's wrist and twisted it, forcing his twin to turn. There was a loud pop as the shoulder dislocated. Hector raised his foot, ready to kick him to his knees, when the clone swung his elbow back for a third time. Hector ducked and caught his wrist, then pulled both arms behind the lookalike's back until he screamed in pain.

From the moment Emilia entered the cave, it didn't just look different, it felt different. A shimmer of light punctured the darkness, leading her deeper toward another entrance, this one small enough that she wondered if she could get through.

She got through without incident and found herself in a massive cavern. The light she had seen shimmered all around her in a rainbow of colors. Try as she might, Emilia couldn't pinpoint where it originated from, and she was too deep for it to be the sun. She stopped swimming and remained suspended in the water, slowly turning in a circle to take in the sheer size of the area. She expelled the last of her air, and the urge to inhale was so strong she had to fight not to drag water into her lungs.

Finally.

Emilia scanned the cavern, but her brain was getting fuzzy from lack of oxygen.

You won't die here.

But she couldn't breathe, and if she couldn't breathe, she would definitely die.

Then breathe.

Emilia fought to hold her breath for as long as she could. Her body finally took over, and she inhaled, ready to choke on water. But nothing happened. Water didn't enter her body. She could almost pretend she was walking on land except that she was deep in a cave.

I've waited a long time to meet you.

Without knowing why, Emilia swam deeper into the cave. She passed a section of rock formations that looked like pillars, and the space narrowed to another entrance as large as a doorway. She kicked her feet and continued through it, only to come out in an even bigger cavern. There, in the middle, sat a huge plant with long, narrow glowing white petals that rose straight from the ground and moved with the water.

Closer.

Emilia swam to it. She tucked her legs and lengthened them down to find herself walking along the bottom of the cavern. The plant towered over her. The petals parted. This was what the vision had shown her. This was where she freed Hector. She lifted her foot and walked inside.

FORTY-TWO

Hector forced the clone to his knees before placing his foot on his spine. Hearing his own screams of agony made him hesitate. Then he remembered what he was fighting for. *Who* he was fighting for.

"I didna invite you into my head, and I willna allow you to remain. I am Hector, King of Sea Greens, and you doona belong!" He thrust his foot forward, severing his doppelgänger's spine.

His double vanished, and with him, the black room. Hector blinked and found himself standing in a familiar cave. He raised his arm to test his theory and smiled when he flexed his fingers. Then he spotted Rhi and Teo.

"Are you...you?" Rhi asked as she stood.

Hector nodded. "Barely, but aye. I'm free of Eurielle's hold."

"Bloody hell. It's about time," she murmured.

Teo nodded, though his eyes were sunken.

Hector scanned the cave for Emilia but found Agathi bound and gagged at Rhi's feet instead. The human glowered at him before turning hate-filled eyes to Rhi.

"She wouldn't shut up," Rhi explained with a shrug. "Lotti and Villette took Eurielle, so you should be good."

Hector wanted to ask about that but was more concerned with Emilia's absence. "Where is Emilia?"

Rhi hesitated as she turned her head toward the entrance.

It was Teo who said, "In the sea."

Terror turned Hector's blood into shards of ice. He raced from the cave, only to be brought to his knees two steps later. He threw back his head and bellowed as pain ripped through his body. It was like someone had taken a dull saw and cut through him. With every beat of his heart, his connection to the island lessened. He dropped forward onto his hands and curled his fingers into the sand. He was sure his chest was being torn open, but when he looked down, there was no gaping hole, no blood.

"Hector!" Teo cried.

He couldn't get words past his lips. He just hoped Rhi kept Teo in the cave. Agony sliced through him, his limbs stiffening in response. He gritted his teeth and shifted. The pain instantly vanished.

Hector launched into the air before diving into the water. He used his wings to propel him forward while covering vast distances in his search for Emilia. Fear coalesced in his stomach the longer he went without finding her. He circled the island once before diving deeper in his frantic pursuit.

There was no way Emilia could survive the pressures of deep water without some kind of aid. He was about to give up and shift his attention to the currents, thinking her body had been dragged away, when he felt a rush of the island's magic surround him. He stilled as it wound around his body before gently tugging him.

Hector leaned into it. When it pulled away, he followed it to the entrance of a cave.

He had to shift to his human form because he couldn't fit through the opening. Once inside the small cavern, he saw another even smaller entrance. He swam through it but had to wiggle and pull himself out when he got stuck. He then found himself in a much larger cavern. The sides of the rock were striated from centuries of water moving over it. Multicolored lights floated around him melodiously. The peace within reminded him of Dreagan.

Magic is magic, no matter where it is.

It wasn't the first time he had heard the magic of the island speaking to him, but it was louder here. The fear that had gripped him since he learned that Emilia was in the water lessened the longer he remained in the cavern.

Hector continued swimming, passing an expanse of stone pillars. It wasn't long after, that he saw what looked like a doorway. When he entered, his gaze was drawn to the plant with its glowing white petals. The flower pulsed with magic, each vibration sending ripples of magic outward in the water.

The long, narrow petals parted so he could see inside. Emilia was at the center of the flower, hanging upright with her blond hair floating around her and her eyes closed. He used his arms to propel him forward. No air bubbles rose from her nose or mouth. He halted before her, knowing she was the one who had removed whatever had bound him to the island—and taken his place.

He touched her cheek, and her eyes opened. Her pupils and irises were white like they had been during her vision, but they had a glow now that matched the flower. Suddenly, Emilia's gaze shifted to him, and she smiled. Her eyes then rolled back in her head, and she went limp. Hector brought her against him, fearing the worst, but he felt her heart beating against his chest.

After he gathered her in his arms, he turned and began swimming out of the flower. It never closed around him, nor did anything stop him as he made his way out of the cave and back into the sea. Hector paused outside the cave and shifted into his true form. He gently held Emilia in his palm before pushing off the seafloor, thrusting them to the surface, and then launching into the air.

He flew to the top of the nearest mountain and landed. After laying Emilia on the ground, he returned to his human form and bent over her. He carefully moved some hair that clung to the side of her face. Several tense moments passed before her chest rose with a deeply inhaled breath. Then her eyes fluttered open. His relief was so great that all he could do was pull her to his chest and hold her while squeezing his eyes closed.

"I thought I'd lost you." He pulled back to look into her cobalt eyes. "I thought you were gone."

She pressed her hand to his cheek. "I am."

He shook his head and tightened his grip. "Nay, lass. I'm holding you."

"The human me is gone," she explained.

Hector glanced at the sea as an image of her within the large flower rose. "If you're no' human, what are you?"

"I was chosen by the magic of Zora to protect Highvale."

He stared at her, letting her words sink in. "Like I was chosen to be King of my clan?"

Her lips curved into a smile. "Exactly like that."

"So, you're a queen."

"Nay," she replied with a quick shake of her head. "I'm merely a guardian."

He moved his thumb against her back. "You broke my bond with the island."

"It was meant to be."

"You could've died."

She rested her hands on his shoulders. "I did, in a way. And I would do it all over again, even if I didn't get to live. Because it would've been for you."

He swallowed as emotion swelled in his chest. Just as he was about to speak, he heard someone clear their throat behind him. Hector turned his head to the side and spotted Rhi's boots.

"Sorry to interrupt, but Teo is losing his mind," Rhi said.

Hector grimaced since he had forgotten about the lad. "We'll be right there."

"Don't forget some clothes," Rhi replied.

Emilia grinned as he called clothes to himself. He also replaced her wet chiton with a dry one before he stood and pulled her up with him. They walked to the edge of the mountain and looked down at the shore.

"Do you trust me?" he asked.

She nodded. "Always."

A bubble of laughter burst from her when he lifted her into his arms. Then he stepped off the edge. Wind howled around them as they fell. The smile on Emilia's face wiped away all the fear that had gripped him earlier. He landed gently and released her legs so she could stand on her own. Rhi appeared in front of them and reached out to touch them both. In the next instant, they were in the cave.

"You were taking too long," she said tightly.

"Emilia! Hector!" Teo shouted and threw himself at them.

They caught him, holding his thin body against them as they exchanged a look of remorse. Hector glanced at Rhi and saw her eyes watering.

Hector dropped down to face Teo. "We're all right, lad. Everything is fine."

"I'm okay," Emilia told him with a smile.

Teo hugged her, his arms going around her waist. Then, the boy threw his arms around Hector's neck.

He enfolded Teo in his arms. "It's all over."

"Not all," Teo said as he stepped back and pointed at Agathi.

The brunette was still bound and gagged, but Rhi had propped her into a sitting position.

Hector stood and looked at Emilia. "It's your call. What do you want to do?"

"If she goes anywhere else, she can harm others as she has here," Emilia answered.

Rhi twisted her lips. "Not if she can't talk."

Agathi tried to talk around her gag, but it came out garbled. No one paid her any attention anyway.

"She did a lot of damage to others on the island. I think there should be a trial where the Highvalers decide her fate," Emilia said.

Hector shrugged. "That sounds fair. It's more than she would give you."

"I know," Emilia replied with a sad smile.

Rhi rubbed her hands together to get their attention. "All right. I have lots of questions, but I think it'd be prudent to put Agathi somewhere until the trial."

"Agreed," Hector said.

Agathi let out a scream as Rhi reached for her. It was cut off when the two disappeared.

"What happens now?" Teo asked.

Hector motioned to him. "What do you want to happen?"

"I'd like to stay with you. Both of you," he amended, looking between them. "You two will be together, right?"

"And that's my cue," Rhi said as she appeared. "I have to get to Iron Hall. Teo, why don't you come with me? Con wants to meet you."

Teo's eyes grew round with excitement. "Really?" Then he darted a look at Hector and Emilia.

"It will only be a short visit," Rhi hurried to say. She leaned close, and, in a loud whisper, said, "I think they need some time alone."

Teo nodded gravely before moving closer to Rhi. "I'm going with her, but I'll be back."

"You do that, lad," Hector said with a chuckle.

Emilia kissed the top of his head. "Have fun."

Once again, Rhi left, and Hector turned his head to Emilia.

"What about Eurielle?" Emilia asked.

"Lotti and Villette are taking care of her."

"And the people? Are they still riled?"

Hector opened his hearing and heard the faint sounds of angry voices. "They are."

"I need to calm them before it gets out of hand."

"I think it already is. Want to make an entrance?"

She gave him a sideways look. "What do you have in mind?"

FORTY-THREE

Emilia would never tire of viewing Hector in his true form. Her first time had been all too brief, but now, she could look her fill. He stood half in the water and half on the beach in all his dragon glory. The sun sinking into the horizon glinted off his scales, making him look otherworldly. He dwarfed her, and she understood why some would fear his kind. Their size alone was enough to make anyone pause.

His idea of making an entrance was flying her into the city. She had to admit, she wanted to be on his back as he took to the skies. It would be a short flight, but a flight, nonetheless.

He lowered himself and watched her with pearly eyes as she made her way to him. She smiled when she stroked her palm along his scales and found them hard and warm. Then she climbed up to settle at the base of his thick neck between two of the horns that ran down his spine.

Trepidation filled her when Hector stood, and she rocked to the side. For a heartbeat, she thought she might fall off. He made a sound that vibrated through her body, then turned to face the ocean and unfurled his wings. She looked out at their long, leathery length as she tightened her hold on the horn in front of her.

Her stomach dropped as he leapt into the air. A rush of wind pressed into her face. He quickly leveled his body and turned them to fly over the island. Hector released a roar that made her ears hurt. It got everyone's attention as the crowd froze and turned to look at them. Emilia looked down upon the crowd, watching them as they gaped at her and Hector.

He circled the island again before returning to the crowd that hadn't moved far from the guild house. Hector remained suspended over them and waited for her, his wings beating loudly. His idea had sounded simple, but that was before she was dangling over them. However, she knew Hector wouldn't let her fall to her death.

Emilia got both legs over the same side and slid down Hector's shoulder. He reached out his hand and caught her before lowering his arm. She stepped out, dropping only a few feet to the street. Then he shifted into his human form and landed beside her. He smiled at her, and she couldn't help but return it.

"Citizens of Highvale," Emilia called out. "A lot has happened today that has set neighbor against neighbor. This island is a sanctuary, and it will remain that way. The cabinet was slain, and the individual responsible has been confined. There will be a trial in the coming days, where Agathi's crimes will be listed, and you will decide her fate."

She paused and took a breath. "We will hold elections for a replacement cabinet immediately. The committee that oversees the elections and the results will accept nominations beginning tomorrow morning. We must remember what the island means not just to us but to all magicals. We don't own the city. We're just its caretakers for those who come after us. I beg you to return to your homes and businesses and carry on as usual. Hector will remain to ensure that nothing else disrupts the city until the new cabinet is in place."

Emilia braced for questions or someone questioning her being there, but none came. The crowd disbursed and returned to life as she had asked them to.

"Why did you no' tell them you're Highvale's guardian?" Hector asked.

"I might one day, but not this day. Especially not when they're looking for leaders. I don't want them to think that's what I am. Because I'm not."

He turned her to face him and smiled. "You're pretty incredible, do you know that?"

"So are you," she said and moved closer.

Desire filled his eyes as he pressed her against him and began to lower his head.

"I, ah, hate to interrupt," said a voice behind them.

Hector let out a strangled laugh and pressed his forehead to hers for a heartbeat. Then he straightened. "Lotti."

Emilia had known the voice sounded familiar. She turned to face the Star Person.

"How did it go?" Hector asked.

Lotti blew out a weary sigh. "We had a small clash, but Eurielle left before we could get to the heart of matters."

"In other words, we still doona know why she helped Agathi," Hector said.

Lotti shook her head. "I'm afraid not. I searched the entire island for her, and she isn't here."

"That's a relief," he murmured.

Emilia nodded and blew out a breath. "But we don't know where she is?"

"Not yet," Lotti said. "We'll keep looking."

"We? You're going to continue working with Villette?" Hector asked.

Lotti shrugged. "She knows Eurielle. And right now, we need her."

"Seems we've been saying that a lot," he stated.

Emilia bowed her head to Lotti. "Thank you for your help. We owe you a debt."

"You owe me nothing. It's what friends do," Lotti replied and looked around. "I don't see Rhi."

Hector said, "She took Teo to Iron Hall. Thanks for being here for me, but I think things are back to normal."

"Ah," Lotti said as she looked between them. "Hope to see you soon, Emilia."

She grinned. "I hope so, too."

"Hector," Lotti said, not bothering to hide her grin before she vanished.

Finally, Emilia was alone with Hector. She looked at him as he looked at her. He held out his hand, and she took it. Then, he led her down the street to the beach. They didn't speak until they were inside their cave.

Their cave.

She faced him and looked into his dark eyes. "I want to say so much, but right now, I just want you. Your body against mine. With no interruptions this time."

"Fuck yes," he murmured, yanking her against him and claiming her mouth in a sizzling kiss.

She was drowning in pleasure, swept away by desire. Her body throbbed with a need that only Hector could quench. She reached between them and slid her hand along the hard length of his arousal. His body went taut before he groaned and deepened the kiss.

Her heart was pounding, her blood running like fire through her veins. He walked her backward into her alcove.

She tore her mouth from his and said, "I want to see you."

In the next instant, their clothes were gone. He didn't hide his tattoo now, and she spread her fingers and ran her hands over his shoulders and through the light dusting of hair on his chest before caressing down his rock-hard stomach. She paused when she spotted his arousal jutting between them. She swallowed to wet her suddenly dry mouth and slowly wrapped her fingers around him, stroking up and down his long length.

He groaned but didn't move to stop her. She released him and trailed her fingers along his stomach as she walked behind him. Tight sinew covered every inch of his amazing body. She stroked down his back, eyeing his spectacular arse.

Suddenly, he spun around and yanked her against him, his mouth descending on her. The kiss seized, it captured.

It ensnared.

She was sinking into oblivion and went willingly, freely. Emilia tightened her arms around his neck to ensure he went with her.

In the next instant, she was on the bed, Hector's hands on either side of her head as he leaned over her. Her heart missed a beat at the sight of his blatant need. It made her knees weak and caused her entire body to shiver excitedly about what was to come.

He slowly lowered himself atop her until their mouths were breaths apart. Then, his lips pressed against hers. He settled between her legs, his cock pressed against her stomach as his tongue swept into her mouth.

Hector had never been so wild for a woman before. He craved Emilia, hungered for her as if she were the very essence of his life force. He cupped her breast and rolled a nipple between his fingers. She tore her lips from his and moaned. He trailed kisses down her neck to her other breast, wrapping his lips around the turgid peak and giving it a pull.

She cried out and rocked against him. "I'm on fire," she said hoarsely, her back arching.

That's exactly how he wanted her. Burning from the inside out with the same desire he felt. He held her arms above her head with one of his hands and raised his head to look at her kiss-swollen lips. Her chest heaved from her rapid breaths. He glanced at her lovely breasts and the nipples that responded so quickly to his touch. And her lips.

He slowly ran his free hand down her stomach to her sex. She sucked in a breath, watching him with cobalt eyes, her mouth parted slightly. He stopped just short of touching her.

"I want to feel all of you." As soon as he said the last word, he slid a finger inside her.

Her eyes rolled back in her head, and her back arched again. He claimed her lips as he delved his finger deeper into her tight, wet sheath. He moved it in and out, mimicking his tongue. Then he added a second finger. She spread her legs wider to allow him more access. He made use of the opportunity by teasing her clit with his thumb.

Her entire body started to tremble as he brought her closer and closer to orgasm, and then he gave her the release she sought. Her eyes flew open, her lips parted on a silent scream, and her walls clamped around his fingers. He watched it all with amazement.

Emilia was soaring high, even as the last vestiges of the orgasm racked her body, Hector's fingers still moved within her, drawing it out. His thumb flicked over her sensitive clit, sending her into another mini climax.

And all it did was make her crave him even more.

She shoved at his shoulder and rolled him onto his back as she rose on her knees over him. His dark eyes watched her, daring her to do whatever it was she wanted. And, oh, the things she wished to do to him. She could spend eternity in bed with him, and it wouldn't be nearly long enough. She reached between them and grasped his engorged cock. He sucked in a breath when she ran her hand up and down his length. His body tensed when she circled the tip with her thumb.

Holding his gaze, she brought him to her entrance. As soon as she felt the head of his rod against her, she lowered herself upon him. She dropped her head back, her eyes sliding closed at the feel of him stretching her, filling her. It felt...right.

Once she was fully seated, she lifted her head and looked down at him. A fine sheen of sweat covered his skin. His hands were braced on her hips, and the fire in his eyes made her stomach quiver. She began to slowly rock back and forth. The deeper his fingers dug into her hips, the faster she moved. She had to brace her hands on his chest at one point.

But their gazes never broke.

She could feel the tightening of her body as passion and pleasure reigned. Their breathing was harsh, their bodies sliding against each other sensually. A moan slipped past her lips as her body wound tighter. The climax hit her quickly, sending her spiraling into oblivion.

Hector ground his teeth, intent on maintaining firm control of himself as pleasure erupted over Emilia's face, and her body jerked around his cock. He waited until he couldn't hold back any longer. Then, he flipped her onto her back and rose onto his knees. He thrust into her hard and deep.

She lifted her legs and locked them around his waist, her ankles urging him to go faster. He looked down into a face branded in his mind. She opened herself and her body to him without any reservations. She touched him—profoundly. Deeper than anyone ever had. His hips jerked a final time, and he buried himself deep, whispering her name as the climax took him.

When he could move again, he pulled out of her and fell onto his back, dragging her with him. He held her close as she snuggled against him.

"Lass?"

She was yanked from sleep by someone rubbing up and down her legs.

"Lass? Did I wear you out?"

Emilia grinned at the sound of Hector's voice. "I'm afraid so."

"So, I doona suppose you'll be wanting this?"

Warm breath tickled her skin. She opened her eyes to see him on his stomach between her legs, his mouth close to her sex. "I'm awake."

"Are you now?" he murmured with a heart-stopping, crooked smile.

She spread her legs wider. "Very, very awake."

He chuckled, then dipped his head, his tongue lightly swirling around her clit. She sucked in a breath as delicious warmth spread through her. He was thorough, tasting every part of her. He was soft, he was hard. He was relentless.

Every lick pushed her closer to climax. As if he knew, he doubled his efforts, gripping her hips with his big hands when she tried to get away from the pleasurable onslaught that bordered on being too much yet wasn't enough. Need spiraled within her, tightening with each heartbeat. She reached for the orgasm, but she also wasn't ready for the pleasure to be over. Everything felt so... good.

With one flick of his tongue, he sent her tipping over the edge into ecstasy. The blissful waves racked her body over and over. Time stopped. The world disappeared.

Leaving only her, the pleasure, and...Hector.

When she finally returned to herself, she could barely remember her name. Her limbs were heavy, her body sated. And yet, she wanted more.

Hector rose and ran his tongue over her stomach to a nipple.

He drew the peak into his mouth and flicked his tongue around it. She thrust her fingers into his hair and held his head as desire shot from her breast to her center. Then he flipped her onto her stomach and raised her hips.

She waited expectantly as he smoothed a hand down the center of her back and over her arse. He repeated the gesture twice more. The last time, his finger trailed down between her ass cheeks to her core. He thrust one finger, then two inside her. Her body hungrily clutched at them. He returned to caressing her back, ignoring her sex that throbbed for his cock or his fingers. She didn't care as long as something was inside her to ease the ache.

"Please," she whimpered.

"Och, lass."

Then his cock rubbed against her. With one thrust of his hips, he filled her. She moaned in response. He began an easy tempo that soon had them both gasping with pleasure. Sweat covered them as his body slapped against hers. He held her hips still, preventing her from moving back against him. Another orgasm began to build.

"Fuck. I can feel you tightening around me," he bit out.

She pressed her cheek into the covers and hurtled toward another climax.

"Emilia!" he shouted.

She felt the tremor run through him as his seed spilled inside her the same instant she orgasmed.

FORTY-FOUR

Hector sat with Emilia on the beach, watching the sun rise on a new day. They'd spent the night pleasuring each other, and there had been little time for talking. He looked over at her to see her smiling with her eyes closed.

"You're staring," she said.

He grinned. "Hard to look away from someone so beautiful."

Her eyes opened, and she turned her head to him. "You make me feel beautiful."

"Because you are, lass."

She nodded and rested her head on his shoulder.

Hector looked out at the sea. "I love you."

Her head lifted, and her gaze met his. Her smile was slow as it spread over her face. "I love you."

Hearing the words loosened the knot around his heart. Hector shifted toward her. "When Eurielle brought me to that room, and Agathi told me we were to be mated, all I could think about was you." He cupped her face in his hands, holding back her blond curls. "I knew in that instant that you were my mate. Did I mention dragons mate for life?"

"So many things tried to keep us apart." She grabbed one of his hands and kissed his palm. "But we were destined to be together."

"How do you mean?"

She brought his hands to her lap and looked into his eyes. "When I entered the flower, the magic showed me everything. I'm not a seer. The visions it gave me were to bring me here, prepare me for you, and make things right on Highvale."

"Did it happen to tell you who created the island and all the dragon statues?"

"The magic did, through others."

Hector nodded and glanced at one of the mountain statues. "I suppose that's why all the sculptures look like dragons I know. The magic saw into the future."

"Something like that."

"Shall we spend the day decorating the cave?"

Her brows furrowed. "Why would we do that?"

"Or we can live in the city?"

"Ah," she said with a chuckle. "Just because I'm guardian of the island doesn't mean I must stay here. I can get back here if I'm needed, quicker if Rhi creates a Fae doorway."

Hector brought her hand to his lips and kissed it. "I think I can make that happen." He sobered suddenly. "We doona have to worry about any other Kings being bound, do we?"

"That's over. The Kings can come and go as they please, just like everyone else."

"That's good. Because they're going to want to see this place."

She rose to her knees and pulled him up with her. "And I wish to see Iron Hall."

"I'll show you the universe, lass," Hector promised. He gazed down at the amazing beauty. "We'll see it all together."

"Together," she whispered before she kissed him.

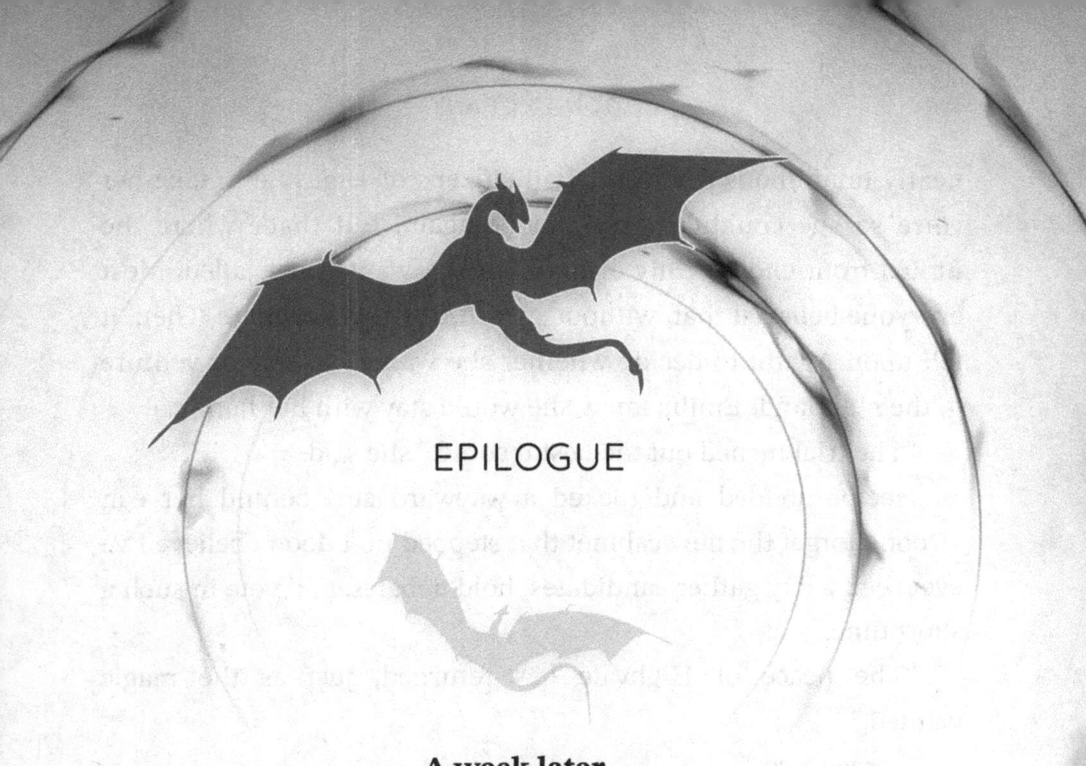

EPILOGUE

A week later…

Emilia stood on the amphitheater's stage and stared at the empty seats. It hadn't been that long ago that she had stood upon that very platform and thought her life was over—when, in fact, it had just begun.

"Going over the trial again?"

She turned and found Hector casually leaning against one of the columns. "I was actually thinking about the first time I stood up here."

"Ah. That," he said and pushed off the pillar to walk to her.

Emilia wound her arms around his neck when he reached her. "You don't have to worry about me thinking about Agathi again."

"You wouldna be human if memories of your earlier years didna rise up now and again. Besides, she opted to remain on the island. You'll see her from time to time."

Agathi's trial had been long and painful. In the end, it was a nearly unanimous decision by all citizens of Highvale to take her voice so she couldn't harm anyone again. But that's where the united front ended. Only a small portion wanted her jailed. Most everyone believed that, without speech, she was harmless. Then, it fell upon Agathi to decide whether she wanted to stay or venture to the mainland. Emilia knew she would stay with her family.

"The trial turned out the best it could," she said.

Hector nodded and tucked a wayward curl behind her ear. "Doona forget the new cabinet that stepped in. I doona believe I've ever seen a city gather candidates, hold debates, and vote in such a short time."

"The peace of Highvale has returned, just as the magic wanted."

"It seems so."

She glanced to the side. "I have something to tell you. Once I was bound to the island, I discovered why those who leave Highvale forget how the dragons are revered."

"How?" he asked.

"It's the island's way of protecting those who live within her shores. The magic knows that if humans crossed the dragon border, they would likely be killed. So, not wanting that for any magical, the magic instilled that bit of fear into those who leave."

He grunted. "Makes sense. Speaking of magic, I have a surprise."

Emilia perked up. "I do love your surprises. What is it?"

"I have to show you. Come on."

They left, hand in hand. Emilia smiled and spoke to those they passed. She no longer sought the fringes of society to hide in the shadows. She had stepped into the light, and she intended to stay.

Hector took her to the cove and stopped, a huge smile on his face. "Remember when you asked if Rhi could create a doorway to Iron Hall?"

"Did she?" Emilia asked eagerly.

"She did, indeed."

Emilia scanned the beach, her excitement dimming when she couldn't find it. "I don't see it."

"That's because it's only visible to Fae."

"Then how are we to find it? And what if someone accidentally goes through."

Hector chuckled and led her into the cave. "I would never let that happen, lass. Only the Kings, their mates, and Teo can freely come to the island. And Rhi marked the doorway for us."

"You always think of everything."

"No' always, but I do try." He turned them into the first alcove and motioned to a set of boulders in the middle that hadn't been there before. "The doorway is between those boulders."

Emilia eyed the empty space. She expected...something that would tell her it was a magical doorway, but everything looked as it had, other than the rocks. "Are you sure it's there?"

"Shall I show you?"

Her heart stuttered as she swung her eyes to him. "You mean go to Iron Hall now?"

"Why no'?" he asked with a crooked grin.

She bit her lip and looked at the supposed doorway. "I might be a little nervous."

"You're going to a place where your new family awaits. Though, there are quite a few of us, so be prepared to be inundated with everyone wanting to get to know you," he added.

A new family. How lucky was she that she had found another?

Emilia drew in a breath and nodded. "Let's go. I want to meet everyone."

"They're going to love you. Just as I do."

She tightened her hand around his as he walked forward.

"It willna hurt," he told her right before they stepped between the stones.

Marcus tried to stay away from the atrium, but it didn't matter where he was. The whispers followed him, always asking for help. With every passing hour, he feared he was losing his mind. It was what had brought him back to the antechamber.

He stood in the domed room, staring down the corridor. No matter how long or hard he looked, he saw no movement.

Help.

"Who's there?" he called.

Marcus waited, his agitation mounting. The seconds felt as interminable as centuries. His stomach tightened with dread, his heart thumped against his ribs, and his hands grew clammy. He couldn't remember the last time he had been so terrified.

Of what was down the hall.

Of going insane.

"Answer me!" he bellowed.

But there was only silence. He dropped to his knees, his head in his hands.

Help me...Marcus...

Thank you for reading DRAGON FORGED. I hope you enjoyed reading Hector and Emilia's book.

There's a bonus short story featuring Hector and Emilia. Grab it here:

https://mailchi.mp/donnagrant/dragonforged

* * *

If you want more Dragon King stories, then you won't have long to wait. DRAGON SIEGED will be out January 2026!

BUY DRAGON SIEGED NOW
at www.DonnaGrant.com

* * *

If you love the Dragon King series, you'll love the next Dark Universe book set in the Skye Druids series, AFTER MIDNIGHT…

BUY AFTER MIDNIGHT NOW
at www.DonnaGrant.com

* * *

To find out when new books release
SIGN UP FOR MY NEWSLETTER today at
https://www.tinyurl.com/DonnaGrantNews

* * *

Join my Facebook group, Donna Grant Groupies, for exclusive
giveaways and sneak peeks of future books.
https://bit.ly/DGGroupies

* * *

Keep reading for a glimpse at AFTER MIDNIGHT...

GLIMPSE AT THE NEXT DARK UNIVERSE BOOK

AFTER MIDNIGHT, SKYE DRUIDS SERIES, BOOK 7

She was always my weakness. Now she's my only hope.

She was my salvation once—wild magic in her blood, fire in her kiss, and a body I still dream about. I touched heaven with her.

Then dragged us both to hell.

Now she looks at me like I'm the enemy. But I see the way she trembles when I get too close. Feel her power pulse when I say her name.

She hasn't forgotten.

And I'll make damn sure she remembers.

An ancient evil is rising beneath Skye—older than our magic, and twice as ruthless.

Only she and I can stop it. We're bound by fate, fueled by everything we never stopped wanting.

She doesn't trust me. Doesn't want to want me.

Too bad. Because I'll fight for her. Claim her.

Ruin her all over again—if that's what it takes to keep her safe.

This isn't just about saving the world. It's about *us*.

What I destroyed.

What I'll never let go again.

New York Times and USA Today bestselling author Donna Grant returns to the Skye Druids, where destiny awakens, secrets unravel, and a love long denied refuses to fade.

BUY AFTER MIDNIGHT TODAY

at www.DonnaGrant.com

ABOUT THE AUTHOR

New York Times and *USA Today* bestselling author Donna Grant® has been praised for her "totally addictive" and "unique and sensual" stories.

She's written more than one hundred novels spanning multiple genres of romance including the bestselling Dragon Kings® series that features a thrilling combination of Druids, Fae, and immortal Highlanders who are dark, dangerous, and irresistible. She lives in Texas with her dog and a cat.

www.DonnaGrant.com
www.MotherofDragonsBooks.com

facebook.com/AuthorDonnaGrant
instagram.com/dgauthor
bookbub.com/authors/donna-grant
goodreads.com/donna_grant
pinterest.com/donnagrant1